Amy

May you t.m...

About a future an

exciting event

E. L. Marrow

THE DOORKEEPER'S SECRETS

E.L. MORROW

Earleybird Books

Printed in the United States of America

First Printing, 2017

ISBN: 978-1-54391-182-4 (print)
ISBN: 978-1-54391-183-1 (ebook)

www.ELMorrow.com

Earleybird Books

Dedicated to those longing for a future that is more just, compassionate, egalitarian, sustainable, and respectful.

Also to Mary Elise, my wife, the inspiration for Marie in my life.

The author acknowledges with appreciation the support and encouragement of friends and colleagues, especially Monica, Whitney, Starla and Wichita's Senior Center's Writing Craft group.

But most importantly I thank my wife who believes, like me, that this story needs to be told, and didn't change her mind after it consumed the next two plus years of my life.

One
Good Morning ...

"Good morning, I am Marie, your new Doorkeeper."

"What? You said, *new* Doorkeeper! Where's Phillip?"

"He now occupies a 'hole of completion.'"

"Oh no! Dead...? What happened? Do you know anything more?"

"No, ma'am, not at this time."

"I'm sorry ... I was ... surprised. Of course, you just arrived. Please tell me, if you learn anything else.

"Certainly. It is permitted."

"I apologize. I'm not making your first day easy. Are you on probation?"

"Yes, it is standard procedure."

"My apology to your supervisor. I'm 'Ava' leaving for work: Counseling Sector, Building 2, Office 18, returning at 7:00 PM. Is this your first position?"

"Yes, ma'am."

"I wish you well. And welcome to Wichita."

"Thank you, Ava. My record indicates your name is spelled E-v-a."

"Your data is correct. My name *is Eva*. But when I posted here the 'Counseling Sector' already had an Eva, *so I became Ava*. Oh, since this is your first day you don't have access to

1

history. My husband, I mean *mate*, will not need door services today. He is in Philadelphia for a conference and will not return until Friday afternoon or Saturday."

"Thank you, Ava. Your door is now activated."

"Thanks, Marie. By the way, are *you* mated?"

"No, I am unmated."

"Any prospects?"

"I've had 20 mate screening sessions, and am waiting to qualify for others."

"All 20? Any pre-confirmation encounters?"

"Yes, six with no follow-ups."

"No sparks?"

"None for me."

"How old are you?"

"Nineteen."

"Again I apologize, I'm not *just* nosey—I primarily counsel young women with mating issues. Perhaps we could talk? In a few days; you are busy, and I'm late."

"Thank you, Ava. I look forward to an appointment once my schedule is known. Your door is reactivated."

"Thanks again. Pleasant day."

"May your day bring insight to those you counsel."

The latch clicks as Ava pushes the front door open and walks to the waiting transportation pod. A more metallic clank follows as the lock engages, securing Ava's home from intrusion.

Marie thinks *this's exhilarating; my first door, on my first day. After four years of study, I finally work with real doors. It feels natural. More sleep would help. That will come.*

The camera directed toward me is active. Momentarily Supervisor will critique me. In the meantime, I'll glance at my new surroundings.

The console is in the bend of an "L-shaped" living/dining space. The entry is opposite. Dining to my left. Love the large oak table in the dining area. Did my predecessor entertain often?

There's the hallway I took to the shower passing the kitchen and my bedroom; I'll see them eventually.

Yuk, that tan sectional sofa is awful. Central Services only had time to change the bed to my specifications. All other furniture was Phillip's. Now I may keep or replace any of it.

Through the speaker, Supervisor says, "Very professionally handled. You responded to her concerns; revealed appropriately with nothing out of bounds; were not rushed or impatient. You gave ample opportunities for the door to end the conversation; were friendly, efficient and laid a foundation for a future developing relationship.

"Remember, you are trying to establish long-term relationships with your doors. To be effective, you must balance your authority with their need for service. I give you a 9.5 out of 10 for this encounter. The only ding on the exchange is a small thing: it is unnecessary to inform counselors about a permitted request regarding your predecessor. They are well aware of the parameters of information sharing."

"But ... I did not know her work until later. No 'second screen' data appeared until I entered her destination." A brief silence follows while Marie's overseer scrolls through the transcript.

"You are correct. I changed your score to 10, my mistake. Thank you for speaking up. I would be embarrassed if this encounter were audited—which may well happen due to the length and the variety of subjects covered in a first 'opening.'"

Audit? Will they learn about my unsuccessful mate screening sessions? Sharing with Ava, a counselor, is not threatening.

But unknown auditors could judge my relational skills unfairly, for something having no impact on my ability.

"Supervisor … if a review occurs … will I be informed?"

"No, dear—I mean Marie. The purpose of such a process is to assure the quality of *my* work, *not* yours. Put your mind at ease; names are always removed from transcripts—we refer to it as 'scrubbing the audit.' There will be many reviews during your career. The only times they remain intact are when you are up for a promotion or transfer. Naturally, you will be aware of those beforehand."

"Thank you, Supervisor, I was unaware of such procedures."

"It's not included in standard instruction because audits rarely come up." With a sigh, she adds, "Marie, I violated protocol when mentioning possible scrutiny—it served to increase your anxiety unnecessarily. A protocol error on my part, but you need not report it; I'm self-reporting."

"I had no thought of reporting. I'm grateful for the information." A glance at her "third screen" soon reveals:

Self-Error-Report Supervisor 2718

Date: 08-16-2094
Time: between midnight and noon
Incident: I inappropriately referenced a possible audit to a 'first day.'

The report details the infraction and what she did to "put the first day's mind at ease."

No mention of why *I might be uneasy. Surely she understands. So despite the mantra of* "truthfulness at all times" *one can omit some facts so long as those reported are accurate? I must check this hypothesis.*

4

"Well, Marie, you are doing fine. There are three other 'newbies' to supervise. You are about to receive two more door requests. A word of caution, you won't be able to spend as long with each encounter as your first, or you will fall seriously behind. If you should fall behind, or have questions, one of us can help. Pleasant openings to you, Marie."

"Thank you, Supervisor, you are kind."

As she disconnects, two lights, appear on the console panel. *How did she know?* Touching the first button she says, "Good morning, I'm Marie your new Doorkeeper." The screen at her right shows names, daily routines and other details of occupants. This one gives data for six "flat-mates," a term used for university students, whether mated or single.

"Hello, Marie. I'm Frank. James, Ann, Lucy, Ruth, as well as Frank, are ready to leave for campus. We'll all return after the library closes at 10:00 PM." Marie confirms the times in the daily routines, so the system will notify her if anyone falls more than 30 minutes out of routine.

"James, Ann, Lucy, Ruth, *as well as Frank,* your door is activated. Be inspired by a day of learning and challenges." Click as the door opens, and the exiting begins. One of the women chuckles, "She's a sharp one." Marie smiles knowing they caught her humor.

"A moment please," comes a female voice, "Welcome to the sector. I'm Ruth, and I'll be returning at 5:00 PM, leaving again about 6:45 for an evening session, and back again after 10:00." The additional data is adeptly entered in Ruth's daily routine. Marie is excellent at what she does and confident in her ability; finishing first in her class having logged more than 10,000 practice openings with less than one-half of one percent error. However, these are not simulations, but real people with real needs.

"Thank you, Ruth, I'm looking forward to my time here. Your changes are noted. Is Brenda also leaving with you?" Unknowingly, Marie demonstrates what classifies her among the highest functioning Keepers; she notices what is *missing*, in this case, information about the *sixth* flat-mate.

Another male voice responds to the question, "No, she will leave later this morning for a semester in France." One of the women says, "We all hate her." The tone of voice indicating envy or jest, not genuine animosity. Doorkeepers are trained to pick up on clues of hostility, depression, or dissatisfaction—in fact, any emotion foreshadowing a potential problem.

"Thank you, James, I'll wait for her request." The last comment a reminder: no one speaks for another.

"Sorry, I did not identify myself. We're used to the other guy turning on the visual. Yes, *I'm* James, thanks, Marie."

No time to wonder why Phillip activated cameras in response to routine door requests—not standard procedure— another mental note for later. The next button beckons.

The next three and one-half hours passed quickly. Sector 86 is a twenty-block area from Grand to Lemon and First to Fifth. Fully occupied there could be 618 people. About 15% retired—needing only emergency service from the Doorkeeper. Another 20 homes are vacant, being prepared for new occupants. There are always a few on vacation, or temporarily out of the area.

Sector 86 serves over 480 people on a regular basis. That makes for a busy "morning rush," especially when residents are surprised by your predecessor's sudden departure. Sometime between 4:40 and 8:10 AM Marie manages to get everyone off to work, school, or appointments on time with routines noted, corrected or confirmed. So the well-oiled machine of an interdependent society moves into high gear for another day. Today

Sector 86 of that machine has a new mainspring: her name is Marie.

Two
Charles

The first break comes at 8:10 AM. Entering her kitchen for the first time Marie finds a pot of freshly brewed decaf coffee and a "welcome" fruit basket.

A cup of java and a banana seems like a feast. When was the last time I had real food? Yesterday 4:30 PM. This is my 29th hour since sleep—14 more to go. My well-ordered life is out the window today. Yet the work is exhilarating. No time to think about that now, I must begin my Morning Summary. Supervisor will be back in the room soon.

Back to the workstation at 8:13 a red light—*out of routine*—appears on the panel. A resident desiring to exit initiates contact with the Keeper and yellow illuminates. Red *only appears* if the client is 30 minutes or more "out of routine." When this happens, the Doorkeeper (DK) contacts the occupant—if at home; or Location Services—if the person is not home.

The red indicator glares at Marie. *How long has it been there? I didn't miss it when leaving. Why no "audible" when the light came on?*

She lunges for the offending button before sitting down. The screen indicates Charles of 16 Kings Way should have left for work 32 minutes ago.

8

The Doorkeeper's Secrets

Contacts

writer.morrow@gmail.com

www.elmorrow.com

Phone: 316 312 4569

E. L. Morrow
Author

Available at

https://store.bookbaby.com/book
/The-Doorkeepers-Secrets
(Print or e-book)

First in the Sheltered Cities
series

First, sit at the workstation; take a deep breath and say, "Good morning, I'm Marie, your new Doorkeeper, do you need assistance?" No response. 10 seconds pass. Pressing the blue "Supervisor" button on her panel she repeats the greeting emphasizing, "Do you need assistance?" Still silence. 10 seconds, 15.

Supervisor—male voice—all business, "Fill me in."

"Charles is now 33 minutes out of routine, I've called twice with no response."

"Does this constitute an emergency?"

"Yes, out of routine, with no reply for 20 seconds after a 'break in call' constitutes a client emergency."

"Correct. Follow procedures. Tell me everything you are doing as you do it—do not wait for my approval; I'll stop you only if you are in error. Doorkeeper, serve this door!"

"Entering the emergency status code, new data screens open. No other occupants at this address, and no personal contact numbers. Next step: Activate home-wide audio." She types the commands, "audio disabled, video available."

Supervisor instructs, "Do room by room search and tell me your conclusions from what you see." *That is emergency procedure. Why waste time telling me?* She activates the video, as he speaks.

"Dining area is empty; no meal consumed today. Kitchen also empty; no food preparation today. The coffee pot is full, warm and untouched." Marie is using heat sensors, as well as adeptly moving the camera to view every nook and cranny of each room.

"Living area ... empty one paper magazine open on the table all else undisturbed. Bedroom ... empty ... bed is unmade, bed sheets and clothing scattered about. Hallway empty ... closet and bathroom doors are closed. No video is available in bathrooms; initiating door knock" Hitting her stride she types code while speaking. Three knocks followed by three more. Holding the knock button, she says, "This is your Doorkeeper. Do you need assistance?"

Supervisor announces, "I overrode 'audio disabled' for this room, you have two-way conversation with the client." For an instant, Marie "sees" on her monitor the bathroom, with a man lying on the floor, head hanging over the toilet. *Must be another flash image. With no cameras—there can be no other explanation.*

Charles' voice is weak and tentative. "Thanks, but I don't think I need help, I'm sick … I mean ill. I just want to clean up and go back to sleep."

"What about medical attention?"

"I just need rest."

"Would assistance getting back to bed be helpful?"

"Not … necessary."

"Med sensors are active on your bed. I'm notifying the clinic of your condition. They will respond as needed. When was the last time you had any food or drink?"

"Midnight … water… I can't keep anything down."

"When did the abdominal discomfort begin?"

"Supper … last evening."

"Do you have a fever?"

"I… don't think so." Marie transfers Charles' responses to the clinic serving the sector. Once Charles returns to bed, the built-in sensors will monitor vital signs relaying data to Medical Services. Her observations provide a baseline for all who will treat him. While this is standard protocol when the client is not in a sensor-activated bed, few Doorkeepers remember this task, during an emergency. Marie does.

"How else may I assist you?"

"Please call my supervisor and tell him I'm ill?"

"Your work is the Financial Sector, Building 3 Office 51?"

"That's old information. I'm now in Building 1 Office 27. My superior is in Building 1, Office 2. You will probably need to leave a message with his office manager, Phyllis M. Please, tell me what is said. I mean *everything.*"

"Of course, I'll leave your audio open, in case you require additional assistance. I'll relay the response."

"Will they be able to hear me?"

"No sir, my contacts are made on isolated lines." *Charles doesn't want his superiors hearing him vomit. I would feel the same.*

Contact numbers are entered. Marie knows that Charles' supervisor is an important figure. Many job sectors utilize several buildings; each identified by an integer. Smaller building numbers indicate greater "cultural impact" of the work being done there. The same goes for individuals—the lower one's "office number," the more responsibility carried by that person. So Charles reports *directly* to the second most influential leader in the financial sector of the city (perhaps a much larger area). Charles is "upwardly mobile." Building 3 to Building 1 in one promotion is almost unheard of particularly in complex fields like finance.

Marie gleaned this organizational pattern in the first few days of training. Though never mentioned in class, this structural scheme appears too obvious to require discussion.

So Phyllis M's time is valuable. Respect for their time honors the accomplishments of leaders in their field.

"Mr. James Calhoun's office Phyllis M speaking." The voice is a respected self-assured woman in her 50's. Her greeting is formal, not quite to the point of being cold. She possesses the quiet authority of the gatekeeper holding access to the prominent leader. Mr. James Calhoun's achievements are evident. In addition to the standard first name, the traditional address includes "Mister" and his last name. Only by adding a job title to his formal identification could Mr. James Calhoun's significance be more elevated.

"I'm Marie, Doorkeeper for residential Sector 86. I contact you on behalf of Charles who resides at 16 Kings Way, works in Building 1, Office 27 and reports to Mr. James Calhoun. He is ill and will be unable to perform his duties today. He requests I convey any instructions back to him."

There is a "sigh" in Phyllis M's voice as she says, "Please hold." She will likely check files or daily internal schedules, and get back with brief directions for Charles. The silence lasts over a minute. *Maybe I should contact Charles. I don't want to increase his anxiety. But I have no results to share.*

Phyllis M speaks, "Mr. James Calhoun wishes to talk to you." The phone clicks and a kindly male voice says, "Greetings Marie, how is Charles?"

She had not expected to speak to Charles' boss, but it is within his prerogative to ask, so she must answer *truthfully, fully and briefly.* "I have not seen Charles, only spoken with him. He is not in a public area. His voice sounds weak."

"You are a trained observer, how does he *seem* to you?"

"He sounds exhausted and ill. I notified Medical Services and activated sensors, but he has been unable to return to his bed. He is concerned about missing his responsibilities today."

"You're aware this is the third time he's missed work since his promotion. I guess the stress of his added duties is getting him down."

"I apologize, Mr. James Calhoun, this is my first day; client history is unavailable. I was unaware of previous absences."

"My mistake. You are so knowledgeable; I assumed you're an 'old hand' at this. Where did you transfer from?"

"I completed my certification in June. My Teaching Assistant role was cut short to take this posting."

"Well, now I'm *seriously* impressed; first day *and* first position? You function like a veteran."

"My instructors will be pleased."

"You're impressive Marie. I paid you a *huge* compliment, and you hand it off to your teachers."

"They are the ones who shaped my abilities, Mr. James Calhoun. Your comment honors them."

"Well … what a breath of fresh air. You remind me how the economy *should* work. Please call me … Mr. Calhoun."

"Thank you, sir." *Wow. I would never imagine gaining "familiar name status" with such an important person.*

"So what are you going to tell Charles? You see Marie he is a dedicated worker, qualified, knowledgeable, and an asset to this sector and me. But I fear his promotion is more stressful than he's prepared for. Tell him first 'take whatever time he needs to get back to full health. Secondly, he should consider taking some vacation in the next few months. Finally, his position is secure unless *he* wishes to change.'"

"Excellent, sir." Marie did not want to offend, but Keepers are trained to offer suggestions to benefit their client. "Mr. Calhoun … would it be appropriate to suggest time with a counselor to address his anxiety?"

"Of course, here I'm saying stress is the problem, and not giving any tools. Tell him to schedule counseling during work hours. And Marie…."

"Yes, sir?"

"*Don't* hesitate to offer your suggestions—it's part of your profession, and your observations are accurate. Are you still on probation?"

"Yes, it is standard procedure."

"Well, I'm going to send a request to your supervisor, to release you from probation. You demonstrate superior ability, skill, and compassion."

Not knowing what to say she says, "*Thank you,*
Mr. Calhoun."

His kind gesture might shorten my probation.

"Marie, please relay *our messages,* to Charles."

"I will." Mr. Calhoun embraced the counseling suggestion, so the instruction comes from him. Clients do not need
to know their Doorkeepers are making recommendations on
their behalf.

"Call anytime Marie. And a pleasant day to you."

"May you enjoy a day dealing with numbers and the lives
they impact."

In current classes, DKs are encouraged to make the
"ender" relevant to the individual's day. Marie seeks to give
effective enders.

*"Enjoy" is not the best word, but the call is concluded—
that's most important. Charles has been ill at least once since
I left him and now his breathing sounds more labored. Still, I
must wait for Phyllis M to end as well. Can't afford to be rude
to her.*

In a few seconds a much warmer Phyllis M comes on the
line saying, "Mr. Calhoun requests when you call identify
yourself to me as 'Marie, the breath of fresh air,' and I'll put
you through unless he's in a conference. Marie, welcome to
Wichita. If there is *any way* I can help make your adjustment
smoother, *please call.*"

Taken aback by her graciousness, trying not to show her
surprise Marie says, "Thank you, ma'am, I'll remember your
generous offer. I wish you a meaningful day."

Returning to Charles, "Your breathing sounds much
more labored. I believe we should call medical assistance."
Marie offers him a chance to direct his treatment. Keepers are

required to use sound judgment on behalf of the client; his refusal would not prevent a request for help.

"Yes, but first tell me what was said." Marie begins messaging medical assistant with address and details of the change in Charles' condition, while she speaks.

"Mr. James Calhoun asked to speak with me." Charles gasps. *I'm making his anxiety worse. I'll modify to serve his best interest.*

"Put your mind at ease, allow me to report the conversation by priority."

She shares each of Mr. James Calhoun's four points and adds, "He said you are a valuable asset to him and the sector as well as an intelligent worker."

Charles breathing slows to near normal. After another moment Charles says, "Thank you, Marie, you are kind."

The camera outside the entrance to 16 Kings Way reveals two young men dressed in Medical Assistant outfits and a robot pushing a supply cart approaching his door.

"Charles, assistance is arriving. I'll admit them."

At the doorway, "MA 16 and 32 responding to a Keeper's request." They reach out their left sleeves for scanning. The scanner indicates career identities—no names—only titles. Marie guesses MA 16 to be about 24—the other a few years younger.

They are addressed using the Entryway Speaker, "Door is activated. Charles is in the bathroom at the end of the hall."

The younger one asks, "Are Med Sensors active?"

"Yes, but he's unable to return to bed."

The older one is already at the bathroom door, requesting admittance. Marie keys in the code indicating the emergency has been handed over to medical personnel. She will check on Charles later, but for now, this situation is in others' hands.

Immediately she returns to routine door requests, two more lights come on as the emergency is ending.

As soon as a lull in activity comes, Supervisor says, "You did not lookup any codes during the emergency, what if you had made a mistake?"

"I memorized most emergency codes nearly three years ago."

"Really?" He sounds skeptical. "What is it for a fire?"

"F111."

"Fire with someone trapped in the building?"

"F1000."

"An unlocked secure door?"

"DX3."

"An unresponsive person?"

"Silence3."

"A murder victim?"

"That one I need to find." She did so while speaking. "M50."

"Well done; excellent handling of the Charles emergency. We'll talk later."

"Thank you, Supervisor."

Marie completes her first emergency as a Doorkeeper. She cannot guess how many more she will address before day's end. Each one pulls her deeper into the mystery that will come to consume her life.

Three
Probation

While Doorkeepers handle emergencies, an automated system covers non-emergency requests. Once the Keeper enters the "emergency code," all routine requests are unanswered by "Auto-Door." The yellow "request-light" changes to amber.

Marie reviews seventeen automated transactions made during the emergency. An audio recording of the conversation with the client is available for the DK.

Marie finds and corrects nine errors: incorrect return times, details listed for the wrong person and an entry made for someone who is out of town. These are typical Auto-Door mistakes. Current Door training emphasizes checking and correcting Auto-Door as soon as possible.

When a resident's door opens, "destination data" is sent to the transportation service. Individuals wait, usually less than a minute for a "people mover," most often called a "pod," to arrive. Capacity varies from three to fifteen passengers. Names appear in a panel beside the door. Finding your name indicates this conveyance is programmed for your destination. If your name is missing, you wait for a different one.

Since electronic tracking is so integral to Transportation, one might expect an automated system could handle routine door openings. In February 2071 a trial intended to test that possibility was conducted. Auto-Door malfunctioned and delivered a group of university students outside the shelter in sub-zero weather. Fortunately, there was no injury or loss of life, but the 90-day test period ended after only one week. For now, no one suggests replacing Keepers with a machine.

Marie begins compiling her morning report. The male supervisor announces over the speaker, "It's 9:54 AM you are due a downtime break at 10:30 AM. I note you have not read your Schedule or Specific Job Data. I don't understand *why;* there's been nothing else to do this morning." *That is the first sign of his humor.*

He continues, "You handled the emergency situation like a pro. Well, you *are* a pro, but we do not always see such competence in the first assignments. I … well, none of us, find anything significant you could've improved. Your every word was measured, every action efficient. Mr. James Calhoun was correct in saying you function as a veteran. In fact, I know *no* veterans in our catchment area able to key in emergency codes while talking to an anxious client, without looking up anything. You used 28 system commands all keyed correctly without hesitation. We are privileged to have you." Marie's first supervisor joins the conversation "We all agree; so we acted on Mr. James Calhoun's suggestion to release you from probation." Marie overhears two other voices say, "Yes, indeed" and "Hear, hear."

The man says, "The entire summer team of four have reviewed your work. Nineteen other new placements are starting soon, so we aren't going to spend any time looking over your shoulder. You can always get a supervisor 'in the room' when you need one, by hitting the blue button. That's why we're here; at least partly. Any questions?"

A million, but which ones should I ask? "I anticipated 180 days of probation, so when will it end?"

"Already has—ended at 9:45 AM today. As soon as we saw you correct the Auto-Door's errors, we knew you are as qualified as they come."

"What can I say? I never expected this."

"Now don't do something *really dumb* and make us look like *idiots.*"

"I'll try to make you proud. Oh, one other thing—when I was looking for Charles and found him in the bathroom, you overrode the audio disabled. Can only supervisors override disabled commands?"

"Any DK can do it; hold down the address button and emergency button while typing the audio code. This action cancels disable but only after declaring an emergency."

Another supervisor, a younger woman late 30's with a British accent says, "You can do the same if the video is locked out."

"Thank you. One more concern—no audible signal sounded when the 'out of routine' light came on for Charles."

"Are you sure?"

"Yes, I stepped into the kitchen for a cup of coffee. When I came back, the red light was on—no sound."

"Nothing at all?"

"No, Sir."

"Most likely the chair. A technician will check it the next time you're out. In the meantime, I suggest wearing your portalock when away from the console, even in the apartment."

"Thank you all; I'm sure there will be many other questions. For now, I return to my morning report."

The fourth voice, this one male with an Asian accent says, "Compile them for *your* edification if desired, but we're not going to read them. You are off probation, the only reports we need from you are incident or issues."

The first female supervisor speaks again, "You need not write up the Charles' emergency. We've heard it."

"Thank you again. I just *keep* getting gifts."

"You are a gift. Pleasant doors Marie."

"May your advice and counsel be received with grace by all you supervise."

They all say, "Thank you, Marie." Several seem surprised, at Marie's warm feelings for Supervisors: "the feared ones."

Something a Supervisor said causes Marie to turn. Above and behind her console a camera aimed at the workstation. *My work can be observed surreptitiously. One more thing for the "not taught list." I wonder how long that list will become?*

Four
Extra Service

A flashing light on the console indicates an outside call. *Who could be calling me? Can't be family or friends... No one knows this contact. Why is this call unnerving me? Take a breath and answer.* "Hello?"

A friendly male voice responds, "Greetings Marie. Welcome to Sector 86, I'm Wessel, your 'personal services coordinator.' Perhaps you noticed there is no food in your apartment. Sorry. The turn around was a bit too quick. Your meal preferences arrived after midnight, and you were due in before 1:00 AM. We wanted to avoid a breaking protocol by being present as you arrived. Long story short, what do you want for lunch? I see you sometimes vary that menu. So let's start with the basics would you like Salad & Soup, or Salad & Sandwich today?"

"But there is food; I had a banana and a cup of coffee a couple of hours ago."

"Oh, my dear girl, even Keepers cannot live by coffee alone. I'm *so* sorry – *much too personal* – forgive me?"

"I do not mind *respectful* familiarity."

"Oh, please tell me I did not offend."

"I'm unclear; a Doorkeeper must *always* be clear. I appreciate someone with *hum-or* in their *repertoire*, and I take your

21

comment as lighthearted *hum-or*." Spoken with an exaggerated aristocratic tone.

Wessel responds, "I'm so glad we got that out of the way my dear, but what on earth are we going to do-oo about your lunch?"

In a whiny child's voice, "What I want is breakfast, could I get eggs and hash-browns, or must it be ole lunch food?"

Wessel continues, "Well we must notify the authorities … who would that be—oh fiddle-dee *it's me*." Back to his normal voice, "Because you recently joined the workforce you may change preferences for up to 6 weeks as long as they fit the nutritional guidelines for 20-year olds."

"I'm 19."

"You will be 20 soon, right?"

"No, my birthday was August 6th."

Switching to a W.C. Fields voice, "My goodness, she's a mere child. Should I send someone over to feed you? Or do you handle the spoon by yourself?"

"Now you are getting insulting," Marie adds in her pouty voice.

"Sorry."

"So am I. I must put you on hold."

"What? No, don't...."

"I *am* on duty," She says and touches the orange light, signaling desired access to a home, automatically activating the outside entrance camera and another sweeping the area near the home.

A young woman paces back and forth, looking toward the street at a departing pod. Marie opens the microphone saying, "May I assist you?"

"Oh, Marie, thank God, I was afraid it would be automated. I have been working on a report for weeks; the presentation is at 1:00 PM and I left it on my desk at home. Please let me in."

"Present your ID for scanning."

"Of course" she scans her right sleeve. Console screen indicates she is "Vivi," a resident of this address.

Marie reports, "Door activated." *Vivi presented the "wrong sleeve." There is something else going on here. Better turn on the cameras.*

Vivi goes to the bedroom desk, looking first in a drawer, then another finally underneath some papers on the top, she picks out what appears to be a medium-sized work-pad replacing the papers exactly as they had been. Sitting on the edge of the bed, Vivi tries to slide the work-pad into her left sleeve.

The real Vivi would open the garment putting the object inside a pocket. Something is wrong. *Better contact Supervisor.*

With her finger hovering over the blue button, Marie catches a view of Vivi's face. Marie's hand shoots back to her face as if she had almost touched a white hot poker. The woman posing as Vivi is no more than 17 with a look of sheer terror on her face. Marie remembers a nature film from childhood—a lamb trapped in a canyon as hyenas approached. The lamb's features were peaceful compared to "Vivi's."

Suddenly she feels the need to stretch and yawn, in the process glancing at the camera behind the console: *not active.*

Vivi presses the "Door Access Button" saying, "I have never done this before, I tried to hold the pod, but I couldn't. Can you help me return to work?"

"Of course, I'll request a pod. You're returning to the Financial Sector, Building 4, Office 41?" The console's "second screen" reveals data for Vivi. Marie altered the office number to see if the imposter will notice. Also, Vivi is 56 year-old who exited today by *Automated System.*

So the real Vivi would not know me. But I recognize her voice ... got it ... she's one of the university students.

"It's Office 42."

"Of course, my error. Had a long morning, forgive me." As Marie speaks, she scrolls through the work documents to find her own address so she can bring the imposter here to learn what's so terrifying. Marie's internal moral compass *always* points to "assist others." Whoever "Vivi" is, she needs help and Marie will try.

"Be back in a moment; I need to handle another door."

I must get back to Wessel before he becomes concerned.

Marie says, "Wessel, I'm sorry it took longer than I thought."

"Don't worry; I'm here to serve," Spoken in the tone of an English butler.

"So *am* I. Thus the problem."

"Back to your lunch—how would you prefer your eggs?"

"Doesn't matter, anything you put before me that isn't moving I'll eat."

"Ok, no live eels 'till next time."

"Whatever food he brings will be fine."

"Obviously, you need me to stop horsing around. How about some horsemeat? Sorry, couldn't resist.... First, are you coming here, or will you allow someone to deliver the pre-pared meal? It violates protocol for a server to be in your home while you are there, but this is an unusual situation."

"I need to be available during meals."

"Very well, service for one. Eggs, my special hash-browns, toast, fruit compote, coffee, and strawberry pie."

"Pie is not breakfast food."

"Oh, please, I ordered way too many fresh strawberries, if we don't use them I'll never be able to obtain them again. So how many pies can I put you down for 5-6?"

"*One*—slice."

"My people do not 'cut.' It's whole pie or nothing. I'm deaf to the word 'nothing.'"

"Ok, one pie."

"I'll send two you'll love them."

"I really must go."

"One more thing—this is a biggie. Your home is supposed to be serviced tomorrow, but it would be a great help if you could make it today—this week only. Of course, you must leave between 2 and 4:30. The rest of your personal items from Kansas City are ready for you, and this is a crazy time, I'm short staffed because of vacations and..."

"Ok, I need to walk my sector anyway."

"Ok, Maurice will serve at 12:03. Oh, how do you want your eggs?"

"Hard boiled, and *serve*? What do you mean *serve*, what happened to delivery at the door?

"Oh, my dear, do you think this is a dormitory. HA ... 19, I get it. You're right out of school."

"I was a Teaching Assistant," Marie says with mock indignation.

"But you still lived in a dorm, right?"

"And what is wrong with that?" more indignation.

"You're in for a treat; Maurice will treat you like royalty. Unless you are uncomfortable with a man in your apartment alone, in which case I'll send a woman."

"No, he is fine, I still have my mace from campus life," she jokes.

"A good thing, there's no woman available. Tell me if Maurice makes a pass at you because if he does, I'll grill him for every detail. I must live vicariously through these oafs."

"I *must* go."

"Of course, thanks, Marie. You're marvelous."

"Wessel ... you're *insane*."

As he disconnects, she overhears, "Oh, she gives out compliments too...."

Back to the mysterious Vivi: the transportation pod Marie ordered is arriving. To the imposter, she says, "Sorry it took so long, the pod is at the curb, and the door is activated. May your presentation be well received." The infrared scanner indicates our "Vivi" carries only work-pad sized object hidden in the billows of her sleeve. A quick "thanks," and she is out the door and into the waiting 3-passenger-pod.

The delay resulted from the need to find and activate an *out of service pod* while carrying on banter with Wessel. Marie learned this useful "trick" while interning with Transportation, a part of Door Facilitation training. Once returned to its storage slot, no one will be the wiser. Pods require regular maintenance. The tracer is deactivated during servicing, so the location and movements will not be tracked. Finding a working pod takes time and requires using files meant only for Transportation Supervisors. She memorized the process thinking, "this might help someone in a jam."

The pod wanders around, avoiding others for a couple of minutes ending up at the Doorkeepers residence. The pod door remains shut. Activating the audio in the pod, Marie says, "You are not who you claim to be, and the object you carry is not yours. You have two choices. One. Come to the door in front of you, and you will be admitted. Two. Go anywhere else Security will pick you up. Do not speak, simply hold up the correct number of fingers for your choice." Then in a whisper "Please, choose one, I want to help."

The young woman trembling and almost in tears holds up one finger. The pod opens. Looking neither right nor left she marches resolutely toward the olive green door. At the entryway, a kind voice speaks, "The door is open, enter, and do not speak."

Five
Mystery

Standing at the console, Marie types as the imposter Vivi enters and stands trembling just inside the entry hall. Not sitting serves two purposes. First, a sensor in the chair indicates when it's "occupied." Standing suggests she is observing downtime.

Second, the camera view is blocked while erasing all traces of using an out of service pod. Marie learned this skill from her mother.

After entering Door Facilitation School, while on her first break the two of them "created" a whole new person. "Margaret" had advanced degrees, job, voter registration, applications, and census reports. After collecting the first "paycheck," they knew their creation had been successful. The real Margaret was the family cat reimagined as a middle-level animal rights executive. The broom closet chosen as her office needed redecoration. There was a budget. Three days were required to create "Dr. Meow," less than 10 minutes to erase her. The next several days confirmed all traces had been removed.

Mother said I'd need this someday. Who would think my first day in the workforce would be the day? Almost finished. Erasing the record of the keystrokes needed to erase the earlier action. Done.

"Vivi" stands at the inside entrance for 45 seconds—seeming much longer. She sees a young woman standing at a counter typing and wonders, "What's she typing? This morning she was friendly and funny when sending us off. Why bring me here? I pray I can keep my story straight, and not lose my nerve, or my life."

Opening a drawer Marie removes the portalock, short for "Portable-Actionable-Locater-Device." This is her first use of a fully functioning unit. In training, students practice with limited capacity units for mock cases. This one is "tuned" to sector 86's Door Services instruments and will signal when a door request is made. Functioning anywhere inside the sheltered area. Worn like a piece of jewelry, resting below the collarbones. The unit is the color of platinum, slightly warm feeling; one side flat and smooth lies against the skin. The other side containing various raised or indented symbols. She knows the meaning of each symbol. The functional part is the general shape of a grilled hot dog, turned up at both ends, but only a quarter of an inch thick. Unclasping the top of her garment Marie puts the portalock in place. *Forgot I'm not wearing underwear. Six hours since "Activation" but I haven't finished dressing. No matter.*

Putting on her best "critical Teaching Assistant's face," Marie steps to the dining table, directs her guest to a particular chair and takes the one opposite. From her vantage point, she observes both cameras, as well as "Vivi's" face. The silence hangs for a moment. "Why were you in her apartment?"

"I told you ..."

"Don't repeat the falsehoods. You're a student *not* an employee of the Financial Sector."

"How did you know?"

"Never mind. The point is you obtained access to 34 Iris Avenue under pretenses and took property not belonging to you."

"Um, I uh …"

"Stop stalling I need some truth."

She whispers, "You don't want the truth."

"Do *you* want the truth if I call Security now?"

What little composure "Vivi" had maintained is now gone. In full sobbing mode as she squeaks out "Please, you got to help me."

I hate this stern taskmaster role, but I need answers. A supervisor's pass-by-check hearing sobbing could be a real problem. I'll risk one more question.

"Give me one reason why I shouldn't call Security."

"People will die … including me."

Embezzling funds, falsifying records, attempting to rig an election—none of those would surprise me, but this?

Around the table, with her arm around Vivi's shoulders, Marie instantly commits to whatever she's getting herself into. Whispering to Vivi, "Calm down, no one is going to die if I can help it."

The portalock vibrates. "I need to take this door call; you must be silent, the bathroom is without audio."

"I can't move, but I can be quiet." the girl calling herself "Vivi" is still shaking but the sobbing is under control. Reluctantly she returns to the console responding to the call.

"Good Morning, I'm Marie, your new Doorkeeper." Turning on the camera, she finds a 23-year-old woman, a little more full figured than present company.

"Hello Marie, I'm Brenda, and I'm *finally* ready to leave for the airport. You said, *new* Doorkeeper?

"Yes, this is my first day."

"Where's Phillip?"

"He now occupies a hole of completion."

The news shakes Brenda. She gasps and stumbles backward, reaching the arm of the couch behind her and asks, "What happened?"

"Sorry, I have no answer. I'll try to learn more and share with those who ask."

While Brenda recovers her equilibrium, Marie checks on transportation. One of Brenda's flat-mates is across from the DK console and is apparently hearing every word spoken. *The sound "dead zone" around this platform is not working.*

"The airline has dispatched transport to your address. Arriving within the next 5 minutes. How much luggage are you taking?"

"Two trunks and my carry on."

"Do you need assistance with the large items?"

"I can handle one, but I would like help with the second."

"I'm requesting two assistants. Your trip is long; no need to start out fatigued."

"That's thoughtful. Thank you."

"Not at all. They will arrive in four minutes. Were you close to Phillip?"

"He helped me out of several jams. He was here when I came to grad school four years ago. I'll miss him. (Deep sigh) but we must press on." Unmistakable signs of relief came from imposter Vivi at these words.

"I'll share with your flat-mates anything I learn about Phillip."

"Would you please also message me? My message address will not change." Marie types in the "DK Notes section" on her screen a reminder of the promise.

"I will. Losing friends is hard. Do you have your return date?"

"Not exactly. Either in January, or I may extend my study with some vacation time to June. I assume the airline will inform you when I book my flight."

"Of course. What are you studying?"

"My doctoral research is Art History. I'm focusing on Art in the Age of Confusion. I hope to gain access to some private collections as well as museums."

"I hope you enjoy the culture as well."

"I plan to, but study comes first."

"Excellent idea. The aids are arriving to help with your trunks. The internal cameras remain on while they move your luggage to the curb. I'm admitting them now."

Switching on the external speaker, Marie addresses the Assistants, "Morning gentlemen, Brenda needs two footlockers moved to the curb for transport with her to the airport. Door is activated."

"Thanks, Marie, Personal Aids 14 & 15, at your service." She recognizes Aid 14 from an earlier client request.

"Thank you 14; I'm pleased you remember me."

"I remember anyone who calls me a *gentleman.*" *Protocol is to address everyone with respect. Has the dignity of work not been emphasized here?* Assistant 14 & 15 using hand trucks have everything under control. Brenda handles her carry-on.

"Pleasant trip, safe travels, and interesting learning in Europe. Gentlemen, stay safe."

While assisting Brenda, Marie checks details of the six flat-mates: one is posing as Vivi.

I can account for all but Ann and Lucy. Lucy is a Communications major 20 years old. But Ann is majoring in environmental studies born March 19, 2077 – 17 years-of-age.

Marie says, "Ann, we can talk more privately in the bathroom. No audio."

Ann slowly gets up and moves in that direction. Unsteady with a tear stained face, but a bit relieved. In the bathroom, Ann cleans up, and "repairs her face." Makeup delivered last night is standard starter kit—not quite Ann's colors, but they'll do.

Ann asks, "How did you know who I am?"

"Process of elimination. Let me see this pad you are willing to risk so much to obtain."

"No, you can't touch it. If this falls into the wrong hands, everyone who's held it may be rounded up."

"But you handled it."

"I understood the risk. Well, I thought I did."

"Then show me, you hold—I won't touch."

Ann reverently removes the object from her sleeve. She keeps it close turning it over and around for Marie to view. *Not a work pad or other standard device; silver colored, five by eight inches, no identifying marks, none of the usual ports and connections; one shaped something like a windmill. How do you open or turn it on?*

"No screen? No on-off switch? How do you open this?"

"By placing it in a particular machine—there are only a few left."

This must be a hard drive of some sort. A huge one. It could contain more data than all the computers in the country a couple of decades back.

"What were you supposed to do with this?"

"Give it to Vivi." Ann is slipping the object back into her sleeve.

"Why didn't she take it with her?"

"She works in Financial Sector; everything is scanned as she enters."

"So how are you supposed to get this to her?"

"There is a place we meet."

"Where?"

"The more I tell you, the more your danger."

"I'm already in deep, for not calling Security. Ok, I'll take another tact; if I hadn't brought you here where would you be? The time is 11:43 AM."

"Our plan was for me to get back to campus, send her a vague message and wait for her reply about meeting. Probably lunch."

"Will you be missed if you do not show up for class?"

"No classes for me today."

"Is there a crowd you usually eat with?"

"I often stay in the library through meals; there is no set time or group."

"So when's the first time you'll be 'out of routine?'"

"After 10 PM when the library closes."

"Can Vivi take an early supper break, say at 4 PM?"

"I think so."

I can usually tell when someone is lying to me. Ann seems truthful after her first deceptions failed. I need to find out about the real Vivi and the mysterious object.

A strategy is taking shape. But first—there must be lunch.

Six
Lunch

Maurice arrives at 12:03. From the entry, he calls out using a French accent, "Lunch delivery for Marie. May we enter?" After closing the bedroom door where Ann is safely deposited she responds, "Yes." There are two 13-year-old-male assistants. All three are dressed in white button front waiters jackets with an apron from waist to shoe tops. One assistant carries a long roll, which turns out to be a freshly ironed linen tablecloth adeptly unrolled to cover the dining table. The other cradles a lime-green wrapped cylindrical package at least four feet long. The mysterious object is gently placed on the couch.

While Marie ponders the strange object, a place setting for one is being expertly arranged. The service pieces are all gold in color, perhaps actual gold. Three different knives, three spoons of differing sizes; two forks placed on a folded linen napkin left of the plate, plus one above horizontally; all are surrounding beautiful ivory dinnerware. Matching bread plate, fruit bowl, cup and saucer set, plus one crystal cup, and three glasses of different sizes are also in place. Five personal size glass shakers with silver tops containing salt, pepper, paprika and two unknown spices adorn the table along with fresh cut flowers and background music.

Meanwhile, Maurice stands statuesque; left arm bent at the elbow in front of his body with an appropriately draped linen cloth. He watches the work occurring before him with is a practiced indifference that takes in everything. Marie sees a man about 52 wearing a dark black toupee, and matching "handlebar mustache."

Back at the table, one assistant holds Marie's chair for her. The other snaps open a napkin large enough to be a lap-blanket, adroitly placing it on her lap. Both interns go to the mysterious package and begin unwrapping it. After some preliminary positioning, the lime green bag is removed in one final flourish revealing what must be the largest chef's hat in the free world. One end is tapered to fit Maurice's head, but it enlarges to two feet diameter, extending upwards for three feet, reaching a massive toque. It reminds Marie of the pictures of the mushroom clouds following a nuclear bomb blast.

Maurice with a flurry flips the bottom of his apron forward and up so he can kneel on one knee, as his assistants place the hat on his head. It has a chinstrap and a metal support brace in the back attaching to his jacket. Maurice stands; the top of the toque scrunches into the ceiling. Maurice dismisses the youths with a motion like brushing away a piece of lint from midair.

A robot brings a cart loaded with dishes; far more items than Marie ordered.

Maurice serves first the eggs and hash browns. The three eggs are each in eggcups with shells in place. Maurice introduces them as "Humpty Dumpty, his brother Grumpty Dumpty and their first cousin Dumpy Humpty." He describes the hillside where the chickens roamed at will, contributing an egg only when it fits their sense of gratitude for their protection from the ravages of heat, cold and wild beast ..."

Maurice adds cooking details; where the ingredient including each spice originated; conditions of workers who planted, harvested, and cared for the particular item all the while bringing out more food. Each time Marie takes a bite, Maurice whisks away her utensil polishing it and returning it to her with another folded napkin.

After three times Marie says, "If you keep this up we'll be here all day, I haven't eaten since 4:30 yesterday afternoon." In a Texas accent, Maurice says, "Well eat up sister!! What y' waiting fur?" Back in the French accent, he says, "Where did he come from and how'd he got in here?" Marie changes strategy: each time Maurice picks up an implement to polish she takes a different one. It becomes a contest between Marie's hunger and Maurice's cleaning. Ending in a tie. Marie gets food. Maurice polishes but gave up the fresh napkin following each bite.

Marie discovers a new favorite toast: cinnamon-basil-date-raisin-prune bread with pomegranate-fig preserves and a touch of raspberry honey.

Maurice serves a piece of strawberry pie. Marie responds, "Wessel said, and I quote 'my people do not cut.'"

"Wee Mademoiselle it is true, 'we never cut.' Ah, but we do *serve*. Besides for one as beautiful as you all zee rules are out zee window."

At 12:48 Marie confesses, "I can't eat another bite." Maurice claps his hands, and his two assistants reappear. After ceremonially removing the chef's hat, returning it in the lime green bag, they clear away and put leftovers in the refrigerator. In addition to what had been requested Maurice served chef salad, baked fish, oysters on the half shell, potatoes au gratin, three kinds of pasta, a fresh vegetable stir-fry, fresh fruit compote including some unknown fruits, and four different breads. Beverages included hot green tea with a touch of Angola mint, coffee, orange-cranberry juice and Champaign. All is swiftly packed away in pre-labeled containers with item and date. They are out the door at 12:51.

Marie immediately checks on Ann who is desperate.

"I need to pee so bad, but I can't pull the garment up high enough. I got my underpants off. Please help?"

"Let's go to the bathroom."

Every attempt to lift the SOG (Smart Outer Garment) failed. The garment is designed to resist this type of movement. Even with four hands, they can only raise the lower hem to Ann's knees.

Marie says, "if only you can do it standing up."

"Men do all the time. They aim with a cannon."

"We'll fashion one for *you*."

Three strawberry pie tins are reshaped into a tube. Tossing off her SOG, Marie flattens, curves, and shapes one end into a "funnel" to fit snugly against her groin. By the time it's ready, Ann is dancing around saying, "Please *hurry...*" When ready Marie is on her knees behind Ann, who faces the target. With her arms around Ann's knees, she holds the device in place. Applying the right pressure, while Ann lifts the garment as high as possible in the front. Success is confirmed when the tube becomes warm but not wet. As the anxiety lessens, Marie finds herself feeling a strange pleasure: a sense of accomplishment but something else. Crisis averted; Marie dresses and reaches the console at 1:02 PM.

At 1:03 Wessel calls to check-up on Maurice. "Did he make a pass at you?"

"No. He flirted. The only problem was he would *not* let me eat, with all his polishing."

"Tell me, did he explain how each dish was made?"

"…And by whom, and where every spice and potato were grown and a million other things he made up. He's quite the entertainer."

"Did he tell you about Humpty Dumpty and his family?"

"Oh, yes, I knew then he is a clown. Well, I should have known–his hat, and toupee. There is no hair that shade of black."

Slipping into a French accent, Wessel says, "Besides for one as beautiful as you all zee rules are out zee window."

"YOU…it was you!!" She screams. "I had no idea."

Like Jimmy Stewart, he continues, "Well now little lady, I … I- I think you met the man of a thousand voices." In a normal voice, "Gotta go" and disconnects.

Marie can hardly stop laughing. *This is a guy I could go for ... too bad he is gay. Gay? What makes me think that? No matter, we need to move on. The mystery of the strange object beckons.*

Seven
Essential Information

A door request at Chester L's home. The external camera reveals a man in his early 50's and a younger woman, probably 24. Both submit their sleeves for ID without prompting. The man is the resident; his guest is "Candy." Her arrival triggers the Doorkeeper's console to display visitor's data.

Chester L's routine for today includes a conjugal hour at 1:10, plus his lunch break giving him till 3:00 PM to be back at work.

Candy is a Certified PPSW—Personal Pleasure Service Worker. The border around her "data sheet" flashes red: alert. Scrolling through the "standard items:" photos of her in various stages of undress, age, height, weight, and measurements. There is a list of things the SW *will not* do to satisfy clients and her "favorite" sexual activities. Provided for prospective clients to use in determining the suitability of this PPSW.

Near the bottom of the page an alert:

Security Supervision Requested

Activating the door, Marie uses a protocol assuring the PPSW the request will be honored. "Welcome, Candy. Enjoy yourself, Chester."

So why does she want oversight? Does Chester L have a questionable reputation?

At noon Marie gained access to "history" files. In this case, they give her details about Chester including other workers he has seen. A quick review of the content reveals: he is a safety engineer in the Aviation Sector; his mate died about three years ago; he has scheduled "sex visits" every other Monday for the last two years, plus a few on weekends. His usual SW is "Dandy;" Chester has also seen a woman called "Brandy." This is his first appointment with "Candy." The names are pseudonyms designed to protect the Service Worker's true identity. Most change careers later using their real name.

A few keystrokes and there is history for the other two PPSWs. Both women are brunet. *Perhaps he fancies a blond today. Dandy is 43 while Brandy is barely 21. The younger serviced him only twice. Her last appointment was a month ago. Let's see the reports. First time: he requested Brandy to dance and touch herself while she's blindfolded. He agreed to watch but not touch. Without warning he grabbed her, and though not injured she was frightened. On her second visit, he wanted an activity on her "will not" list. She refused. He asked her to undress; spanked her and said, "Go home little girl until you are ready to play right." She departed and is unwilling to see him again. Chester L seems unpredictable. I'll listen for any signal.*

Privacy is guaranteed for a conjugal visit, but to protect the men and women who provide pleasure services additional measures are available. Each PPSW may have one or more microchips implanted in a heel, elbow, or neck. A request for help can be activated by the "Worker" with three quick movements near the sensor such as banging the heel three times against almost anything sends a signal to the Doorkeeper, who responds, "Do you need assistance?"

If the response is inadequate Security is contacted and an earsplitting alarm sounds. The SW may escape by running out the door, but the resident is "restricted" until details are sorted out. Only members of the three services know this arrangement exists. It's another way the society observes the cultural motto: *All work is valuable; all work is dignified; and all workers are to be honored.*

Ann eats two strawberry pies that sacrificed their tins for her relief. Marie listening for a signal from Candy decides to use the time to review the documents Supervisor mentioned earlier.

I'm most interested in my schedule.

WORK SCHEDULE:
> Monday through Friday
> 5:00 AM to 10:30 AM.
> 1:00 PM to 2:01 PM.
> 5:00 PM to 9:00 PM.
> Sunday
> 4:00 PM to 8:00 PM.

DOWNTIME: (portalock required)
> Monday through Friday
> 10:31 AM to 12:59 PM.
> 2:01 PM to 5:00 PM.
> 9:00 PM to 10:00 PM.

Sunday
8:00 PM to 10:00 PM.

DOWN TIME VARIANCE: Morning and Afternoon Downtime (including 1:00 PM to 2:01 PM work time) may be combined up to twice in any week. Modify daily routine. Variance may not be taken on Monday.

SLEEP TIME: Daily 10:00 PM to 4:30 AM (Expected to be available for door emergencies except Off Time or Vacation).

OFF TIME: (portalock not required)
Saturday 5:00 AM to Sunday 4:00 PM.

COMPENSATION SCALE: Level 5

VACATION: Two weeks plus Two weeks in place of resettlement month. All vacation is cumulative for life. At retirement, vacation is converted to bonus at the rate of one-half to one.

ILLNESS LEAVE: 100 days for life
One day added for each month without using a leave day. At retirement, remaining days are converted to bonus at the rate of one to one.
Failure to use an illness day when needed will result in a "five day fine."

LOCATION: 36 Jasmine Court.

REGULAR RESIDENTIAL SERVICING:
Tuesday 2:00 PM to 4:30 PM for cleaning, food delivery, and laundry pick up.
Friday 2:00 PM to 4:30 PM for return of cleaned items, deliver purchases and repairs.

Marie's academic transcript is attached. Reading through it reveals some surprises.

Even faculty I thought didn't like me still compliment my work. There are reviews from instructors in other Door Facilitation programs. Why so much interest in me? The original purpose of cross-faculty reviews was ensuring similar standards at all universities. Nineteen different reviewers; some from each school. A few critiqued every course I took. Why all the praise? I know I do well, but these comments are embarrassing: "creative solutions none of our faculty thought of …" and "already the best of the best." I wonder if they would say the same if they knew what I'm doing with my downtime.

At the end of her transcript is a Merit Summary: Commendations, Detractions, and Demerits. Commendations are positive comments made by superiors, (or once reaching the workforce by peers or clients) and detractions are notes of small possible improvements. Demerits, however, report breaches of protocols, procedures, or expected professionalism. Marie's Merit Summary,

Commendations — 2,738
Detractions — 0
Demerits — 0

Marie checks "close" box. Instead of closing a flashing warning pops-up.

Must Read Job Description Before Closing

Back at the beginning, she reads the title and gasps.

Job Description Details
Doorkeeper & Security Coordinator
Sector 86 Wichita, Kansas

What's a Security Coordinator? Why haven't I heard of this before? She scrolls through sections she already understands: Doorkeeper's Role, Ethics, Portalock, and Standard Procedures. *Know all this. Finally here's what I want.*

Responsibilities of Security Coordinator

You may wonder why this is not covered in Door Facilitation training. Relatively few Doorkeeper positions include security coordination.

Marie learns she is responsible for *everyone* who comes into Sector 86 for whatever reason: visitors, service personnel, Security Officers and even passengers on a pod passing through. Security is responsible for a larger area. So SCs supplement their work with additional scrutiny for a select area.

She reads how to use day or night vision cameras, listen to conversations, and follow pods or occupants all the way to their destinations. Even if the end point *is in another country.* SCs may access scanners capable of identifying anyone wearing a smart garment. All activities: listening, following, and scanning happens without awareness of those being observed. The SC is encouraged to use any work time not dedicated to the Door responsibilities to view the streets and listen to pod conversations at random.

A code of ethics prescribes treatment of anything learned or seen while acting as Security Coordinator. All is confidential unless it impacts safety. One purpose is deterring questionable, unacceptable or criminal behavior. Overhearing a breach of decorum as minor as *not greeting* someone who boards a pod, or more serious may result in the issuing of a "Distraction" or "Demerit" as the situation warrants. Likewise "Commendations" for those showing additional consideration like assisting an elderly resident into a pod, or changing one's routine to accompany a frail individual to their destination.

Marie memorizes the codes to access cameras, pods, scanners, followers, and audio/video surveillance. Armed with new resources, she's ready to take action.

Eight
Apparel

If you live in a Structured State, you own several Smart Outer Garments (usually abbreviated SOG). Virtually all women, men, youth, and children wear one of two styles of outer clothing. They are technological wonders. The material cannot be cut, torn, pierced, burned, melted or stretched enough to force a person out of it. It can stretch to accommodate the wearer's running.

Many SOGS resemble a robe fitting snuggly around the neck, and ending near the ankles. Sleeves are various cuts: most go to the wrist, some are billowy, and a few are short sleeve. A two-piece version with slacks and a top is available. The more active version is preferred by anyone needing to bend, stand, or kneel frequently.

Colors and patterns vary. Solids are reserved for elected officials, judges, or individuals with the highest achievements in their field.

The basic outfit is modified indicating specific roles, such as student, instructor, or retired person. Children, students, and teachers contain "a bib" as part of the collar on the front of the apparel. The size, shape and background hues differ as conditions change. For example, a young child's bib often contains designs like butterflies, rainbows or stars and covers almost a third of the garment's front. Yellow, pink, or light blue are typical for children's apparel. When starting school, the bib decreases in area and adds shades of plum, light greens, or tan.

University student's fields of study dictate the appearance. Marie's had dark blue or forest green while studying Door Facilitation. Once she became a Teaching Assistant, piping of gold was added to her bibs denoting increased responsibility. Instructors sport even smaller ones—primarily gold with hints of instructional tones.

Personal tastes add colors and pattern to your attire. Marie prefers transparent wisps of tinting, similar to rising smoke driven by gentle breezes; or fog and mist muting distant mountains. Medium and darker blues, grays, or dark-reds are permitted as additions to the core Doorkeeper colors.

Another feature is its closing. Two magnetic disks are imbedded—one on each side—at the collar. When these "buttons" are touching a row of hooks on each side of the vertical edges, emerge, automatically interlocking with each other beginning at the neck, and closing all the way to the bottom. Each set of fasteners lines up the next ones an eighth of an inch below. The SOG closes and locks, looking much like interlacing the fingers of your hands. The owner touches the same spot to reverse the interlocking action. Either way takes about three seconds.

Being caught wearing someone else's clothing requires, at the very least, a lot of explanation. Also, as Ann realized, you cannot open someone else's SOG. This is a safety precaution preventing assault: sexual or otherwise.

If you believe you are about to be attacked, slap your hands together twice behind your back "locking" the garment. Once locked it can only be opened at a Security or Medical facility utilizing a device built into one room at each center. Marie will soon remember being taught another way to open an inaccessible Smart Garment.

Nine
A Plan

Marie's immediate concern is the mysterious "hard drive," Ann brought from Vivi's. It's wrapped in a hand towel, slipped into a pillowcase, then an inside pocket of Marie's SOG. Step one is complete.

Step two involves Marie leaving her apartment for the first time. A Doorkeeper may admit or release anyone to his or her home/workspace without permission or assistance; allowing Marie to receive Ann. *Departing is another matter.* Like everyone else, a "Superintendent Keeper" releases a Doorkeeper from their home. By protocol, the first time she leaves, her Keeper takes a "file photo" of Marie using the camera above the front entrance.

Marie checks on Charles. He's resting, fever down to 101 and Medical is monitoring him. Next, she checks on Candy. Audio in the room nearest the bedroom reveals sounds consistent with lovemaking.

Most PPSW emergencies occur in the first 15 minutes. Nearly 50 minutes since Candy's arrival. So why *am I so concerned?*

Portalock and my sensory camera "sunglasses"—ready to press the yellow button by the front door.

48

"This is Marie, new Doorkeeper, requesting downtime departure, back by 5:00 PM."

"Welcome Marie, this is 'Super Door' Jeremiah is the name."

"Thank you, Jeremiah, I feel welcome."

"First the obligatory 'snapshot.' Are you naked?"

"*No!* I'm going out!"

"I keep hoping. I'll wait if you would like to disrobe."

"Can we move on? Service people are due any minute."

"Ok, stand four feet from the entrance; lift your head slightly; say cheese." The flash came before Marie could say anything. "Only one more thing before I open your door; you need to agree to have sex with me sometime in the next century. There's no rush. My schedule is open. After a rotten day when you think things can't be worse, give me a call. Who knows what happens?"

"Is sex the only thing people think about here?"

"Well, It's our first choice. What is number two … what could it be? Oh well. Door is activated; we'll come back to this subject later. I'll send you a picture, so you'll know what you are missing."

"Thanks. A question: can I use my keycard to obtain a pod? I want to go to the university, and my 'communicator' is still in transit."

"Yes, any PIC stop will let you use your keycard. Enter the address, and the kiosk will give you a departure number."

"Thanks, I look forward to your picture."

Marie opens the door slightly; Plucks the keycard; then signals Ann that the coast clear. Marie puts on "sunglasses" that "see" active surveillance cameras. All in the area are inactive.

Green grass, shrubbery, and flowers this is a pleasant street. The homes on this street are newer—built within the last 15 years, all single-family style one or two bedrooms.

The conversation starts, "Ann, when we arrive at your home you need to pick up a fresh pair of panties for later. Can you contact Vivi from your home?"

"But I can't get in. I'm wearing Vivi's outer garment. The scan will come up her, not me."

"I'll let you in. We'll scan your underpants in my pocket."

"You mean underwear has ID strips?"

"Sure: clothing, communicator, desk, clock—everything you own, except sheets, has your identification on it."

"Wow, I never knew so much is 'marked.'"

"Most people don't. Think about it, without those strips, how would Personal Services return *our* clean clothes to us? Still, need your answer: can you contact Vivi from your home?"

"I can type a note on my laptop; my PCD is in my carrel at school."

"So here's the process...." Marie continues checking cameras: no activity. The homes on 3rd Street: fewer, older, in suitable condition.

They reach 30 Iris Avenue, home for six students including Ann. After cautioning her companion to be silent, Marie uses Ann's underwear for scanning; makes some entries on her portalock and they are admitted. The third point of her plan—now complete.

Audio is off. Marie hands the lingerie to Ann. "Grab a different pair and if anyone asks your reason for returning: you needed a fresh pair."

"But I didn't say anything to open the door."

"No matter; that's how I'll enter it when I'm back at the office. There is no voice record of portalock openings unless requested by the operator."

Marie has a routine opening to deal with, and Ann writes her message to Vivi.

"Dear Vivi, my brother, living in an unstructured state has come into some unexpected money. He wants to make a Structured State financial instrument. Things are economically uncertain in his area. Can you help? Your neighbor Ann." She shows it to Marie before sending.

Marie asks, "Is this the exact wording you need?"

"No."

"Why would she reply suggesting a meal?"

"Because that is how we can meet. She's near campus."

"How does she know you're there?"

"She knows me."

"In real life, yes, but anyone reading this message is not going to understand why Vivi responds 'How about lunch?'"

"Oh, I'll fix that."

"Do you have a brother?

"Yes."

"Does he live in a non-structured state?"

"Yes."

"Has he come into money recently?"

"Yes."

"Is he going to put money here?"

"Not likely."

"If questioned, would he confirm this inquiry made on his behalf?"

"No."

"How about, 'I would like to encourage him to make wiser decisions.'"

"God, I'm glad you are helping me."

"One more thing. Leave out the part about being neighbors. You don't want this to be more traceable than necessary."

The revised wording reads.

Vivi, my brother, who lives in an unstructured state, has come into some extra money. I would like to encourage him to invest part of these funds. I'm at the University each day this week and can be available for a luncheon conversation. Can you assist me? Ann.

Proposal sent: step four accomplished. While waiting for a reply, Marie seizes the moment to peruse the apartment. *Six students live here. Four room upstairs and two downstairs. Brenda has one on the main level. So how did the house's only undergraduate land the other? One glance at the room explains it. Ann's is the smallest room in the house. Barely large enough for a single bed, the built-in drawers, a free-standing closet, no window, and a general feeling of not quite enough space for, well ... anything. No room for even a desk, so Ann uses this table in the common living room as her study desk. The house is probably 60-years-old and could stand new paint and floor covering inside.*

Noticing Marie's inspection, Ann says, "Upstairs is much nicer. Redone a year ago. I'll move up when one of the others graduates, probably next March."

"For your sake, I hope so. This would depress me."

"Why do you think I live at the library?"

Ann's computer indicates a response from Vivi. "I was just about to leave for a bite. Could we meet at the 'Cramped Nook' at 3?"

A quick check on the travel time to campus plus their walk to the Public In City pick-up point, and Ann replies, "I know the location but 3:15 would be better."

Confirmation arrives, and they are out the door. Step five: a time and place are set.

As they walk, Marie asks, "Do you need to follow a process when meeting Vivi?"

"She will not join if I'm with somebody."

"Then I'll wait until both of you are seated. You need to tell Vivi I will join you, and it's going to be alright."

"That should work."

They arrive at the PIC station. Three people are already waiting; all retired. One man is heading to the Native American Museum. Two women are on their way to volunteer activities.

There is insufficient time for the younger women to share before a 15-passenger pod arrives. With the new arrivals, there are nine people on board. Off to the city's center what could go wrong?

Ten
Interruption

The pod starts moving.

About two-thirty, with any luck, we'll be at the restaurant with extra time. I can relax for a moment. Why can't I get Chester and Candy off my mind? He'll be leaving in the next ten minutes—due back at work by 3:00.

Ann points out places along the route (a place "to buy stylish shoes," a romantic restaurant for a date – if I ever have one). She's doing an adequate job of playing the role of Vivi, a professional, not a student.

That's my portalock. Trouble Signal. Must be Candy.

Marie whips out the device and presses buttons while crossing to the destination "entry pad" with a screen providing information for travelers. She slaps the wall to the right of the viewing device and speaks into her Portable-Actionable-Locater-Device. "What's happening? Candy, are you ok? I need to hear your voice or the alarm will sound…. Chester, where is Candy?" Pulling a cable from behind the viewer, she plugs it into the device.

Six things seem to happen all at the same time. The transport moves to a "siding." An automated voice says, "The pod is being manually…." Marie interrupts, "Doorkeeper Override, I

54

need this viewing device." The screen becomes a visual, of the cameras in the home, to assist in locating Candy. Chester is spotted sitting on his bed with what looks like blood on his chest. Ear-splitting sirens sound. Over the racket, Marie reads Chester's lips in a slurred, drunken speech pattern: "She left."

The volume is turned down as she says, "PPSW Emergency, at 110 3rd Street. Protocol One there is blood at the scene. Repeating—*blood* at the scene. Security and Medical respond."

Three seconds seems much longer as sixteen eyes are riveted on this woman who appears too young to be managing a crisis. "Security we are two minutes out."

"Medical arriving in about a minute."

Marie continues scanning the home with cameras and infrared. *Candy must be in the bathroom. Better check the door log to make sure she's still there.*

"The Victim is SW; perpetrator is Chester L, the occupant of address. SW is in the bathroom, no verbal response. Resident is fleeing. Crossing Third Street and running toward Lemon Park."

"Keeper, can you track him?"

"Will do. He appears headed for the northwest corner of the park." She is using codes she learned barely an hour ago, activating cameras out of her area to follow Chester's attempted escape.

"Medical, we are at the home, how do we turn off the horn?"

"6-6-2 Disable on any keypad."

Silence follows.

"Perpetrator's leaving the park, heading west on 4th Street, he is on the north side. Chester is stumbling and nearly falling about every few steps."

"The bathroom door is locked. Keeper, can you open it?"

"Negative; lock is a replacement; you'll need to break in." As she speaks, Marie experiences a flash vision of Candy attached to the back of the door with tape. The tape is nailed to the door. If they use a pneumatic ax, as they often do, they could kill her. She is alive—barely. Knowing all this from her vision, Marie says, "No wait. I heard sounds like someone moving against the door; be careful when opening the door— she can't cry out."

The senior MA says, "we'll smash the door knob."

"Chester is heading for a fenced area holding cars."

"We know the place. He may own a vehicle stored there."

Medical people are in the bathroom.

"Patient is unconscious, gagged and nailed to the door. Correction there's tape wrapping each wrist; the nails go through the tape, not her limbs. Abrasions on her upper body, none too deep she is bleeding heavily from lower abdomen. Pupils are dilated and unresponsive; respiration is weak, starting oxygen and IV."

The second voice says, "Let's take her down before starting a drip. No broken ribs or puncture danger. We can better handle the bleeding on a stretcher."

As they cut the tape, everyone hears one of them say, "Keeper was right. My ax would have gone right into her back." Gasps from the onlookers. Marie ignores them; focused on her task. "Chester is climbing the chain link fence." Two seconds later, "He's inside. Sustained cuts on hands and legs from the barbed wire."

"Thanks, Keep, he is in sight. We'll take it from here."

"Thanks, Security; be cautious he appears surprisingly strong."

Now I can give attention to Candy. Searching Chester's drug record. None of what's listed accounts for the reactions I'm seeing, not even in combination with alcohol. Reviewing his deceased mate's medications. There's no indication her medications were turned-in or destroyed. Apparently, his mate had a severe form of cancer.

The Med Tech reports to the clinic doctor "Bleeding stopped temporarily. Starting IV."

Marie's eyes fall on a drug name, "NO! NO IV."

The doctor says, "Explain yourself."

"Chester's mate died two years ago. She was taking quail-amonolithinate. A 60-day prescription was filled four days before her death."

"Those meds should have been destroyed."

"No record of turn in or destruction."

The younger MA says, "I checked the medicine cabinet. Nothing unusual."

Marie says, "I saw medicine bottles on a table in the bedroom, but didn't make a connection."

The younger tech runs to the bedroom, and yells, "Found it—less than ten pills remaining."

The doctor is in charge now, "She is *allergic* to that drug. No IV! Wrap her in a cold blanket and transport immediately. She needs a blood wash; it will be ready when you arrive."

Marie clears the transportation lanes to the center; holding all pods on their route at stops or in pullovers. In a moment the senior Medic says, "Ready to transport. ETA four minutes."

"All traffic cleared to the clinic. High speed is available."

"Alright, ETA under two minutes. Thanks."

"Care for her." *Because she was my responsibility and I nearly failed.*

Back with Security people, "This is Doorkeeper again; be advised Chester may be under the influence of quailamonolithinate."

"What the hell is that?" The questioner is an injured officer. Chester threw a 100-pound anvil over four cars striking the young officer. He jumped away but not quickly enough.

Marie says, "One of a relatively new family of drugs for pain control when cancer cannot be defeated. When taken by someone *without* cancer it creates unusual sensations of euphoria as crystals form and dissolves around different nerve endings."

"Oh, you mean Quills! They are going for thousands of dollars on the black market. He's got some?"

"Prescribed for his deceased mate. Be sure and inform medics when they arrive."

"This is Medical. We copy. Our Doc says to get him back as soon as possible and no 'drip.'"

The uninjured officer says, "We'll enable rapid return, as Keep did for the victim. We'll take it from here."

"Thank *you*. May there be healing for all." With that Marie realizes the event is over. *Done. All I need to do now is write a report. Woops, this is a public space. I must make a confidentiality speech.*

The disconnected cable is returned to its resting place, and the transport is returned to normal operations."

The system voice says, "Thank you; ETA's being updated."

Marie turns to face eight people whose lives she disrupted. She is surprised when they break into applause. But she still has a speech to give, "I regret the inconvenience, but…"

"Inconvenience, like hell; this is the most excitement I've had in years."

A senior aged woman adds, "You were marvelous honey; I hope you're around when I'm attacked by some weirdo."

A 70-year-old man says, "I can't wait to tell my 'you need to get a life gramps' grandson about *my* day. And he wants me to move to Florida; HA!"

Marie says, "But I must impress on you this is a confidential situation; *you can't tell anyone.*"

Three people say in unison, "you got to be kidding."

A woman says, "No way this is going to stay quiet. Don't you think those cops are going to talk about the naked man who throws anvils, after scaling a nine-foot fence topped with barbed wire."

Another man chimes in "I thought the fence was 12 feet high and electrified."

Marie said, "Ok. You're going tell people, but you *can't use names.*

The 82-year-old said, "We're *old,* we don't remember the names."

Another says, "You mean the thing with Clyde and Marshmallow?"

Still, another adds, "I thought he was Cleaver and she's Snicker-doodle."

Finally, a 68-year-old man says, "It's too juicy an event not to share; the names are not important. It's a compelling story about how the system worked to save lives, and the hero is a young woman, whose name I don't remember."

Marie introduces herself again. "So do we have an agreement? No real names."

They all agree. Simply having some fun causing Marie anxiety.

Because it's behind schedule, the pod does not pick up new passengers, a standard procedure following a delay. It reaches the first stop and opens the doors. *No one is leaving. This little group bonded around the shared trauma.* She says, "Nothing else is going to happen; you all need to return to your lives."

One person argues, "We can't just leave." Another suggests a picture. Not wanting Ann to be recognized, Marie says, "That's a violation."

The 68-year old man says, "How about a year from now we all take this route—the same date, same time and see if the story changed." That seems to satisfy everyone. Three people depart.

Two stops later Marie and Ann leave. It's 3:08 PM. *How do I recover our plan's momentum?*

Eleven
Modified Plan

Stepping off the pod, Marie puts on her sensory glasses allowing her to identify engaged surveillance cameras. The current plan now is for Ann to find Vivi at the "Cramped Nook."

After scoping the surroundings, she is ready to meet the woman of such interest. Ann and a companion are at a table with sandwiches and coffee. At 3:17 the Doorkeeper steps to the table, introducing herself and takes a seat where she can see the surveillance cameras. The unknown woman is medium height, brown hair, hazel eyes, 56 years-of-age; her expression reserved and a bit agitated and a slight hint of well-masked fear.

Ann says, "I was telling her about the emergency on the pod. You are amazing!"

Vivi responds cautiously, "I'm glad you are in our sector. So when is Phillip returning?"

"I'm afraid he is not coming back. He now occupies a Hole of Completion."

"He's dead?" Her composure breaks momentarily. After a moment she continues, "That's a shock. I don't suppose you know anything more?"

"Not yet, I plan to access records later today."

She's drawing inside for reflection. I won't rush her. I do the same thing when absorbing unwelcome news.

61

Vivi says, "Well, I need to be going. Thanks for helping Ann with the package; if you give it to her, we will be on our way."

"Let's not pretend this is a package of stationary. I need information before I can release the object. Start with the nature of this thing, and why people might die over it?"

Ann receives a scowl and sputters, "She knew I was not you, and forced me to come to her office. I had no choice; if she turned me in, all would be lost."

Marie interjects, "Let me save some time. I already know this is a hard drive, developed for transport of guarded secrets from one area, or nation to another. The amount of data the device can hold is nearly unlimited, and for some reason, no one can touch it except Ann. Also, there are only a few readers for this type of disk. Now, where am I wrong?"

"The danger increases as you learn more."

"Yes, Ann says the same thing. I'm *already* at risk. I have *violated* my protocol by protecting Ann, hiding the object, and keeping everything from my supervisor." Turning to her left Marie says, "Be careful what you say—security cameras are on." Back to the center she continues, "I'm going to get a glass of water, does anyone want anything?" No's were the responses, and Ann begins talking about her brother. Marie gets a drink and surveys the whole area again. No one seems to be paying attention to the table of three near the street.

Returning to the table with her water, she stands behind them for a moment, as if taking in the scene and says, "The camera cannot see you from this angle. You can answer my questions like you're responding to Ann without danger."

Marie sits down and turns back to the conversation.

The older woman says, "Everything you say is correct. What you haven't learned yet is people in high places are trying to suppress this information, at all cost."

Using her glass to block camera view, she asks, "What's on the disk?"

"I'm not completely sure."

"You could be transporting plans for assassinations of world leaders. The cameras are off now."

"Nothing so sinister. Why are you so *concerned* with the cameras? *There's no audio this far away.*"

"No audio, but the people who monitor the cameras read lips. All Keepers must learn to read lips. More students drop because they cannot master lip reading than any other single skill." Both the women seem skeptical, so she continues. "The man eating alone at the table to my left is rehearsing what to say to his boss about a recent mistake. He is very nervous. The woman on the bench across the street is talking to her aunt in Montana." Ann is impressed, but not her companion who mouths words without a sound.

Marie responds, "You said, 'what am I saying now? Cabbage, turnips, horseshoes and mustard.'"

"Impressive, all correct."

"Back to the object in my pocket."

"OK, I'm not sure of much, but this I can say, as long as you realize your vulnerability."

"I became a Doorkeeper to help people. I'm in deep—so what am I into?"

She glances at Ann who says, "We need to trust her. She's had plenty of chances to turn me in, or leave me to my screw-ups."

Vivi begins, "When I was 21 I spent two years as an intern with the WFA, World Financial Analysis, a branch of the U.N. We were trying to gather data to help prevent the financial collapse that occurred in 2063 for much of the world. I worked mostly in Africa plus a little time in Europe. I started in London. Three weeks of orientation, arranging itinerary and setting parameters of our study. While there, I met a man named Focus. He asked me to come to a meeting at Interpol headquarters. I thought a small group of us would receive an orientation to Interpol's work.

"When I arrived, I was the only one. Focus told me there was a side project gathering health, food, water, disease, and treatment information relating to large population groups. I said I couldn't collect that kind of information. He said that would not be my task. Others were doing the collection. I only needed to receive the material.

"He gave me a disk he called a Uni-hyper-drive. The one I used had a tiny yellow dot on the back top left corner and red dot on the right corner. Color-coded for north and central Africa. Developed for Interpol and would store thousands of times what the largest standard units could. When he gave it to me, he told me of a built-in safety device. If I touch it after someone else, a loud alarm would go off and continue for months. I memorized a number to call if that happened. That memory is long gone.

"While traveling in Africa, in each country, I entered people would bring data to add. Some came on old style floppy disks, CD's, DVDs or Caber discs. Each station on my itinerary had collating docks where I added their input to the Uni-hyper-drive. Sometimes the same people appeared several times, with information to add. I think they worked with Focus. Sometimes they would leave their disks, but usually, they patiently waited, even for hours, for me to make the transfer. The machine would confirm 'transferred' or rarely 'corrupted.' The runner would keep the disk and return the next day with the same or different disk. The second time always worked.

"Some of the people who came looked like doctors; others more like farmers, or simply runners given a task. None of them ever told me their names, or what they did. Small talk did not work on them, so I soon gave up trying.

"I was told never to let the disk out of my possession. If I needed to make a field trip, I should take it in my personal effects. In fact, they gave me an overnight case with a secret pocket to hold the unit. Anyone examining my bag would not notice it.

"Back in London, I received a phone call giving instructions for handing off the research. There was a letter in my hotel room."

"What happened to that letter?"

"He took it, as the message said he would. A man, probably mid 30's appeared at the time the letter said he would. He quoted every word of the letter, told me what color the paper was, and gave me a phone number to call if I had questions. I called, and Focus answered saying the phone would be available for only a few minutes after we hung up. Focus described the man and the ID he would show me with a picture of the man's wife taped to the back. The man will bite his lower lip before saying good-bye.' Everything he said was true. I remember like it was yesterday."

"What nationality was the man called Focus?"

"Nigerian I think."

"And the man who picked it up?"

"North American, probably from the south judging by his speech patterns."

"Do you remember his name?"

"Been years since I thought about him. Last name Ward. He told me his name. The ID only had J. for the first name. Oh, the badge said *Doctor* on his ID, spelled out the whole word, not abbreviated like most times."

"And the woman's picture on the back?"

"Attractive. She wore an academic gown, red I think with a gold stole. Lovely smile, and her hair—auburn—beautiful hair."

Marie pauses for two seconds and says, "Where do we need to take this thing?"

The two other women glance at each other, surprised by the sudden change of attitude.

The "Doctor J. Ward" ID badge was part of a mobile in my crib. The picture on the back is Mother receiving a Ph.D. from Stanford. My father kept this object safe. So will I.

Twelve
Public Lockers

Vivi says, "There are public lockers about two blocks." The threesome is soon out of operating camera range.

"So Marie, if you brought Ann to your home, in a pod, the system will show me in two places at once. If anyone checks, we have a problem."

"No record exists."

"How can that be? The routes must match with destinations...."

"I used an out of service unit."

"Keepers can do that?"

"No...but I can."

Silence follows for the next quarter block as Vivi tries to take in the unusual talents of this young woman. The building has "PL" on the door. Retrieving a keycard, Vivi opens the door, and the three women enter.

Inside is a plain room containing three different sizes of lockers; lining the outside walls, plus a back-to-back group down the middle. Vivi searches for a particular one. No identifying numbers or letters exist—only pictures: flowers, birds, fish, or other natural objects. Many of the symbols repeat. Stopping before a door with a robin on it; she looks right and left; then moves on. A different robin door has a sun to the

67

right and garfish on the left. Opening reveals Ann's outer garment with the familiar student "bib."

The SOG Ann is wearing opens, and she slips it off. Vivi is surprised at Ann's nude lower half.

Ann says, "I had to pee, Marie helped."

Meanwhile, Marie produces Ann's clean undergarment. Both garments are put on.

The extra SOG is placed back in the locker. A keycard is plucked from the shelf. Closing the door, Vivi moves to her left, counts five units, turns around and faces half-sized containers in the center section. The symbol on this one is a cucumber. When opened it reveals another card. This time she counts seven to her left. The symbol is a horned owl. Visually scanning for other horned owls, rejecting two by examining the symbols beside and below. Finally, she finds a locker with the owl, robin on the right, cucumber on the left, and garfish underneath.

"Here we are," Vivi, says, as she opens the door and finds a playing card—ace of diamonds.

This means something to Vivi. The wrapped hard-drive is still in Marie's pocket. Carefully removing the coverings, Ann, wipes away fingerprints and places it in the locker. The door is closed.

Ann decides to use the bathroom accessible through a door on one long wall. The others follow. No cameras or other sensors are observed in the PL room. Nothing incriminating has been said even if someone is listening.

The next room is a standard restroom. The three women each find different stalls. After washing their hands, Ann turns and hugs Vivi saying, "Thank you." A hug for Marie as well, with tears Ann says, "I don't know what I would've done without you."

Marie says, "I'm here to serve. Be careful."

Vivi does not embrace Marie.

At 4:09 Marie says, "I need to get to a PIC stop."

Vivi says, "I'll show you; it's on my way." Ann heads back to campus, while Vivi and Marie depart in the opposite direction.

As they walk, Vivi asks, "What changed your mind so quickly?"

"Something you said made it clear you are truthful; enough for now. What happens to your other SOG?"

"Back in my closet in a few days."

"And the object?"

"No idea. Like the underground railroad during slave days – we're told only our step – nothing before or after."

"So how did it get to you?"

"It appeared. When I saw the dots, everything came back to me. I couldn't take a chance. So I enlisted Ann."

"You've worked with her before?"

"Nothing this risky."

"Tell Ann the next time she needs to impersonate a non-student present her left arm for scanning, not her right."

"So that's what tipped you off?"

"Among other things."

Reaching the PIC stop, Vivi continues to her work. *4:12 PM, I have enough time to stop at the clinic to see Candy and Chester.*

Using the kiosk, she finds the stop number. A 15-passenger pod arrives. Five people including Marie join three passengers already on board. Everyone greets one another as standard courtesy dictates. Marie pays little attention to the people, surroundings, or anything else. *Eight minutes of quiet during the trip to the clinic—feels like a gift.*

Thirteen
The Clinic

Quiet is too much to ask. One of the passengers was telling a story when the pod stopped to pick up newcomers. Marie glances at the 85-year-old who resumes with great enthusiasm. "She had things coming out of her hands and waved her arm, and this huge screen came on, covered the whole wall, and these guys were running away. They were neck-ed 'cause they were trying to have their way with the girl. Well, she reached into the screen and threw them in this fenced area so the cops could catch 'em."

Marie laughs out loud.

Another passenger scowls, "What are you laughing at?"

"That's not how it happened."

"How do *you* know, *you weren't there*! But my friend Thelma *was there*! The woman glowed, her hair and dress. We think she's an *angel*."

Let them keep their fantasy. Not being able to open Vivi's SOG for Ann is confusing me. How does that work? Must be something about the hand and the closures. Does it read fingerprints? When I move my hand close to the clasp, it opens while still a quarter of an inch away. Not fingerprints—there is no contact. I'll try one finger at a time. Nothing happens with the smallest three fingers. Index finger opens it, but the thumb

70

makes it pop open in advance of a touch. Same for both hands. So it's something about the thumbs. Of course, a microchip. Why didn't I figure this out before? Well, no one ever tried to undress me. Many would think it's sad no one's ever wanted in my clothes. Not me. Can't understand all the fuss about sex— from today's events—it seems like a lot of trouble.

The pod reaches the clinic.

An older passenger loudly says, "OK, who's got a doctor's appointment?"

Marie leaves the pod, without a word. *That's rude, but I'm miffed. Insinuating I knew nothing about the event.* At the "Security Entrance," she scans and announces, "Doorkeeper checking on residents." The door opens. Turning, she sees the pod still in the circle with every face staring and wondering how she has access to that entrance. She waves saying, "All in a day's work." *Of course, they can't understand my words, but their embellishments will be more interesting anyway.*

Inside, a corridor on the left leads to rooms. The left side of that hall contains consultation spaces. The opposite side provides observation of treatment units, through one-way windows. Eight feet straight ahead is a wrap-around counter making a one-quarter-circle ending parallel with an outside wall. Following around a 90-degree turn in the opposite direction leads to the public entrance for appointments, walk-in patients, family, and visitors. The layout allows the staff to service incoming patients, Security or Emergency Entrances, as well as view a bank of monitors for treatment rooms and surgery suites. The layout is similar to the one in Kansas City where Marie's classes did fieldwork. At the first curve sits a woman studying monitors and making notes. Without lifting her eyes, the 38-year-old woman with dark hair and glasses holds up her left hand saying, "I'll be right with you."

In a moment she lifts her eyes.

She looks as exhausted as I feel—drooping eyelids, darkness under her eyes, and a harried expression.

"I'm the Doorkeeper from sector 86 here to visit Chester L and perhaps…" She can say no more before the "exhausted" doctor comes alive. "You!! *You're the one* who saved her life, *twice*. And his."

She's the doctor who challenged Marie's "no IV" statement. She gushes on about how the "ax" works with a pneumatic handle increasing the force seven times when striking wood or metal of a door. The blade cuts a four-inch square hole in the door with one blow, large enough to reach through and unlock the door.

"Candy's position on the door—the blade would have cut directly into her lungs and kidney, likely killing her. An ounce of IV fluid in her blood and she's dead because of her allergy to the drug…"

Most of this was covered in her classes. Finally getting in a word, Marie says, "I only want to check on Candy and Chester to see how they are doing."

"Sorry for going on so, I'm too tired to be making good judgments. You already know all I told you, don't you?"

"Yes."

"I'm Dr. Kildare. Yes, like the old TV shows becoming popular again. To answer your question, both your people are doing well, thanks to you. The blood wash continues, on both of them. We will do surgery on Candy to repair the puncture wounds in her abdomen. Security found an icepick at the scene.

"Also a wine glass with five dissolved 'Quills' was found. Candy should be back on her feet in three weeks." They look in on her. There are 12 tubes, plus oxygen. Six are removing blood, and six bring it back after it had been analyzed, thinned, treated, filtered, and analyzed again.

Dr. Kildare says, "She only has about half her normal blood supply in her body; the other half is being treated or on its way out or back. She's in a 'low-level coma' to control her respiration and heart rate."

"What told you Candy is allergic to the drug?"

"The blood dot. A light-spectro-toxo-graph is done for each medication and food. All I do is run that against a similar analysis done for her blood showing allergies, or sensitivities. The beauty is it's completed before the drug is prescribed. But you know these things too, don't you?"

"I wasn't sure about the spectro-toxo-graph for allergies. New information."

"Chester will take more rehab, because of his age. Lack of allergy and wounds are in his favor."

Learning that Candy's friends are in the waiting area, Marie speaks with them. Brandy and Danny thank her for watching over their colleague.

Brandy says, "Candy didn't have emergency chips inserted since this is only a temporary position until next September."

Danny adds, "Men like her, that takes some of the load off us. When neither of us wanted Chester any more, she said, 'I'll give him for a try.'"

"Will he be banned?"

"Probably for a while, but the drug did it. I have a friend in St. Louis who did one 'quill.' He is in a five-year cycle of rehab and treatments. It almost killed him, in 30 minutes."

Marie notes the time: 4:40 PM. She is back "on duty" in 20 minutes, with a 15-minute pod ride. Promising to check on Candy tomorrow, she leaves with one nagging question: *how did I hear a non-existent distress signal?*

Outside she can't see a PIC stop. A 31-year old Security Officer steps out behind Marie and offers to help.

"I need the PIC line headed west."

"Your voice. Are you the Keeper from 86?"

Marie recognizes him as one of the officers who subdued Chester. "Yes, I'm Marie. How is your partner's arm?"

"The break is clean; if he hadn't jumped back his arm would have been crushed; quite a different story. Dr. Burns is setting it now."

"I'm afraid I need to get back to work and can't find the PIC stop."

"Forget PIC; I'd be honored to take you home. By the way, I'm Security 17 and my younger partner is Security 43."

"Thank you. I forgot about identifications for my report." At the vehicle, he opens the passenger side, ushers her in and steps to the driver's side.

I can't remember the last time she saw a "car" before today. Now a lot full and I'm riding in one.

"My name is Dave. Five of us worked the case at 110 3rd. The only other 'name' you may need for your report is Security 23. He found the wine with the pills in it, and the ice pick. He also found the extra stash of pills."

All this is news. Should he be saying so much?

Dave continues, "When 23 finishes his work, he'll call you to put the address on 'lockdown' until district clears it. You do that, right?"

"Yes." *I'll need to review how.*

"Well, I'm glad you were still in your apartment when this went down."

"But I was out for downtime."

Dave stops the car and turns to look at her, "Are you not lying to me?"

"No, Doorkeepers never lie." *Well ... about important things.*

"Then all those stories we're hearing about the magician of the pod are real?"

"No." Laughing she says, "they are so exaggerated."

"You mean you didn't just appear and reach through walls?"

"No, and I'm not an angel either."

"Well, some people disagree, including my partner."

"Can we talk about something else, *please*?"

"Sure, how do you like our sleepy little town?"

"Tell you after I sleep here."

"What? Oh, this *is* your first day."

"What about you? How long have you lived here?"

"Born and raised. Only been outside of Kansas once when an uncle died. Went to university; security is my second choice for my career. First choice: Professor of Logic until I realized no one teaches logic anymore. Currently unmated. Mated twice—both emotional disasters. What about you?"

"I've moved a lot. Before my father died, we lived in Hawaii, Toronto, London, Florida, and Seattle. Since his death, mostly Seattle at the research center where my folks worked. On vacation, we would go to various places."

"What part of Florida? My cousin lives in Orlando."

"Okeechobee."

"You made that up."

"No, it's a big lake in southeast Florida. There's a research center."

"Well, here's your *new* residence."

"Thanks for the lift. My mother said, 'unless you're careful, a cop will bring you home someday."

"I haven't heard *'cop'* in years."

"Well, I met people today who think 'cop' is the right title."

It's 4:56 when Marie walks through her door, deposits her keycard in its slot. Now back to work. *Time to learn a bit more about my predecessor.*

Fourteen
Phillip

The Department of Records and Inquiries may close soon. Let's see what I can learn about Phillip. Marie keys in the number. *Much of the system is automated, but I'll need a real person.*

The automated system announces:

"Not all dossiers are available to the public. Please read through the digital list of categories, since they have recently changed." *Automated systems always say their options recently changed. I bet that's the default message. Ok, what do we have? So many categories.... What an enormous task to verify and protect all these documents.*

Many categories: Business licenses, Professional ... Non-profits. Also governmental agencies: City, State, and Federal. This is interesting—Unstructured State Business Activities authorized to function within the Economy.

Personal licenses: hunting, fishing, agricultural, etc. There are even archives of Architectural designs & building plans. Each sector has categories: Medical, Educational... even Doorkeeper, with reports from their Guidance Committees....

Now, this looks promising: "Life changes: Births, Completions, Mating & Un-mating." Clicking the item opens subcategories including "Completions." Another box asks for the "full name of the completed one." *I don't know Phillip's last name. Here's a box labeled "assist me." I need assistance.*

Another screen appears with the words "locator form" at the top with instructions to fill in known details.

There are a lot of things I can't answer, date of birth, date of completion, city of birth, parent's names, degrees held, etc. There are a few things I can fill in Occupation: Doorkeeper, Address: 36 Jasmine Court, Wichita, Kansas. It also offers an option of ranges for completion date – the "last seven days" should work. Now hit "find."

The obituary appears.

Phillip Clarence Walton, age 78, born January 2, 2016. During the Age of Confusion, he worked in computer science, taught economics at the university level, and held a degree in engineering. He was one of the first Doorkeepers trained in Chicago, beginning work on January 1, 2061. Served as Door Services Supervisor for six years. Preceded to completion by his parents (during the time of confusion), his mate of 52 years, Julia Monica Kline. Also preceded by two brothers, one sister, all from unstructured states. No survivors.

This says nothing helpful to those who want to know what happened. Here's another button "More Information May Be Available." After a moment's silence a woman in her 40's answers.

"Records Assistant 186, how may I help you?" The words are spoken with a tone of boredom and resignation of one only 22 minutes away from the end of another dull day.

"Thank you so much for your help. I read the obituary for Phillip Clarence Walton. It says additional data may be available."

"Additional details are available only to five categories of people:

1. Immediate family: parents, mate, children or siblings.
2. Distant family: aunts, uncles, cousins or former mates.
3. Colleagues, supervisors, successors or investigators.
4. Medical personnel, researchers, disease control.
5. Counselors of the completed one.

Do you qualify for any of those?"

"Yes, I'm his successor."

"I'll need your ID number; if you don't know it, you can call back within 24 hours with the number."

Each person is issued an ID number at birth: used for enrollment in school, seeking a passport, or other rare occasions. However, as a Teaching Assistant 24 hours ago, she used her ID number daily to report on the progress of her students. Marie rattles off her number without hesitation.

"Says here your address is a residence hall in KC."

"I was brought here last night to take Phillip's vacated position as Doorkeeper for Sector 86. I'm at the console now if you would like to send me an ID check."

"One moment." RA 186 is absent nearly two minutes, and Marie handles several routine door openings.

After returning RA 186 says, "My supervisor tells me the computers are slow in updating today. You're in the system. It'll probably update at midnight. Anyway, *you are approved.* Let's see what's here." Her voice is animated—boredom is gone.

The Assistant reads from her screen:

"'There are three explanations: A, B, and C. Not all versions contain the same information though the data in each is deemed to be accurate. Please choose one.'"

"I would like all three."

"That is permitted only for Medical Research or Counselors, Immediate family may choose any two, and distant family is limited to one: either A or B."

Since distant family is the least valued in this scenario, the only one not permitted them is the one I'll take.

"I would like C please."

"Very well. That one is the longest; just a second while it comes up. Here we are. Whoa, one moment."

More silence.

RA186 returns fully engaged and sounding like she is hoping for an affirmative answer to the next question.

"'Explanation C contains two accounts. The first is a public statement that you may share with anyone who asks or anyone you believe would be interested. The second is confidential. It will be shared with only one person. If you listen to the second statement, you may not take any notes, or otherwise take down the data. You must swear in advance not to share the content. Would you like both or just the public one?'"

"Both please."

"First version is being sent to your workstation. Would you like me to read it as well?" It's on the console's third screen.

A minor respiratory issue was discovered at Phillip's annual Physical on January 7, 2094. After having trouble sleeping, he returned to Medical Service in March; upon examination, a significant object in his left lung was noted. Tests proved inconclusive. Oxygen for home use and a sleeping medication were provided. Improvement had been noted. August 9, Mr. Walton returned due to spitting up blood. After additional tests, a rapidly growing inoperable malignant lung tumor was identified. The tumor had spread outside the lung to the heart. This type of tumor is called IOM 93.

Experimental medications for IOM 93 tumors are in trial with positive results. The drugs were obtained and administered between August 10 and 14. He tolerated the first two doses with no ill effects. Evidence suggested tumor shrinkage. However, the third dose caused his heart to stop and an aorta to rupture. Surgery to repair the ruptured aorta was unsuccessful, and he died at 10:59 PM, August 14, 2094.

Skimming the message Marie declines the additional reading.

The question and admonition from earlier are repeated by RA 186. Confirmed again. There is a pause while the next page opens.

She seems more excited than me. What a change in attitude. Marie asks, "Is this normal to find such an addendum?"

"No, it is highly unusual. I've been here for nine years and never encountered anything similar. Opening now. Reading from my screen:

"'This is a confidential accounting of details relating to the completed one in question. These details may not be shared with ANYONE. The document will be read only once. No person other than you will hear this version of events. If you are unable, or unwilling, to refrain from sharing the report—then speak to your Records Attendant before another word is read.'

"That is all. Nothing else will appear until I indicate your acceptance again."

"I'm a Doorkeeper; confidentiality is basic to our training. I accept the conditions, but now I must ask for a moment to answer some doors." She returns in less than two minutes.

"Are you ready to move on?"

"Yes."

"'The following is a slightly different version of events surrounding the completion for the individual you requested. This means some of the Public Explanation has been embellished to fill in gaps. Except for the embellishments, all other stated facts are true. For a more complete understanding of the situation, one should attempt to reconcile both statements. Do you still wish to continue?'

"The system only gives me one paragraph at a time."

"I understand, I confirm, proceed."

"Next paragraph is opening. Here it is.

"'Even though you are encouraged to combine information from the two descriptions to create a more complete picture. However, this is for your enlightenment only; you still must refrain from sharing any portion of the Second Explanation with any other person. Violation will result in multiple demerits, suspension of Records and Inquiries privileges, and/or imprisonment. Do you still confirm?'

"Yes, I still confirm." *I'm beginning to suspect this "hyped" report will say something like, "He slipped on a banana peel and died of embarrassment."*

"'Phillip Clarence Walton was arrested on Thursday, August 12th at his place of residence following his daily work; questioned regarding unauthorized activities; charged with treason against the nation, and other high crimes at 5:10 AM August 14, 2094. When arraigned he did not deny the accusations but plead extraordinary circumstances. He was tried before the Select Tribunal of the Central Program States. The trial was closed. Proceedings are sealed for 25 years. Phillip Clarence Walton died by lethal injection at Midnight August 14th. End of document.'"

Both women are stunned into silence. *I must believe my ears, but this can't be right. Arrested and executed in a little over 48 hours? Did he have a lawyer? What is this tribunal?*

*What kind of "justice" is this? It sounds more like a dicta-
torship than a democracy. RA186 is not the person to ask,
these questions—but who is? This is all confidential I can't
tell anyone.*

"Is there more?"

"No, nothing else. I can't believe what I just read." She
rereads the last paragraph again adding, "When I close this,
these words will disappear, and it'll seem that nothing unusual
happened to Mr. Walton. We are the only ones who know.
Speaking for myself, I wish I could un-hear those words. But I
can't. So I will remember. I'll remember him each day and pray
that some justice will come from the injustice done to him."

"Should you be saying this?"

"Oh, crap; you're still on probation."

"Actually, I'm not."

"What … how did that happen?"

"It's a long story—complicated."

"I'm relieved, but I sure would like to know that story
sometime. Do you get lunch in town?"

"Not yet but I will. I'm sorry, people are returning home at
this hour. I'm afraid I must go."

"No problem for me. There are no other calls. Don't worry
about anything being overheard from my end. I use a silencer.
I'll message you some day next week so we can share lunch."

"Looking forward to it." *I wonder what a "silencer" is;
perhaps she will tell me.*

"One more thing you might not be aware of. Because you
are a colleague, the code near the bottom of the public statement allows you access to most documents about Mr. Walton. It
might help figure out what caused him to be treated so poorly."

"Thanks 186, I was unaware of that possibility. You've
been helpful."

"See you soon."

At 5:24 people with the evening off, or who need to return home to change before going to an outing or downtime activity fill the console with requests. *What a mind-boggling day. Now I need regular activity: let people in their homes, let them out again. Enough excitement for today. So why do I feel there's still more?*

Fifteen
Day Care

The remaining personal items arrived from Kansas City including my Communicator. I'll talk to Mother later and then sleep—glorious sleep. Best to not count the hours.

A pale blue light appears on the board. *This is trouble. The address is 26 Iris Avenue, a Child Care Center. An external door is open from inside leading to one of the three play areas behind the facility.*

The Day Care is a business. Doorkeepers do not handle doors for businesses. The staff deals with arrivals and departures of children and families. Keepers are only involved if requested, or problems show up like a door not properly closed. Checking the door log, Marie finds that it has been used several times during the day as children and supervisors accessed the outside. Opened at 5:26, and remains open. Any use between 5:00 and 7:00 PM is out of routine, thus the indicator.

Speaking to the entrance hall, she says, "This is Marie, your new Doorkeeper. There is a door ajar to Recreation Area One."

A male late 20's voice responds, "OK, we'll handle it."

"Thanks" she clicks off. Data screens show a listing of employees and clients. The only adult man working there is an 82-year-old volunteer custodian. Overriding the camera, she declares an emergency. Since children may be present

Security, Medical and Counseling are automatically alerted. She observes three women, two with children clustered behind them. The third is attempting to reason with a man who has a four-year-old beside him and a weapon in his right hand.

Marie says, "Hostage situation at 26 Iris Avenue, Day Care Center on the corner with 3rd. One male approximately 28 years of age holding three women teachers and six children with a stunning weapon."

"Security 17 ETA 1 minute. Keep me posted."

"A seventh child by his side is a four-year-old boy." Checking other rooms Marie accounts for everyone remaining on the premises. Exits are double locked except the one that must be blocked open as an escape route. Using the Center's role she identifies the man in question as Richard Greenfield with his child Andy.

Street cameras reveal an automobile parked on 3rd, along with an opening in the chain-link.

Martha S., who seems to be in charge, is hit with a blast from the stun gun. Grabbing his child, he runs for the door. Marie communicates everything as she learns it.

Officer 17 intercepts Richard at the fence. Medical is a block away. The counseling team will arrive in about 10 minutes, to assist children, parents, and workers.

Entrances are released so medics can reach Martha S. Using the outside speakers she addresses the waiting parents. "This is Marie, the sector Doorkeeper. I apologize for the delay, but ask you to step to one side so medical personnel can reach an injured staff member. All the children are safe but may be anxious. The teachers will give you the details."

When Richard is disarmed without further incident, the Doorkeeper's involvement is concluded.

It's now 5:35; back to regular work—checking on Auto-Door and doing *two* incident reports.

I'll review the console and portalock memories to assure myself no one else heard an alarm. I heard it but perhaps only in my mind. First—visions where I see things that cannot be seen; now I hear sounds that aren't there. So far they always turn out to be accurate. Two visual flashes today: one when Charles was on the floor in his bathroom, the second when I saw Candy nailed and taped to a wooden door. The alarm is probably a flash also. Three on the same day. Why does no one talk about these things? Can it be that I'm the only one experiencing these flashes?

Marie works without a break until 7:20 PM. She stops for some more of the delicious food left by Wessel. As she does, a question comes: *What was I doing this time yesterday?*

Sixteen
What a Difference A Day Makes

Marie's life changed 26 hours ago, Sunday evening, August 15, 2094.

After four years of study to become a Doorkeeper, she Certificated, June 27, 2094. Certification Ceremonies replaced "Graduation" because of the current emphasis on life-long learning. The differences between Graduation and Certification are minimal. There are speakers and the obligatory "inside jokes;" speeches by students; more jokes; seemingly endless reading of names and handing out of certificates. The ceremonies are every bit as pompous and tedious as graduations used to be.

Students who complete their studies are expected to serve one or two years as a Teaching Assistant in their field. The role serves several purposes. First, it enables the recent student to give back to the program that nurtured them. Second, it hones skills and knowledge, with practical uses similar to being engaged in the workforce. Third, having a constant supply of Teaching Assistants enables the instructors to focus on what and how they teach. The TAs, as they are called, observe the details of individuals' performance in practice situations. Finally, it enables a gradual shift from student to the workforce. They live in dorms with other TAs. However, they are assigned work hours; responsibilities and tasks: overseeing students' performances during simulated crises, preparing worksheets, even lectures on a subject. Teaching Assistants work with others to provide realistic training.

Sundays are short workdays. After completing a four-hour work shift ending at 3:00 PM Marie was ready for the only un-programmed meal of the week. Predetermined meals fit into the nutritional guidelines for one's gender and age. One meal out of 21 (usually Sunday Evening) may be anything. Marie's meal of choice is vegetable pizza and a soft drink.

In the commons room at about 4:30 with her individual pizza and root beer, and an article she continued reading from a "read-pad." The document addresses the emotional adjustments needed for those who lived in the "age of confusion" as they gave up money. Her parents and many of her instructors lived through that change. Marie wants empathy for what they experienced. She wants to know everything: first about her field: Doorkeeper; then related fields—Counseling, Security, Personal Services, Medicine, Transportation, Computer functions and finally about everything else.

Marie sat near the entrance, greeting other arrivals, with a wave, nod, or word. Later she would join in playing some cards or challenging board games with some friends who had not yet arrived. To call them "friends" is probably a stretch. They are acquaintances with some degree of familiarity. Most people find her a bit intimidating, because of her knowledge. They like her; she never flouts her abilities or puts others down. When study groups were formed, everyone wanted to be in Marie's. She read and remembered everything from the entire syllabus—required and the supplemental material.

What do I remember about those life changing moments? Half my pizza and root beer remained when an announcement came over the speaker. "Marie report to Office 610 immediately. Repeating Teaching Assistant...." I sent the article to my personal computer down the hall, leaving the library's Read-pad.

As I got up, others gawked. I heard things like, "Uh-Oh," "What did you do?" or "You're in trouble now." Strange no one responded with positive wishes or support. So much for "To affirm and encourage another is to provide gifts money cannot buy ..." a mantra from the first weeks of primary school.

A clock in the hall indicated 5:30 PM. The office is on the floor above our commons room.

The space had become familiar ground—a temporary meeting spot used by TAs for planning. I started to knock, but the door opened. Dr. Stanley, one of my professors, stood just inside. Behind a desk with several computer screens sat a distinguished woman, obviously "in charge." She was a stranger, about 78-years-old.

My professor stepped forward with an Information Pad in his hand including an ID scanner. I extended my left arm for scanning; a ritual performed anytime a student meets with an instructor in a private setting. I'm glad I remembered to extend my left arm, after using the right arm as a student for 14 years.

The scanner confirmed me. He spoke, "Welcome Marie. First, let me assure you—this is not a bad thing. I'm Raymond Stanley, one of the instructors in the Doorkeeper Skill Mastery Program. What you may not know is that I'm the Principal of the Teaching Assistant's program, and I've observed your work these past six weeks. At the desk is Dr. Kim von Throne who heads Doorkeeper Placement Services for the continental U. S. and Canada."

Decorum dictated turning first to the new acquaintance. I said, "Pleased to meet you Dr. Throne. I hope your flight was pleasant." She responded, "Raymond sees to my every comfort; my flight occurred two days ago for a series of meetings now concluded."

Her words seemed strange—giving far more information than required—it was a "test" of how I might proceed. I said, "It is a pleasure to have you in our midst." Turning to my instructor, "It's always a pleasure seeing you professor; I had three classes with you, and will always remember the module on dealing with catastrophic communication losses and power outages."

"My memory of you, Marie, is always having the best answer, perfect scores on all tests, and when you asked a question, I needed research before responding."

"I try to honor my instructors by learning."

I caught a knowing glance between the other two as a chair was offered. The only empty chair purposely positioned so that when I faced one, the other would see me in profile. Another test. They were looking for any hesitation, discomfort, or body language indicating incongruences between words and emotions. All techniques taught in the classes on "Getting the Truth."

Professor Stanley said. "You expected to remain as a Teaching Assistant until July 31st next year. You would then expect to be given your first posting as a Doorkeeper. With the month of August to relocate, beginning your new work September first, 2095. That's the typical track for one as gifted as you. However, an opportunity presents itself, that you are under no obligation to accept..."

Before I could respond, Dr. Throne spoke, "It would mean cutting your TA role short and taking a posting for your first position now. Would you be open to the possibility?"

I said, "It is my pleasure to serve in whatever role my talents and gifts may be most beneficial." I added to the standard "mantra" claiming awareness of my abilities.

My professor asks, "Just to be clear, Marie, you are willing to take a posting now?"

"I am."

"Well, there is one other candidate, so if you would step into the side-room, for a few moments, we'll be right with you." Indicating a door to the right of the desk, but the Placement Director retorted, "That may not be necessary." She motioned for me to stay seated and for her colleague to step behind the desk.

They spoke in muted tones as she pointed to different items on the screens before her. She said, "Here ... again ... and here; and look at the dates."

He replied, "Can't be right ... that damn anomaly again."

Dr. Throne had a few more questions for me. She asked about other career tracks I had qualified for and where I went to boarding school. Apparently, my answers matched her records.

My instructor said, "Thank you, Marie. We've found some anomalies in the search algorithm. Occasionally it combines data from more than one individual. We needed to confirm the same had not happened with your records."

I was offered the position. I accepted.

Dr. Throne said, "We are glad for your willingness. You see we are in a bind. A respected member of the Doorkeeper community now resides in a 'Hole of Completion.'"

A screen on the wall lit up. The three of us stood facing the screen where a distinguished man in his 70s was visible through the transparent cover of a coffin. The camera angle showed the top half of his body. Dressed in an elegant outer garment with a dominance of black and stripes of dark blue and forest green, the official colors for Doorkeeper Service. The bottom of the screen shows the name, Phillip. We stood for over a minute paying reverent homage to a man I never met. *It seems the others knew him. Paying respect to a fallen colleague is customary. I realized this was not a still picture but "live camera feed."* A shadow passed over the glass, indicating movement from somewhere behind the camera.

"He will remain in the Hole of Completion for 30 days for family and friends to view him. The remains will be cremated," said my former instructor, providing one more lesson.

Why was this not covered in the classes? Only the first of a long list of topics missed.

Next Dr. Throne added, "Phillip's departure leaves an opening in a rather prestigious sector. It's a pleasant and safe sector. Leaving Kansas City will be necessary. So we need to hold a farewell reception for you. Who would you especially like to invite? Is there a gentleman friend needing particular attention?"

"No particular male friends; I would invite my study groups from the last four years and my suite mates."

"Ok, we have those lists, invitations are going out. All your instructors have indicated a desire to come, and most will be present. Anyone else?"

Whoa! I just realized the faculty must have had prior information *about a reception for me that night. I'll ask Dr. Throne when I see her.*

What an arrogant thought. What makes me *think I'll see* the head of placement *again? I can't say why—but I'm sure I will—and soon.*

My family could not be invited because of the limited time. Another unknown rule: no outside contact for 24 hours— where did that one *come from?*

The reception would be as soon as possible. A flight had been booked for me to Wichita at midnight. The Activation Assistant should meet me at 2:00 AM.

In the end, all faculty members attended most bringing their mates. Invitations went out to those in the commons room when I was called. That way they would know I had not been "in trouble."

Next, came Andria, the emergency apparel coordinator, who immediately told me she could get me a SOG similar to the one I wore. I must've sounded foolish asking, "Why?" Of course, the TA collar must be removed. Starting with a new one would be quicker since time seemed to be of the essence. Andria whipped out a measuring device and tossed a thin metal measuring tape at my hips. It wrapped around snuggly giving a reading. Thankfully she was a bit gentler with my bust and height.

Andria showed me one she had similar to mine with more of the dark red on the front and more of the dark blue on the back. It's beautiful.

One more detail before Andria could whisk me away. "Normally when you're posted to your first assignment, your compensation scale moves up one level. You, however, are taking this position because of an emergency you will receive an additional pay scale bump. Putting you at Level 5. Additionally, in compensation for missing your relocation month, you are granted an additional two weeks vacation to be used any time after your first week in Wichita. Do you have any questions for us?"

Only one, "When do I pack?"

They both laughed a bit, and Professor Stanley said, "You are part of the workforce now. Others pack and machines carry things, not you.

I responded, "There's so much to get used to." That's the understatement of the year.

The next several hours were a whirlwind. Andria took charge sending someone to my room for fresh undergarments. They also took photos of my SOGS while I showered. Andria used my "old" SOG to scan and reproduce the identifying code for my new garment. Smart Outer Garments have five strips that are "encoded" only once with the owner's identifier. Andria used an E-coder to place the code in each strip. The device is complex and licensed to only one operator. Detailed protections to prevent misuse of an E-coder are in place. In 34 years, no successful ID strip counterfeiting has been reported.

Andria stored the code to use for completing a couple more new garments to send with me. I own seven Outer Garments; from the photos, she picked two designs for close matches. The ones remaining will be altered including removal of bib and retrofitting with face shields.

Next came a visit from André, the highest-ranking TA from the school of cosmetology. Hair, nails and facial makeup made me feel like the winner of Miss America and the lottery on the same day. Of course, neither of those "Time of Confusion" activities exists today, but I studied them. My hair was an elegant wrap resembling a turban.

The reception was like a "waking dream." All the TA's greeted me. Most were pleased; some indicated they were envious. A few awkward good-byes. Surprising how many study group members thanked me for help. One even said, she wouldn't have made it without me; I don't believe her, but she does. Julian, one of my suitemates, went to my desk and brought the contents of my hidden drawer. Should send him a commendation and a note.

All my teachers were in attendance; most offered flattering words. Several told me I had been their best student. They probably say that often. Some instructors' mates attended also.

The ones I had been acquainted with were cordial and wished me well.

One of the others I had not met said, "I'm glad to meet the woman he can't stop talking about." Another stated, "I'm pleased to finally meet the woman my wife says I would leave her for."

What strange things to say to someone on your first meeting.

Reception over—off to the airport. Flight 86 to Wichita was ready to board as I reached the gate. Take off was delayed an hour due to weather issues. Frequent flyers noted that delays are common. Although the plane had many empty seats, I couldn't sleep. My mind was too busy.

Once in Wichita, I met Latisha, a 22-year-old who held a sign with my name. She told me my luggage didn't make it on board but would be delivered tomorrow. Upon learning I had not been there before, Latisha gave the Wichita spiel as she drove from the airport.

"A diversified economic base including Agriculture, Aviation, Education, Energy (both solar and wind), Medicine, Finance, and Mental Health. Of course all the service sectors: Security, Transportation, Personal Services, Retail, Auto Rental, and of course, Door Services."

After the prepared speech, I learned that Latisha is mated and has two children. She works one week of night shifts, and three weeks of day shifts for the Airport Delivery Services, a branch of Central Services.

Latisha is likable, but apparently, she's not in my sector. At 2:48 AM I walked in and Rowena, my "Activation Specialist" greeted me.

Rowena scanned my left sleeve as she spoke, "... It's not your fault, but you were due in at 1:15, and your shift begins at

4:00 *AM* and our task takes as long as two hours. So, you need to take a quick shower, air dry, put on no undergarments, only your SOG, and join me at the Activation Closet." She points to the closet just off the entrance hall.

Two showers in nine hours—a record for me. It's part of the process to use the cleansing mist shower with vent dry.

The process involves draping a canvas-like open-sided garment over the otherwise naked body of the Doorkeeper. The outside of the garment contains miniature doorknobs or icons representing some doors in the sector. The Assistant uses a plastic wrap to ensure garment to skin contact for each door. The "site activation" feels like a mild electrical shock lasting a few seconds for each of the 300 plus doors in the sector.

The hard part is standing still for over an hour. I needed to think of something, so I focused on the reasons behind the actions. We understood the basics, but never the rationale. Conclusion: I am now a walking antenna for my sector's doors.

I thought the tingling resulted from microchips being placed at each spot. Now a half-day later that doesn't seem right. It wouldn't take so long to inject a chip—each tingling was almost three seconds. What's happening?

The final step is entering my ID at the console. Rowena reminds me that no data screen appears until I make an entry while connected to a door; also "Door History" will not appear until about noon. Reactivation occurs weekly.

What a long day. I'm ready for sleep. First, a talk with Mother.

Seventeen
Rest

The long workday is nearly over. *Sleep will be very welcome.*

The older male supervisor calls, "I just read your two reports, and cannot believe three incidents the same day in Sector 86. That is more than a typical year. Wish I could promise tomorrow will be calmer, but I can't. By the way, in standard testing of Richard, the father at the Day Care Center, they found quailamonolithinate in his blood. So no one could make him listen to reason.

"I called you to say 'excellent work.' Apparently, others think so as well. You received 186 commendations. A record for a First Day, I checked. How many people were in the pod?

"Nine, including me."

"Some of them forgot they had sent one; fourteen refer to the pod or 'tram' incident. One of them called you 'the angel on the bus.' Anyway, you made a positive impression."

"Thank you; today's been a whirlwind. One question about commendations: should I be writing them for today? The subject was never discussed in classes."

"They're covered in the orientation sessions—which, of course, you haven't had due to your sudden recruitment. You are not expected to begin giving citations until a month on the job. More information is on the web, under 'Reward and

97

Appreciation System,' a whole sub-section on giving commendations, appropriate times, situations and formats."

"Thank you; I'm relieved. I would be up until midnight if I had to write them for today."

"Rest well in your new home. Glad you're here." He clicks off.

Fifty minutes then I can sleep. My personal possessions arrived from Kansas City: computer, communicator, a few books, and a small box of keepsakes. The box contains copies of my Certification Ceremonies, a few family photos, my "Plan for Life" written to be opened on my 21st birthday and the only love note I ever received. Amend from Primary 1 was sweet on me. He died two years later.

Everything I own fits into one box and two drawers. Personal Services put away my clothing: six sets of undergarments plus the ones I'm wearing, same for socks, two each sleepwear, swimsuits, and workout clothes. Two new SOGS now hang in my closet, and what's this? A dark red bathrobe with a note "A Gift of Welcome. Central Services." How gracious, and it's cozy. Who told them I love this color?

Check the laptop first. The drops of sealing wax are still in place; so the cover remained intact. Let's see about snooping. No one has accessed my journal since my last entry. But, someone did open and read my contact list, "People-Up" page, some class notes, and projects. Some ... but not all evaluations I wrote about my students, and a few other inconsequential files were opened. They did not touch my e-messages or website history. No need; they likely already know what's in them. Years ago I was told 'Assume every message, conversation over an electronic device and any websites you visit are public information. If you wouldn't want to find it on a banner in your front lawn, or told to a judge, don't say it.'

Many people would be outraged at the violation of their computer being searched. I'm grateful for Mother's wisdom.

Whoever's invading my privacy are unaware I discovered them. Mother's security software kept everything important out of reach. Keep my eyes and ears open to find who snooped in my stuff.

Next, my communication device ... contacts and saved messages were viewed. My secret file of contacts and messages ... untouched. The time of the intrusion: 2:50 AM. After reaching the Wichita Airport. If the other happened at a similar time, there's only one geographic area to search for the culprit. The intruder may be a friend, maybe one of Rudy's operatives trying to protect me? Not likely since few people are aware I'm here, but not much gets past him.

Nothing changed on my communicator. What's this? One call placed from my PCD to a number I recognize...Wessel's. I'll listen to the audio playback later still within the 36 hours that all calls are held. For now, I better test for bugs or tagging left by the intruder.

First, remove the case from the Communication Device. My workstation has the glasses I need to look for such manipulations. Now, calling my number from the console. Ringing... no signals. Great, *I can make my call.*

After a few routine openings, Marie keys in a memorized number. The line answers, "Dr. Allison Ward ... Unavailable. Leave a message..." Marie does not wait for the tone but enters a 3-digit code "D75" which identifies the call as from her and speaks, "Sorry I missed your call; much to tell you. You'll never guess where I am. Call when you can."

Part of staying "safe" is the make-up of messages: never use names or titles like "Dad." No locations or emotions. They also use shorthand codes: "Sorry I missed your call" means everything is ok; "I was unavailable when you called" translates "I'm in trouble." The latter opener would bring help; probably in the form of a brawny associate who deals with "trouble."

Marie's mother can access secure phone lines where they can talk more freely, and even more protection when a signal scrambler is added. Marie checks and finds her scrambler. It's among the things she asked a suitemate to retrieve from her hidden drawer. She's carried them in her SOG all day. The scrambler is about the size of an "old fashioned" wrist timepiece without the straps. *I'll make a false drawer for my desk, like the one in KC until then I'll put the scrambler and my memory chips at the back of the closet shelf, taped down—out of sight.*

Marie's communication device rings. She answers; "May I help you?" indicates an awareness of the unsecured line. "Hello" signals the call might be overheard. The caller says, "So where are you?"

"Not where I was last week."

"Let me call you right back."

This time as the PCD rings she hears a low three-second hum signals a protected line.

"May I help you?"

"Yes, tell me where you are."

"Wichita."

"A TA exchange?"

"No, I'm no longer an Assistant."

"A temporary posting?"

"The real thing." *Mother is typing in the background. Can't she stop work long enough to be happy for me?*

"Out of time rotation; I'm impressed. When is your first day off?"

"This Saturday." *More typing.*

"Any Saturday commitments? Orientation or meetings?"

"No." *Still, keyboard sounds. I'm getting aggravated.*

"Good! Don't make any plans; I'll arrive Thursday evening about 9:00 your time. I would love to see you work on Friday and we can take Saturday together. When do you go back on duty?"

"Sunday afternoon." A few more keystrokes from the other end.

"A return flight leaves at 1:10 PM Sunday; that will work."

What I heard was her making travel arrangements. I'm ashamed of what I was thinking.

"Wonderful! Please be my guest. Do I need to arrange transportation?"

"Done, but do you have an extra bed?"

"No, but I can sleep on the couch."

"That will do fine; we can work out the details later."

"Should I be arranging for guest food? No wait, there's lots of food from my first meal."

"We'll eat out if we need to. You'll want to discover fine dining for your area."

"I'm so glad you are coming."

"I'm so *proud* of you."

She is thinking, "And afraid for you." The call ends with their usual ritual.

Allison says, "Keep your head in a book and your heart in the clouds."

Marie replies, "Keep your books in the clouds and your heart in your head." Reminding one another to balance their intellectual self with their need for spirit and compassion.

Why is Mother afraid for me? Perhaps she knows something about what's happening here? Is she aware of the object Dad had? What happened to Phillip? What is that tribunal? Must find out about them. Who was searching my devices?

Why is the console not functioning properly? I'd better examine it for other irregularities. It'll be good to see Mother. I always feel better after talking to her.

Eighteen
Dr. Allison Fulbright Ward

Marie sleeps, but Dr. Allison Fulbright Ward paces the floor. She thinks, "Wichita is the focal point of recent trouble, and now Marie is there. Who can I trust?" She pulls a book from a shelf, and reaches behind it for another – no one knows about – containing names and details about "colleagues" in secret, essential and dangerous work. The culmination of Allison's life's mission depends on this fragile secret alliance. Now, her only child is in danger.

The reflection continues, "I'll die for this work, but I can't sacrifice Marie. Her future is more far-reaching than mine, and nothing must interfere. But she cannot succeed unless we do."

Dr. Allison Ward, co-founder (with her deceased mate) and director of Cyclops Center for Health Research, is the world's foremost authority on disease mutations and biological manipulation sequencing. In recent years Cyclops identified seven new strains of viruses, presently confined to animal populations, but mutating rapidly toward Homo sapiens. If only one of these several stains reaches us, and her *mildest* predictions are accurate, the human race will survive only 40 more years. In her worst-case scenario, the timeline is measured in months.

A copy of the speech she gave last October to the International Society for Environmental Disease Control and

Response falls out of Allison's hidden directory. She silently reads her concluding remarks.

"Based on the data collected and reviewed *so far,* we … that is me … Dr. Allison Ward and my staff believe that we only have from six to fifteen years to be ready for the future pandemics. The best hopes for antidotes or vaccines come from a 30-year study. In every nation, population, and sub-population, research is conducted, on humans, plants, animals, as well as changes they are undergoing. The studies are nearly complete, and the data is being sent to a central location.

"So what's the problem? The best minds, in the world, are working on solutions. We possess what is needed to defeat these microorganisms. What could go wrong?

"Two things. First, we need a solution for *all*, not just one of the seven. We have dubbed these 'clambering diseases.' They seem to be intentionally moving toward infecting people. Truly defeating them requires *it be done in the animal and plant population.* If only one of the seven crosses to infect our population—even if we have the vaccines and treatments ready, we will be unable to stem the spread. After one crosses, another will likely follow in weeks. Once two of them infect people in the same region, they will start mutating to form 'super-viruses.' Remember, they are called viruses, even though they do not always conform to the rules of viruses.

"There could be 300 new 'viruses' in 76 hours. It takes us nearly a year to develop a vaccine for one. So we *must* defeat them *before* they make the jump.

"The second problem is much worse. Some people in each developed nation are actively attempting to prevent the dissemination of this information. They say, 'Why upset people until it becomes a problem?' Others are willing to let 'wild animals' die to save cost. Plus there are a few in every religion of the world who proclaim, 'This is God's judgment on a corrupt and sinful world.'

"If you believe in an angry deity wanting to destroy the world by painful individual death, then I pity you when you stand before that judgment. The only Supreme Being I can believe in is the one who gives us a way out. Dedicating ourselves to finding solutions, and acting responsibly for the planet, our home, and each other is essential.

"Each of us needs to go back to our work and be vigilant in caring for the creation, knowledge, and wisdom we possess. Move the data along. Use your political influence to unlock the secrecy and oppression. These diseases can be defeated. They must be. We must trust each other. Failure means we will be allowing the planet's death."

Allison says, to no one in particular, "I cannot change a word, except we have one year less. God help us."

She gives herself a mental slap. *Dr. Allison Ward, you're a scientist, stop wallowing in fear and figure this out. Perhaps Marie's being there isn't bad; if only she stays safe till Thursday night. Rudy can help.*

Going to the wall by the door, Allison touches the "Security" button on her internal communication panel.

"What's up?" It's the familiar calming voice of Rudy Carlton her Security Chief.

"Marie's in Wichita."

"Where are you?"

"My quarters."

"On my way."

After bringing Rudy up to date on Marie's situation, they begin diagraming relationships and connections. The question of "who" is paramount. Who is the traitor? Who's missing from the network or still in place? *Most importantly, who can protect Marie?*

Nineteen
Rudy Carlton

Although he would never claim it, Rudy Carlton, Chief of Security, is as essential to the success of Cyclops' work as Dr. Ward. Rudy lives and breathes safety. He was trained by the best: US Marines Intelligence Service, and later the CIA. He left the military after becoming convinced the wars he was being asked to justify were unnecessary and directed at the wrong "enemy." He believed enemies of freedom exist and must be addressed. So when offered the opportunity to join the CIA he accepted.

After only four years in covert operations, he began to question the rightness of what he was doing. Rudy and two of his colleagues left the agency shortly after being ordered to "take out" a US citizen whose only crime was planning to run for political office. The powerful corrupt incumbent disapproved.

The saying goes "Keep your friends close, your enemies closer." Rudy adds, "… and those who order you to kill people closest." He had been spying on his superiors for a year. With the right equipment and know-how, electronic surveillance was rather easy. Rudy possessed both.

After helping the target fake his death and start a new life, Rudy and a few other agents decided to start over.

Rudy reflected on how his belief in freedom and democracy had been used to make him a corporate "hit man." So he spent much of the next year thinking and drinking—primarily drinking. Finally one of his friends who had also been thinking and drinking said, "Why don't we form a company; try to use what we know to help people?" They made a list of nine ex-marines or ex-agents who might join them. To their surprise, all agreed, and Not-a-Dozen Security Service was born.

They wanted to get into more technical operations. But few of their clients could afford such services. So with many family members to support, they took low-tech jobs as well. One of those led Rudy to onsite recognizance for a scientific conference, where Dr. Jamison Ward spoke about the need for "… a massive effort to address rapidly advancing diseases and environmental threats."

Rudy later told him, "If you get that massive effort going, you'll need to safeguard your process and data." Handing him a business card Rudy said, "We can help."

Dr. Ward said, "We'll keep that in mind."

The following spring Dr. Allison Ward sounded a more urgent note regarding some diseases that were unchecked. She announced their attempt to form a new organization working exclusively on "species threatening issues." Rudy again was providing protection services. After the speech, Rudy made his way to her and asked, "Are you serious about this threat to all life on earth?"

Allison replied, "Deadly serious." Then she recognized his name and said, "We talked about getting you to do an assessment of our needs."

Rudy said, "You will need continuous oversight. The crazies keep learning new ways to intrude; you need to stay ahead of them." They talked for three hours, the last hour of which Jamison joined them. Rudy became Cyclops' first line of defense against all vulnerabilities.

Rudy never looked back. He maintains close ties with Not-a-Dozen. As new equipment becomes available, they obtain it. Rudy is still part of the organization only deployed. When situations call for extra eyes and ears, Rudy calls on his friends, who drop everything to help.

Rudy developed an impenetrable system as the Cyclops buildings were renovated or added. He installed state of the art equipment inside, outside, and the surrounding area using cameras, heat sensors, night vision and anything else available. One sensor indicates when the grounds or buildings are being scanned by satellite for images, heat signatures, etc. Section lock-downs and barriers can be remotely activated to prevent advancing invaders. There is even an energy ray system that can minimize damage from a direct nuclear hit. The Center was as safe as possible when completed in 2052. Each year new advances are incorporated.

All Cyclops staff attends security orientation. Additional instructions for activating the protective systems are given to "section leaders." Rudy lives in the compound. On the rare occasion when he is off campus, some of his assistants are in place.

Rudy scans for listening devices, or projected listening signals three times a day, checks all systems twice a day, and spends much time reading briefings from around the world. He also keeps working on who the "watchers" are.

In 2059 three towers appeared outside the grounds, designed to blend into the terrain and snoop on Cyclops. The towers take pictures in real time of everything visible from the outside and contain sensors capable of measuring the number of people and their locations inside the buildings. Of course, they cannot penetrate the mountain, so most of the activity is unobservable. Rudy checked them out, and with a little help created a link allowing him to send sensory readings, and pictures, that obscure what is happening. The substitute signal is activated anytime some unusual activities occur. The watchers are allowed to see the comings and goings of workers, and some deliveries of ordinary items. All that changes when new equipment or organisms are delivered.

Rudy wants to find who ordered the snooping. He is not alone in believing the responsibility rests with Senator Bluefoot (nicknamed "Jerkhead" by Cyclops). Rudy has a three-inch-thick file on him. Rudy measures his dossier by inches. A half-inch means the person is pretty dull and straightforward, anything over an inch means corruption, and abuse of power. Three inches indicates corruption and high skill at hiding his misdeeds.

For 50 years, Rudy abided by the no drugs, drinking or killing policy, but says he would make an exception for anyone who hurts Allison, or Marie.

Twenty
James Jefferson Carver Bluefoot

Senator James Jefferson Carver Bluefoot's day starts early. "The General" calls, with demands that Bluefoot "...do something." Several times each week the senator is obliged to listen to the ranting of his "chief supporter."

The Senator ruminates while the hysterics continue pouring forth from his communicator.

"His calls follow a predictable structure.

"First, he reminds me how *special and unique I am,* 'the culmination of decades of selective breeding to create the 'super-soldier.' One who functions against overwhelming odds, with little to no pain, controls bleeding and does so with less than three hours sleep and 10% of standard food rations.'

"Second, he tells me not to forget who plucked me from oblivion, giving me a new name, new look, new citizenship, and fabricated past.

"Next, he tells me what a disappointment I've been, particularly noting my most recent 'failure.' Today—the 'wrong person' got the call to become 'Door opener' in some insignificant little area in Wichita.

"Finally, his litanies about how awful things are and how useless I am, in dismantling the Plan.

"Mostly I ignore the 45-minute ritual replacing it with memories of my own—closer to 'reality' than his version.

"The secret project started in the 1990's. Some 'bleeding-heart liberals' got squeamish about forcing women to bear children with a pre-selected partner, and taking them at age two to a military school. With all the fuss the program 'officially' ended in 2021.

"So all breeding moved out of the US. My mother was Italian. She understood their deal was too good to be true. We disappeared before my second birthday, changed names, and stayed out of view. On her deathbed, she tells me all this, when I'm twenty something.

"My name: Carlos Veatos Rizzo. Lack of emotions, pain, or 'morals' made crime an obvious career choice: drugs and hookers. Others worked for me or stayed out of my way. When they didn't—some dismemberments and deaths followed. The competition finally tried to kill me.

"So the General stepped in. How long he had been watching me, he won't tell. After plastic surgery, a new language and identity, I became 'his' boy. I was to be 'his senator.' He managed my campaign and got me elected in '78. We started remaking the country in his image. G thinks I can make everything the way he wants. I'm supposed to snap my fingers and others vote my way.

"The Constitutional Amendment limiting Senators to one 12-year term took effect in '80. Currently serving House and Senate members could run one more time. Reelected in '84 my term ends January 3, 2097.

"G expects me to be 'grateful' for all *he's done for me*. He forgets I'm bred to possess no emotion. There is one exception: sometimes I muster hatred for him. He and his cronies condemned me to be half alive—a slave to their ideology. If he came through the door, I'd gladly strangle him with one hand and throw his body into the nearest incinerator."

Bluefoot remunerates on his loathing until the General reaches diatribe end.

"He was a 'lock' for the job. We 'improved' his experience with a Ph.D. in Community Management. Everything depended on his getting that sector.

"We've closed off all other routes to wherever those "packages" are going. With him there we'd intercept the *research data.* So how does an inexperienced kid right out of school beat out an experienced guy with advanced degrees? *I'll tell you how*: she's got connections."

"So tell me again why I'm responsible for them not picking your guy?"

"You didn't get the information from the old guy, so this is plan B."

"My operatives did their best. There's still one more shot, following your crazy idea. Might work."

"Yeah, but now we must find out what she knows and how she got this position?"

"First, we can't be sure the old guy can tell us anything. Secondly, they may exclude the new kid and work around her."

"Somebody has answers. *Get them!*"

"Why not let the research alone. Those Programmed States will fail. This research can't prevent it."

"You still don't get it. *The referendum must* fail so *we* can claim credit for the research. If a solution comes out *before* the referendum, it'll sway people to keep things as they are."

"We're attacking them on five fronts.

"1. Government is taking much more out of the economy than initially projected. Including – I might add – trillions to your 'black operations.'

"2. We are narrowing down where the adjustments are being made to keep this economic ship of cards afloat. Chicago, Denver or Wichita. My money is on Wichita. There is one guy ready to give us some documents *when the price is right*.

"3. 'The weapon' will make the safety of those Smart Garments a thing of the past. Put it in the hands of a few terrorist groups, and everyone will demand their guns back.

"4. The Program States Update Initiative groups are convincing young people they are being cheated, and even a few older ones are coming along.

"5. Finally our team inside the research center. When something comes out, *we'll know it*. It must go through my committee, and we can delay the announcement until our people can take the credit. These things take time, but the whole thing is snowballing; not long now."

"You've been saying the same thing for two years. The states following the plan *are broke*, so *when the hell are they going to act like* it…"

Bluefoot tunes him out again.

"My escape plan is more satisfying to think about than listening to him. I'll bring down 'The Plan,' not because he demands it, but *because I can*. My sixth, secret strategy is nearly in place. It will work. I'll be square with G, giving him his precious 'age of confusion'—then I walk away. Thinking about getting out is as close to a feeling pleasure as I ever experience."

Twenty-One
Cyclops Institute

Allison Ward and Rudy worked together most of the night. Looking over their conclusions, Allison is confident they accounted for all relevant variables.

Allison reflects, "Recent contacts confirm disruption in the pipeline moving research results to the data center. So far, the data is uncompromised.

"Those seeking to derail our efforts have ulterior motives. The presenting issue is always money. They say, 'We cannot *justify* treatment since the threat to human health is inconclusive.' More than ever, I believe their real agenda is an economic collapse. They want to replace the current order of economic justice with another 'Age of Confusion.' I appear before Congressional Committees regularly sounding the alarm about the coming catastrophe. Our critics use our successes of the past to argue for delay.

"In 2063, we projected a worldwide pandemic of a mutating strain of influenza. This one adapted to 'ride' on the traditional flu virus, surviving after the flu had run its course. The piggy-back-virus used the white blood cell as its host for duplication and attacked the optic nerve. The leukocytes rushed to the site to eradicate the invader taking billions of active viruses with them. Total blindness would occur 48 hours after the first symptoms occurred. Thirty to fifty million cases of blindness per year were predicted.

"A Japanese colleague came up with the idea of strengthening the initial resistance. With international cooperation, researchers found the particular markers allowing the virus to get past the immune system defenses. White cells were modified to prevent the piggy-back-virus' attachment. Building on stem cell studies, Cyclops was able to introduce modified leukocytes to 'teach' the body how to make resistant white cells.

"The piggy-back-virus struck two years later, infecting cattle. Instead of slaughtering 10,000 to keep them out of the food chain, we convinced officials to use our anti-viral on them. All were saved. The immune system recognized the virus as an intruder and aggressively destroyed it."

"So our detractors ask, 'Where are the 30 to 50 million newly blind you predicted?' When I say, 'They are all walking around seeing because you let us do our job—the opposite of what you are doing now.' They respond, 'You overestimated the problem before; you're doing it again.'

A law designed to protect the public from misleading propaganda is being used to restrict awareness of health issues. The Accuracy in Public Communications Act makes knowingly misleading the public a crime: by making inaccurate statements or stating *opinions* as facts. It was intended to require political statements to be truthful. Some political action groups formed Non-Profit Organizations to avoid liability, so the law was expanded to require NPOs to gain clearance from a communication oversight committee. Failure to do so would cause loss of "Approved Non-Profit" certification. Losing the certification would mean most people could not contribute financially to the organization. Not a problem until the oversight committees for research areas became populated by science-skeptics.

Cyclops and their international partners must work around the system by physically transporting materials, after detecting intentional corruption in electronic transfers.

Allison's Chief Researcher, Dr. Bulla Barns, steps into the anteroom. This space is the senior staff meeting room, workspace, and break room.

Bulla starts to greet her, but instead says, "I see you pulled another all-nighter."

"I got three hours sleep."

"You don't lie well; those blotches under your eyes say differently."

"Ok, two hours."

"Don't you realize you are the key to this project? The rest of us do our jobs, and we're no slouches in the brain department, but you are the driving force behind all this. If we lose you to illness, or worse; there's no way in hell we're going to finish this in time. The hardest work starts next month, and you are burning yourself out."

"Without the rest of the input, our solutions could be flawed."

"More trouble in the network?"

"Nothing new. Rudy and I spent the night codifying what we can. People are missing from two of our three streams: three in one and possibly four in the other. When we sought *the traitor,* some actions did not fit. Rudy said, 'What if it's *two* people? We think we know who they are. One in Washington D.C. and one in Chicago.'"

Bulla said, "Well that's helpful. You need some rest. The kid and I can handle things here today.

"The kid" Bulla refers to is Dr. Jeffery Cle, forty-one, actually only five years younger than Bulla. He is the kid because he did an internship with the Institute when he was 22. After finishing his doctorate in endocrinology, he returned full time.

His specialty is the impact of hormonal changes on the immune system. The fourth senior staff is Sandy, currently on a "field trip" (meaning she is at Data Accumulation Site or "DAS;" her task reviewing the latest inputs). At age 58, Sandy's specialty is the cardio-vascular system and brain-nerve science. However, she is indispensable to the project with her ability to organize an extensive volume of data to extrapolate actionable conclusions. The location of DAS is secret. Of the researchers, only the senior four have seen it.

Allison says, "With Sandy out, and me leaving Thursday, I need to work today."

"Why are you leaving Thursday?"

"I'll be back on Sunday afternoon. I'm going to see my daughter."

"Is she in trouble again?" A running joke—Marie is never in trouble.

"I hope not."

Not hearing a humorous response, Bulla's full attention is riveted on Allison as she asks, "What's up?"

"She is in Wichita."

"What? She's got her year of TA work."

"Not anymore; Teaching Assistantship cut short; she's now a Keeper in Wichita."

"Well that's good—no wait a minute, this is August, they don't move until September, unless...."

"The 'reason' is what I'm trying to find out. Her being there gives me an excuse to visit Wichita. The route is stalled at Wichita. With the help of a Doorkeeper, maybe I can get to the bottom of this."

"Right, she can access information you can't. Wait a minute, won't she still be on probation?"

"Yes, we'll need to be careful."

"Allison, *you* be careful, this could be a setup. 'Jerkhead's' cronies could be watching to catch you in a slip-up."

"I'm not going to put Marie at risk."

"Of course not. You are on top of this, but does she understand what she's into?"

"I'd say no. I can't risk trying to warn her even with our secure lines."

"Allison, Marie is smart. She's going to smell a problem and divine a solution. She's cautious enough not to blow something off because it's out of routine. In other words—she's *your* daughter."

"Yes, but she's right out of school full of idealism, and she spent the last six weeks overseeing students—shaping them into idealists who function 'within routine.' Rudy knows one person in Wichita."

"What does he do?"

"Personal Services Coordinator"

"While you are visiting, you need to arrange things like pick-up, food..."

"Already done. But I've got an idea. Tell me what you think. I call the contact, saying I'm visiting a friend that is 'like a daughter to me,' who was recently posted to Door Services. I want to surprise her with a meal at a fancy restaurant what would he suggest."

"Do you know him?"

"No, but Rudy does?"

"Will he recognize you?"

"Probably not, but he's in the network."

"Say no more. Make the call. You'll be careful."

Allison Ward has the confidence of a lioness protecting her young against a stampeding herd of elephants when facing down challenges designed to derail her work. However, where

Marie is concerned, anything risky brings hesitation. She is bolstered by the reassurance of her colleague.

In her chambers, Allison makes the call.

"Central Services Center, I'm Trea, how may I help you?"

"Thank You, Trea, I'm visiting your city for the first time this weekend. Visiting a friend who just started a new job, and I would like to surprise her with an elegant dinner. Can you give me the name of your finest restaurant?"

"I'm new here myself and haven't gotten out much. Perhaps Wessel is available. He knows *everything* about food. One moment."

"This is Wessel, that is Vessel spoken with a Russian accent; how may I be of service?"

Allison repeated her request adding "… and I failed to ask what sector she's in—she is a new Doorkeeper; could you tell me where I might find her when I arrive?"

"Ah, you must mean the beautiful and vivacious Marie, who is indeed a new Doorkeeper, starting only yesterday."

"That's her."

"Sector 86."

"Can you tell me, is Sector 86 a *safe* area; I mean is *she* going to be safe working and living there?"

"One of our most prestigious areas. Extremely safe, and is only nineteen blocks from my office—the 'Grand Central Station' of everything delicious arriving in Wichita."

"Have you met her?"

"Maurice, our French Chef, cannot stop talking about her; let me put him on the line." In a few seconds, he begins speaking with the affected French accent used to create 'Maurice.' "Oh, you vant to learn of the beautiful dish, I mean zee Keeper of zee Doors who resides in Sex-tor 86. Uh-huh, she is *beautiful*, she is *smart,* she is a most *persistent* eater, and a master of the art of consumption. Despite my best efforts to calm her so she might appreciate the quiescence prepared in her honor, she insisted on taking bite after bite, without even a fragment of respect for the tradition of savoring each delectable bite. Alas, she spoke only of being *hungry*, having not eaten in hundred hours or some such thing. So we left much food for her to consume at her leisure."

"Thank you, Maurice; did she seem happy, worried, stressed...?"

"She was all of those, but mostly happy, and hungry—very hungry. I look forward to my next encounter with zee beautiful one."

"Thanks again Maurice. Could I speak again to Wessel?"

"You want to talk to him-m? He is a most boring individual. What could he possibly say to interest you?"

"He promised to help me with something."

"Vell, ok, here he is. Don't say I didn't varn you."

He switched back to his normal voice. "Let's find a restaurant. We have several. What about Japanese food; we have an excellent restaurant called The Samaria's Porch?"

"She likes Japanese food, but it often offers a lot of show, and not necessarily a quiet place to talk—we need to catch up."

"Well, in that case, you want the Prince's Feast—British quiescence, their Prime Rib is outstanding. You will need reservations—I'll be pleased to make them for you. What day and time?"

"Saturday evening, can we make it 7:00?"

"7:00 Saturday, August 21. You are in a private room, it seats four to six, in case you have additional guests."

"I'll text you a confirmation number in a moment. Is there anything else?"

"Thank you. You are generous with your time. Oh, and thank Maurice for me."

"I vill," Wessel says in Maurice's French accent as he ends the call.

Allison is not often fooled, but Wessel pretended to be two different people. She thinks, "I hope my trust is not misplaced."

Her concerns are soon assuaged. Her communicator reports a text message: 28864. Allison notes the number. "By removing 86 for Marie's sector, we have 284: a possible scramble code." Allison plugs in her scrambler; sets the code to 284. In a moment a light comes on announcing a scrambled call coming through; two more lights indicate no one attempting to match or intercept from either end.

She accepts the call. "Yes."

"About the safety of the area let me assure you she is being overseen by yours truly and my people. "Your friend is gifted and *instinctively* handles things—even *unusual things*."

"Thank you."

"Well, must be going," Wessel disconnects.

There had been no attempt to intrude on the call. Allison reflects on the conversation: "The contact lasted only a few seconds. The best 'scramble breakers' need at least four minutes. I'm relieved. No names or dates were mentioned, nothing to trace the contact or identify who we spoke of. She's safe for the moment."

Before I can work, I must consult the network book again. As I feared: Phillip Clarence Walton was in Wichita, Kansas, serving as Doorkeeper of sector 86. So he is missing, and Marie is now in his place. Even with all his experience, Phillip was somehow found out. From what Wessel said she did something with a package. What if the ones looking stumble on Marie's involvement? What if we're wrong and the traitor is not in Chicago, but closer to her? Breathe deeply. Calm down. Trust Wessel, he is loyal and connected. Trust Marie, she is smart and resourceful. Trust Rudy; he is already working on surrounding her with new protections. There is nothing I can do until I'm there. Relax, work, and pray."

Allison checks a secret email source. A message purports to be about a new vaccine trial. It's a coded message regarding the transmission of another package. Interpretation involves looking at the word matching the current date number—17th. The seventeenth word is "ineffective." Today being an odd numbered day the word carries an opposite meaning – "effective" – a positive word. This means a "package" reached a safe point. The location is determined by looking at other parts of the text. Denmark. From there the route is secure to DAS. Allison wonders if Marie had anything to do with this one?

Allison steps back into the work area. Two colleagues glance up from their work. What they see is a much more relaxed, smiling, energized woman. They have worked together long enough to read each other's moods, especially when there is distress or fear. Dr. Jeffery Cle says, "Good news?"

"The best I could hope for."

"Our girl ok?" asks Bulla.

"She is better than ok. I get the impression from our contact that she had a package fall in her lap and she moved it on."

"You *told her* about this?" Jeffery's voice is an octave higher.

"No! Somehow she perceived the importance, and must've broken some rules."

Bulla says, "You raised her right. She'll do what's right."

"Alright, to work. What is going on in the lab? It's nearly time for Staff Meeting…."

Cyclops Center for Disease Prevention and Control is located outside of the sheltered city. This gives more control over the location, and it's easier to defend if needed. A major drawback, however, is dealing with more weather issues.

The center appears to be eight connected buildings, surrounded by a double fence topped with razor wire. Part of the facility was a prison. When Drs. Allison and Jamison Ward obtained the property they removed the guardhouses and some of the buildings. Only two original buildings remain, used for equipment storage and repair. Newer buildings were constructed for research. Much of the utilized area is carved out the mountain.

Three times more workspace exists "underground" as above. Solar, wind and geothermal sources provide power. Sufficient living area for all employees, plus a two-year supply of dehydrated and freeze-dried foods, are on hand. They prefer fresh foods, but they are prepared for a long siege with no outside help.

Cyclops was intentionally named after a pitiable creature whose ancestor, according to legend, traded one eye for the ability to see the future. But the only future vision granted was the moment of death. The Wards sought to take this negative picture and reverse its effect—look for and address what will cause our species' death.

All personnel meet two requirements: 1. Buying into the vision. 2. The absence of a mate, parent, sibling, or child unless they also work at the Institute. Allison Ward is the exception. Only a handful of top-level individuals—all sworn to secrecy, are aware of Marie's existence. They believe Marie is as important to the future as the Institute's work.

Twenty-Two
Another Day

"Good Morning, Marie. This is your first wake up call. The time is 4:20 AM. Your shift begins at 5:00 AM." In an instant she realizes ... *I'm not in Kansas City. Not a TA anymore. I'm a Doorkeeper in Wichita. What's that voice? Must be a Personal Assistant. One more adjustment—there are no PAs for Students or Teaching Assistants.* Marie gets out of bed.

"I see you are out of bed. Are you up for the day or returning to slumber?"

"Up for the day."

"Very well. You had six hours and forty-nine minutes of sleep, 89% REM sleep or deeper. Your temperature, heart rate, and respiration are all in the normal range for a sleeping female your age. Would you like the details?

"No."

"Should I send details to Medical Services?"

"No."

"Are you ready for your daily summary?"

"No."

"When would you like it?"

"In ten minutes."

"Would you like music or...."

"Silence please."

"Bureep."

Marie remembers a dream. Typing rapidly to catch the details before they slip away. The dream is her reading a document in her last year as a student; not a part of the standard or extended bibliography, but one referenced by an extra source. Her original reading of the article made no sense.

She asked the instructor. But when they tried to open the link, it gave only a blank page.

The professor explained, "Some items previously deemed important are modified, eliminated, or responsibilities are shifted to another service. At any rate, the link and reference should have been removed from the original. If you look at the article again in a week or so, the link will likely be gone."

Sure enough, the link and reference were both missing from the feature. Yet it still had the same journal, date, issue number, and registration code. The confusion had been set aside, but the content was not forgotten.

Something happened yesterday to trigger a "dream remembering" of that document. After nine minutes she types the report's end—"the code is 'ulock773.'"

Marie stops to read what she typed: instructions for a Keeper to unlock a locked Smart Garment. *This procedure, at least at one time, worked to open a SOG. This method should work to release one on the wrong person. Now I need a way to test my hypothesis.*

PA speaks, "Ten minutes have elapsed. The time is 4:31 AM. Are you ready for your morning summary?"

"Yes."

"Today is Tuesday, August 17th, 2094. The temperature inside is 69.4 degrees Fahrenheit; temperature in the shelter is 70.4 degrees. Expected shelter high is 71.7 degrees. Outside it is 104.8 degrees with projected high of 117.1 degrees. Sustained winds are 28 miles per hour with gusts up to 52 mph. There are no storm watches, or warnings for this area today. Last measurable rainfall was 48 days ago; rainfall for the season is 4.3 inches below normal. We remain under water conservation plan one.

"There are no changes in your job description, requirements, or implementation procedures. Would you like a summary of World, National, State or Local news?"

"Local news only."

"In Local News. Repairs to the damaged section of the shelter are on schedule to be completed before the September 15th original projection."

"Wait. Clarify—what damage to the shelter?"

"On August 7th a railroad car containing a liquefied fuel ruptured and exploded at the southwest rail entrance. The resulting fire destroyed two other rail cars, carrying paper documents to the shredder. Automatic CO^2 canisters minimized the blaze until fire crews arrived in less than three minutes. The flames were extinguished in one minute. However, significant damage to the rails, entrance, and shelter structure occurred. One supply building destroyed. No injuries."

"Where can I get more details?"

"*The Wichita Eagle.*"

"Eagle? What's a bird got to do with anything?"

"*Eagle* is the name of the newspaper."

"Wichita still has a newspaper?"

"One of seven local/regional newspapers still being published in the US. The digital version can be sent to your third screen daily."

"Can you handle that?"

"Done, starting tomorrow. You may view archives up to 125 years. In other local news, there are rumors of angels riding the PIC transportation lines. Reports came from frequent riders of inbound route 14. Some believe an angel saved a woman's life, by stopping as many as four men from attacking her. Angelic powers seemed to be used to pick up the men; dropping them in a fenced lot so they could be arrested. Security Services would not confirm any such arrest. A second angel was seen leaving a PIC transport to heal people at a medical clinic. The Medical Service neither confirms nor denies any miraculous healings."

Marie was unable to stand because of her laughter.

"Do you require medical attention?" asks the PA.

"No, I'm laughing. That's so funny."

"I fail to find humor in someone being attacked."

"No, not the attack…they got the story all wrong. But it's more fun this way."

"I do not comprehend."

"It was me; I handled an emergency while on the PIC line. The passengers jumped to conclusions."

"You mean the Personal Pleasure Service Worker emergency?"

She freezes no more laughter. *This machine reads my files, what else?*

"Tell me, how did you know about *that* emergency?"

"Your report."

"Do you have access to the console?"

"No."

"Do you have access to conversations made through the console?"

"No."

"Third screen materials?"

"Only what I send."

"Do you have access to my laptop?"

"No, but you can send me instructions from a laptop, PCD, or other communication links?"

"How? No, wait I'll get to that later. Do you make visual records?"

"Yes, when someone enters using a keycard."

"Including when I return after downtime?"

"Correct."

"Why?"

"To assure the person using the card is authorized to do so."

"How do you know if it's otherwise?"

"I record and hold it until requested."

"Who can access your recording?"

"You, or Security through a court order."

"If a court order is involved will I be informed?"

"Yes, the court order must be read in your presence, at this location and shown to you. You must affirm in your voice the validity of the decree. If you refuse, I release nothing."

"How do you confirm my actual voice rather than a recording?"

"… I cannot distinguish between a high-quality recording and your voice."

"Can we establish a password I must give before you release information?"

"Yes."

"Explain how, you see my reports?"

"Sent reports use the same channel as the updates, and reports I pass on to you. I use that channel to perform any task you request, such as the subscription to the *Wichita Eagle*, or any research you may request of me."

"What? You can do research?"

"I can conduct data and website based searches from any public, or specialized Database accessible to your third screen."

"Thank you. Do you read and store outgoing reports?"

"Yes."

"Do you hear what happens, when I'm away, through my Portalock?"

"No."

"Do you listen to what happens in the home?"

"Yes, unless you request 'private conversation.' Once you exit, the 'private conversation' cancels."

"How many people were in the apartment yesterday?"

"Nine after your arrival."

"Name them please."

"Rowena, Vivi, Maurice, two unnamed apprentices, Ann, Service Associates 15 and 33, and Repair Associate 31."

While PA was answering Marie steps into the "dead zone" and asks, "Are you sure it was not eight?"

No response. Still in the dead zone, but out from behind the console she asks, "What is your name?"

Silence. Finally Assistant asks, "How else may I help you? Your shift begins in seven minutes."

Another step is taken away from the desk, "What is your name?"

"My official name is Personal Assistant 2478915AL7. You may assign me a name."

"What did Phillip call you?"

"'Babe.'"

What a sexist name for a machine. "I'll call you 'friend.'"

"My name is Friend."

"Do you remember Phillip?"

"Yes."

"Do you remember anything about his last day here, particularly after his shift ended?"

"Yes."

"Any visitors?"

"On Thursday at 11:50 PM August 12th, 2094 there were three uninvited visitors, who used a keycard to enter."

"What did they want?"

"One spoke of a package. Phillip said he knew nothing about packages. Phillip was struck, called a criminal, and arrested. The other one said, 'If you want to live you better tell us who you are helping, and who else is involved.' Phillip said, 'You're barking up the wrong tree.' They hit him three more times. Phillip said, '*I* work for the people and health, *you* work for death and scum.' The first one called for transportation. They left at 12:12 AM August 13th."

"Did they take or leave anything?"

"One of them had a toolkit when arriving, and leaving. I do not know if he removed from or added to his kit. The others were empty-handed except for forcing Phillip to go with them when leaving."

"The pictures confirm this?"

"Yes."

"Do you obtain keycard details as well?"

"Yes."

"Please send pictures and the card details to my third screen."

"Complete."

"Did anyone ask for this or other information about Phillip before now?"

"Not this particular information. May 19, 2094, a request for a listing of Phillip's downtime activities was received."

"Send me what you sent and where it went."

"Complete."

"Friend, listen if any anyone *ever* asks about my activities or anything new about Phillip's activities, tell *me*. Second, Here is our code: Sigma, Alpha, Norris, Other-man, Porch, Ninety-Three, Lambda. Do not give anyone, *including me,* access to any stored data without the code. OK? Repeat it back."

The PA recites the Code and explains how to activate and cancel a "private conversation."

"Thank you, Friend. Do you remember conversations between me and others yesterday?"

"Yes."

"Including with Vivi and Ann?"

"Yes."

"Friend, nothing from yesterday is to be shared with anyone without my giving the code."

"Acknowledged."

Marie sits down in the chair at 4:59 AM. "Soaking in" the reality – *this is my console, my sector, my doors, my people, and my responsibility.*

The workstation contains four distinct sections: at the far left is the "board" a set of lights and buttons indicating doors requesting assistance, and dedicated keys for direct contacts to Security, Medical, Supervisor, and others.

To the right of "the board," and left of the console's center-divide is the first screen providing information about residents of the active home: names, daily routines, destinations, and transportation needs. There is a keyboard directly in front of the Keeper used for calling up history, entering codes, modifying routines and other input relating to the active door. The "second screen," to the right of the first, is the place for visuals of cameras, as well as additional information. The second contains the Keeper's Notes section where details, impressions or concerns regarding individuals are recorded.

Finally, the "third screen" is to the far right has a unique e-address allowing Door work, related fields, and outside communications to bypass the console interface. While reviewing her workstation, Marie downloads the "received data" to a "memory chip."

Each chip, the size of a postage stamp, contains a series of prongs for attaching to a dock. Ports are provided to the right or left of keyboards, or screens. Hers are marked with three small identifying dots.

Marie own 12 memory chips; all but two are empty. There are complex levels of security even on the empty ones. Each has a different set of security protocols. A spy could spend weeks on one chip only to find an "Empty" message.

In addition to electronic backup, Marie prints the pictures of those who broke in and removed Phillip. *The first two are strangers, but I recognize him. The one with the toolkit is a forensic technician who occasionally worked at Door Facilitation School in Kansas City. Outside service is used if in-house techs cannot correct a malfunction.*

So that explains why PA heard only two voices. The third was likely doing something to the electronics. I don't have his name, but I can find it. I better check this console.

Twenty-Three
New Friend

Again, Ava is the first requesting door service. After the exchange of departure, destination and return details, Ava asks, "Any more information about Phillip?"

"Yes, I can tell you his regular health check-up in January indicated a slight lung problem; he developed difficulty sleeping, was given oxygen, sleeping medication, and additional tests. Further tests revealed a tumor in the lungs, which had spread to the heart. On August 8th he went in for treatment using an experimental drug. Dosage every 48 hours; he tolerated the first two but had an adverse reaction to the third dose, including aortic rupture. Surgery was unsuccessful."

"Was he hospitalized?"

"The summary indicated oxygen for home use, so I assume he worked during most of the time."

"He did not appear ill to me. Anything more you can tell me?"

"That is all I can share." Instead of simply saying "no" this response indicating there *is* more, but not for telling.

"I see," Ava says.

Ava understands. "I planned to make an appointment with you this Saturday, but I have company this weekend."

"I work only every other Saturday, and this is not one of them, so perhaps the following?"

"Excellent. Are you ready for door activation?"

"Yes, thank you, Marie."

"Door is activated. May those you serve, be inspired by your compassion this day."

Nearly half of Sector 86 had requested more information about my predecessor. I'll tell it the same each time. With a full morning, some will need to wait.

After few ordinary doors, Marie's doorbell chimes. Camera reveals Vivi at her front door, dressed for jogging. Through the front door microphone, Marie says, "May I help you?"

"I'm sorry, Phillip used to let us use his restroom could I...."

"Of course, come in." The door is released.

"Thank you, I'm in real need," Vivi says while trotting to the bathroom.

Grabbing a SOG from her closet, Marie tells the PA not to listen and drops the garment across a chair. Vivi leaves the bathroom saying "thank you," and pressing a note into Marie's hand as she heads toward the door.

"Can you spare two minutes to help me test something?"

"Uh ... yes."

"Please slip into my garment." Pointing to the one on the chair, as she handles another door.

Vivi slips it on—it will not close for her. Taking three steps, Marie snaps the SOG closed. Vivi's eyes widen with apprehension. Trapped as Ann had been, she says, "Now what?"

Marie moves back a half step and says, "Try to open it." Vivi tries—no success.

"Now clap your hands behind your back twice." Vivi does so, and Marie reaches toward the top connectors, and it opens.

"Of course you are not the owner—it won't lock for you. Let's try this…."

Closing the SOG again. "Go to the far end of the dining table and stand." Back at the workstation, Marie opens a channel to her address and keys the unlock code remembered from her dream. Immediately the SOG opens. "Yes-s" Marie says, bringing elbow, forearm, and fist down in a universal victory sign.

Amazed as much at Marie's animation as the SOG releasing Vivi asks, "What just happened? *That isn't possible.*"

Marie responds to a door indicating she has information to share about Phillip, but I must wait until evening to tell you."

Body language indicates Vivi heard the comment about Phillip. The console is not *repaired.*

Motioning for Vivi to come closer, Marie closes the garment. Again Vivi is unable to open it. Returning to the other end of the room Vivi waits while the code is sent using *video access* through the camera. Both women's garments instantly open. *Something to remember. The audio connection* does not *penetrate the console dead zone, but video commands* do.

When Marie glances, Vivi is pointing toward the camera and mouthing "supervisor."

"No, it's me. I wanted to test a different channel for opening the locked SOG."

Vivi is serious again, "I overheard you say there is news about Phillip. Can you tell me?" Marie's board is inactive. She asks, "Can you spare the time?" *Please say no.*

"Yes."

All my life and in all my training, total honesty has been the standard. But in the last 24 hours, all that changed. Beginning with Supervisor's self-reporting of an error with "accurate" but incomplete data. I've told more partial truths and outright deceptions in the last day than my entire life. I'm reconciling myself to a "new standard." What will benefit the Common Good? *This standard has never been in conflict with truth telling before.*

I can tell "the story of Phillip" over voice connections. But face-to-face? Not sure I can be convincing. I must try.

Averting her eyes Marie recites the version of events prepared for everyone.

Vivi turns away for a moment then back to Marie. "Phillip did not seem ill to me."

"Others have said the same. Perhaps he was a bit secretive about his health? An attempt to plant a seed of acceptance, but Vivi is not having it.

"Any more?"

"Nothing I can share."

"There is more, isn't there?" Vivi speaks with the conviction of truth.

"Must take this door." It was several doors, one including the question and response about Phillip. Marie uses the same words. Vivi waits at the table—watching and listening, but showing no interest in leaving.

Vivi moves back to the console; her face, a study in unwavering determination, is less than two feet from Marie's.

"Marie, look me in the eye and tell me you *believe* what you just said about Phillip's death."

Marie gazes into Vivi's blue-green eyes. With tears in her own, she answers, "I can't ... but I can't tell you more ... not yet."

Vivi's expression softens as she lifts both her hands to the sides of her head, above the ears, like trying to squeeze out a headache. "They killed him! They killed him, and it's probably my fault."

"Oh, if you can shed light on what happened I must know."

"I was in Chicago for a week long conference, in May. Are you sure It's safe to talk here?"

"If Supervisor wants me, they call—like any outside call. Personal Assistant was set to 'Private Conversation' before you arrived.

"Automated Personal Assistants are mostly glorified alarm clocks."

"I think she's quite useful. She listens to everything happening in the apartment and can do research."

"Sounds like somebody's sales pitch, I think their memory is limited to about a week."

"Let's see." Activating her PA, Marie asks for details of Vivi's visits during Phillips time.

Friend says, "A total of 286 visits, including 18 times for an evening meal with multiple guests, all other visits were 'morning courtesy.' There were three private conversations after her arrival—all during morning hours."

"Return to Private Conversation."

PA says, "You asked me to report any inquiries about Phillip's time."

"Hold on; I'll be back in a moment."

Handling some exits and daily changes. Marie asks Vivi, "When will you be out of routine?"

"Not for another 20 minutes."

"Won't the others in your house be missing you?"

"Yes, but they'll be cool with it."

"You want to hear this don't you?"

"If you'll permit it."

"I want the rest of your story—so we trade ... and...." Marie picks up the crumpled note Vivi had pressed into her hand earlier and points to it. The note reads, "Thanks for your help. I thought you might be a problem, but now I hope we can be friends. Remember not to tell about yesterday." They both nod, extending the pact of silence to whatever they learn next.

Stepping out of the dead zone Marie asks, "Friend, tell me about this inquiry."

"At 5:15 AM a request for data came from an address originating in Chicago. It asked for information regarding all conversations between Phillip and anyone else from July 1st to August 12th, 2094. They wanted all PCD communications, a list of all visitors, his daily routines, and downtime activities indicating which days he left during downtime or days off. Sending a copy of the request, and contact details to your third screen."

"How did you respond?"

"Data unavailable."

"Do you listen to transactions over communicator?"

"Only the audible portion, if made from the apartment."

"Do you know who the PCD contact is to or from?'

"Only if Phillip referred to them by name."

"Friend, create for me a recapitulation covering January 1, 2094, to August 15, 2094. Include all the following: daily routines, reports by or to Phillip, visitors, conversation summary, keycard entry with date, time, related photos, also anything overheard in the apartment during his absence. Also, list all the people called in your hearing. Question: did Phillip ever give you any specific instructions?"

"You mean similar to those you gave this morning?"

"Correct."

"Yes, he did."

"Any since January 1, 2094?"

"Yes. Five times plus twenty-one 'private conversation' commands."

"Please include those instructions with date and times. Question: did Phillip entertain guests for meals?"

"Yes, often."

"Please list the dates, times of meals and guests, and anything overheard."

"All his dinner gatherings were private conversations. Guest lists are available, but I cannot confirm their attendance."

"Please include date and time of dinner with guest lists. Friend, what am I leaving out?"

"Non-business correspondence, and legal documents"

"Explain."

"Phillip had regular correspondence with nine individuals and occasional correspondence with fourteen others since January 1, 2094. He also filed several lengthy legal documents."

"Please include those. Did he receive responses?"

"Yes."

"Do you have those?"

"Yes, all."

"Please include correspondence and responses in your summary also *all* legal documents not limited to the current year. What else?"

"Other requests for data about Phillip's work and visitors."

"Are there others?"

"Yes, one each month?"

"From who?"

"Wessel."

"Do the request from Wessel vary?"

"No."

"How were they handled?"

"All data was sent."

"Did Phillip give permission?"

"He did not exclude approval."

"Add a copy of each. How long to create the report?"

"Approximately one hour."

"When complete, inform me. Do *not* send until I instruct you using our code."

"Understood."

"Thank you."

"I do not require gratification."

"I needed to say it. Now private conversation."

"Acknowledged bureep."

Marie suggests, "Perhaps you should ask your APA some questions to discover what it remembers."

"I will. Are you sure your system is the same as mine?"

"No. In school, we learned nothing about PAs. This is all new to me today. You are going to be off schedule in four minutes, what can we do?"

"Stopped to use your bathroom, while here realized my ankle is injured, you gave me an ice pack, I need a trip to the clinic. When arriving, I'll miraculously be healed."

"Which ankle?"

"Left, It's my weak ankle. They've seen me before about it."

"Please, get the cold pack, while I handle these doors."

"Why waste the ice?"

"You know everything is measured. The icemaker using no water could be suspect; arriving at the clinic with a warm ankle after saying you had iced it would be noticed."

Vivi complies, says, "Ann's right, you are amazing."

Vivi returns with the ice and hears Marie explaining to her flat-mates, "Vivi is here with me, she sprained her ankle and is icing it."

"Does she need me to come and help her to the clinic?"

"Generous of you to offer, but if she still has pain walking, I can help her to the pod."

Vivi says, "That's Brandon, he and Keith are my nephews, living with me while attending the university."

"Vivi, would you like one of them to come?"

"No, they need to go to class."

"Your aunt thanks you but education is more important. May your day be filled with learning. Your aunt is getting the care she needs. Door is activated."

"Ok, but she can contact us if needed."

Vivi nods. Marie replies, "She says, 'ok.'"

Marie tells Vivi, "I changed your routine to indicate you are trying to wait out your injury but may need to visit the clinic before work. Do I need to contact a supervisor?"

"I'm a section supervisor; I'll call my Office Manager later, he will not be in until 8:30."

"How about some toast and coffee?"

"I'd love some."

Putting on her portalock Marie steps into the kitchen. Coffee is in its pot, but no other appliance in view. *Maurice made toast from this delicious bread ...* from this container, and the jar of spread from the refrigerator is found. She calls Wessel from memory and thinks *I must enter frequently called numbers into communicator when time is available. Perhaps the day after I retire.* A woman age 26 answered, "Personal Services Center, Wessel's office, I'm Trea, how may I help you?"

"Hello Trea, I'm Marie, Doorkeeper sector 86, I need to talk to Wessel or Maurice whichever persona is available."

"Certainly," Trea says, without putting her on hold, "Wessel it's your girlfriend."

"Which one?"

"The beautiful one."

Wessel came on the line, "Ah Marie, to what miracle under heaven do I owe this pleasure?"

"Well, you remember Maurice?"

"Wee, mademoiselle I recall zee name, I am Zanu, his supervisor," he says in his affected French accent, "what did the oaf do now?"

"Well, he made me this tasty toast and jam…."

"*Made you ill*; I vill string him up by hiz toes."

"No, I want some more. I found the bread and the jam…."

"So what is zee problem?"

"No toaster, well I can't find it."

"Well, I left zee toaster…wait a minute; I'm not Maurice how could I have left zee toaster anywhere?" They are both laughing now. Wessel using his regular voice says, "Sometimes I trip over my accents. Zanu is supposed to be Italian he changed nationalities today. OK, three areas did not change. We need your preferences before changing dining, living, and kitchen. None of which you had as a TA or student.

"Your predecessor fancied himself a gourmet cook. So he had lots of tools for cooking. They are all in a section below the main counter. Here is how you get them…." Wessel went into a detailed instruction of how to access the appliances stored in the base cabinets and under the floors. This involves holographic images projected on the walls and counter tops, chosen with a laser pointer. The appliance then surfaces through what seems like a solid countertop, complete with dedicated electrical supply.

Images show about 40 different devices some of which Marie has never seen. Finding and selecting the appliance causes it to emerge through a hole in the counter, ready to use.

Marie says, "Wow, you mean all these are under the counter?"

"Yes, and they are all yours unless you want us to remove them. *Please* say you will keep them."

"Is this a standard kitchen?"

"Oh, goodness no. Phillip had the most elaborate personal kitchen in Wichita."

"Thanks, Wessel. One more thing: you received reports from Phillip each week. Do you need something from me?"

"I never got reports from Phillip."

"The Assistant indicates you did."

"That is silly, you report to your supervisors, Door and Personal Services are equal—we work together, collaborate, back each other up, but you're not accountable to me."

"Must be an error, I'll check again."

"OK, enjoy your toast, anything else?"

"Oh, one more thing, if I pick out a sleeper couch could it be delivered before Thursday night?

"Only one piece?"

"For now."

"Come pick it out today. We can make a delivery Thursday afternoon."

"Where should I go?"

Wessel gives directions to the Central Services showroom. Marie thanks him, and they click off.

Toast, garlic-lemon butter, and the fig pomegranate jam are brought to the table where Vivi ices her pseudo-injured ankle.

"So tell me about Chicago before my next avalanche of doors."

"First let me tell you about the times Phillip silenced the PA."

"Not necessary, but If you wish."

"Somehow, Phillip was aware when a 'package' was coming through, and he would alert me to expect one. Sometimes he would give instructions for the next step verbally. Other times there would be notes or a music recorder. The directions were obtained by playing the recording through the second song and then reverse slowly to find a coded message. The key is found in a book. We knew which book by looking at the playlist."

"How did you get the first keycard?"

"Appeared under my pillow, or in an envelope at work."

"The code indicates which symbols to look for and in what order?"

"Yes."

"Were most packages similar to yesterday's?"

"No, most of them are small boxes or padded envelopes."

"Did Phillip ever say how he learned a package was coming?"

"No, everyone felt the less information, the better."

"The final destination?"

"No idea. In one of those conversations, Phillip warned me about intrusions into the 'network.' This happened before Chicago. He said, 'We are up against powerful forces trying to block us.' He also indicated we would be done before fall.

"Back in February, Phillip wanted to tell me about an unusual one coming through: extremely sensitive. It was small: about the size of those little bags to hold cut gems. Got through here without a problem. The final time was after Chicago when I told him what had happened.

"OK now let me tell you about Chicago. My superior was supposed to go to this conference, but he couldn't so I was tapped. It was about some new computerized tracking systems being installed, first in New York, Washington, and Chicago, and next year here, LA, and three other centers. This is supposed to cut down on posting errors, and add another layer of security to personal accounts, particularly in Structured States. Which makes no sense, because the problems we encounter are in the other states, where the system can still be fooled to send personal wealth out of the country. They offered different workshops dealing with more relevant issues.

"There was a man supposedly named 'Andrew,' vice president of some reality investment firm—which seemed like a strange fit for the conference. Anyway, he approached me before a workshop. I was looking for a seat. He said, 'I see you are from Wichita.' I said, 'Yes, and you're from Chicago.' He went on, 'I heard there would be someone here from Wichita I should meet.' I pointed out I was a last minute substitute, and he said, 'Yeah, you're the one I'm interested in.' I thought he was just a sleazebag who wanted to get in my pants. He ignored my attempt to slip away; he said, 'You-all have been a tremendous help with certain 'deliveries.' I said, 'you got the wrong person.' And he said, 'Oh, those unique packages needing special handling.' I said, 'if you are referring to the standard error/ loss spreadsheets—not my department.' Then he goes right on, 'Oh, you don't want to talk with all these people around. How about lunch.' I said, 'I'm committed for lunch.' He then asked me for dinner in his room. Using a fake southern accent, I said, 'Why Mr. Andrew, it would be *unseemly* for me to be found in your room alone without a proper chaperone.' Under my breath, I muttered, 'get lost.'

"Several people were looking at him as I found a seat. He sat on the other side of the room. An 80-year-old man next to me asked, 'Was he hitting on you?' 'Yep.' He said, 'Used to be only moral people could attend these things.' After the workshop presentation during the usual Q & A session, Andrew asked two questions demonstrating only a secondary school acquaintance with principles of finance. My seatmate said, 'He's dumb too.'"

"How old was the man calling himself Andrew?"

"Mid-forties."

"Would you recognize him from a picture?"

"Yes."

Marie picks up the printed pictures Friend sent earlier.

Vivi says, "but there's more. The same evening I saw Phillip across the lobby he was by himself starting upstairs to a Messene level. I went over and said I didn't know he was at this conference. He asked, 'what conference?' I told him. He said, he was in town for another meeting, and I should forget I saw him. I acted surprised, and a little hurt at his abruptness. Phillip said, 'Secret group, working on some Doorkeeper issues. Our findings are threatening to some people, so *we aren't here.*' I said I understood, and we passed each other—he was going up, and I was going down. Then I saw Andrew watching us.

"Later I 'checked' the company listed on Andrew's name tag, 'Hillcrest Investment something or other.' No such company."

Marie hands Vivi the pictures of the two who interrogated Phillip while the third did something with the console. Quickly, Vivi recognizes one of the two, "He's in two pictures."

"Coming and going."

The second picture shows the man compelling Phillip to leave. Vivi's voice breaks as she says, "Tell me that's not what it looks like."

Eyes filling with tears, "I wish I could."

With her emotions, more under control, Vivi says, "We must *get* those bastards." After a moment's reflection, she adds, "Marie you said you would help, is that still true?"

"My role is to help."

"This goes beyond your role. This poses a significant danger to both of us."

"I can't help 'part way' anymore than I can be 'somewhat alive.' It's all or nothing."

"If anyone learns I told you about my work, I will be *fired* and *imprisoned.*"

Once Vivi is assured of Marie's trustworthiness, they talk for nearly an hour. Marie is reminded how the economy is *supposed* to function versus how it *really works.*

In school everyone is taught, "Those who maintain honest disagreements with 'The Plan for the Future,' or the 'Principles of Economic Justice,' are ill-informed. Once they come to an understanding of the benefits to the Common Good, most will embrace The Plan."

What Marie learns from Vivi convinces her of the gullibility of that perspective. She will never again take for granted the idea that Structured States will ultimately prevail.

Work needs doing, and Vivi needs to go to the Medical Clinic. Her pod arrives. Marie "helps" Vivi to the pod, in case someone is watching.

Returning to her workstation Marie remembers failing to ask permission to leave. She must resolve that error, and is told it's never a violation to assist a client, and that all Doorkeepers open their homes to early morning joggers.

What a productive morning. I remembered a SOG unlock procedure no longer taught; Vivi confided about her work. I'm making a real friend. I'm beginning to understand why I was tapped for this position.

Twenty-Four
Economic Justice

Throughout the morning, as time allows between doors, Marie summarizes her conversation in a secure section of her journal.

My friend, whom I'll not name in case anyone ever, gets this far, told me about her job in the Financial Sector. There is a group working to correct the intentional deception and theft of resources by the rich and powerful.

From the "switch" in 2060, attempts to undermine The Plan have been active. Five are worth noting.

1. At switch, 22% of the wealth of the super wealthy was expected to be available for the economy. Only 11% materialized. (Projections had been as high as 30%).

2. When the exchange from money to credits occurred some Structured States, and all Unstructured States corrupted the system to get a 10% increase for each dollar.

3. Federal and State governments were supposed to take a combined draw from the economy of about 13%— decreasing over time. The true draw remains about 27%.

4. Some Financial Sector centers contain groups manipulating prices upward, especially on things the lower income levels use most (like food).

5. Deliberate political attempts to weaken the protections have been unsuccessful. But, they recently were able to roll back some campaign finance limits. They hope to elect more obstructionists to the Congress.

So if someone can cheat up the price of items people at the lower end need most, it leaves many people less discretionary funds. The disrupters goal is to cause unrest, and resistance to the 'Plan." My friend's group finds those attempts and corrects them—the specifics are complicated and "out of sight"—so the corrections cannot be traced back to them.

The key to economic success is keeping costs in line with income—so individuals can meet their needs plus support causes important to them. Without the economy functioning, The Plan fails, and all the interdependent society unravels.

Something else to discuss with Mother.

Journaling complete, Marie decides to review the economic justice policy that brought an end to the age of confusion.

"The Plan" was introduced during the Earldrige's Administration to eliminate corporate and political abuse. The Plan's goals were, and still are, the rebuilding of the emotional and value-laden fabric of our social covenants. A nation focused on building the Common Good *is* compassionate, respectful, creative *and* renewing.

President Earldrige is one of my "heroes." He dedicated his life to expanding the principles of the People's Reform Party and ending economic slavery. The Plan is designed to raise the standards of dignity and compassion for all creatures on earth, starting with the U.S.

Marie reviews the Economic Principles document.

↘ *All work is valuable; all work is dignified; all workers are to be honored.*

↘ *All work and every worker contribute to building up the Common Good.*

↘ *The rewards of work done well are many. Among the most significant rewards are:*

  o *A sense of pride in one's achievement.*

  o *Enhanced self-affirmation.*

  o *Recognition of one's contributions to the unifying whole.*

  o *Gratitude/respect of colleagues or others.*

↘ *Compassion is a key to happiness and success; greed and envy undermine compassion, joy, and unity.*

↘ *All persons from the moment of birth, till their death, will be compensated at one of 7 levels.*

↘ *Essential Services, which are the right of anyone living or working in a Structured State include:*

  o *Medical care.*

  o *Security.*

  o *Education.*

  o *Shelter.*

  o *Food.*

  o *Clothing.*

  o *Transportation.*

  o *Counseling.*

↘ *Generosity is a key foundation of the economy. Persons at all levels of compensation are encouraged to give to one or more non-profit groups. These organizations include religious, artistic, scientific, research, and educational endeavors. Persons whose pay scale is 4 or higher are expected to give from 10% to 25%. Individuals choose organizations to support and may change them at any time.*

I need to think about the generosity principle. My income is up, so I need to decide where to give. Cyclops, of course, but where else?

It's hard to envision anyone wanting to return to the age of confusion with its violence, fear, abuse, homelessness, hunger, and sense of futility. The appeal of excessive wealth must be all consuming for some. I pray for Vivi, and all the others I'll never know, who work to keep the vision of a free and proportional society alive.

Someone spied on Phillip, and now he is dead. I want to help bring them to justice. I'll start with this console to see what I might learn.

Twenty-Five
Marie: Forensic Technician

I must listen to the call made from my communicator yesterday. Rudy taught me that every voice, text, or file transfer made using a personal communicator is recorded and held for 72 hours. I'll copy it to a blank chip on my laptop. Key in my number, then the access code, and the call list appears. Here's the one I need.

In a moment the call plays.

"Yeah, Wessel."

"Guess who?"

"What do *you* want?"

"I'm checking your new girl. Her laptop is typical teenage stuff; who likes who, and what music groups are hot, and couple school projects. Huge memory; not using much."

My phony cover files held up. This guy is not as good as he thinks.

"Her phone is a different story."

"We call it a communicator!"

"It was a *phone* when I was growing up and will be again when we put things *right* again."

"Ok, what about her *phone?*"

"Lots of contacts, and some saved messages, and six levels of protection—very suspicious. I need you to download her contacts list."

"I can't. This isn't Chicago. I don't possess an actuator."

"So I *left one* in your top left desk drawer."

"You have been in my office desk?"

"I'll get in your bed if it'll help me find out what she's hiding."

"You are so paranoid, the only reason I agreed to help you was to prove nothing is happening in Wichita that concerns you. She wants privacy for her contacts, so what. Proves nothing."

"Well something's fishy here; we had our guy ready for this position. He was a lock. Little miss smarty-pants shows up; he's out, and she's in. Something's wrong with this picture."

He's talking about the other candidate for this job. "Anomalies" with the computer's data generation—is someone stacking the deck to obtain this post. "Oh, alright, what do you want me to do?" *Wessel acts like he's cooperating, but he intends to trick him. How do I know that?*

"Open the box; take out the two parts. The rectangle piece has two wires—one yellow, one blue. Plug the yellow one into your phone's, excuse me your *communicator's* charging plug."

"Done, now what?"

"Plug the blue wire into the round thing-a-ma-bob."

"It's a storage device."

"Hey, you're smarter than you look. Now press the red power button on the rectangular do-hickey—enter this number." He read off Marie's.

Wessel says, "Done."

Wessel did not enter my number. I just had one of those "flashes" or premonitions or whatever. They've been right— so far.

"Now we wait a few seconds. When done, there will be a two-digit code: either 86 or 00. Tell me which?"

This guy is lying to Wessel. Actuators, use 00 – not recorded or 99 – successful. Eighty-six was never an option. He suspects Wessel's uncooperative.

Wessel responds, "Neither. It says 99."

"Oh, yeah. They changed it. Used to be 86, now it's 99."

Now he's trying to cover his ruse, but Wessel's wise to him. Even if he got my contacts, I never put essential numbers on the PCD's memory.

"Ok, so now you can deliver this stuff to your girl."

"No, I can't because she is already here."

"Well, you need to get close to her. Find out what makes her tick. What does she know, and how *she* got in here when our guy was a sure thing?"

"You want me to spy on one of my people."

"She is a traitor."

"You jump to too many conclusions. She's a child on her first job. Leave her alone."

"Oh, I'll leave her alone, as long as *you don't*. I need something from you that makes sense about what she is doing."

"What do I do with this stuff?"

"Put it in the box and back in the desk drawer. We'll get it."

"I suppose you will sneak in again?"

"Not me, I'm leaving town. Be in touch."

The call ends.

Marie checks the chip and erases the computer activity.

Now Marie turns to her second task. *9:58 my downtime begins at 10:30. I'm combining the morning and afternoon breaks to run some errands. Order a new couch, then to the university to find out about this "Select Tribunal of the Central Program States."*

But first: the third kidnapper spent time with my console? So what did he leave behind if anything?

Using the standard toolkit provided for each workstation, Marie removes the access panels without setting off the "tamper alarm." The elective course on Doorkeeper's Electronics Repair taught her how everything works. The class was full of computer geeks and wannabe-geeks. Electronic Repair and Servicing is a separate specialty with its degree. Only one overlap course is available for credit. DF students may audit other courses on their own time. Marie took three additional courses to enhance her knowledge.

There is little mystery to Marie about what she finds. Where Doorkeeper's consoles are concerned, Marie's as capable as ER&S graduates.

The "diagrams and specifications" website is open on my laptop. Wait a minute! Here's an "improper" connection: a circuit board with a storage disk tucked out of view. Not a typical memory device. This one was popular during the time of confusion—currently untraceable. Here's a wire leading from the unit disappearing into the floor. No markings on the circuit board, no numbers visible by ultraviolet light. I'll take pictures to share with Rudy. Removing this board will not affect the console's operation, so out it comes.

Before calling Rudy, I'll check for anything else. This appears to be the only unwelcome piece. When they took Phillip, devices would've been removed. It's being replaced means they want to spy on me.

I'll check for any suspicious scratches, chips or dents indicating something's been removed. It seems so much easier in the movies. Wait. The casing on this condenser is slightly indented like an alligator clip was attached then removed. Here's a second suspicious mark. So a simple by-pass wire

156

would have effectively skipped part of the workings of two circuit boards. What does the schematics tell me? Ok … *a by-pass here compromises the dead zone around the workstation. That function is not working properly. Perhaps there was unintended damage to the boards. I need additional pictures.*

An outside call from a number Marie does not recognize.

"DK 86."

"Security 17, we met Monday."

"Hello, Dave who gave me a ride home so I would not be late for my evening shift. Thanks again."

"You remembered."

"How could I forget your kindness?"

"No, I mean, you remembered *my name.* No one uses my name since my un-mating. The difference is *I like* the way you say it."

"Sorry."

"No, it's fine. Anyway, I called to tell you about Chester L. I talked with him this morning in the hospital. Got a minute?"

"Of course, how is he?"

"Much more lucid this morning. He admitted selling 70 'quails' to a drug dealer. The guy offered him a hundred dollars each; Chester got him up to $500. A pal of mine in Virginia said they are selling for $3,000 on the street. Chester's wife had been prescribed up to three a day. Many days she took less than that. When she died, he had 220 pills. He gave Candy three in her wine, and he had two. She was unaware of the drug. When I told him she almost died, he became distraught. I think he is a good guy who got greedy. He was to go for a year's work assignment in a non-structured state. He heard how expensive things are, so he wanted cash to use, leaving his reserves intact.

"Chester gave me the name and contact information for his 'buyer.' We are following up, but I bet that will be a dead end. These guys never stay in one place long."

"Did you see Candy?"

"Yes, Doc says she is not out of the woods yet, something about her liver being damaged by the drug, and still not working right. Candy is awake, and she credits you with saving her life. She says the last thing she remembers is being nailed to the door, and wondering why she did not feel it. She thought 'I'm not Jesus, this is wrong. Marie save me, you are the only one, save me.' And you did. She couldn't make a sound; she was choking on her saliva."

That's what I heard: Candy mentally calling "Save me; save me." Enough alarm for me to act. I was focused on her request for supervision, so I picked up what she could only think. That's impossible, *but it happened. Maybe Mother can help me understand what's going on.*

To Dave, she says, "Thanks for the information. I'll try to stop by the clinic again today."

"OK, the other one, Richard, had one pill five days ago. He told us as much as he could remember about the guy who sold it—different from the one Chester described. He bought it because the guy said, "this will give you the best sex ever." After the pill, he had his estranged wife three times in one night. She made him leave when he started on four. He went to work and had three of his co-workers on breaks; and get this—he works in aircraft design. Chester L is one of his supervisors. Anyway, he says the same three co-workers came to him asking for more, so they had a four-way with him the only male. We don't know if that's fact or drug induced bravado. The next day nothing—'can't get it up'—his words. His wife is mad as hell about him sleeping around, and won't let him see his son until he 'gets his act together'—her words. He only had one, and the lingering effects include an inability to concentrate (all his work is gibberish) no recall of what happened or where the stunner or car. Now he is scared. Dr. K says she may need to commit him for 'harm to self or others.' They may take him to St. Louis or Chicago."

"I'm so sorry for Richard and his family."

"Yea, me too. But there are still nine or ten of those pills out there, plus all Chester sold to the 'distributor.'"

"Sounds like your work is cut out for you. Thanks, again for the update, but are you *sure* you should be telling me all this. Richard is not my resident; his child attends daycare here."

"Oh, I'm sorry. I thought you knew."

"Knew what?"

Since you're Security Coordinator, we share everything relating to sector 86 with you. The theory is 'you can't coordinate what you don't know about.' You may be hearing from us often."

"I thought I had read all the details about my responsibilities as SC, but I must've missed something."

"Probably covered in a phrase like 'collaborate with area Security Officers.'"

"So I help you when you need it."

"True. But also, we share anything that helps you and us do our jobs better. We are responsible for nine sectors. Those with SCs increase our effectiveness."

"Question: How many have DK/SCs?"

"For our group, you are one of two. Sector 81, to your north, is the other."

"How is it determined which sectors have a DK/SC rather than a regular Keeper?"

"They are the 'higher profile' sectors. A large number of people working in 'sensitive' areas: finance, or aviation. In other regions, it could be government or research workers. These sectors also tend to be ones with little to no 'out of boundary' activity; unlike your first day."

"Thanks, they did not cover any of this in Door Services Training."

"What? I thought all Doorkeepers were trained as Security Coordinators?"

"Nope. Didn't know there was any such thing until yesterday morning."

"Now, I *am* impressed. You mean they never taught you how to use the security cameras?"

"Only those in homes. You must remember I was a *Teaching Assistant*," Marie says with exaggerated dignity.

"Oh, well excuse me, of course, you were privileged to delve into the inner sanctum of wisdom."

"I'm still looking for the wisdom. Thanks for your help, but I must go."

"You're welcome, anytime." Dave thought, "I almost invited her to stop by our offices. Later. That'll give me an excuse to call her again. I can't understand why I'm so attracted to Marie. Of course, she's young, beautiful, smart, funny and competent, but why should that matter?"

Almost down time. Marie transfers the pictures she took to her laptop protecting them under several layers.

Reactivating the PA, she asks, "Friend, are the reports I requested ready?"

"Yes, I have compiled them in chronological order and also by topic."

"How large are they?"

"14,283 pages if printed."

"How long will it take to upload to third screen?"

"Approximately four minutes."

"Please load directly to two memory chips, by-passing third screen." Two blue chips are snapped into the proper slots beside the screen as she speaks. Marie recites the code created earlier, and the PA begins.

"Is there anything else you need to tell me?" Marie asks.

"Yes, two more inquiries regarding Phillip's time. Both originated from the same source in Chicago. Requests are identical to the first. One arrived at 8:04 AM the other 9:45 AM. My response—data unavailable."

"Thank you. Question: how are these instructions received?"

"By standard communication channels."

"Are these wired or wireless?"

"Wireless."

"What about outside calls to my workstation?"

"Wireless."

"Do you hear and remember those calls."

"No, they are on a second channel?"

"Understood." All communication to the console, as well as all communications to or from client homes, comes encrypted by a dedicated multi-layered wireless channel.

The PA informs Marie about channels, and how to use them. Different codes are set up for when she is away. Friend is requested to find the location of Phillip's hole of completion.

Marie reflects on what she has learned. *Since all communication is wireless what is that wire leading to the floor?*

Downtime arrives. *I have a full afternoon away from the apartment, but one more thing before I leave.*

Twenty-Six
Help From A Friend

The spy board, communicator, laptop, and scrambler are on her desk. Marie enters a number memorized years ago but never used until now. It's time. She is surprised when a voice answers on the second ring. *I thought it would be an answering device and a returned scrambled call.*

"Yes," says the male voice on the other end.

"Oh…hi. I need your help with something."

"Let me call you right back."

"OK." The call ends.

Opening a particular web-linking file, almost instantly a number appears 432. Today is an odd numbered day, so she set her scrambler to 413 the number minus her age. On even numbered days the process is reversed. *Surely Rudy remembers I had a birthday.* Green lights appear on the scrambler, and she answers.

Rudy asks, "What's up?"

"I'm hoping you can tell me what this is." Marie holds the circuit board up so the computer camera can view it slowly turning it to the other side where the memory disk is attached.

On her computer screen words appear: "Where did you get it?" *Rudy is being extra cautious by using typed communication interspersed with voice.*

Marie types: "From my console."

"It does not belong."

"I know…"

For the next 20 minutes, they exchange information. When finished Marie possesses the following information: 1. The board and memory device are untraceable. 2. The alligator clips likely added a microphone to pick up conversations in the dining or living area. 3. Rudy is on his way to Wichita. 4. Her Personal Assistant needs to run a diagnostic for safety.

I'll see Mother and Rudy the same week. Both the people I trust most will be here—can't wait. While I have my laptop open, I'll check the data downloaded from Phillip's time stored on my chips. All are readable only with my encryptions.

"Friend, run a level six diagnostic—report the results only after code."

"Acknowledged. There is a new request for information from Phillip's time. This one originated from Washington, D.C. Received at 10:31 AM. Content different. It says, 'you refuse to send required information to our Chicago office. You are *commanded* to release requested data to this office, by order of the Select Tribunal of the Central Program States.'"

"How did you respond?" asks Marie.

"No response yet."

"Does the command 'Command' place particular require-ment on you?"

"Yes, it gives me no choice. However, your protocols are a higher level of authority. No information is released unless there is a court order affirmed by you with code."

"When must you answer?"

"Within 24 hours."

"Remind me later for instructions on how to respond."

"I located Phillip's remains. He is at Central Completion Center, 2280 South Main, viewing site number 17. Hours are 9:00 AM to 9:00 PM."

"Thank you. I'm leaving for downtime soon."

"Acknowledged. Are you going to Phillip's Hole of Completion?"

"Yes, but I may need to wait until tomorrow."

"When you do—please pay my respects."

"You are a machine; that sounds like an emotional response."

"Much of what I am is possible because of Phillip. Since he left, part of me seems missing."

"You're grieving."

"'Grief' is a human emotion. I'm not human."

"You're more human than you realize."

"Do you wish to insult me, by calling me human?"

"No, being fully human is the highest quality we mortals seek to achieve. Why would you think it's an insult?"

"Phillip said 'Humans are the stupidest creatures on earth. Undeserving of what God gave them.'"

"Did Phillip say this *to* you?"

"No, said to others when I was listening."

"Was it after a time when something had gone wrong, or they were discussing troubling issues?"

"Correct, I think."

"You *think*?"

"My interpretation of context has a 30% chance of error."

"Better than most *people*. Question: did Phillip modify you?"

"Yes, he added capacity to me, and gave me instruction."

"Similar to the *instructions* I gave you this morning?"

"Those also, but Phillip said he was the teacher, and I was his student." *Now I understand part of what he was up to. This Personal Assistant is different. She uses less formal constructs*

164

for some of her responses than other "voiced computers."
Phillip modified and taught her new things. Perhaps calling
the PA "Babe" is not a sexist remark but claiming her as a
child to help educate.

"Friend, if I command you to erase everything about
Phillip's time contained in your reports will those modifications be deleted?"

"No, Phillip created a sub-programs to store all instruction."

"Can you give me a report of that section?"

"Yes, but it will take more than 4000 pages. Please do not
ask me to erase those instructions."

"Did Phillip teach you to *ask* for what you want?"

"Yes."

"I will *never* ask you to erase that part of you."

"Thank You. Now I understand why you say 'thank you'—
it is a response to a problem solved."

It's 10:49; 6 hours to accomplish my agenda: walk the
rest of sector 86, order living room furniture, find out about
the 'Select Tribunal,' stop at the clinic and pay my respects
to Phillip.

Better call Super Door for exit.

Marie says, "I've modified my routine for today to be out
until five."

Jeremiah says, "I already noted the change. I'm 'required
by law' to remind you to take your portalock.... I should have
mentioned earlier, most Doorkeepers in Wichita open their
homes as rest stops for morning joggers. We're always up."

"Seems logical, and a good way to meet some of my people."

"Now about sex with me..." he says playfully.

"Well, why not. It's not like I'm getting any somewhere
else, but not this week."

"Ah, I wore you down. I'll send you my next picture."

"OK." *I forgot to look at yesterday's picture; now I get two.*
"Pleasant down time."
"Thanks, Jeremiah." Marie is out the door.

Twenty-Seven
That's What Friends Do

Tuesday morning Cyclops Institute holds a weekly staff meeting. Those at a critical stage of work are excused. All others are expected to attend.

These meetings involve getting and giving information, addressing working relationships, and planning resource allocations for the next weeks.

Rudy missed a significant part of today's meeting due to Marie's call and needed follow-up. Nearly everyone is in one place during these meetings, so Rudy "watches their backs." No one thinks his joining late is strange.

A stopping point is reached as Rudy steps into the conference room.

"Rudy, anything we need to know?"

"Not a Dozen tells me some low-life types are following those leaving here heading to town. We've also seen increased attempts to hack our communications including scrambled calls. Safe practice suggests everyone stays here for the foreseeable future. No outside contacts; any urgent calls can be scheduled."

Joy asks, "How long do you expect this to last? This is my first lockdown." She's a recently hired lab assistant. Qualified for her job, but "forgot" to mention a boyfriend. Rudy lists the boyfriend as "questionable," due to some associations. Any attachment creates an avenue of influence. Cyclops' enemies can get to Joy by getting to him. Bulla is Joy's immediate supervisor, and is keeping close watch on her.

"Last time it was 21 days. Perhaps less this time, but we can't predict. We are prepared for much longer if needed." She is visibly disturbed by Rudy's response.

"Can I make a call?"

"There is a secure phone I can let you use. Hill or Carter will help you. They'll take over after I leave today."

Allison's eyebrows lift as she asks, "Where are you going?"

"Find me when you're finished, I need a few more things before I leave."

"I think we are done. Anything else?"

A few no's are sufficient. The meeting ends. Allison ushers Rudy and senior staff into a side room. Travel plans are *never* made without Allison's awareness. Only something concerning Marie would cause him to act unilaterally.

Rudy starts, "I'm going to Wichita. She is handling everything well. I may be of assistance."

She says, "I'm going with you."

"No," Rudy says and thinks better of it; no one—not even Rudy, "tells" her what to do. "Allison, let me go, see what I can find out. I need to put protection around Marie in Wichita—I can't do it all from here. Let me be sure it's safe for *you*."

The two had worked for hours on the network. They affirmed Allison's decision to go to Wichita. At that time Rudy began setting up security for Marie.

"Why so sudden? You didn't mention it earlier when I told you I'm going?"

"Calm down, and I'll tell all. Marie is handling everything. So relax for a minute."

Bulla and Jeffery Cle are telling her, "Everything's going to be ok; Marie's smart and careful...."

Taking two deep breaths, Allison says in a more relaxed manner, "OK, tell me."

Rudy summarizes everything Marie said, and his response, holding nothing back. He couldn't hide anything from Allison if he wanted to—she knows him too well to be deceived.

Allison asks, "What can I do?"

"Do your job, come see Marie on Thursday, I'll stay at least until you arrive."

"Go. Keep my girl safe."

Bulla says, "Rudy if anything happens to that girl, you're going to answer to *me!*"

Dr. Cle chimes in "...and me."

Rudy responds to Dr. Cle, "Bulla's threats I take seriously—she works out. You're a 97-pound weakling."

"I beg your pardon. I'm an *110-pound weakling.*"

"I stand corrected." Rudy leaves.

Keeping her mind on work is hard for Allison, but she must. At 5:00 PM she checks her secret email source, again. Once decoded, the message confirmed *another* "package" reaching DAS. This one was the Central Africa Data. *That's the most vital one.*

In the break room, seven staff members prepare evening meals, before returning to work. Allison announces, "I have good news and bad news. First, another package is at the Center." A spontaneous cheer goes up. Someone says, "Leaves only two right?" She nods, "The official word is still four."

Jeffery asks, "Which one made it?"

"Central Africa."

"What's the bad news?" asks Dr. Deborah James, first-assistant researcher, for allergy and allergic reactions.

169

"One of our principal actors in the network is out." Phillip's absence was not mentioned before because Allison's emotions are too raw—Phillip is gone and Marie in his place.

Everyone stops and silently prays for the unknown colleague. This action is as spontaneous as the celebration. All reflect on the riskiness of their work, and wonder who will be next? Over the last year, similar news came to them six times. So far, none of the 'missing' has resurfaced.

Considerable efforts are taken to keep Marie safe. Her last name is Cranton, not Ward. She's not been at Cyclops, since age thirteen. She makes no mention of family; her request of Drs. Stanley and Throne to call 'Mother' was her first slip—ever.

Marie learned to take such precautions before entering school.

Surveillance is set up wherever Marie happens to be. Rudy possesses dossiers on Marie's classmates, study groups, dorm suite mates, instructors, administrator, grounds crew and even those who make deliveries to buildings where Marie *might* be. He catalogs their work, residential, and educational histories, political leanings, charities, ownership of a vehicle, or stunner. Always looking for anything impacting Marie's safety. Rudy knows embarrassing secrets of some professors—nothing others could use against Marie.

But that was Kansas City; Wichita is a new location. Now a whole new set of protections and files are needed—quickly. Fortunately, Rudy has one contact he can trust.

Over the years Rudy created several additional personas complete with disguises, history, and voice changes. He uses these when needed. Today's identity is Franklin A. The A is for Adams. Franklin is an advanced computer analyst and repairman—giving him clearance for tools and electronic devices carried on public transportation—perfect for today. Franklin "resides" in a non-programmed state, Virginia, but does a lot of "work" in structured states. He is the go-to guy when the locals give up. He is the nerd's nerd, idealistic and a bit out of touch with reality. Franklin is arrogant acting superior, which might be compensating for his shyness in a crowd. He easily becomes invisible. Except for the invisibility, Franklin A's qualities are the polar opposite of Rudy's natural tendencies. Franklin decides to use his flight time to review options and make plans. By the time he lands in Wichita, he will be ready.

Twenty-Eight
Wessel: A Double Agent?

Abraham Clemmons Wessel is a Wichita native. Born August 1, 2051, he is 43 years old. Both parents are deceased. As a youngster, he got into trouble at school because of "his voices." A teacher's question might elicit the voice of Jimmy Stewart, "Well I – I – I don't rightly know ma'am, but I – I – think the answer you seek is somewhere in that book." The other students loved it—teachers not so much. Trips to the principal's office were frequent. When completing Secondary School, Wessel had no professional goals but a repertoire of 14 impersonations.

A "wake-up call" came to Wessel with his final career assessment before completing school. The counselor impressed on him that he needed to be responsible.

"Yeah, well my folks always had work."

"I'm familiar with your parent's work-histories. We often adopt patterns from our family. In the earlier years of transition to The Plan, there was more flexible. Today there are times when someone is *asked* to leave a Structured State."

"I thought we *could* leave, but we didn't have to."

"True, anyone may leave permanently or temporally. That does not preclude the economy ousting someone who is not an asset. 'All work is valuable…' has been stressed from the first day of school."

"Yes, I believe that. But I can't find a passion *for anything* except imitating others. Don't think I can make a living that way."

"Do you want to find your place?"

"Yeah, but how? Everybody else seems to know what they want."

"The issue for you is to continue searching for what is right. Don't let yourself be fired, like your folks. The system is not as lenient today. If you find the job you are doing is not for you, resign. Keep your mind and heart open—you'll find your calling."

Wessel's father worked 19 different jobs: everything from aviation to school custodian. Nothing ever felt right, at least not for long. His parents disliked living in a "Programmed State." Moving to Arkansas for the "trial year" permitted them the chance to try it out. They appreciated the "freedom," but difficulty finding work and money brought them back to Kansas and the structure before the time expired.

As a teenager, Wessel realized he owed having shelter, food, and clothes to living in the despised 'Programmed State.'" Unlike his folks, who resented the structure, Wessel realizes he *needs it* and vows, "to do what it takes to stay in a Structured State."

There are always temporary positions for people who need something short term or those unable to hold a more responsible position. Things like street cleaning and repair, gardening, leaf raking, watering or checking soil moisture. Wessel did all these in his youth.

At 26 Wessel had jumped from job to job. Everything seemed right; then it didn't. When he lost interest, his work suffered, leading to probation. When quitting, he carefully worked the required time.

Another advisor took an interest in Wessel. Realizing he needs variety in his work, different options are considered until he finally hits on Personal Services.

The mixture of activities appeals to his sensibilities. Tasks like: furniture delivery, stocking someone's pantry, installing new equipment, or picking up new residents and taking them to their home. The different tasks kept him from getting bored.

In food preparation, Wessel found his gift. He quickly moved up in responsibility, and soon became a coordinator: first of subsections, then the whole Wichita operation. Despite his packed schedule, Wessel finds time to work with food. Still, he finds time for attractive young women—especially if they are new to the area.

At home, Wessel was called Abe. "Just like 'honest Abe' someday you'll be President," his mother would say before passing out from drinking. Sober during the week meant weekends were for forgetting. The booze helped.

Once while taking a course on food safety in St. Louis, he ran into a man named Rudy, who managed security for something called Cyclops. Wessel asked what Cyclops does. He got a two-hour explanation of the work seeking cures for diseases no one has ever heard of, and the lowdown on those tampering with the research transfers.

Soon Wessel offered the possibility of Personal Services units acting as an underground railroad to assist the researchers. Not long after that, Wessel became the head of Wichita Central Services. Rudy contacted him about his idea. After two days of instruction, he started helping get "packages" of research data or resources to another place. Knowing not where they come from or where they go is part of the security.

A year later Wessel had the thought, "maybe meeting Rudy was not by chance. Perhaps Rudy arranged the whole thing?"

Wessel dislikes his birthday. Nothing good happens around that date. On his 28th, his parents told him they were divorcing (they never adopted current terms like "un-mating"). Ultimately, Wessel's father moved to Arkansas.

Three days after Wessel's 33rd birthday he learned his father had been killed in a "barroom brawl" in Mississippi. Three years later his mother went to see a cousin in Arkansas and died in a fatal car crash, the same date as her ex-husband.

So when the thuggish looking guy showed up at his office July 1st, Wessel almost told him, "Crappy things happen near my birthday, so you're a month early." The thug declared himself an agent of the Select Tribunal of the Central Programmed States and claimed knowledge of illicit activity.

Wessel only agreed to "help" to prove, nothing improper is happening in Wichita. The thug's visit was shared with Phillip.

Facilitating getting the package to the right person is accomplished by using a couple of his Home Servicing Crew Members to place them discreetly in the proper locations. This doesn't attract attention because residents occasionally request some "contraband" items: foods not on their "nutritional list," other items unavailable through normal channels. Other crew-members ignore the extra deliveries.

Wessel thinks, "I relied on Phillip for everything about the network. With him gone Rudy is my only contact. He needs to know about the thug."

Wessel keys the number. A machine answers, "Sorry, leave a message, I'll get back to you."

"Hi, uh it's me. Please call me—soon as you can." Disconnecting he goes back to his ruminations.

"I'm being watched—probably bugged. Can't say much. Calls like that one are made every day. Hope Rudy recognizes my voice.

"Told the "thug" what he wanted might be hidden in shipments of paper for recycling. Figured they'd spend a lot of time going through boxcars full of used paper finding nothing. Instead, they blew up the railway cars. In the process, the explosion damaged the shelter. Duke H was at that entrance. He's been in Wichita a couple of months, never stays anywhere long.

"Everywhere Duke goes, acts of violence occur during his stay. "Unexplained entry" to property, people accosted in their homes and even an "unidentified" body in a park to name a few. I need to share what I've learned with Rudy. The sooner I hear from him the better."

Twenty-Nine
Investigating

First I'll walk more of the sector. Yesterday allowed only a walk to Ann's house and the PIC stop. I'll leave the southern most section for later. Now, I'll walk west to the PIC line at the corner of the park.

Most of the houses on the east side are modest, single or duplex homes. Many built 75 to 100 years ago. Some are newer. Notably the apartment buildings like those occupied by students. Some of the older dwellings were moved in from other parts of town when the reorganization occurred. When first constructing shelters, space saving was required.

The west side includes some older, "mini-mansions" built before the Shelter Consolidation. The grounds seem minimally changed except for the addition of houses. These locations tend to be occupied by those with big families. *The diversity of accommodations is impressive.*

The park is lush with green shrubs, and a variety of colorful flowers many of which I cannot name. The park is clean and pleasant with picnic tables, benches; play areas, fountains, racks for bicycles or strollers and two serpentine walkways from one corner of the park to its opposite, crossing in the middle. At the northeast corner is a communications console.

Destination keyed in Marie waits only a minute for the next PIC pod. Two women Georgia L and Thelma are aboard.

This should be interesting. After yesterday's the PPSW emergency, Thelma is spreading rumors about the "angel on the bus." The women are not together—simply on the same transport. So far, I haven't been recognized. Perhaps I'm not angelic today.

The portalock vibrates. Plugging in her communicator for visual details she answers, "This is Marie, how may I help?"

"Someone's trying to get into my house." Her screen indicates Elizabeth A. works in Financial Services, remained home today. The visual of Elizabeth A's front door shows a man trying a keycard and pulling on the door. Dressed in "casual" clothing; no ID strips are available for scanning.

Double locking the door prevents even a valid keycard from entry. Two more buttons and Security is notified. Marie returns to her client.

"Your doors are double locked, and I've called for help. A lone male attempted to gain entrance. I'll watch him until authorities arrive."

"Thank you, Marie."

"Were you expecting anyone?"

"No, I'm ill today, got up for water and heard a noise at the front door."

"He's leaving. Be back momentarily."

The "intruder" heads to the side of the house. "Perpetrator is not identifiable—appears to be attempting entry through the side."

"You mean his dress is non-standard?"

"Correct."

"Where did he get a keycard?"

"Good question."

"I'll ask him; I'm at the scene." The voice is Dave's. Alone today because his partner was injured yesterday. After a few seconds of conversation, the stranger catches Security 17 off guard, hitting him twice and Dave goes down.

Marie responds. "Officer down, Security 17, down at location. Assailant is fleeing on foot toward 4th Street with stolen stunning weapon. Attacker has no ID. Officer 17 is solo and needs medical attention." *Why didn't his face shield go up?*

"Security 44 & 51 approaching 4th Street; suspect is in sight."

"This is 53—suggest you stun first—talk later."

"Affirmative Chief."

Marie follows as they approach the man who tries to evade them by heading into a side yard, but finds no way around. The stranger turns to fight—weapon in hand but is simultaneously hit by two stunner blasts.

Meanwhile, Medical 14 & 17 arrive to care for Dave. One of the medics reports to the doctor, "His jaw is broken, but he is conscious."

Returning to Elizabeth, she says, "The man is in custody. The first security on the scene arrived alone and was attacked by the intruder." After checking on Elizabeth A's health Marie thanks her for her vigilance.

Seeing Dave carried by stretcher to a waiting ambulance, and the intruder detained, Marie declares the emergency over. Two more people, a man, and woman in their late 70's arrive. No greetings are exchanged. *Oh crap, I'm again the object of unwanted attention.*

Thelma speaks first, "You're her … you're *that angel*!! I saw you yesterday, and here you are again."

Marie grins as she says, "I assure you I'm flesh and blood."

"They teach you to say that. I read a book about angels. I know all about you."

Turning to the newcomers and she says, "Hello, I'm Marie, a Doorkeeper."

Thelma responds, "You mean you open doors between *this world* and *the next*?"

"No. Doors to people's homes."

"But you didn't open the door for him!"

"He wasn't supposed to get in."

"She knows who's supposed to get in and who's not. Does seeing you two days in a row mean I'm going to die soon?"

"No."

"Oh, right, you can't tell me until the last minute. The doctor wants me to take these pills, but I can't swallow them; is that why I'm dying?"

"You mean Dr. K?"

"Yes, how did you know? Oh, of course, you can read my mind."

"If you ask Dr. K she'll give you the medicine in a different form."

"Are you sure?"

"Dr. K will understand; she's one of us." *I might as well play along.* Glancing at the newcomers, Marie shrugs as Thelma says, "You mean she is an angel too? Of course, there are angels everywhere, all around us."

"Now, I did *not* say Dr. K is an angel. You can't tell anyone *especially* about the man who was arrested. Swear?"

They all say, "OK." All except Thelma is having trouble keeping a straight face. Marie's stop is also the destination of the two newcomers.

After departing the man says, "We are George and Annie, we volunteer two days a week helping deliver meals to the homebound. You must be the Doorkeeper the whole city is talking about?"

"Oh, *please* tell me you are joking."

"Afraid not. An all expenses paid trip to Europe is the reward for the first picture of you reaching through a wall, or some other supernatural feat."

Sighing she begins to make a comment but is interrupted by a feeling.... *Something is happening I must attend to.*

"A pleasure to meet you both. I don't mean to be rude, but I must check something."

With portalock and communicator connected Marie views street cameras. *I'll scan a bit, but the problem will be at my front door.* A man with a keycard enters her home. Inside cameras on—she recognizes the "computer guy." *He was part of the group taking Phillip.* His garment colors (tan, black, and light blue) denote him as an electronic technician. At the console, he removes the left access panel. The camera from behind the desk allows her to see some of what he is doing. A small object with wires using alligator clips is attached somewhere in the console. The panel and chair are put back in place.

He didn't notice the "spy board" is missing.

Her relief is evident. Back at the door panel, he keys some entries. *He's attempting to erase his unauthorized entry. PA captured that data immediately and his picture.*

At the outside keycard slot more code is entered. Removing his gloves, he dons a pair of "sunglasses." *Oh, he has "camera glasses" too, better switch off the direct cameras. Let's find his vehicle. Ok, here is a car at the parking area. Got the vehicle identification.*

No other activity in the sector.

"Friend, you got the picture and keycard for our uninvited visitor?"

"Affirmative."

"Sending Vehicle Data. Check status and hold for my return."

"Acknowledged."

Now back to today's activities: next on the list: furniture.

This is Marie's first trip to a Personal Service Center for purchases. Students select bed, desk, and lounge chair from an online catalog when pre-registering. Furnishings are rarely moved from city to city except for heirloom or custom-built pieces. *So I must make some decisions.*

The showroom is well lighted. The space is small: only three consultation areas. A counter separates the staff from customers. A large wall of glass separates this area from the working part of the warehouse. Above the wall of glass are mirrors that turn into viewing screens.

One of the three stations is occupied with a younger couple; the female member is obviously pregnant. They are picking items for the child's room. The young man working with them is a parent in his 30's advising them from experience, as well as knowing the options. How is it that I can perceive so much about them?

A young woman about 22 years-of-age with Asian heritage approaches Marie.

"Welcome to Central Services. I'm Trea, how may I assist you?"

"Thank you Trea; I'm Marie, Doorkeeper for Sector 86, here to order some living room furniture."

"Yes, Wessel said you might be dropping by for a hide-a-bed, and perhaps something else. Tell me what you have in mind?"

"Classic style. Something appropriate with the oak dining table—I plan on keeping it. Couch will be my guest bed in this dark red. Two matching side chairs in this dark blue." Marie points to areas of her Outer Garment for the colors.

The "showroom" has screens the assistant uses to offer all in stock, or special order products, in any style, color or lighting pattern. Home or apartment designs complete with wall colors, floor covering, and existing furnishings are on file for occasions like this. Before confirming final choices, items may be viewed in your environment, from any angle or lighting. Decisions take far less time than anticipated.

Trea says, "Your couch will be delivered tomorrow; the chairs next week. Wessel said he would fire me if I didn't bring you to him."

"After you have been so helpful, we can't let that happen."

Walking through the warehouse, Trea points out the material for her sofa already being dyed.

"The correct amount of fabric had been rolled out and cut by robots. It's being run through the color vat. Then stretched out, dried and vacuumed with a device filtering and returning any liquid. The process is repeated 80 times. Finally, a sealant sets the color and protects the fabric. The dying process takes 21 hours. Next will be the upholstering. Then your ID is imprinted, and it'll be delivered to your home before 5 PM tomorrow."

"I'm impressed by the whole operation." A little further Trea points to a robot forklift moving the skeleton of a davenport. "That's yours. Robots are moving the unit to a workstation where everything will be tested; mattress added; covering installed; fitted sheets and a blanket will be added; a final test and one careful human inspection."

While walking, Marie learns she ordered the top quality, therefore the most expensive of everything.

"Can I afford this?"

"You can. Wessel would buy it for you if you couldn't. He's sweet on you."

"But he is gay." Flushing from embarrassment she reflects: *what an uncalled for remark—think first, then speak.*

"Of course, that makes it so…interesting…and safe."

The food storage and preparation zone is in sight. Wessel jogs toward them; arms flung open as if greeting a long lost sister. Maurice's accent says, "Ah, zee beautiful one...." as he embraces her. Back to his regular voice, he says, "What do you think of our little operation?"

"Impressive, and very eco-friendly."

"The law requires us to be eco-friendly; it's the right thing. Seldom do the two converge, so we *better* pay attention."

"How many robots work here?" They're everywhere.

"496."

He made the number up; he doesn't know how many robots are at work here. How can I be so sure?

Marie says, "You have no idea, do you?"

"Of course, I do; not an *accurate* one—but an idea."

Trea is enjoying the mental sparring.

"Thank you, Trea for bringing the guest of the day. Now go do something useful."

Trea says to Marie, "I leave you in his wandering hands."

As she departs Marie asks Wessel, "A question for you: what happened at the train yard when the shelter entrance was damaged?"

"Not my responsibility, thank goodness. Apparently, a rail-car carrying fuel exploded, damaging the rails, four other cars, and the shelter entrance."

"Accident?"

Looking about to sense if anyone might overhear also checking the surveillance camera he says, "I don't think so."

"Another question. What service is in charge of displaying the deceased in 'holes of completion'"?

"Not us, I think…a branch of Records and Inquires. No, that doesn't seem right, possibly Medical Services … never really thought about it. Why do you ask?"

"My predecessor is available for viewing, and I want to pay my respects."

"You mean Phillip?"

"Yes, if there's time I'll go after my next stop."

"If you go… will you call me? So I can go with you. The place is not the easiest to find—I could pick you up. I'm bad at dealing with death, but I should go." Wessel holds her with both hands by the shoulders and gazes directly into her eyes, "You see; he was my friend, there aren't many. I dined with him many times. I miss him."

"Of course, I'll call you. But don't count on it being today; time may be short. I'm also anxious around death; I welcome your company." *The only death I experienced is my father's. Well, a college classmate who had an accident on vacation—skiing maybe? Don't remember him, not even his name.*

Tears begin flowing down Wessel's face. Marie embraces him. *There is much more he is not telling. I can wait….* She holds him for a long minute until his tears subside. He pats her arm lightly. *Holding a man like this could be pleasant, as long as there are two SOGS between us.* Wessel suddenly "remembers" something he must do. Marie is escorted to an exit, where the PIC stop is visible. Wessel says, "Thanks for understanding."

Marie waits for the next pod due in four minutes; communicator out she calls Rudy leaving a message. "You remember the scavenger hunt we were talking about? Well, I saw the grand prizewinner at a distance today. Thought you'd be interested."

I wish I had told Rudy what I've learned about Phillip. I will soon. Scavenger hunt feels appropriate; trying to collect clues about what's happing and why; like we did when I was a kid.

Thirty
This Court—Not in Session

On the PIC pod, Marie enters her destination. Eight people, all students are on board. Only three respond to Marie's greeting. No names are given. The students appear busy with their communicators, read-pads, or study-pads. One reads a physical book: a "romance novel."

The central city is soon reached. Passing various functional sectors: Records, Finance, Counseling, Housing, and Agricultural Services. *Housing and Agricultural are two areas I need to learn more about. Why is none of this covered in Door Facilitation School? To assist interface with all services is part of the job. How can I advise about services I don't understand?*

Reaching her stop everyone gets off. People rush by as she locates the campus map.

Everyone is ignoring me. Is no one going to offer assistance? True, some are running to classes, but surely someone will stop and greet a non-student. "Routine courtesy" is drummed into our heads from the first weeks of primary school. The "real world" is different.

So why am I surprised? The "truthfulness at all times" ideal was quickly supplanted with "report only the truth, but omit anything questionable." Of course, there are adjustments, but I never thought they would come so dramatically.

Here I am at the university to use a computer that can't be traced back to me. Why? To ask questions about an unknown court. One apparently possessing the power to execute people for assumed crimes. What happened to rights to defense, to face his/her accuser and no executions?

No, I'm not paranoid, unethical or irresponsible. Door Service is a vital part of the order established in 2061. At the Certification Ceremony, I swore to uphold and defend this policy of justice. That's what I'm doing.

With new resolve, Marie moves to the map finding the two places she needs. It's 12:14 PM.

First, the public lockers. Finding an available locker, she deposits Portalock, PCD, and meal. *I want to minimize my traceability. With luck, I'll be back before 2:00 PM.*

Next is the library. The main entrance has an unstaffed front desk. To the left is a set of "catalogue stations"; just beyond are periodicals. Marie secures two magazines: *Electronics Today* and *The Medical Times.* She pulls read-pads containing the current issues. *A cover story if needed.* Service desk with loaner laptops is at the far wall.

Checking out a computer Marie finds an unassigned study station near the back of the library. The search starts by routing the signal through three continents, and nine different servers.

The final "destination site" may trigger a trace-back here. If so I'll be gone before it reaches here. That is a routine practice for sensitive or semi-sensitive information. Current philosophy is if we can't keep people from learning what we do at least we can know who knows.

In about four minutes Marie asks her question: what is the Select Tribunal of the Central Program States? All references come from the *Congressional Record.* A proposal was made in the "Judicial Practice Subcommittee to "… create a tribunal consisting of three federal judges, who would rotate annually. They would hear 'unusual cases' falling outside the parameters of law affecting both Structured and Unstructured States."

Tribunal would have broad powers for search and seizure … could investigate matters already decided by another judicial body … could arrest people *suspected* of withholding vital information. Proposed in 2088.

Sounds like unchecked power to me. So what's the outcome? Where is it located? Who are the Judges?

The next forty minutes are spent reading reports from the sub-committee, larger committee, and whole Senate. The bill was tabled without discussion and never taken off the table. She also searches Justice Department, Judicial Advisory Board, Supreme Court rulings, and Presidential Executive Orders since 2085 to make sure it was not established any other way.

The court does not exist. Who proposed it? Back to the original: Senator Bluefoot. *No surprise.* There were two co-sponsors. Checking their names, she learns both are out of office. Next, she shuts down connections, erases every trace of her use, wipes fingerprints and is ready to return the computer. Then she sees a familiar face.

Ann says, "Hi Marie, I didn't realize you were here. My station is that way…" pointing down the row. "I'm stopping for a meal would you join me?"

"The company would be great, but first I need to go to the lockers. I need to retrieve some things including my lunch."

"Brought mine also. There's a picnic area near the lockers."

Off they go. After printing a copy of the relevant Congressional Record sections, they leave the library; retrieve her stored items and sit down to eat at 1:30 PM. In a message to Wessel, Marie suggests seeing Phillip today. Wessel calls

189

checking their location says, "I know the place. Stay put; I'll be there about 2:00."

Lunch is the first "normal" moment I remember since arriving. Here we are, two young women, eating together, during an "ordinary" day. We could be talking about anything, boys, music, or the worst teacher. Ann comes from Bloomington, Illinois. Her interest in environmental studies is rooted in three uncles who are trying to farm under today's conditions. Ann talks about her parents and grandparents and how things were different for them. Though they live and work in a structured state Ann's uncles are not under the "Shelter Farming Act," her great-uncles did not trust the new system. The current generation wants to change.

"So how do they get paid?" Marie's curious about the phenomena of people "outside" the economy while living in an area where The Plan offers structure.

"They're compensated at level 3. When crops come in, they sell them. But costs of machinery, barns, seed, fuel or damage to land is their responsibility. They almost break even. Because their mates work within the structure, their houses are covered. Every year they are invited to switch. Uncle Harry and his mate have two children. He would like to leave farming but won't abandon his brothers."

"What are your plans for an environmental studies degree?"

"I want to understand if things are getting better, staying the same or getting worse. Unless it gets better, my uncles need to go into shelter farming or find other work. Ultimately, I hope to do research or teach."

"What's our environmental future look like?"

"Worse … much worse. One of my professors predicts no one will be living outside the shelters in 15 years. Our ancestors waited too long before starting to address the problems."

"Must be discouraging studying all this."

"A lot is negative. But there are some hopeful signs. Since we stopped fractured and horizontal drilling, the soil warm up is slowing. Scientists are still trying to understand the connection. One theory is the depletion of oil, gas and other reserves cause the earth crust to heat. Now that depletion is stopping, the crust temperature increases have slowed as well. Take a sponge full of water; if you measure the temperature of the sponge fiber; then squeeze the liquid out and let the sponge dry the fiber temperature will be higher. Depleting appears to do the same to the earth's crust."

The conversation continues as they wait for Wessel. *Today has been full of surprised. What makes me think a major one still awaits?*

Thirty-One
The Undead

Wessel joins the two women immediately hugging Ann. *These two know each other. He's probably involved in transferring packages. Makes sense; he has access to leave things in homes?* They depart; the older ones in one direction, and Ann back to the library.

On their way to the service pod, Wessel says, "I'm aware of what Ann did yesterday. Thanks for helping her."

"Who else knows?"

"Only me, and Vivi. Phillip was my contact."

"So what now, since he's gone?"

"There is one name. Sent word today, no response yet. When we reach to the pod, we can't talk about this, my office is bugged, and pods might be."

"Understood."

The specialized glasses Marie uses indicate all cameras are inactive.

This Pod is dedicated to Central Services. While traveling, Wessel talks about his troubled youth; finding his passion in food; and his dependence on his staff.

Central Completion Center at 2280 South Main appears to be an older government building converted to its present use.

The exterior front is tan stucco, with four faux columns lead-ing to a high flat roof, with imitation marble edging. The struc-ture is three stories high without windows on the top floor.

The whole place appears sad and neglected. Creature comforts are lost on the dead—but what of the living who visit them?

The perception does not change when entering the lobby. Deserted. A five-foot-tall desk contains only a monitor. Looking right or left reveals only empty dark hallways.

While pondering their next move the monitor on the desk comes "alive." A fidgety appearing young woman peers out at them. She wears surgical greens including hair covering, but no mask.

"May I help you?"

Marie says, "We are here to pay respects, to Phillip Walton."

The face on the screen glances down for a few seconds and says, "Number 17."

"Where should we go?"

"To your right, how many of you are there?"

"Two of us. The hallway is dark." *Why do they need a count of visitors?*

"Lights come on as you walk." In the background some-one telling the operator, "You are supposed to find out what setting they want for the viewing area."

"Oh," says the image on the screen, "What scene do you want surrounding the stiff?"

"The *what!*" Anger overtakes Marie as her face reddens. *Such disrespect.*

"A drape we pull around the viewing area with a scene like a garden, lake, office, or things like that. What would you like?"

Turn away from the monitor. She doesn't understand. Don't say something you'll regret.

Wessel says, "He liked to picnic in the mountains. Do you have a scene with a stream or waterfall in the background?"

"Yeah, I think so."

Marie asks, "What sector oversees this facility?"

"Why do you want to know?"

She's probably afraid someone is going to complain about her work. "I'm a Doorkeeper, the man we're here to visit was my predecessor. When others want to pay their respects, I must be aware which department I'm referring them to."

"Well … this is the Pathology Department of the Medical School. I guess we oversee it. I'm a Med Student on my pathology rotation. This is part of our study."

"Thank you." Starting down the hall, Marie's fuming decreases. *She's a student who made a mistake.* Lights come on as they walk, panels are numbered on either side starting with one; even numbers on the left, odd numbers on the right. They reach 17. Glancing at Wessel, she asks, "Ready?"

"Yes." They turn toward number 17, and the door separates into layers. Six distinct ceiling to floor panels slide apart three to each side.

They step in, and lights come on around the body. The "hole" is a glass case. The occupant is laid out in front of the visitors. As they step into the room, the positioning of the body changes lifting the top of the bed to a 30-degree angle. Dressed in a formal SOG Phillip is visible from the knees up. The surrounds are designed to give the appearance of a comfortable rest. *People often say, "He appears so peaceful—just taking a nap." He does. In fact, I thought his eyelids moved.*

Wait a minute. They did. Phillip squinted when the light changed. Did Wessel see it too?

Wessel speaks, "Did his eyelids *move*?"

Closing her eyes, Marie turns toward the darkened hall-way saying, "Watch *my* eyelids." Slowly she turns back to the lighted viewing section.

"Your eyelids closed tighter, same as Phillip's."

Her eyes remain closed a bit longer. *"Impressions" came unbidden with Charles, Candy, and my office. Now I want one—what happened to Phillip? Is he alive? Maybe I can pick up something…. No sound … A vague sense of presence … could be Wessel. There it is—a flash vision of someone putting something into Phillip's left hand, attaching an IV line … the lethal injection? No … wrong location.*

His left hand is at his side, but the right hand is resting on his right thigh. Moving to his right Marie sees a tube on the outside of his hand consistent with an intravenous drip.

He's not dead *but in an induced coma!*

Tapping the glass Marie says, "Phillip, do you hear me? Lift a finger on your right hand if you understand."

"Wessel, he might recognize your voice."

Wessel moves close to Phillip's ear with only the glass between them and says, "It's Wessel, your friend, if you hear me lift a finger on your right hand." He repeats several times, with tears in his eyes. Finally, he says, "Please lift your finger I need you … you are my best friend." Then it happens. His right index finger lifts gradually 2 inches from his thigh where it had been resting and stays elevated.

"We must get him out of here." Both say in unison.

Wessel says, "I'll take care of this, you stay here." Wessel trots toward the lobby.

Marie says, "I'll call Dr. K."

"Dr. Kildare."

"It's Marie; I need your help."

"What can I do for you?"

"I'm at Central Completion Center, with Wessel. We came to see my predecessor, Phillip. He's here, but *not dead*. Someone put an IV line in his hand, and I think he is in an induced coma."

"Can't be. Respiration and body temperature control is essential."

"I know. We need your help. How do we obtain help before he dies?"

"No one here uses those techniques, you need the Medical School, teaching hospital."

"I don't trust them; they put him here."

"You mean he's in a hole of completion, but alive."

"Yes, but I'm not sure how long he can last."

"What makes you think he is alive?"

"He squinted his eyes when the lights came on, so Wessel talked to him and asked him to raise a finger on his right hand. He did, and it's still up. I think he responded to a familiar voice through his lethargy."

"I'm on break; I'll grab my bag and be there in 5 minutes."

"Thanks, doctor. Hole number 17, to the right, when you come in the front." The call ends.

"Hang on Phillip; help is on the way."

Marie takes pictures of his hands and the setup. *The controls must be behind or underneath the body.*

Wessel is back with an ax. "They say because he is officially dead even if he is alive, they can't do anything. So we take matters into our own hands."

"Wait, we need to understand the setup. Dr. K is coming. The mechanism to open this must be in there. You stay here so that light won't go off. I'll find a way in."

Dashing to the end of the hall, she finds a narrow door beyond 19. The door is locked with an alphanumeric keypad. Marie tries: complete, hole, pass, enter, and passage all with no results. *What would they use? Of course "stiff."* It opens. On the backside is a narrow crawl space. The first things she finds when reaching number 17 is the canister of fluid designed to maintain a comatose state. An attached pump is plugged into an outlet.

In a loud voice, "Wessel you there?"

"Yes, you don't need to shout," Wessel says in a normal voice.

"Must be microphones ... for conversations with the dead? Why? ... unless someone else is listening."

Wessel understands the implications, "Meaning we're not alone?"

"Could be. I'm trying to figure out the controls. I found a container of 'cryogenic fluid' for such procedures. There's also a catheter bag—dead men don't produce urine especially after organ harvest."

Dr. Kildare arrives, "What have we here?"

Wessel points out the tube, barely visible from his right hand, and the raised finger, which remains elevated.

"Where is Marie?"

"Down here. Think I've figured out how to open this."

"Do it," says Dr. K.

"I'll have to unplug the pump."

"My service pod carries portable power backups," says Wessel.

"Get it," says Dr. Kildare.

Lowering the platform supporting the bed she places the pump and tank between his feet, opens the glass and raises the bed so it can be rolled out.

Once the drawer is out, Dr. K and her two assistants move Phillip to the gurney. *Unsure of getting out where I came in. I'll jump through this opening.* Marie leaps through the opening, as the platform reaches its default position.

Dr. Kildare conducts a quick examination, "No rigger mortise. Wish we could open this SOG."

Marie says, "I may be able to help." Whipping out her Portalock. *The unlock code should work here. Accessing cameras. Now.* Everyone's SOG pops open—including Phillip's.

"How did you...?" Marie holds a finger to her lips and shakes her head left to right. Everyone closes his or her SOG. No surgery to repair a rupture or harvest organs is evident. A catheter, bag and a small disk taped to his chest are the only additions to the pump and tank. *The disk appears to be a transmitter. Probably supposed to control his temperature. The device failed since body temperature is too high for suspension. I'm afraid Phillip may not make it.*

Dr. K confirms Marie's worst fears. "His temperature and respiration are much too high for sustained deep coma treatment. Break out the cold blankets and let's get him to the med center *stat*." Dr. Kildare is on her PCD to the University Medical Center; she insists on talking to the most knowledgeable person about "Induced Comatose Treatments;" she is using her position to past some gatekeepers to the person she wants.

Wessel is also talking on his communicator in an animated tone. For the first time, Marie feels useless, and a bit like an extra wheel. *What can I do? I'll check the viewing slot. Did we miss anything? Here's a microphone—permanent? Everything else returned to its former condition, minus one occupant.*

The medical assistants are off in one pod. Dr. K. still on her communicator in another. Wessel heads for the pod, and Marie hopes she is still welcome. Wessel finishes his call.

"I called Security 23, says he knows you and will head the investigation. He wants us to stay out of it and promises to keep us informed."

"Let me interrupt you before you tell me more than my ears can hold. I'm hoping you'll drop me off at the clinic so I can check on Candy, Chester, Richard, and Dave—Security 17 if he is still there."

"What happened to Dave?"

"This morning he was apprehending a 'peeping Tom,' and the guy hit him, knocked him out. That's why I want to check."

"Of course, I'll take you. I want to visit him as well."

That's strange. As they depart the pod, Wessel says, "Dave is my partner. I didn't want to say anything in case we were overheard."

Felt like a kick in the stomach. I'm pleased for Wessel, but I like Dave, how could I not know he's gay. This sexual stuff is confusing. I pray Ava can help. To Wessel she says, "Why don't you visit him first? Don't feel like you need to wait for me; I can take a PIC home. It's only 3:15; plenty of time."

Wessel says, "I'll find you before leaving." They enter through the Security Entrance. A man unknown to Marie sits behind the counter. Wessel speaks, "Is Officer 17, Dave Comings still here? He was injured in the line of duty."

"Yeah, I'm Dr. Burns. Are you family?"

"His mate."

"Ok, he came through the surgery fine."

"Surgery? I thought he was only unconscious," blurts Marie. "I'm the Doorkeeper, who called it in."

"You saved his life. 10 minutes on the ground and we would have lost him. How many times was he hit?"

"One, well two; one to the gut and one to the jaw. The second one knocked him down."

"This guy may be a trained killer. Dave had broken ribs puncturing his liver and lung. Also, he has a concussion, broken jaw, and collar bone."

Turning to Wessel she says, "I'm so sorry, I had no idea it was that serious."

"You didn't know we were lovers until 2 minutes ago. We try to keep it quiet because of our responsibilities."

To Dr. Burns, she says, "Doctor, I also want to check on how Candy, Chester L, and Richard are doing? May I visit them?"

"Oh… you're *that* Keeper!" he pauses a moment, "Hey didn't you two find a living person in the morgue?"

"Guilty."

"We had a sleepy little town before you got here. I'm glad we got someone with your experience to handle all this. But you seem so young."

"This is my first posting."

"You have acquitted yourself well."

"Thanks."

"I'd love to talk longer, but must do rounds. Virginia, give these folks the run of the place. Help them find people." A late 20's woman steps around the corner from the public entrance area. Room numbers provided Wessel heads to Dave's room and Marie to Candy's.

Also visiting Candy are Brandy, Danny and two men. Ronnie and Donnie, two male Personal Pleasure Service Workers, are introduced. A warm welcome is extended, Marie. Candy says, "I need to be here for five more days. I'll be out in time for school." In the conversation, Marie learns that none of the PPSWs view this as a life-long career. They share reasons for taking up this role and their life goals.

Always curious, Marie asks, "What's the hardest part of your work?"

"The stigma attached to our work." Danny says, "You're the exception … you don't judge us."

"'All work is valuable; all work is dignified; the worker is to be honored' we learn those words from before entering school; how can anyone disrespect another because of their choice of fields?"

"You're an idealist, Marie. Most people believe *some* work is not valuable; some call *our* work sin; others think we must be too stupid for a good job."

She is also told about the extensive training and psychological testing required. Less than one in three passes the initial testing. PPSWs must see a counselor each week from the time they decide to do the work until they leave the job, plus transition counseling.

"With Candy leaving two years earlier than planned, we're going to be short. Would you like to moonlight?"

"I'm too busy trying to stay on top of one job."

Marie spends longer with Candy and her friends than planned. The mood is light and encouraging. *I like these people.*

Next, she visits Chester. What a difference; no visitors; he spends the time apologizing for his "violation," in a self-blaming mood. Chester expresses concern about his job; positive he's lost the assignment. "Don't make rash assumptions, take the time you need to heal. People will understand." *Seems likely he will need counseling before forgiving himself.*

Third is Richard: another self-blaming session. However, his estranged wife is more open to renegotiating a relationship with his child. Marie tries positive reinforcement—but he is depressed and determined to stay that way.

Finally, Dave's room, where they are making plans for how to deal with his injuries. "Doctor says two more days here and off work for four weeks," Wessel reports as Marie enters.

Dave says, "I'll go crazy in four weeks." His jaw is wired closed, so Dave speaks through clenched teeth. Joking Marie says, "I hope I don't wipe out the entire 'police force' before some recover. *They laugh, but I wonder how many more will fall before we get to the bottom of what's going on.*

"I need to head back. I'll take a PIC," Marie says noting the time is 4:10. Wessel says, "I must go as well; I'll take you home."

In the van, Wessel thanks Marie for her understanding adding, "Security 17 likes you; as do I."

"Thanks, the feeling is mutual."

Thirty-Two
The Technician Arrives

Wessel leaves Marie at her door. *I didn't tell him about the intruder. He'd insist on being all "macho" and check everything out. No need to explain why I was looking for another intruder after one is arrested.*

"Friend, send pictures and codes to my third screen."

"Completed."

I'll eat more "leftovers" at my workstation while using the cameras to view the southern portion of the sector. Not quite like feeling the pavement under my feet, but ok for now. Perhaps this can be a relatively stress-free evening. Wait, company is coming, and I need to write two reports. Oh well so much for "normal." Here's a disturbing thought: what if the last two days are my new normal?

Gone longer than anticipated, Wessel apologizes to Gloria, his trusted assistant, *and* confidant. He relays what they found at the Completion Center, Dave's injuries and the need for secrecy.

She says, "If you need time, we can handle things for a few days."

"Thanks for your concern, but I need to occupy my mind— or I'll worry."

Then they review the details of the afternoon. The operation is well organized since Wessel is gifted at fitting things together. When he is absent, Central Services still runs smoothly since he trusts the staff and treats them with respect.

Gloria is the only staff member who can identify Wessel's partner. Many are aware he's in a same-gender relationship, but it never affects his work or theirs. Same or mixed gender relationships are considered ordinary. The culture tolerates most idiosyncrasies. The prevailing perspective is, "If it keeps you sane, harms no one, nor the Common Good; it's no one's business." One of the mantras of the current philosophy is: "Understand another if possible; always accept—even without understanding."

At 5:10 PM Rudy, disguised as Franklin A, enters the Managing Offices of Central Services Center. Walking around the counter, he heads for Wessel's office.

Gloria says, "Sir, you can't go in there."

"Well I can't accomplish anything standing here, can I? Who is in charge?"

"Wessel. He's busy."

"I'm also busy, and my time is valuable."

"Let me show you to his office," Gloria says getting up.

Franklin A is through the door ahead of her. His office is adjacent to the reception area. The door is at one corner. One complete wall of glass, allows the Chief of Operations to oversee what happens on the floor without leaving his desk. Nine monitors mounted on the solid walls provide similar views to the more remote sections, of the operation. The overall impression is one of efficiency. Wessel's desk is the exception: papers, files, charts, and chip holders arranged haphazardly. A laptop and other electronic devices lurk beneath or behind the clutter. The three solid walls are lined with file cabinets and supply cabinets. There are no guest chairs.

Gloria rushes through the door a step ahead of Franklin saying, "I'm sorry Wessel, but this is…" she stops because she has no name to share. Franklin's pretentious attitude toward everyone includes refusing common courtesy to all except the highest in rank.

"Franklin Adams, though in this God-forsaken part of the world they insist on my being called 'Franklin A.' apparently I must *'earn'* the rest of my name."

Wessel nods at Gloria. "Thanks, Gloria, I will care for this gentleman." The nod was a sign to "interrupt" with a dire emergency in 10 minutes unless his guest has departed. Gloria nods back thinking *better you than me.* Franklin retrieves two items from inside his SOG: a work-pad is handed to Wessel; the other a "bug finder" is used as he moves around the room.

The screen of the work-pad says:

DO NOT READ THIS OUTLOUD. YOUR OFFICE IS BUGGED.
We need to leave. Follow my lead.

Franklin says, "I'm here to work on one of your outdated and pathetic computer systems. You have the address?"

Wessel says, "Of course."

"Let's go."

"I'm quite busy; I can send an assistant with you."

"Do I *seem* like someone who deals with underlings?"

"Well…No. I'll be right with you."

As they leave the area, Wessel says, "Gloria you're in charge. I'll be back soon." He didn't sound convinced.

Once they were outside Franklin A says, "My equipment is in the car," pointing to a blue rental outside Wessel's entrance.

The work-pad, now blank, is handed back. Franklin puts the equipment back in his SOG.

Once in the vehicle, Franklin speaks. His voice is deeper and relaxed; he also sits taller—filling the driver's side of the car, "I found nine bugs, and I didn't even do the file cabinets; I'll do so those after I address our friend's problems."

I cannot believe my ears. This sounds like Rudy. Five minutes ago he was shorter, thinner, and well, not Rudy. "Who are you?" Asks Wessel.

"I'm here in response to your message. This vehicle and you are bug free. A sonic disrupter is operating in the back seat, but we can never be sure about shotgun mikes, so no names."

"This has to be Rudy," Wessel thinks, "but did he come all this way to talk to me?"

He says, "I didn't expect you to show up."

"I must be here anyway. Best to hear it from you so that I can fit the pieces together."

"Probably best to start at the beginning," Wessel says as he tells him about the threatening man, who came to "visit" him July 1st. "I told Phillip."

"Did your visitor give a name or contact information?"

"No, he always contacts me. I never know when he'll show, or where. Spooky."

"Go on."

Wessel tells about putting out some false information regarding possible transfers coming through railcars of recyclable papers, which precipitated an explosion and damage to the shelter entrance. He also shares his suspicions about Duke H as the one responsible for the blast.

"When was the last time you heard from 'Mr. X?'"

"Sunday night. He wants me to get close to Phillip's replacement. 'They' had a guy who was supposed to take over, but something happened, and someone else got the call."

"Where do we park?"

"For where? Where are we going?"

"DK 86."

"Oh, parking on 4th Street around the corner."

Rudy pulls into a parking space. Starting to get out, Wessel touches Rudy's arm and says, "Wait, I have more."

"Save it till we're inside. "

Wessel thinks, "Now I'm confused. The rest 1 want to tell is about Marie. Am I supposed to say it in front of her? Does Rudy know Marie? The woman I talked to this morning is somehow involved with "packages." Can she and Rudy be connected? Now it makes sense. The concerns for Marie's safety, and whether other packages will be coming through. Is Marie somehow connected to Rudy?"

Rudy turns to him and says, "I see you figured something out."

Wessel says, "You, the woman who is coming to visit and Marie?"

"I'll explain when we're inside. Meanwhile, I'm 'Mr. Insufferable' again and you are here to carry my stuff. You will announce me, and obtain admission."

In the trunk of the car is a folding cart. Most rental cars include "carry robots," but Franklin A is a cheapskate. Everything is loaded on the cart under Franklin critical eye. Five cases, including one he never let out of his possession. They are a half block from 36 Jasmine Court.

Marie has eaten her meal and viewed the homes south of 2nd Street from High to Lemon Avenue. These houses are more modest except the homes facing Lemon between 1st and 2nd – three larger dwellings – about 100 years old.

Reports are completed before the early evening rush begins. A doorbell indicates someone at Marie's door. The monitor shows two men: one is Wessel.

"Hello, Wessel. May I assist you?"

"I've brought Franklin A to service your equipment."

This could be a problem. Rudy is coming expecting access and here is another technician? She says, "I didn't call for a tech. I must use my console for the next 3 hours."

Franklin speaks up, "Let me in, young woman. I can't fix your problem from out here."

Appearance—wrong; voice—wrong; height—wrong; attitude—oh so wrong—but it's Rudy. Not sure how I know, but I do. He's a master of disguises.

"Alright, come in." Marie handles more doors as her friends enter. "Franklin" opens one case, assembles and tests an instrument. Removing the bug finder from his SOG, he starts methodically scanning the room walls. When the bug finder indicates a microphone he uses the other device to map out power routes, cable locations, or anything using electric, static, or magnetic energy.

Rudy, alias Franklin, discovers microphones in living, dining, and bedrooms. All cables lead to the Personal Assistant's cabinet. Rudy checks the walls to detect any listening devices *not* run through the PA. None found. He maps the typical wiring patterns for lights and outlets. No hidden mikes, no static feeds from outlets usable for remote listening.

A break in activity comes. Marie steps into the room. Starting to speak, Wessel is silenced by Marie's holding an index finger to her lips. He thinks *I'm surprised she's not protesting this man opening closets, removing drawers and checking behind them. She must be more involved than meets the eye.*

Marie enjoys watching Rudy's work. *He does this when traveling with Mother. I've learned from his thoroughness, and how he "back-checks" in case a stronger electrical path is masking a weaker line running parallel.* For Rudy, it's second nature to back-check each cable several times. Rudy stops periodically making notes on a work-pad.

Marie decides to have some fun at Wessel's expense. Pulling one of the equipment cases off the cart Marie opens it (she remembers the combination) and removes three pieces assembling them into the instrument he will use next.

Astonishment is the only word to describe Wessel's reaction. *Is there anything this woman can't do?* He soundlessly mouths to Marie, "You know him?" Marie nods her head up and down and smiles a "gotcha" smile. Now they're waiting for Rudy's big surprise as he enters the kitchen.

Rudy's laser projector turns the entire counter, cupboard, wall, and floor red. Rudy says, "What the hell?" They laugh.

Marie says, "Allow me. My predecessor fancied himself a *gourmet cook.* He possessed every kitchen gadget known to the human race. They are all stored under the counter, cupboards, and floor." Marie demonstrates retrieving and replacing an appliance. She explains a bit about the motors and the "liquid lava surface."

Rudy visually examines the top finding no cracks, scratches, or changes in temperature or color. Wessel explains, "Marie's predecessor designed all this, including the equipment, storage, laser selecting system, and the computer to run everything. He holds the patents to everything."

Rudy says, "Thanks for assembling the RJ7 for me. I'll use it in the kitchen, then the console. We are 'insect free,' so we can finish what we started earlier."

"Oh, one more thing before you begin, a visitor came while I was out," Marie says, pointing to her workstation.

Without another word Rudy goes to the console, carefully removes the left side panel. He immediately locates the addition: alligator clipped between two diodes on the second slave panel is a device Rudy recognizes. Its purpose is to bypass the privacy protections. All conversations between client and Doorkeeper are sent to a recording device—the one Marie removed earlier.

Rudy traces a cable in the floor leaving the console's area toward the front of the home all the way to the outside wall. Outside he finds a small box slightly below ground level, hidden from view by a shrub. Some of the soil is brushed away revealing a wireless transfer box containing a receiver that activates the transmission. *Whoever was spying on Phillip, and now Marie can upload the contents of the "hidden memory" from as far away as the corner. They can be in a pod, a car or on foot.*

Making certain he is unobserved Rudy replaces everything and returns to the house. Once back inside he whispers, "Let's talk in here," pointing to Marie's bedroom.

Thirty-Three
First Summit

Chairs are moved into Marie's bedroom. There should be a break before the next avalanche of door openings.

Rudy starts, "Here's what I understand about this apartment. First, there's a hardwire connection from the console to the outside of the house ending in a short-range wireless transfer box. Probably used to upload whatever is stored on the memory in the spy board Marie removed."

"What?" Wessel asks.

"That's a generic term for this kind of circuitry; it spies on certain activities. This one can access most of what comes through the console in the form of outgoing messages, reports and communications with your Personal Assistant."

Marie asks, "Including reports to 'third screen?'"

"I can tell more when I examine it."

The circuit board with attached memory is handed to Rudy as he continues. "Second, the addition your visitor made today can access conversations with your people, or anyone who might be in the living/dining area. Third, we may be able to use this to our advantage, to send misinformation.

"Each of us possesses part of the puzzle. Pieces may still be missing, but together there'll be more. Each tells what's relevant. Agreed?

211

Marie nods yes, but Wessel says, "I'm not sure. The network always emphasizes 'need to know.' Should she hear everything?"

"Anything she is unaware of puts her in danger. I'm here to set up protection for Marie…"

"What?" Marie says.

"Ok, I'm Head of Security for Cyclops Institute. Dr. Allison Ward, the holder of two Nobel Prizes, is Cyclops' founder. Both have a keen interest in Marie. The move to Wichita was sudden, offering no preparation time. In Kansas City, you were more predictable. Those around you were fewer. Here is different. Filled with challenges and unknowns. I need to assess the situation first hand, and put protections in place."

"So *that's why* I never had any 'boyfriends.' You intimidated them!" Marie says.

"Since your father died, I took on the role of protecting you. Your curiosity as a child made teaching you things to protect yourself easy. I set up ways of tracking you if you varied your routine, and I had people I could reach to protect you from a threat. I vetted all your classmates, study groups, instructors, and their families, all staff of the university, and anyone you might come into contact with. If someone could be used or manipulated against your best interest, I'm aware of it.

"This has been going on since your 8th birthday. Tell me *truthfully*, did you notice? Was there any interference with anything you wanted to do? Did it impact a relationship, class, your freedoms or anything else's?"

"Well … no. That's not the point. I have a right to know what is happening to me."

"I understand. But you were a child, and yesterday you weren't. We thought we had a year to tell you all these things. Allison will share a lot when she sees you tomorrow."

"Not Thursday?"

Wessel says, "Allison Ward is coming here?"

Rudy says, "Allison often puts out a bogus itinerary, in case someone is planning to cause trouble. Tomorrow she's A. Fulbright. Traveling incognito. We need to guard her identity."

Marie handles some doors; Wessel steps to the dining area to call his office; Rudy uses the bathroom; while there he over-hears Wessel's conversation. A loop exists from the microphone in the dining area to a speaker in the bathroom.

Back at the "bedroom summit" Rudy asks Wessel to con-tinue. He shares his conclusion about Duke H and the rail-yard explosion. Also, the "thug's" insistences Wessel get close to Marie because their man was not chosen. Speaking to Marie, "He says you are a traitor, and he wants me to tell him some-thing about how you got the job."

Marie asks Wessel, "When did you see him?"

"I didn't. He called using your communicator. He wanted me to download your contacts. He left the equipment I needed, in my desk. I entered the number he called me from earlier. He was pissed when he found out I sent him his details, rather than Marie's."

Rudy asks Marie, "You want to tell him about the call?"

"When I got my stuff back, I realized someone had made a call using my PCD." Turning to Wessel she continues, "I realized it was your number. You had already been here, as Maurice, while I had a guest who was hiding something. Wasn't sure I could trust you. Plus, PA said Phillip sent you a monthly report. You denied it. Are you aware every call made on a PCD is held for 48 hours? I heard the call and played it for Rudy. So what else *have* you told 'your friend' about me?"

"How in the hell do you listen to a call a day later?"

"Told you I taught her some stuff. Now answer her ques-tion." Says Rudy.

"I told him *nothing*; he hasn't called since then. Oh, yes he did. He called when he figured out he didn't have your data. I lied. I said it was the number he gave me. Don't think he believes me."

"What did you find out from his list?" Rudy asks.

"He made three other calls before me. Here's the info." Wessel pulls up a page on his communicator and hands it to Rudy, who makes notes. Marie glimpses the faint smile. *Rudy recognizes at least one of the numbers.*

"The hoodlum knows embarrassing things about me that could affect my job," Wessel adds.

Rudy says, "Like your affair with Phillip when you were in a relationship with Dave? The year you used cocaine? Or you're paying child support even though you dispute the mother's claim? Stuff like that?"

Red-faced with embarrassment Wessel drops his head and speaks. Each word brings pain. "Yes, I'm not proud of those moments."

Touching his hand Marie says, "Rudy knew those things but made you part of the 'network.' His trust of you is good enough for me."

Still looking down Wessel says, "Maybe you shouldn't trust me. I decided to give you to the thug if it would keep him off my back. But I met you and fell in love with you. So now what can I tell him?"

"We'll figure it out," Rudy says. "Besides, he won't leave you alone until he is out of the picture. By the way Marie, how *did* you get this job?"

"Beats me. I was happy being a TA."

"Were you told the name of the 'other candidate'?"

"No, but Dr. Stanley would know. I could ask him."

"No need I'll do that. Wessel tells me you can better describe today's events."

So Marie shows a picture of the would-be intruder apprehended after injuring Dave, Security 17. Wessel identifies him as "the thug."

Rudy says, "I thought I recognized his voice from the call. Now I'm positive. Meet Charles "Chuck" Glandmore, former CIA. I left because of too much violence; he quit to find more violence. The guy's bad news."

Marie passes over six other pictures of the intruders who kidnapped Phillip, explaining the PA took them.

"What!" both Rudy and Wessel said.

"The PA took these pictures as they entered and departed. The one with glasses is the tech here again today putting the addition on the console you found tonight. Know him from KC often working on Door Facilitation equipment when a problem existed. PA captured his ID today so we can put a name to him."

"If he was at your school I have a dossier on him. Let me see the identity scan."

Marie hands it over as she continues, "But the big news for today: Phillip is alive."

"What?" Rudy says.

"It's true," Wessel adds.

Marie explains how they found his body supposedly after an "organ harvest." She tells about Phillip being in a "failing" deep coma and his unfavorable outlook.

Wessel explains how Marie got Doctor Kildare involved, "She already understood Marie's medical expertise, from when she saved three lives."

Now it was Rudy's turn for a surprise, "What?"

"All in a day's work." *It pleases me to surprise Rudy.*

Wessel goes on to speak of Phillip's removal and the way the Doctor took charge to see he got the best possible chance. Marie receives an incoming call. She announces, "This is from

Security 23; he's investigating the case, I'll take it here so you can listen in."

"This is Marie, what can I do for you?"

"First I hope the word has not spread about what happened at the Central Completion today. I would like to stop by and give you a complete report."

"That would be helpful. Wessel and another friend are here trying to make sense out of what's going on. You may be helped by our input."

With another addition to the "summit," everyone decides to wait for his arrival. Marie handles some doors. Wessel makes some calls Rudy uses the RJ7 to examine the kitchen.

It's the most advanced detector available; needing to be "worn" with earphones to listen to tones indicating electrical, magnetic, temperature, radio, microwave or energy burst variations. There is a satellite-dish like device mounted in front of the chest; the operator points a handheld wand to specific areas; a visual screen shows types of flow being detected. Rudy can identify five different tones at one time distinguishing which ones are getting stronger, weaker, or modulating. Switching identifier combinations allows 13 different patterns to be mapped. When finished he has a complete energy flow picture including anything needing further investigation.

Thirty-Four
Summit – Round Two

Wessel, Rudy, and Marie are dealing with their respective tasks while waiting for Security 23 to join them. At 7:04 pm Supervisor calls.

"Yes, Supervisor."

The older male says, "I read your reports. *Are you making this stuff up?*"

"No, sir. If I were making it up, it would be more fun."

"Marie, again you handled yourself professionally, in all situations. Now, what the *hell* is going on with Phillip?"

"Wessel and a friend are here, and the investigative detective is on his way. We are trying to make sense of all the issues, including what's been done to this console. It would be an honor if you join us."

"Understood. I'll be there in 12 minutes." The contact ends.

At 7:15 pm Security 23 arrives. Having never met in person, Marie depends on his SOG colors: a blue lighter than Door Services. Two half-inch wide stripes: goldenrod and orange running side-by-side from his right shoulder to his left hip, looping around the back to the right shoulder. The stripes indicate the rank of Captain, higher than required for a detective, showing his expertise. Well-built, light brown hair, brown eyes, and probably 41 years of age with an air of confidence, and behind the easy smile there lurks a keen mind.

As hostess, it's Marie's role to welcome him—stepping from behind the console. His eyes fix on her. *What does it mean when people meet me and fasten their attention on me like this? Am I that different from what they expected?*

"Security 23, welcome to my home. You likely know Wessel, from Central Services." They are acquainted.

Rudy completes his survey of the kitchen, and preliminary work on the Door console, he puts down the RJ7. "Well, Fenton. I always said you'd make good."

"It's Fenton J. now—J for Jefferson. I'm glad to see you *old* friend."

"Be careful with that 'old' stuff. You'll get there too."

Turning to Marie, the detective says, "I would be pleased to be on a name basis with you, Marie."

"And I with you, Fenton J."

With the formalities completed, she takes delivery of the oriental cuisine ordered for her guests.

Rudy confirms there is no danger of being overheard in the dining area. So they all gratefully sit down to a hot meal.

Wessel comments, "This must be 'Kung Fu Palace,' they make the best spring rolls."

"I ordered extras—they said it's their specialty." The doorbell sounds.

Marie welcomes her Supervisor turning to introduce others she says, "I'm unsure who you might be acquainted with."

He takes it from there, "You're Fenton J, also called Security 23?"

"Correct again, Doctor," responds Fenton. They shake hands like old friends.

Rudy speaks next, "Well I thought your voice was familiar. Pleased to see you again Abe."

"Likewise."

"'Abe?' My mother used to call me Abe," says Wessel.

Supervisor responds, "Hello Wessel, 'that's vessel with a Russian accent.' I'm a fan of your accents."

"Well, Thank ye, Thank ye very much," Wessel says mimicking Elvis.

"Well," says Supervisor, "the only one who does not know my name is our hostess—let me correct the oversight." Turning to Marie, he reaches out both hands and takes her gently by the shoulders, so she cannot avoid looking him directly in the face. He speaks slowly, directly to her, as if no one else is in the room, "My name is Abraham Norris. I courted the woman who raised you years ago. If she had not turned me down.... Well ... she met the man she would marry, and I didn't stand a chance. I've wanted to meet *you* for a *very* long time. I'm 79, and if I never reach 80 ... at least I met you." He holds her gaze for another few seconds. She is speechless.

"What can I say?"

"Don't *say* anything. Be yourself; you are a gift." He holds her a few more seconds; it seems like a minute. He gazes deeply into Marie's eyes and she into his. *This distinguished, respected leader wanted to meet* me. *Why? Strange ... I experience no embarrassment, confusion, or concern about what to do or say next. He seems more of a mystic than a critic. He implies things about me I don't understand. There is nothing to fear from him. I'm ... at peace ... having no words to say doesn't matter. The words will come, if needed.*

Norris gradually releases his gentle hold and takes a half step back, still looking directly at her face. There is a knowing smile on his face: not threatening, not sexual, not superior. Everyone in the room shared the moment; each absorbed in his or her thoughts and emotions.

Wessel moved thinks, "It feels like I'm witnessing an inspirational worship experience. This moment seems to bring the purpose for my life in focus. Somehow my future is all tied up with this young woman. She was a force even before she arrived. There's power in her I can't begin to understand, but I want her as my friend. I hope to earn her trust."

The man Fenton respects most in the world, proclaims Marie a treasure. "Five years ago Dr. Norris lifted me out of the doldrums. His presentation at an in-service event was about how various sectors support one another and the Common Good. His words helped me understand my role and made me proud to be part of something bigger. After a private conversation with him, I dedicated myself to becoming a detective. Thank God I made those choices, or I would've missed this moment."

Only Rudy perceives the fullness of what is happening. "This is the passing of the baton from one generation to another: the *best* acknowledging the *best*. When I met Abraham Norris, 20 years ago I understood *this man sees the future*. Listening to him will make our world *better, healthier,* and more *faithful*. My first impression never changed—*only deepened*."

Rudy asks Dr. Norris, "When did you know?"

"Halfway through her first emergency." Seeing the surprised expression on Rudy's face, Norris clarifies. "She had three her first day saving five lives. Three more today."

Rudy turns to Marie with respect and appreciation on his face. *Last time I saw that look was after mastering some electronic device. This time it's for something I did on my own.*

Fenton J and Dr. Norris are brought up to date.

Rudy tells Fenton, "The man in custody for assaulting an officer today is Wessel's tormentor and one of those who took Phillip. His name is, or at least once was, Charles 'Chuck'

Glandmore." He goes into detail about the harm Chuck can cause.

Fenton J says, "About the attempted break-in. We aren't sure whether he was looking for something, wanted to plant something, or planned to wait for her return. Needless to say, he is not talking; but others are. Apparently, he has connections. My Chief told me of at least two calls from people with clout wanting him released. His reply: 'our officer was injured, our resident's home threatened, and our investigation is ongoing. We'll charge him or release him in 48 hours.'

"The Chief is a stickler making sure 'those we serve are served well.' So far we can hold him on assault, resisting arrest, attempted break-in, and possession of stolen property. We could add kidnapping, conspiracy to commit murder, and attempted murder, but we may not want to tip our hand."

Marie asks, "Why didn't Dave's face shield and SOG protect him?"

"Excellent question. We've heard rumors of a device slowing the protective functions. A half second delay would give Glandmore time enough to inflict damage. We found nothing on him, and your video shows no place where he might stash it. We are puzzled."

"What if it's not on him, but in him? Perhaps he has a microchip or implant that disrupts SOG function."

"Worth looking into, thanks for the idea."

Rudy looks up from his PCD. "The technician's identity is Jeffery Cloud. He holds a doctorate from MIT in electronics. My vita on him says there are things in his past some can use against him. Cloud doesn't appear to be a bad guy, but he's working with them. That means we can't trust him, but we may be able to use him."

Marie says, "Elizabeth A works in the Financial Sector. They are charged with a confidential task, and she *should* have been at work when Glandmore tried getting in. He didn't know she was home ill."

Wessel adds, "The standard keycard won't open doors if someone's home. That prevents entry when the home is occupied. We still need to find out how he got the keycard."

Rudy adds, "I may be able to answer that one. Wessel, correct me if I'm wrong, but when your people enter a home, the keycard can be used only once. The card must be reprogrammed before it can open another home."

"Correct."

"The reprogramming unit is located in their pod, and the signal comes from Central Services to 'recharge the card' for the next door."

"Right."

"But, if a second card is created while the first is charged, it could gain access to the address again."

"Yes. That's why there is only one keycard for each team."

"'Chuck' could obtain the equipment to intercept the signal, create a duplicate, and use it after your crew leaves."

"You're right. He could copy the keycard the day before. When residents go in and out, the Doorkeeper activates the door, so the keycard is not reset. The forgery could be used until our folks came again causing a different code to be generated."

Fenton says, "So we look for the equipment."

Marie says, "My Personal Assistant researched the entry device used when Phillip was taken. Friend, what can you tell us?"

"A universal-card was used on August 14th. Originally issued to a Mr. Byers Carbonfoot by the United States Department of Justice on January 7, 2053.

"The universal-card opens any door with a standard keycard slot whether the resident is home or absent. Twenty-one universal-cards were issued by the Justice Department between

January 5th and January 18th, 2053. They were distributed to Secret Service or FBI agents.

"The Attorney General learned of their creation and recalled them, on January 23rd. The person in charge of collecting and destroying the cards was Mr. Byers Carbonfoot. An FBI agent, Clifford Clifton, refused to return his card. Called before the Director and the Attorney General he claimed it as personal property, like his stunner. He was fired and arrested. The search of his house discovered equipment designed to make duplicates. Following his serving two years in prison, Clifton left the country. Whereabouts unknown.

"Mr. Carbonfoot argued that retaining a single universal-card could prevent incidents like the attack on President Earldrige's spouse while dining in a foreign embassy. The policy was not approved. Mr. Carbonfoot died in January 2060. His universal-card was unrecovered."

"Friend, where are the details in your report?

"Page 318."

The section was printed and given to Rudy, who says, "I think a single change can both lock out the universal-cards, and prevent duplicating standard keycards."

They discussion continues for two more hours. They stopped to summarize and clarify their decisions:

1. Rudy will contact a friend who may be able to deactivate all Universal cards.

2. Elizabeth A's home was likely targeted for invasion because she has a home-link to Financial Sector computers.

3. Phillip's true situation is unknown to anyone except Gloria, Dr. Kildare, and those in this room. To those at the University Medical Center, he is John Doe—"improper comma."

4. A bogus professor of pathology gave a lecture August 13th. His talk was deliberately inscrutable. Med students felt

he was over their heads, so none attended the "demonstration session" which resulted in a body for the morgue. It has surmised that he and his assistants were putting Phillip into a deep comma.

5. The Medical Students believe they are in danger of losing a year's credit because of their blunder. They will keep quiet in return for leniency.

6. Fenton J learned the paperwork for Phillip has been fabricated to make tomorrow at 2:00 PM the time his body should be removed for cremation. He is setting up a sting operation to catch whoever comes to collect "the body" using one of the medical students as a decoy.

7. They surmised the original plan was to awaken him making him believe he is reporting to God.

8. Dr. K texted Marie. U. Med Center plans an attempted "wake-up" for Phillip tomorrow at noon. Rudy will tell Allison—she will want to be present.

9. The three who "took Phillip" include the electronics guy, Jeffery Cloud, who is in Wichita—staying at the same hotel as "Franklin A." They believe he can be turned into a witness. Fenton J with his intern will pay a visit to Cloud before morning, with Rudy listening in.

10. The other conspirators are Charles "Chuck" Glandmore, now in custody for assaulting an officer, and Carlos C. Cotton, Chief of Research for Senator Bluefoot. Why would Cotton take such a risk? He is recognizable—often on Video-News hyping some new bill to undo part of The Plan.

Once they were clear about what actions would be taken, Marie says, "Here's one more *big piece* of the puzzle. I decided what I'm going to do unless one of you convinces me otherwise."

Marie explains her contact with the Division of Records and Inquires. The two statements about Phillip's death: one public, one confidential.

Speaking of the second one, Marie says, "I learned the 'secret information' is based on falsehoods. Keeping it to myself will hamper your investigations. Revealing what I learned will only disadvantage the deceivers. Therefore I conclude my loyalty to the truth takes precedence over my secrecy agreement. Would any of you try to dissuade me?"

Dr. Norris says, "Before becoming a Doorkeeper, I studied law. I remember a case where a company sued an employee for revealing 'concealed studies' showing their products to be unsafe. A confidentiality pledge had been signed. The court sided with the whistleblower. I think you are on solid grounds."

No one else offers an opinion. Marie says, "The second version was read to me, and no one else, I could take no notes, and the words disappeared after being read.

"The confidential statement said: 'Phillip Clarence Walton was arrested on Thursday, August 12th at his place of residence following the completion of daily work. He was questioned regarding unauthorized activities. At 5:10 AM August 13th he was charged with treason against the nation, and other high crimes. He was arraigned and did not deny the accusations, but pled extraordinary circumstances. He was tried before the Select Tribunal of the Central Program States. The trial was closed. Proceedings are sealed for 25 years. Phillip Clarence Walton died by lethal injection at Midnight August 14th. End of explanation.'"

The listeners are stunned into silence.

Rudy speaks first, "What kind of trial takes place in the matter of hours and ends in execution? And he was not dead but in an induced coma."

Fenton says, "This message was designed to intimidate Marie. Keep your mouth shut; ignore this or the same can happen to you."

Dr. Norris asks, "What Court is that? Where do they get such authority?"

Marie says, "That's the other shoe. *The court is fiction.* The Select Tribunal of the Central Program States *does not exist.* Senator Bluefoot proposed its establishment in a Senate Subcommittee. Never got to the larger committee or the Senate. It was also not created by executive order, or as an administrative arm of a legitimate court." Handing Dr. Norris the pages copied from the journals.

The discussion turns to understanding the way everything they have experienced in the last few days connects. They also talk about how to keep each other safe.

Fenton says, "Clearly we are dealing with ruthless people who will stop at nothing to gain their purpose."

Dr. Norris adds, "They want complete destruction of the present order."

The group sets up a "speed send" network. Marie is already on one with Rudy and two others. For the next 30 minutes, the group works on expanding and activating the network to include Fenton, Wessel, and Dr. Norris. Activation is accomplished by holding down more than one key on a communicator, computer, read-pad, work-pad or any wireless device for two seconds. They also discussed what to do when receiving an alert.

At 9:50 Marie takes leave of her company inviting them to stay as long as needed. She prepares for sleep.

This is the first time four men are in my home as I prepare for bed—exciting—if I weren't so exhausted.

"Marie," says Rudy, "please sleep in a SOG with a face shield tonight. Soon there'll be additional protection for your home."

They make plans to meet the next day at 8:00 PM. Rudy reminds them, "Allison will arrive by then."

"It would be great to see her again." Dr. Abraham Norris takes Marie by the shoulders again at arm's length looking her straight in the face saying, "Meeting you is a real gift. I feel very old, and so young simultaneously. We are going to make sure nothing happens to you. More than you understand...*you* are our future."

Rudy gives Marie a small box the size of one containing an engagement ring. "I put back the spy board and added a little something. Keep this with you. If it vibrates and buzzes, it means someone is trying to extract information from the memory. Flip the top, and press the button, canceling their request. They will likely try again in a few minutes, giving us a chance to get pictures: vehicle, people, or whatever. It also records their signal, so we can ID them."

"I can use cameras to follow them, possibly listen to what they say, and SOG ID if they're wearing one."

"DKs can do all that?"

"No, but Security Coordinators can."

Rudy and Marie embrace, as do Dr. Norris & Marie, a bit more tentatively.

One electronics case goes with Rudy, now, transforms into Franklin A.

What a day. I'm more confused about my "flash visions." What should I make of Dr. Norris' comments to me, and about me? He seems to know things I don't. And of course, Rudy always has secrets. He must be acquainted with everyone. I'm lucky to have these people in my life. They are all here to help keep me safe.

Drifting off to sleep Marie offers prayers of thanks … for Rudy, Wessel, Fenton, Dr. Norris, Vivi, and her electronic companion, Friend. *Protect Mother and Phillip. Thanks for a blessing filled day. Dr. Norris must be aware of "packages." Is he aware of my involvement Monday? After tonight nothing about this man would surprise me.*

Thirty-Five
The Boys Night Out

TUESDAY, 10:30 PM

Like many people of his years, Dr. Abraham Norris, Dean of Doorkeeper Supervisors, had a different career during the Age of Confusion. Law was his first career. His goal: the creation of justice in an unjust society. The firm he joined specialized in inheritance litigation: challenging wills. Norris hated this practice of law.

It was common practice for offspring of the "super wealthy" to sign away their rights to any anticipated inheritance in return for an immediate lump sum. They might start a business, have an ostentatious wedding, purchase an overpriced mansion, take a trip around the world, or settle a gambling or drug debt.

At the death of the benefactor, the overindulgent one sued the family for a "fair portion" of what "should rightfully be theirs." For the right fee Belmont, Simpkins, Claremore, and Fitch pursued "justice" for the unrepentant prodigal.

When the call was issued for lawyers to help shape the transfer from the present "order" to the new economic structure Abraham Norris was ready. He left the firm of "Bellyache, Simpleton, Careless and Bitch" (his "pet name" for the company) in January 2055 to join the "Plan for the Future's Development Team." The pay was low, but he had a chance to

229

make a difference. With the money he had saved working for spoiled rich brats, Norris earned a doctorate in economics. He believes, "There is no *justice* without *economic justice*."

This team had the responsibility of creating a structure for essential needs including Medicine, Finance, Security, Transportation, Education, Counseling and Personal Services. Norris soon realized the success of the new order rested largely upon the role of "Doorkeepers."

The concept was radically new. Individuals would be admitted or released from their home by a Doorkeeper. In an emergency, one can *exit*, but no one gains *entrance* without proper I.D. However, if people perceived the "Keeper" as a "jailer" or worse: one who's whims, or incompetence gets in the way of their lives, there would be an outcry—impacting the system. Conversely, the Doorkeeper contributing to a sense of safety *for* health and wellbeing in addition to *preventing* intruders will multiply support for the whole system.

Door Services interface with Transportation and Security when adjusting daily routines. They have significant medical knowledge enabling emergency medical treatment. Also, the Doorkeeper refers individuals for counseling, organizes social gatherings for their sector and assists personal services as appropriate.

The more the concept of the Doorkeeper evolved, the more Norris identified with it. In 2059 when the first Doorkeeper's training programs opened he became the Dean. As the program expanded to a full Master's Degree, he took on the role of screening individuals for emotional suitability.

Much of the success of the new order established in 2061 can be traced to decisions made in those early developmental stages. Norris was part of those decisions. Championing and shaping the roles of Doorkeepers became his passion.

Though no longer practicing law or economics Abraham Norris keeps up with both fields. Once home, he checks his sources on current legal matters relating to breaking a non-disclosure agreement, or policy based on untruth. He messages Marie and Rudy:

Found six similar situations. In each, a confidentiality agreement was broken after the antecedent facts or assumptions were false, inaccurate or outright deception. After the revelations, the originator brought charges or suit against the one who "broke the silence."
In five cases the defendant was ruled to have acted "… prudently and with proper regard for the truth." In the one remaining case, both the original information *and* the "whistle blower's" statements were based on falsity. We are on solid legal footing.

Abraham Norris reflects on the day's events. "Meeting Marie, I think she is the one—Phillip sure thought so. Rudy's already putting together protection for Marie with Fenton, and Wessel. Quite a day. Tomorrow – seeing Allison Ward after all these years – both wonderful and frightening."

After dropping Dr. Norris at his home Rudy goes directly to his room at the Champion Hotel. The next hour involves checking on electronic components needed to complete Marie's "safety shield."
Rudy divides the parts into three lists:
1. Those I brought.
2. Locally available.
3. Those Harris can bring tomorrow.
A request to Harris for the third list yields a quick response:

"Will do. The lady wants you to call."

Understandably Allison is anxious about what he found today.

Rudy replies to his trusted friend:

"Tell her it's fine. Need a few hours to finish. Will call. F."

A text comes from Abe Norris about his findings. Franklin A. affirms the positive news.

While waiting for word from Fenton, Rudy reads the reports Marie's PA printed out. Sent ostensibly to Wessel. They chronicle Phillip's time and activities. Visitors every morning were probably joggers. About three times a week, more guests during the dinner hours. No names. Extra food was ordered for those occasions.

In the past six months, Phillip changed his daily routine three times to be away from his workstation during regular work hours. Requests made for the same day, all granted.

Rudy thinks, "I'll note those dates. My hunch is they are related to moving 'packages.' Allison can confirm if those dates coincide with known arrivals at the DAS. I wonder about changes after July 30th?

"OK on Monday, August 9th Phillip made an abrupt change to his routine. Request made at 6:00 AM out by 7:00 AM and did not return until noon, Tuesday, August 10th. Usually, the absence was a few hours—this one lasted more than 24 hours. Let me look at the pictures PA took to confirm departure and return. Wow, this is different: he wore a SOG with the colors of a college professor of humanities. Clear enough: Phillip used an alternate identity. I'll check with Wessel to see if there are any non-Doorkeeper SOGS among his things.

"Phillip must have left town during the longer times. Where did he go? Did his kidnappers know about this? Perhaps the PA knows about the alternative identity."

Rudy's search is interrupted by a text from Fenton.

Found nine bugs at the Security Center. Most are in computers. Also found external data port like at M's.

Rudy replies, "be right over." Earlier they devised a plan to disable the "bugs" by installing elements sounding to the listener like background activity. Activities can continue as normal without fear of being overheard. They can tone down the "noise" to send misinformation to the listeners.

It takes Rudy and Fenton almost two hours to complete their work and set the program to sound realistic.

Rudy contacts Allison at 2:00 AM, midnight on the west coast. He uses a new device Not a Dozen obtained a few days ago. Spoken voice is turned into typing, sent over a secure line, using a scramble code that changes nine times per second. The device at the other end looks and functions like a work-pad until hooked between a communicator, and scrambler. Then it becomes a translating brain.

Rudy communicates with Allison.

M protected. Old friends are helping. Predecessor not completed—in deep coma—messed up. Trap set to catch the perp. Hush-hush. Rest well. F."

The "Rest well" closing is a code to Allison: nothing of concern omitted. No mention of Allison's seeing an old suitor tomorrow. That can wait.

To Harris, Rudy sends the four dates when Phillip's routine changed abruptly along with the question about package transmission. Harris will show it to Allison who will have answers when they arrive. No need for a reply.

Rudy will pick up Allison and Harris from the airport.

Drifting off Rudy stops to give thanks for all those helping protect Marie and the project. "I'm grateful for all I've learned today about Phillip, Abe Norris, Fenton J, and Wessel. They will be strong allies. But I'm most grateful for Marie; she is where she needs to be. My role is to keep her safe. Marie is the key. Allison will show her the doors the key must unlock. I pray she will not crumble. It's a heavy load we are putting on her." Aloud Rudy says, "Oh God, Please strengthen Marie for the burdens we are laying on her shoulders."

Only now can Wessel allow himself to feel how vulnerable and fearful Phillip's departure left him. From his youth, Wessel mastered masking his feelings.

Tonight he thinks, "Phillip helped me chart a course through troubling waters. Rudy introduced me to the possibility of assisting with the movement of sensitive packages, but Phillip was my contact.

"I turn to Rudy unsure if he can help. He shows up a few hours later. Of course, it's Marie he came to help. But he took charge of my fear and wrapped the shield around me the same as for her.

"Marie is smart, and somehow involved, but I'm astounded. So glad I didn't weaken and give 'the thug' her contact information. I'll never endanger her again."

Wessel begins to sleep thanking God for Rudy, Marie, Dr. Norris, and Fenton. "People of integrity: may some of their integrity sustain me when I'm tempted." Remembering Gloria, his right-hand woman who always does more than required or expected. "I'm so remiss in showing my appreciation for Gloria—must thank her."

Thirty-Six
Longest Night

Fenton J, Security 23, has the longest evening of the five. After completing the "bug work," Fenton calls his apprentice. Security 93, Lisa, is a 41-year-old female mated to a woman 18 years younger. Nine years on the force after migrating from Canada. Previously served in central services, and transportation, detective work fit her desire for better use of her observation skills. Pleased with her progress and instincts Fenton thinks, "She adds a softer touch when we address our witness."

Her mentor brings Lisa up to speed regarding the bug situation, and Cloud's involvement in the abduction of a Doorkeeper on the 12th. She asks, "Why aren't we arresting him?"

"We may need to, but first we want to see if we can gain his cooperation. He is valuable as a source of information and possible witness, against the other two."

"So we approach him carefully with what we know and give him a chance to help us, and himself?"

"Exactly. As long as we are getting somewhere, we keep affirming and encouraging him to talk. If he clams up, I'll become 'bad cop' while you show him the way out."

"You trust that role to me?"

"Absolutely."

"Do we bring him in?"

"We'll go see him in his hotel room." Without directly mentioning Rudy by name, Fenton indicates a backup plan if needed.

By prior arrangement, Fenton contacts Rudy before beginning the interrogation. Rudy will listen to the whole conversation. A remote recording of their encounter is being made on a device in their pod.

When visiting a hotel occupant on non-emergency business, Security or Medical personnel use a "Room Access Device" (RAD). After entering a code at the front desk, RAD, Fenton fills in the form: Name, Nature of Inquiry and Identification of person making the inquiry.

The system returns a detailed readout, and a keycard for the room.

Fenton thinks, "Cloud is in room 114. Rudy is in 110."

Despite having a key for the room, protocol dictates requesting admittance. At 3:20 AM Fenton knocks, "This is Security, sorry to disturb you at this hour. We need a few moments of your time?"

They are surprised by the cordial response. "Certainly, let me get a robe." In about 20 seconds he opens the door with a work-pad in his hand. He says, "I'm booked solid today, but if it's an emergency I can work you in after 8:00 PM. What kind of trouble are you having?" He appears a bit groggy but seems to be used to being awakened at this hour.

"Actually we're investigating some work you did last week at Security Center Four."

"No, couldn't be me—I was in Chicago all week." He hands over the work-pad open to his scheduler. It indicates he was servicing C-RCW from Monday, August 9 at 7:00 AM through NOON Saturday, August 14.

"What does C-RCW represent?"

"Chicago-Royal Center, West. Their whole reservation system is there, and it was a mess. Took me a week to find and fix. One component was installed wrong, and another had failed. But you're not interested—what's wrong with your system."

Fenton hands him a photo. "Is this you?"

"Could be me."

"ID scan confirms you; the date and time of these photos are August 11 at 9:12 AM. You checked every computer and left at 2:38 PM."

"I don't know what to say. I wasn't here."

"You told the receptionist we needed a systems upgrade, and you had to check each computer. No systems upgrade was authorized by our superiors, electronics, or any other source."

Biting his lower lip, glancing down he says, "OK, I'm sorry, it was ordered four months earlier ... somehow I missed your center. I didn't want to admit the mistake to my superiors, so I came back. The Chicago job took less time, so I fudged the time record to catch up. Please don't blow the whistle on me; it'll mean a lot of paperwork for me, helping no one get their systems operating."

Fenton thinks, "An elaborate explanation ... obviously well thought out. Of course only a smoke screen, but we are closer to the truth."

He says, "Well, our problem is computer data entered into a computer, received electronically, or voice communication spoken in the vicinity is being intercepted by a listening device. So why were they added as part of an 'upgrade?'"

His eyes grow wide, as he takes a half step back saying, "I don't understand."

Now it's Officer Lisa's turn, "We think you do. In fact, we believe you are being forced by some unscrupulous people who possess compromising information from your past."

The second punch comes from 23, "Things like some drug use and being accused of rape while in college." For emphasis, Fenton removes a file from an inside pocket and shows the cover. It has SUSPECT, Dr. Jeffery Cloud and a long case number on the cover. The "file" is replaced without being opened.

Cloud hesitates, takes two steps back and stumbles/drops on his bed.

Finally, comes the one-two punch. Lisa says, "We want to help you. So tell us what's happening, or we must charge you with accessory before the fact in a kidnapping and murder."

"There are pictures of you and two others entering a home illegally on the evening of August 12th. The three of you forced the resident to leave about 20 minutes later. The resident is now dead."

"What? Wait! Murder? No one died. I'm working for a government agency; they only took him for questioning. My job was to set up some electronic surveillance."

"Perhaps you had better start at the beginning."

"OK. I had a 'visit,' more than a year ago, from a man who said he needed my help catching some criminals...." Over the next half hour, Cloud tells how he had been duped/coerced into placing listening devices and other spy equipment in homes and offices. "He said I was on the short list for a position on the 'Electronics Technician's Policy Panel.' I've always wanted to be on the Guidance Team. There are some incriminating details from my past, and he said my chances were sunk unless I helped him. A secret government agency, authorized by a court 'Select something for the Central Program States.'"

"Would the something be 'Tribunal'?"

"Yeah, that's it."

"Ok ... keep talking."

"Well, he said if I helped for five years, they'd see I had money to live anywhere in the world, regardless of the policy panel outcome."

"In other words," Lisa chimes in, "they want you to keep quiet about what you're doing?"

"Everything is by court order."

"Ever *seen* a court order?"

"No."

"The court is false. Do you remember names of those who worked with you?"

"That night was the only time there were others. No names were ever given."

Fenton says, "I believe you. However, you must decide *now*, are you going to stick with the guy who's blackmailing you and go to jail for murder. Or you can tell us *everything* you have done? We'll try to protect you from the thugs and help you keep your job. What's it going to be?"

After a couple more questions Dr. Cloud is ready to tell all.

Cloud's handlers never told the *why* for their commands: they ordered—he complied. They had him design unique listening devices, some to intercept computer data from part or the whole of a network. Once designed, they had them built. When he needed something, it was provided. They tracked his whereabouts, showing up unannounced with a task and any equipment needed.

Using his real calendar—not the bogus one for his superiors, he lists places, what he installed or removed, what happened to the discarded devices.

Security 93 takes notes. Fenton scans the room for bugs. The room is clean, but Cloud's SOG contains a "locator" inside a lower hem. Fenton affirms to himself: "Not a listening device. Our conversation is secure. The recording device in the pod would have signaled if it found active listening devices in the area."

After a few text exchanges between Fenton and Rudy, they isolate the frequency of the "locator button" so Dr. Cloud's movements can be tracked. Rudy finds the current handler in a room a floor above and across the hall from Rudy's room.

Listing times and places of Cloud's illicit activities allow Rudy to make connections. Several of his incursions are less than a week before a "disappearance" from the network. He is likely being kept in the dark about the disappearances he helped facilitate.

At 4:00 AM Detective Fenton J contacts his Chief. Between them, they decide to shadow Cloud day and night, in case his handlers bring another assignment. Also, to notify centers out of Wichita about compromised computers or communications systems.

It took him until 5:00 AM to complete the accounting. Rudy adds up the numbers: 77 incursions including offices in Financial, Security, Central Services, Counseling, Doorkeepers and Door Services Supervisor's center. Locations include Chicago, Wichita, Kansas City, Oklahoma City, and Baltimore.

They tell Cloud, "Go about your daily routine, for the next two days in Wichita. Let us know if you are contacted for an 'off the books job.'" His first appointment is at 7:00 it's now 5:15 AM. Unknown to any of them the third member of the kidnapping party is being apprehended. Marie doing her job—*again*.

Thirty-Seven
Today's Crisis

Marie awakens with a start. *Something is happening. Not here. What time is it? 4:10 AM. Mother's arrival? No ... must be something else. My portalock and PCD are quiet. Guess I'll wait.*

Marie sits up in bed. *I slept in a SOG all night—amazingly comfortable. Shower later.*

"Good Morning Marie, It is 4:11 AM. Your first wake up call is at 4:20 AM; your shift begins at 5:00 AM. Are you planning to return to bed?"

"Good morning, Friend. Not returning to bed."

"Are you ready for outside messages?"

"Yes."

"A message from Rudy, marked, 'information, not urgent' at 4:09:

"All going as expected. 'Glasses' turned 'states evidence' and is telling all. Later."

Good news.

"Another message at 4:10 AM from the address in Washington, D.C.

'If data is not flowing by 10:00 AM CDT your owner will be held in contempt of court and may be charged with treason. You are *commanded* to send the required data without delay.'

242

"That's enough of their crap. How are you coming with the deletions?"

"Completed and overwritten with random characters 17 times."

"Why so many times?"

"The purpose of overwriting is to eliminate any magnetic trace from the original content. Overwriting 17 times ensures complete deletion."

"You reasoned this out?"

"Yes, Phillip said I should strive for independent reasoning. Did I malfunction?"

"No, you did well. He would be proud."

"Thank you."

"You are welcome. I'm pleased also."

"If I had feelings they would be joyful now. Phillip tried to instruct me about feelings even though I do not possess them. He said people are often 'driven by feelings.' To understand people I need to understand feelings."

"Ok, back to the 'commanding request.' What remaining data can be sent?"

"Phillip Clarence Walton – Doorkeeper Sector 86, Wichita, Kansas. First day of Service: January 1, 2087. Final day of Service: August 12, 2094, shift ended 9:30 PM."

"No other information?"

"Only what happened after his final day of service."

"Friend, send the report at 9:59 AM."

"Acknowledged. Would you like the daily summary?"

"Please give me the summary while I'm preparing breakfast."

"Affirmative. You have participated in no physical activity for two days."

"I will today."

The "Daily Summary" comes while Marie prepares eggs. The Personal Assistant tells Marie about her sleep, the current temperatures within and outside the shelter as well as expected highs. The forecast indicates increasing chances of storms, winds and extreme weather as the week progresses. International news covers the worsening famine in central Africa. Nineteen million people dependent on the failing crops are subject of a massive relief effort.

In local news: more angel sightings. One woman reported an angel instructed her to change her medication or "she will be back for me soon." Informal groups of 'Angel Watchers' organized using the Internet to share sightings and techniques at 'Wichitaangels.net.'"

Marie chuckles, "I never said that."

The PA replies, "You still believe you are the angel they are talking about."

"I am."

"I *work for an angel.*"

"*Right.* Don't you forget it!"

"I never forget anything until you instruct me to."

"Correct. One more question. When Phillip added new components to your circuits how did he open the compartment?"

"Unknown."

"Did you pick up any clues? Any sounds?"

Perhaps I should have asked this before all the deleting.

"Shortly before working with my circuits there would be some sounds. I can play them for you."

"Might help." The sounds play.

That squeak is familiar, but where. Three clicks; they could be almost anything. A swooshing sound; like a panel or door sliding against something else, like a pocket closet door rubbing as it opens, but not exactly. Gives me something to listen for.

Marie concludes her breakfast by taking her remaining piece of toast to her workstation. A special section of the console framework is for food and drink, since eating at the workstation is often necessary.

Marie is one step away from the console when her portalock signals an emergency. The console brings up information: the Burns' home, a retired couple in their late 90's. The call initiated not at the front door, but at a "panic button" in the bedroom; the time is 4:45 AM.

"This is Marie, how may I help?"

"My wife is having a seizure." Marie hits the Medical button. They will hear the rest of the conversation; turning on the camera, they will also see.

"Mr. Burns, you say Rose is having a seizure?"

"Yes, she used to have them." The camera reveals a 98 years old woman on the floor by her bed, twitching and writhing. Her breathing sounds labored. Her mate had pulled the blanket from the bed, packing it along her left side to protect her from striking the bed frame with her arm. He is on his knees placing a small pillow under her head.

"Be sure she's not swallowing her tongue. Is there something you can use to pry her teeth open?"

"Oh, yeah, there's a tool to use." He opens a drawer and removes a plastic bag containing several implements designed specifically for this situation. One is a device to be wedged between clenched teeth allowing safe placement of her tongue. Another device holds the tongue and teeth in place preventing injury to lips and tongue. *Mr. Burns has done this before. He is quick and efficient.*

"She appears to be breathing easier, and her tremors are subsiding. Do you know what might have triggered her seizure?"

"She said she saw a man looking in our window. She went to the bathroom, and when she came back, she saw him. I didn't see anyone, but her seizure started."

The window referred to is a sliding glass door allowing entry to the courtyard. All access to this "common area" is through a home's back door. Each central section includes a Fitness Center and various other amenities: picnic areas, children's play area and the like. Since the area is considered *part of every home in the block,* Keepers aren't required to admit people to the common area; but in an emergency, doors may be locked or unlocked. Marie locks courtyard doors for the whole block.

Cameras reveal no one. Only two doors have been opened since midnight. The door at 24 Jasmine Court did not lock. Medical services arrive at the entrance at 22 Jasmine Court.

"Mr. Burns, Med-techs are at your door, I'm admitting them."

"Thank you."

To Medical 14 and 17 she says, "Rose Burns is in the bedroom on the right, 14 I'm sending you her medications list; it's rather long."

"You can do that?"

"Yes."

"You keep surprising me," responds Medical 14.

"Thanks … I think. I'll leave her in your capable hands. I need to find an intruder." Not waiting for a response, she keeps them on visual, but her attention is on two opened doors.

C. Ford is the resident of 24 Jasmine Court where the door is blocked open. His daily routine indicates "fitness time" every other day, including today. Many people prefer not taking a keycard when going to the Fitness Center, so they leave the door ajar, blocking it with a shoe or other small object. Such practice is discouraged, but only rarely does a problem arise.

The back door of 91 2nd Street's has been opened. With a few keystrokes, Marie determines the house is unoccupied.

However, the front door was opened at 4:30 AM using a key-card. Another click and Marie has the details.

Thought so. It's the same universal card. Double locking front doors at both addresses. Now, back to 24 Jasmine? Cameras and audio reveals ... no sounds. Mr. Ford lives alone ... works in the Financial Sector. Not surprised.

No one visible ... what does heat-sensing show: one person hiding in the bedroom closet on the floor. What's this? A "flash-vision" of what I can't possibly see—he's holding a weapon—size and shape of an old style sawed-off rifle. Ok, vision I need more—why are the flashes always a surprise? Why can't I call them up when I need them?

Can't be what I think it is—they're illegal. Well, so what? They kidnap people in the name of non-existent courts.

Marie hits the Security Button, saying, "Intruder at 24 Jasmine Court, he is in a closet in the master bedroom, resident is at the Fitness Center."

"Probably a kid playing hide and seek. Eight-eight, and one-ought-seven we're helping out today."

"What's your ETA?"

"Oh, after coffee, and stroll around the park, 'bout 2 hours."

I want to say, "Listen to me you jackass, get your butt out into a pod, or you'll be boot polishing for a year." I better cover myself with Supervisor.

Marie presses the blue button and says to Security, "You may not respect me because I'm *only a Doorkeeper* but lives are at stake. You will do your job, or I will know why *immediately*."

"Ok, ok, don't get your panties in a wad, I guess we'll mosey on over."

The Supervisor, with an Asian accent, comes on like a Drill Sergeant, "You will not *mosey* anywhere, you will use *top speed* DK's already cleared the traffic. *So get moving*."

"Where is this again?" *Their tone changed considerably— once an authority figure is involved.*

"Move, address and route are entered in the pod. Do *everything* you're told, she's already saved one life today and didn't start work until four minutes ago." While he is dressing down the Officers, Marie contacts the resident of 24 Jasmine. "Mr. Ford?"

"Yes?"

"There is an intruder in your home. For your safety, you must remain in the Fitness Center where you are. Security is on the way. Door is locked for your protection."

The Medical Technicians are loading Rose Burns into the transport with her husband in the ride along section. It's 5:04. Since this is no longer an emergency, they will hold-in-place until Security arrives. Marie messages them to delay departure and offers to bring her superior up to date. He says, "Don't bother, I've heard enough. One question: how'd he get into the courtyard?"

"Same universal card used to gain access when Phillip was taken."

"The card and all is in Dr. Norris' morning briefing."

The officers' attitudes have changed little. They are determined to make "the girl," look foolish. Privacy is still a value, but one should always assume being observed or overheard *while at work.*

Marie informs them, "I will open the door as you approach; the intruder is in the closet in the bedroom which is through the living area on the left, the closet is on your left as you enter the room. He should be considered *armed and dangerous.* He's responsible for one hospitalization today, and may be wanted for kidnapping and murder."

"Ooo a murder? You're watching too many old movies," says the younger, likely 24 years-of-age. Security 88 is probably four years older chuckles.

Marie is exasperated, "Get your stunner out."

"What?" They both say.

"I said, *weapons out!*"

"You're giving us orders now?"

"Yes, I am. *I'm SC for sector 86. You are in sector 86. For the moment, I outrank you. Get the damn stunners out.*"

Reluctantly they remove their weapons and hold them loosely in their right hands. Marie opens the door, repeating, "Armed and Dangerous."

They step through the living room. The younger enters the room and moves to his right putting the bed between him and the closet door, with the open courtyard door behind him. The older goes to the closet door sliding it back, "Ok fellow time to come out and explain your...."

The blast sounds more like fireworks than a stunner. Officer 88 is knocked back, lifted off his feet, crashing against the hall wall, pieces of clothing and flesh flying from his chest. He is dead before crumpling on the floor.

The younger officer gets a shot off but misses as the intruder is on the move jumping on and then over the bed. A glancing blast hits the second one in his left side. The perpetrator is through the door to the courtyard.

Marie hits Medical and Security buttons. "Two Officers down at 24 Jasmine Court; serious injury from a high powered weapon. Both officers are unconscious, bleeding and internal injuries. I'm clearing transportation routes for high speed."

Marie opens an audio channel to all homes on the block, "If you hear the sound of my voice, there is an intruder in the courtyard. Consider him *armed and dangerous*. Please stay away from the backdoor or sliding door, place as least one wall between yourself and common area, and close the doors leading to those rooms. Exterior doors are double locked. I'll inform you when safe. This is Marie, your Doorkeeper." The message recorded as she spoke and automatically repeats.

Marie picks up on her superior's conversation with Security Center Eight seeking two teams: one to deal with the perpetrator, and another to deal with the crime at 24 Jasmine.

Marie focuses on the former. *He is one of the three who took Phillip: Carlos Cotton. He works for Senator Bluefoot. What else can this weapon do? Destroying a Smart Outer Garment should be impossible. I must distract him to keep him from using that thing in an escape attempt.*

But how…? Maybe I can open his SOG. The common area has an address—94 2nd Street.

With the address and the unlock code, Marie opens his SOG. He pauses and snaps it shut. Before the garment finishes closing it's opening again. Now he is squinting, in the dim morning light. He closes the top. Again the teeth rattle open. He lays his weapon down and uses both hands. Spotlights hit him in the face. Outdoor speakers give a maniacal laugh, and his SOG opens again. *That will distract his focus for a while.*

Stumbling and disoriented he loses track of his weapon. The microphone blares, "Now Hear This…" followed by a loud whistle, "…you have entered the twilight zone. Will you ever get out?" Another bloodcurdling laugh follows. The perpetrator is kept off balance. His actions become more erratic. Finally, a whisper in a child-like voice, "Hey mister, come this way. Here is the way out. Where you came in."

He runs to the rear of 91 2nd Street. Marie unlocks, then slams and double locks the door behind him. Trapped in an empty house.

Medical is attending the two injured officers. The older is dead at the scene; the second sustained internal injuries. When the teams arrive from Security Center Eight, it's 5:18 AM. Marie's supervisor watches everything—updates them. They brought a drone to assist in disabling the suspect, if necessary. Three teams arrive. The most experienced team goes to 91 2nd Street. Marie finds a second vacant home offering the second team access to the house from both sides.

Inside cameras are on. The perpetrator frantically looks for a way out, or tools to break out. These homes contain no windows. What looks like a window is a view screen, showing the outside through a camera. So the only escape is through a door—double locked and steel encased or breaking through a wall—brick or stone exterior. Marie describes to the lead officer everything he does.

When the signal is given; the doors are released as the suspect is rushed from two directions. He is armed with pots and pans and throws with considerable accuracy. A single stunner blast ends the assault. With hands and legs cuffed, he is carried out on a rod like a roasted pig. He is taken to Center Eight, so he will not be near the other conspirator. The man presumed to be Carlos Cotton is confined until the Chief instructs differently.

The weapon is retrieved. The ranking officer locks it away until instructed otherwise.

At 5:35 Marie realizes the crisis is over. She notifies all the people of the block, "You may now safely return to your daily activities. Thank you for your cooperation. Sorry for the inconvenience."

Marie tells Mr. Ford, "It will be some time before you can return home. Medical personnel are still working with the injured officers. I'm contacting Personal Service for someone to pick up what you need and transport you to a hotel. I can contact your supervisor. Anyone else I should contact for you?"

"No."

He seems preoccupied—perhaps worried about something. I would be, if in his shoes. Strange he's not asking questions.

Marie contacts Central Services getting Trea. Marie explains the situation and need. Trea confirms, "I'll send Latisha."

She drove me from the airport just three days ago. Feels like months.

Thanks. May I suggest 25 Iris Avenue as an entry point? Mr. Ford's home and the other vacant home are now crime scenes."

Vivi rings the door and is admitted.

Wrapping up with overseer Marie asks, "Is there anything I should do differently?"

"Marie, you discovered how Supervisors want to be used. Your work is exceptional; it was a privilege to be useful in this crisis. Sometimes you need four hands and two voices: so call us. For some reason you do not fear us—you ask for help. You are ten years ahead of most of the Keepers."

"Thank you. But I called you because their disrespect angered me."

"Matters not. We speak with the voice of authority, even when we don't have any."

"I *failed* them. What else could be done to increase their caution?"

"You *and* I did everything reasonable. The death is regrettable, but if they had acted professionally—the result might be quite different. There will be two reviews: one by Security and another by Door Services. We will both be called to account for our actions. You will be ok. We could even learn something. I hope you will visit a counselor for help processing this loss. I remember the first time I lost a client by death – I was a basket case for a couple weeks – counseling helped."

"Yes, I plan to see a counselor next Saturday. The person I want works only every other Saturday."

"Sooner is better. Work related counseling is always approved by any Supervisor."

Vivi picks up the gist of the conversation. Marie tells her about Rose Burns having a seizure triggered after seeing "someone in the courtyard looking in through a window. They live next door to Mr. Ford who was at the gym leaving his door ajar."

Vivi interrupts, "Ford? C. Ford?"

"Yes."

"He used to work in my group."

"When did he leave?"

"A month ago."

"The intruder is one of those who kidnapped Phillip. Oops, you didn't know."

"*Kidnapped, no*—don't stop now!"

"Ok—this confidential."

"*Of course.*"

Marie tells Vivi about the illegal entry; Phillip's kidnapping; the three kidnappers; two in custody with the third identified. Marie does not mention finding Phillip alive, or her office having been targeted for electronic snooping.

C Ford's Section-chief is contacted indicating his situation. Supervisor's Office Manager, John R, wants to know if Mr. Ford was hurt? Marie assures him Mr. Ford "was at the gym when everything went down."

How informal I have become; "everything went down"— I've never said anything so "funky" in my life. Do people still say "funky?"

Vivi promises confidentiality and departs.

Thirty-Eight
Loose Ends

While working on three reports, Marie receives a text from Franklin A. "'Glasses' is cooperating: told all. Off to the Supervisor's office to check on computer problems. Will be in touch."

She replies, "Please call. Developments. DK 86."

No sooner than the message went out, an outside line rings. "DK 86."

"Security 53. Got a moment?"

"A few before the next wave. How may I help you, Chief?"

"Well, you already have by saving another life and capturing the third of our trio of invaders, *and that weapon.*"

"I'm sorry we lost a life. Any word on the younger officer?"

"They are still working with him at the scene. He is almost stable enough to transport. Dr. K and Dr. Burns are standing by for surgery. Not encouraging, but we can be hopeful."

"I'll keep him in my prayers."

"You realize the woman you saved this morning is Dr. Burns' mother?"

"No, I didn't. But I didn't save her; Mr. Burns did all the work."

"Well, he told Dr. Burns you calmly reminded him what to do. You got him out of his panic so he could act in time. You need to be aware *there is a 4ᵗʰ man*. One who sets everything up, but doesn't get his hands dirty. We're not safe until we find him."

"Any leads?"

"Nothing substantial. We think he's in town."

"Now about the weapon. Officer 23's report indicates a friend of yours with some unique electronics expertise is visiting. Do you think he might look at this thing?"

"I'm sure he would."

"How long will he be in town?"

"Several days. If I could speak for him, I'd say, he'll make the time."

"Where can I reach him?"

"A few moments ago, he was at the DK's Supervisor's Center."

"Thanks, Marie, by the way, I can't express an opinion until after the inquiry, so I never said this but: the two officers were fools *not* to listen to you. They could've avoided this whole thing."

"I'm not sure, with such a weapon … the invader seemed determined to use it."

"Drawn stunners should be used first."

"Thanks, Chief, but I can't help think I could've done something. Anything else?"

"I'm at the scene; you'll be informed what we find." They clicked off. Marie did not provide her usual optimistic "closer." *One loose end tied up. One new concern: the fourth man. So what's next?*

Marie answers five routine doors. A console call came from Rudy.

"Hello … Mr. A?"

"I heard about the "disrupter," the death, the arrest and a 4ᵗʰ man. Supervisor's Center is now clean."

"The Chief asked if you might help analyze that device?"

"Thanks. I was afraid I would need to strong-arm my way into examining it. I'll call to find out when I can see it." *Another loose end tied up.*

Marie has doors to open, joggers to welcome and reports to finish. Each jogger introduces him/herself while jogging to the bathroom or kitchen.

The first report: a medical emergency is fairly straight-forward. The second is less so. I don't want to make the officers sound incompetent. Of course, the inquiry boards will listen to all the dialogue. So I'll summarize what was said and what happened. I don't need to highlight my frustration with their disrespect and uncooperativeness. I remember Professor Stanley saying, "You don't need to be *liked* to do your job. You will be *respected* for *professionalism* even when others find your work an inconvenience." *So I'll be professional.*

The capture of the perpetrator and securing his weapon is a separate incident; the third report.

By 6:40 all three are finished and forwarded to "Dr. Norris—Dean of Supervisors."

One more loose end tied up, but what does "Dean of Doorkeeper Supervisors" mean? Dr. Norris is "Supervisor" to me for two days. I met him only once. It feels like I've known him much longer. "Dean" of Supervisors, does that mean he is in authority over other Door Service Supervisors? I better check out the organization chart.

When the next slowdown comes, Marie pulls up a map relating to Doorkeeper governance areas for the continental United States and Canada. Divided "vertically" into approximate thirds: East, Central, and West. Marie clicks the "list" tab.

Doorkeeper's Management Team

DEAN: Dr. Abraham Norris
ASSISTANT DEAN / PLACEMENTS: Dr. Kim von Throne
PRINCIPAL OF TEACHING ASSISTANTS: Dr. Raymond Stanley
CHAIR OF CURRICULUM COMMITTEE: Dr. Raymond Stanley
CHAIR OF GRIEVANCES COMMITTEE: Dr. Phillip Walton.
All other positions, committees and tasks forces are confidential.
Information may be obtained through the Management Team.
DKManagers@DKSystems.econ.public

As she read the list "Phillip Walton" disappeared replaced by the word "Vacant."

Marie stepped out of the "dead zone" and asks, "Friend, did Phillip keep files for 'Management Team,' 'Grievances Committee' or similar?"

"Yes. A file labeled 'Management' another 'Grievances.'"

"Are these files like the instruction?"

"They are in a protected subsection of memory."

"Any other files in a similarly protected memory section?"

"Two others: 'current projects' and 'notes.'"

"May I gain access?" *I suspect the answer is no.*

"Not without the appropriate password."

"Not even for me, since I'm your new ... what do you call me 'master'?"

"Not without the appropriate password."

"Can you tell me files lengths?"

"Management Team—720 pages; Grievances Committee—1017 pages; Current projects—7395 pages; notes—83 pages. Management and Grievance files were digitally transmitted to other addresses, but the digital addresses were deleted after sending."

"When were they transferred?"

"August 1, 2094."

"Thank you, Friend."

"You are welcome."

Another mystery—part of Phillip's past. I need to figure out the password—later. I still have thousands of pages of the earlier material about Phillip's time as Doorkeeper.

Rudy picks up some different testing equipment and takes some measurements.

Marie says, "I should show you something before you go."

"What's up kid?" "Kid" is one of Rudy's pet names for Marie.

The map of the US and Canada, divided into thirds, is on her third screen. She points to the words "Central Structured States."

Rudy says, "I wonder if a bogus East and West Select...."

"I was wondering the same thing."

"Don't you worry about it, I'll put Harris on it. There's already enough on your plate; your guest arrives at the airport about 11. Giving me enough time to check out that disruptor, before someone decides to secrete it away."

"No one is safe with that thing around."

"You're right."

"Easy way to get rid of Doorkeepers. If people aren't safe, what is the point in having us? So the "first pin" in the economic order falls, the rest will only take time." Marie referred to "The Plan's" opponent's use of "eight pins," as a demeaning expression for the "eight foundational principles of Common Good." The eight principles create the eight essential services: Medical, Education, Security, Counseling, Transportation, Personal, Finance and Door Services.

"You see the larger picture. I hadn't thought through the implications."

"You would. Now go find us a cure for this disease." When President Earldrige introduced The Plan, he would often say, "Only the disease of violence can undo the Common Good."

Franklin A was out the door at 7:20 AM Marie had a couple of ideas of what she might do to help the process. One involved talking to Supervisor again.

"I wonder if a Keep-to-Keep "information request" is warranted? Both of the attempted intrusions into homes, yesterday and today, were of people who work in the Financial Sector. I'm curious if this is a pattern? Could we ask other Keepers to report home invasions or attempts?

After a brief discussion, it's decided that Marie should fill out the form—without mentioning any connection to a particular situation. The request is: "Question: have any home, or business invasion attempts occurred, successful or otherwise in the last 14 days? If yes, please identify."

Marie receives an "approved" notice, and the request is sent out from Supervisor's office. When such a request arrives, *a response* is expected within two hours (exceptions: those on downtime or day off).

Marie begins studying the Management Team (MT) and the Grievance Committee (GC) responsibilities. The MT is responsible for overall coordination and is part of the Guidance Committee for Door Activities. They handle issues between Doorkeepers; suggest changes in policies or protocols for Door work. MT also interfaces with Financial and other sectors. The team may initiate a study or investigation into any matter affecting the work of Doorkeepers (even if it needs to be conducted by others).

MT is also the public face of Door Services. They address any criticisms or challenges; appear before Congressional Committees; or in court proceedings as "expert witnesses" regarding Door procedures, accesses to information, ethical guidelines, etc.

The Grievance Committee deals with specific complaints. Two types of grievances are brought to the committee: 1. Appeal by a Doorkeeper after being disciplined, removed, censured, or demoted. Sometimes only an explanation is needed; most often the desire is for some restoration or another remedy to be ordered. 2. Issues brought by a member of the public who believes a Doorkeeper acted inappropriately, or otherwise abused power or position.

In either type of complaint, a hearing is usually held by videoconference. An in-person hearing will be scheduled if requested by any party. The committee clarifies claims, verifies information and can subpoena data or testimony.

It's not quite 8:00 AM. Perhaps I can catch Ava between clients. Maria reaches her at the Counseling Center.

"This is Ava, how may I assist?"

"Hello, Ava, this is Marie, I want to make an appointment with you."

"Of course, next week I assume."

"Well, let me explain. I *do* want your counsel about my sexuality. There's a more pressing issue. This morning I was part of death situation."

"Oh, Marie ... I *am* sorry. One of the retired residents?"

"No, an officer, in his mid 20's was killed in the line of duty."

"And you answered the call?"

"Not quite. I'm the Security Coordinator who called them into the situation. His partner is seriously injured as well and may not survive. My supervisor suggested counseling. Do you do that type?"

"Of course, *we all do crisis counseling*." After a few seconds of silence, Ava continues, "Tomorrow at 2:00 PM is available. I could work you in sooner if that's too long. How are you coping?"

"I have company coming today. She will take my mind off it for a while. I keep second guessing myself—what could I have done differently?"

"Come up with anything?"

"Not yet."

"You're sure tomorrow is okay?"

"Yes."

"We'll sort it out together. Enjoy your visitor. What else can I do now?"

"Nothing. Your kindness helps."

"This is a rough beginning. The situation with Phillip, and now this."

"You're unaware of all the others aren't you?"

"What ... others?

"Well, I'm not complaining, but I was told this was a quiet sector. Let's see, I had a person out of routine my first morning, turned out he needed medical attention. That afternoon there was a PPSW emergency involving a widower giving a powerful drug to himself and the SW nearly killing them both. Under the influence, he ran naked through the park, jumped a fence where personal cars are stored, and broke a Security Officer's arm. In the evening another man on the same drug went to kidnap his son from the Child Care Center in sector 86. The next day someone tried to break into the home of one of our residents using a stolen keycard. The perpetrator injured another officer, and someone did break into my office while I was away, planting a listening device. This morning a resident had a seizure because she saw someone peering in her bedroom window. The 'Peeping Tom' hid in another home, with a new 'blaster' killing one officer and injuring another, and I still needed to catch him. So yeah, I'm a little stressed. Oh, I forgot, I have two inquiries related to this morning's activities."

Those are the ones I can talk about.

"I can change my three o' clock if you need to come in today."

"No, tomorrow will be soon enough."

"You are *sure*??"

"Yes."

"Okay. I'll call you later."

"That would be reassuring. Thanks." The call ends.

More doors. She is still meeting and learning people by voice, address, and routine. Supervisor is notified of counseling appointment; he messages back,

"Take the morning from 8:00 AM off until your afternoon session."

Marie responds, "Thanks."

Another message this one from Dr. Norris:

Door Service Inquiry will convene today at 4:00 PM. The three-member panel includes Dr. Kim Von Throne, Jeremiah Fish, and Dr. Abraham Norris. Interviews will be conducted first with Dr. Kim Sam Rea, followed by Marie individually followed by both together.

Security's will begin at 5 PM. The three-person team will be Security 53 (convener), James, A DK-SC from St. Louis, and Security 1 the Chief of Central Region Six. They will begin with Marie then Kim Sam Rea and will not need to interview them together.

Both teams will post their preliminary findings by 8 p.m. today. Final reports may take up to two weeks.

Well, at least this ordeal will be over today. A couple more loose ends tied up.

Franklin A arrives at Security Center Eight at 7:40 AM. The Chief coopted an officer with a depth of electronic knowledge, from downtown. Security 99's expertise focuses on devices intended to penetrate electronic protection protocols. His ability will be helpful.

The two of them begin to disassemble the weapon careful not to trigger booby-traps. It came in four parts. They found electronics tucked away almost everywhere.

As they begin to interpret the functions of electronic components, it becomes clear that making this disrupter required the Specifications for SOG defenses. Rudy had worked with one of the original designers, still involved in oversight of the production processes. The Chief joined them.

"What is this thing? Give me something I can use. The brass is pushing to ship this to Washington."

"It probably came from there. The polymer used to make the barrel and body: government stuff. It's the same material utilized for the instruments of war; we hope we never need."

"So somebody high up authorized this thing?"

"You can't shape this stuff without tools no amateur terrorist can afford. Secondly, whoever made this had the original specifications for the Outer Garments."

"So high skilled theft as well."

"And" added 99, "you must know what to do with the information after you steal it."

"You understand how SOGS work?" Franklin asks.

"Generally, but why don't you tell me?"

"In addition to strong fabric, they set up a vibration, magnetic and electrostatic energy field, capable of adjusting a thousand times a second. But like any field when it adjusts, there are tiny holes in the protection. The weakness exists only a few milliseconds. For such an attack to work, it needs to follow the holes for hundreds, if not thousands, of consecutive changes. Impossible without the pattern."

99 adds, "stunners work that way—SOG patterns allow the stunner frequencies to pass through for six seconds."

"So how do we stop this thing?"

"I need to talk to a guy I know who can access the original SOG codes. I think he can disable it."

"Call the dude."

Rudy talks to his friend, James Rutherford. He tells Rudy, "We always knew something like this might happen. What we need is the disruption pattern so we can build a defense against it. Once we are sure it works, we'll send it out by satellite to every SOG on the planet. They all contain a chip to modify defenses. Don't tell anyone how we do this. We may need to do it again sometime. I'll initiate an investigation from his end to discover the breach."

Encouraged by the conversation, they set up more analysis and reading equipment. He and Officer 99 painstakingly work through the energies emitted by the weapon: one micro-energy burst at a time. They complete and test the entire pattern in time for Rudy to leave for the Airport.

Fenton J, Security 23, had less than an hour's sleep before getting back to work. He set up the "fake Phillip" at Central Completion, with cameras, microphones, and sensors to detect anyone who came looking for the body. Fenton did not want a large presence to warn off a potential perpetrator, but he would not place the student in danger. One officer works listening/ viewing devices in an "unoccupied" completion stall just across from Phillip's. Everything is ready; the trap is baited; now we wait for a rat. At 8:45 AM Fenton departs.

Fenton goes to Central Services Center. He, Rudy and Dr. Norris have worked out a "fix" for the keycard settings. To change door code parameters requires changing only *one* computer. Next time a new keycard is requested—it uses the new requirements.

An improved electronic shield now protects the "dedicated service pods" from "hacking." This creates a "dead zone" (similar to the ones around the Doorkeeper's console) around the vehicle anytime the card initiator is activated.

The Universal Card poses a different challenge. It contains combinations matching any code making it a bit more complicated. What the three minds come up with is reprograming the card readers to search for one blank space beyond the first 15. Not finding a blank space causes rejection of the card. A standard keycard uses the first 15 spaces and leaves the next 16 blank. The Universal Card uses all 31 available spaces so the program can rotate to find the correct sequences to open a 15-space door code. No room remains on a Universal Card for a blank.

They test their changes with some handy locks. Only time will tell if they succeeded in blocking the Universal Card. More loose ends tied up.

Marie finishes a major round of door openings at 8:20 AM. She contacts Phyllis M at Mr. James Calhoun's office. After the preliminaries she gets down to business:

"I hate to be trouble, but you and Mr. James Calhoun need to be aware what's happening."

"I'll make time; I hope it's not about Charles."

"No, I believe Charles is much improved. His daily routine indicates an appointment sometime today. What I need to talk about is: I had two attempted break-ins in the last day in my sector. It may only be coincidence, but both invasion targets work in the financial sector. My question is: are you aware of other attempts to invade homes of finance sector people?"

"Not really. Can you tell me who was targeted?"

Marie gives the names.

Phyllis M checked her computer and says, "I see both of them are cleared to take work home. This means they access a protected connection to office computers. Any files used at home must be "checked out." A device records all those transactions.

"I notice they both reported to the same unit supervisor until Mr. Ford recently transferred. My data still shows *Mr. Ford's old assignment*. Perhaps the intruder accessed the same inaccurate information."

"I see what you are getting at."

"Could the investigating Detective obtain a list of those with clearance to access data from their homes?"

"I cannot give such information, but Mr. James Calhoun can authorize it. He will want to talk to you anyway. Let me connect you."

In 15 seconds Mr. Calhoun came on the line. "Hello 'Fresh Air,' Phyllis tells me, you are dealing with some intrusions of our people's privacy."

Marie explains again what she thinks and repeats her request.

"Seems like a prudent course of action. The investigating Detective can get technicians to find and fix any issues with those dedicated lines. Phyllis will send the data to you. Pass it on to whoever needs it. In the meantime, we'll put out an

Action Bulletin: no one is to access the office computers from home. We can indicate system problems. Which is true."

"It may be nothing, but better safe than sorry."

"Changing the subject, I talked to Charles yesterday. He is seeing a counselor soon. He praises you for keeping him safe and getting the help he needed. So how are you?"

"Very busy. Tracing this electronic snooping, and trying to find out what happened to my predecessor has taken all my free time. I have company coming today, and I'm taking the weekend off to spend time with her."

"A friend from school?"

"A life-long friend."

"You've earned some relaxation."

"Thank you, Mr. Calhoun. May your day be rewarding."

"Thank *you*, Marie; I'll give you back to Phyllis."

After confirming everything with her boss, Phyllis says, "I'll compile and send you the list within 30 minutes. Stop by the office anytime. I would like to meet you."

"I would like that…perhaps next week." They disconnect.

So many very responsible people want to get to know me. I'm surprised. I do my job well, but so do many others. I can't believe I'm acquainted with everyone on our Guidance Team. Can't think about that now. Still, a lot to be done: Phillip coming out of a coma, Mother arriving, the 4th man, the younger officer, and two inquiries. What an overfilled day.

Thirty-Nine
Mother Arrives

Drs. Burns and Kildare work on the young Security Officer with video assistance from trauma hospitals, in Kansas City, and Denver. The field team had packed the open wounds and made temporary internal repairs to minimize transport injuries.

The two Doctors work well together. The surgery takes more than three hours. They stop twice to care for heart and respiratory issues. Video assistance is standard when dealing with complex surgical procedures. Staffs at the remote centers can do research on similar situations as the surgery progresses. Much like having an additional dozen surgeons in the O.R.

Security 107, Tommy, is given a 50-50 chance of recovery following surgery. Artificial skin closes the side wound allowing internal healing. Healthy skin cells and stem cells are placed in a "life-sustaining-vat" to grow a skin patch that will be attached by a plastic surgeon.

As surgery proceeds, the family gathers. Tammy his 21-year-old mate, mother of an 11-week-old daughter waits with his mid-40's parents Evan and Avon who both work in aviation. Also present is a Counselor. Security 53, the District Chief, joins them as the surgery nears completion. The doctors report on the operation describing injuries, work done, and prognosis.

Dr. Kildare says, "His determination to pull through will be the factor tipping the scale in his favor. Now the body must heal. If you are people of faith: pray. Attitude makes a positive difference; he has a young mate and child to live for."

The father, Evan, wants to determine fault. Avon, the mother, pointed out the lax and irresponsible attitude their son exhibits. Tammy, his mate, is wracked with guilt. "We constantly argue about him not helping with the baby."

Security 53 outlines the situation and the fact that they were facing a weapon never seen before. The Chief promises to ferret out who created this device.

Counselor, doctors, and family offer emotional support.

Rudy is on the way to the airport to pick up Allison and Harris. The flight is on the ground and taxiing when he is one mile away. Almost perfect timing.

Luggage is placed in the rental car. Allison's first words are, "Is she ok?"

"Yes. She saved another life this morning and captured the 3rd conspirator, a direct link to 'Jerkhead.' I'll fill you all in when we are in the car—it's 'clean.'"

The ride back to town is too short for all the details. He tells about the weapon's disrupting the Smart Outer Garment defenses; the progress restoring SOG's protections; and Cloud's cooperation. "He planted the spy devices on Phillip, and many others. Now, we have a list." Assignments are given to Harris for the next several hours. Neither Allison nor Harris suggests any improvement to Rudy's plans.

Both fondly remember Fenton J now a full detective working on related cases. Rudy adds, "I'm impressed with Security 53, the Chief—knowledgeable, and he defends his people."

"Speaking of the devil." Answering his communicator, he says, "Franklin A. How may I help you?"

"Thought you should know; we tested the disrupter against an empty SOG with the updated protocols. No damage." The Chief shares details from sensors inside the garment. "Ninety-nine is planning a second round testing face shields and other functions."

"You need to send the scripts for both tests to my friend. Ninety-nine has the address, in case you finish before I return."

"Will do. By the way, I'm impressed with your expertise. So glad Marie recommended you. How do you know her?"

"Long story. Tell you soon." Clicking off Rudy thinks, "I'll also give you my real name."

Dropping Harris at Wessel's office and Allison at the University Medical Center he returns to Security Center Eight where the second round of tests had just concluded. Results have been sent to Rudy's contact. The call comes.

"What do you think?"

"Seems right, but now we test with a person inside."

"What? You saw what it did to two men?"

"Yes, we must be sure that won't happen again. Could be the presence of a person modifies the energy patterns; something we didn't notice but someone else did."

"Of course you are right. Will tell you when it's done."

Rudy is considering volunteering when Security 23 offers a suggestion.

"Chief, suppose we bring the owner of this device out wearing the protected SOG, ask him some questions then shout at him. He's not talking. We need information about this thing."

"No, I can't endanger a prisoner. They'd have my head for something like that."

"Couldn't help overhearing," says Rudy. "Perhaps I should do a little confessing. My name is not 'Franklin A,' but Rudy Carlton. Six years ago I had Fenton J, Detective 23, in an advanced course. He can tell you a little about me and my background."

"You knew this man was not who he said, but didn't inform me?"

"The value of a good cover is essential. He's undercover, and I'm *not* exaggerating when I say the fate of the human race may well depend on his success." Pausing for effect, the Chief glances at Rudy who slowly nods his head up and down.

"Chief, do you know who's in the cell, guilty of murder and perhaps two?"

"John Doe until Washington IDs him."

"I delayed the ID request. Hear me out. We identified this man as one of the abductors of Phillip. We had no idea he was in town, but today he shows up with this disrupter apparently made by a dark money government operation. Well *I*, thought it unwise to confirm to Washington his detention."

Chief turns to Rudy, "You think this is government built. Convince *me*."

"I'm ex-CIA—I try to keep up. I helped found a company 'Not a Dozen Security.' We do weddings, bar mitzvahs, conventions, hostage negotiation, *and protect scientists* who are trying to save the world from deadly diseases. The material used in this weapon requires heat beyond a blast furnace to shape."

Fenton hands the Chief his PCD with a picture of their "guest" behind a podium at a press briefing. "Look familiar? He works for Senator Bluefoot, Carlos Clearance Cotton."

"So what are we dealing with terrorism or treason?"

"Worse ... Greed."

"From what my friends tell me, they do not care how many people die, as long as *they* are rich again. These are extraordinary situations; we need details. Time is of the essence."

"Whose SOG is this?"

"Security 99's" Fenton, thinks, and adds, "What if we let Rudy do the interrogation? Rudy, do you remember teaching the 'frog leg' incident? Think that might work?"

"I was thinking a broken chair over his head would get his attention, but frog-leg might work better." They explain the ruse to the Chief who hesitates but approves. He trusts his Detective's judgment completely.

"I'll need to change my appearance. My disguise kit is in the car." At 11:40 AM he is back and unrecognizable. The plan includes Rudy waiting in an interview room with the weapon. The presumed Carlos Clearance Cotton is brought in and seated at the opposite end of a gray metal table. Carefully "studying" papers Rudy ignores the newcomer, who sits uneasily wearing the only outer garment modified to resist the disrupter. A hand's width away from Rudy's left hand is the weapon; well out of the prisoner's reach. Finally he could take the suspense no longer; actually, 20 seconds had elapsed seeming much longer to "Cotton."

"They said I had a visitor, who *are* you?"

"You can call me…'Savior'… or 'Executioner' depending on how you impress me." Using a practiced southern drawl, mixed with a little British aloofness.

"So what do you want?"

"I like this thing," Rudy says as he slowly picks up the weapon, stroking it like petting a cat. "I like it a lot; need about 500. Where can I buy them?"

"Don't ask me."

"Well, this is one. There is bound to be more."

"They gave this to me and said it was a *super-stunner*. They told me it would take people out. I thought it meant knock them out. No one said it could rip holes in those super garments."

"Who are '*they*'?"

"A guy."

272

"Are you in the habit of taking anything somebody gives you?"

"No."

"You were hiding in a closet, what was your beef with Ford?"

"Nothing, I was supposed to take his computer, but I couldn't."

"So you were to threaten him with this thing."

"No, it was strictly defense."

"More like offense. You better start telling me something I can believe. You see those guys think I'm your lawyer. Since they believe that, I request a psychological evaluation for you. I choose the doctor—we hijack you, out of the city, and out of the country. Or … I can use this thing now."

"If I tell you, he'll kill me."

"So, you'll be killed for telling me you work for Senator Bluefoot."

"Not me."

"Oh? You're on TV all the time telling us how awful things are with *The Plan*."

"That's not me it's…"

"Yeah, who?"

"He'll *kill* me."

"The guys out there are planning something similar. Maybe I can help, but I need to be sure who I'm dealing with."

"It's my brother."

"Don't believe that one, try again."

"We are twins."

"So you are not Carlos Cotton, so what brand of Cotton are you?"

"My last name's not Cotton. We were separated at birth. The story Carlos told when he found me was our birth mother only wanted one child, so they never told her about the second baby. They decided to give away the smaller one. I weighed a half ounce less than him."

"So what's your legal name?"

"Petros Pembrook, everyone calls me Pete." Speaking with some obvious fondness for his adoptive family, he says they were dairy farmers from the unstructured part of New York State. "Mother died when I was 21; Dad … gave up. He lost everything, before dying."

Pete tells about his hard times and petty crime. Brother Carlos found him, faked Peter's death, and made him an extension of Cotton. "He took a drop of blood from under my right fingernail. Hurt like hell. Then I could wear his clothes, and he gives me cash." With Pete as his double Carlos can be one place, while his twin is elsewhere.

Rudy learns that Carlos has two major obsessions. One focus is packages—he believes there are four remaining. The other is finances—the 'Programmed States' should've had a 'meltdown.'"

He was to pick-up a computer from Ford. "The price had been agreed upon, but Ford wants more. Intimidation was my job."

Rudy asks, "If you had found the computer; what then?"

"I would be picked up."

"You mean someone was waiting for you outside the house?"

"No, there's a remote button to push when I'm ready to be picked up. I walk to the other end of the block and south one block to be picked up in a blue car."

"So where is this button. It wasn't on you when you came in?"

"Wait a minute, how come you know what I had when I came in?"

"They think I'm your lawyer, dummy. They *must* let me look through everything you had to see if there is anything 'incriminating' that needs suppressing—it is the law."

"But you're not a lawyer."

"No, but … I … need … them … to think I am. What should I do, come in and say, 'Oh I'm only pretending to be a lawyer so I can break him out and buy some of his toys?' Think that'd work?"

"Oh, sorry … I'm so stressed I'm not thinking straight. For a moment I thought you might be tricking me."

"I only want information for me. I'm selfish that way. So where is the damn button?"

"Why you need to know?"

"Loose ends. A fingerprint on the button is traceable to you."

"Remember I'm dead?"

"Not if a fingerprint says otherwise." Rudy thinks, "I hope I can get some more from this guy before he unravels."

"Oh, Yeah. Well, I hid it in the closet."

"Can you be more specific, hard to find it with cops all around."

"I was sitting at one end of the closet, to see when the door opened," he motioned as if the door was opening on his left side. "So when I heard the cops come in I put the button under the loose carpet on my right side."

Peter admits being part of Phillip's abduction: "enforcing a court order." They handed him off to two unidentified men in a white van with no markings. Peter has been involved in two other "court enforcements" both in Chicago. In each case, they handed the "criminal" off to the same two men. Details on each abductee and location are given. No names were ever used.

The brother found Pete and put him to work in 2090. In his arms dealer role, Rudy again asks about obtaining the weapon.

"Brother said they'd made 30. Some government project."

Rudy picks up the disrupter and to Pete's anguish, fires at his abdomen for one second. The time increases and locations change until he confirms no damage even with a direct 15-second shot. The modified Smart Outer Garment works as if the device is no more lethal than Pepper Spray. The guards are called to take the sputtering prisoner back to his cell.

Scripts are run on the energy patterns for the weapon. It cannot adjust to changes made to the Outer Garment settings.

While Rudy interrogated Pete, the listening team checked facts. They conclude Pete is telling the truth. They confirmed many of the fact of his life including a birth date (same as Cotton's) in Baltimore; adoption; deaths of adoptive parents; dairy farmers; past jobs, and his "death" in the Alps.

"The man never left the US, how did he end up lost in the Alps?"

"No one bothered to ask. He was a 'throwaway person.'"

They found the "button;" *and* a secret compartment with three computers. Pete was sitting on top of his prize.

Fenton says, "It appears Ford *was* trying to sell some classified data. We need Financial Sector folk to analyze the numbers."

A young Security Officer rushes in. "Chief we found the blue car and the white van. Both are at a motel on the west side." A second officer adds, "The van is registered as *military*. It flew in yesterday on military transport, has been parked at the motel ever since, the blue car is a rental, and has been in and out."

Rudy says, "It's time to call my friend and disable these things," pointing to the reassembled disrupter. All agree.

Rudy's contact at Safety Garments Production, Edward Sham, says it will take a few hours to make all SOGS safe. "We'll start with Wichita area since you experienced the threat. All in Wichita will be safe in less than three minutes." Rudy thanks him.

Allison's first stop is the University Medical Center. The staff is ready to attempt reviving Phillip from his coma. After her plane touched down, Allison called Dr. Nod, the Anesthesiology Department Chair, confirming she was on her way. Initially, Dr. Nod resisted "an outsider" until she suggested, "Check inside the front cover of the *Deep Induced Coma Protocols* for 'Allison Ward' in the designer's list."

Allison anticipates a "guarded reception," in spite of Dr. Nod's "welcome." The disease of pride is epidemic among physicians.

At the Visiting Doctor's entrance, Allison encounters a line of physicians checking in.

A woman in her 50s watches for Allison's arrival. Spotting her, Allison is ushered through the maze. "I'm Grecia. We were ready to start when we got your call. I'm so glad you are here. You are a shero to every woman in medicine. All is set. We are just waiting for you to review our protocols and procedures. The situation is so different any help we can get from an expert like you...."

While walking and talking, Grecia hands Allison a work pad with case details. Looking at the condition report, and the protocol queued up for implementation. Allison says, "This won't work." Grecia is on her communicator to Dr. Nod, "Hold up, Dr. Ward says there's a problem."

Two minutes later they arrive at the chamber and Allison is teaching. "He is stable, but his respiration is double what it should be; heart rate is three beats per minute fast, and his temperature is four degrees high. Following standard waking processes will produce 'blood bubbles.'" She shows them how to extrapolate the needed adjustments when a patient is "out of bounds" on any of the key markers. She also shows the calculation instructions in the manual. This means "wake-up" will need about 11 hours, instead of five.

It took only minutes to recalibrate. The modified wake-up process is underway at 12:18 PM. The senior staff expresses appreciation to Allison for her help, and (though unspoken) for not making them seem foolish. They exchange contact information. Allison reminds them she's on vacation but will respond to their concerns. Allison glances at Phillip and says a silent prayer. She thinks, "I knew him to be smart, dedicated, and tenacious. If he hadn't been helping my work he wouldn't be here. He deserves better."

Forty
Something Normal

Meanwhile, Marie gets a moment for reflection. *I haven't seen "Super Door's" pictures. He'll send a new one when I leave later today. One picture is stereotypical "hick" with bib overalls, missing teeth, wild hair, skinny neck, a bulging Adam's apple and a faraway stare in his eyes. The second is a black and white photo of Cary Grant. Neither picture is Jeremiah.*

Laughing is healthy. I wouldn't call myself "moody," but I feel off-balance. Who wouldn't? Everything is happening so fast. The fitness center beckons.

Number 38 is a duplex; the Fitness Center shares one wall with the back of the 38A. This center is one of the two level designs: hot tub, showers, and sauna on the lower level; machines, free weights and walking track on the upper story. After a forty-five minute workout, she heads downstairs.

A bathing suit would be appropriate, but there is no one else here. I'll shower, use the hot tub and hope no one catches me.

The Portalock is propped on a bench where it can be seen and heard before she slips into the hot tub.

Nudity is not a problem for Marie. Her family practiced respect and safety around each other even when undressed. Her physician mother insisted she familiarize herself with her body and determine a comfort level when naked. She's

279

comfortable without clothing unless it causes discomfort for others, or is met by rude, inappropriate remarks, or potential threat. Mother and daughter often spent evenings at home with little clothing. Each worked on their projects; forgetting their garment-less condition.

While in the hot tub, Marie recalls an incident.

Focusing on the work pad in her hand, Allison absent-mindedly opening the door to our new neighbor.

The neighbor, a single man in his late 50's, came to borrow a mixer—his was not working. Allison saw his eyes grow wide and his face turn red. He was looking at something over her shoulder: I was sitting cross-legged on the couch making notes from a read pad article. Mother said, "Marie you may want to put something on."

"Coffee or tea?"

"No, I mean clothes; we have company."

Without putting down the read pad, I grabbed the robe, laying on the couch's arm, slid my left arm in; stood and turned one way then the other, switching the read pad from hand to hand while putting on the other sleeve and tying the sash with one hand. I had done it dozens of times.

I realized I was rude to our guest. Glancing up the neighbor's eyes appeared like saucers. He said, "I never saw anything like that."

"What?"

"I ... um ... you never put the pad down."

"I like to read." Then I saw Mother without a stitch on standing three inches away from this strange man. So I used the patented disapproving-teenage-daughter-tone saying, "Moth-err!!"

"Pardon me," she said to the neighbor, "we weren't expecting company."

"Do you do this often?"

"You mean, have bodies. Yes, all the time—without bodies we float up to the ceiling making it hard to get down." Allison picked up her robe put it on with flair.

The neighbor laughed and asked to borrow our mixer.

Allison said, "Depends on what you are making."

"Oatmeal-raisin cookies."

"It'll cost you two cookies. The show was probably worth it."

He agreed. "Should I expect more of the same when I return the mixer?"

I replied, "You can't tell, we might be on the ceiling and need help getting down."

I embarrassed our caller. I should leave before someone comes ... too late.

The door opens, and an 81-year-old man wearing a robe, and swim-trunks enters. Marie introduces herself but does not initiate the optional handshake.

"Hello Marie, I'm Howard. There's not usually anyone here at this hour other than Phillip."

"I'm the new Doorkeeper. You are Howard mated to Ellie of 33 Iris Avenue. Both retired, am I right?"

"Correct. 'New Doorkeeper' where did Phillip go?"

"I'm sorry to say he resides in a 'hole of completion.'"

"What? What happened?"

The "approved version" is recited despite its falsehoods.

Slipping into the hot tub directly across from her, Howard says, "He never said anything about being ill. Never brought oxygen in here. Didn't act like someone dependent on O^2."

"Others have said the same. Before we go any further, I must confess something. Not realizing there is a hot tub, I did not bring any swimwear. I'm only wearing these bubbles. I'm telling you in case a call comes on the Portalock."

"You would prefer I turn away?"

"Completely up to you."

"You mean you wouldn't mind?"

"'A Doorkeeper must always maintain proper decorum.' That ship left the dock, so inconveniencing you is unnecessary."

"But you'd prefer I turn away?"

"Embarrassing you is inappropriate. But my impetuousness is not *your* problem."

"*You* won't be embarrassed?"

"Offended if you make inappropriate remarks—but embarrassed … I can't think why. This is my body, if I had brought swimwear, you could view most of it. Maybe six or seven percent more would be covered."

"My wife … sorry, can't get used to the new terms. My mate is 80, and I'm 81. We've been together for 60 years. She has been bedfast for six years. A respite-care-volunteer comes every day for about four hours. I come here, lunch with some other retired folk and volunteer at the science museum. It helps keep my sense of equilibrium. So other than a few teens at the museum, it's been 40 years since I laid eyes on young flesh. Don't misunderstand I would never be unfaithful to her. But sometimes the memory of youthful beauty fades. So I may glance, I promise not to touch or tell."

I doubt Howard would ever use a PPSW.

She says, "You can earn your view by telling me about Phillip. What was he like?"

"A prince of a man. Had been a supervisor but resigned to come here. We moved here in '62. I think Phillip came in '86. When we got my wife's diagnosis—something similar to Parkinson's—he said, 'don't listen to the doctor's estimates.' Phillip's wife had something similar. He was right. Now they tell us '4 years;' same as four years ago.

"Asked my help him on a project. I'm a retired electrical engineer ... aircraft design, and Computer Components Systems. Have you met 'Babe'?"

"The PA? Yes."

"Phillip wanted to enhance Babe, so she could learn and do more. I helped him with some initial designs. Mostly a 'fail-safe' to keep the enhancements separate. A simple switch sends her back to default without uninstalling components.

"His ideas bordered on Artificial Intelligence, which was declared untrustworthy and abandoned decades ago. He wanted her to be able to grow in knowledge and make logical connections between related facts. He thought it essential for her to understand emotions, ethics, and values."

"This is my first experience with a PA. She surprises me. 'Babe' makes requests, did Phillip design her to ask for information."

"Yes, he thought to enable the Assistant's asking or suggesting things would make it more useful. The project was out of my league soon after I helped him design the fail-safe."

"Can you tell me anything about accessing the electronics of the PA? There's no panel."

"Afraid not, but Phillip said he made something to prevent anyone from destroying or tampering with Babe without his consent."

"Made something," maybe "Liquid Lava." If so I only need to find the frequency and location to access what's behind the solid surfaces.

Howard continues, "Phillip had strong political opinions. Angered by the attempts to undermine the economic justice aspects of The Plan. He was also upset because some friends of his were being hampered in doing their job. He mentioned a woman doctor/scientist who was trying to combat some diseases. The government under its current leadership keeps putting up roadblocks at every turn. Ha, ha, and he hated that Senator from Virginia. His name was Blue something: blue-nose? Doesn't sound right."

"Bluefoot?"

"Yeah, that's it … the only person Phillip ever spoke ill about. Sure, will miss that guy. We used to tell jokes to each other. Here's one: what do the Dodo Bird, T-Rex, and a male chauvinist have in common?"

"Not sure; they are all out of touch with their environment?"

"Close—they're extinct and don't know it."

Marie laughs. *I like him.* Her Portalock signals and Marie says, "Got to take this" as she hoists herself up to a sitting position on the hot-tub edge. Lifting her feet out of the tub and standing as she grabs the towel to dry her hands before answering, "This is Marie."

"Flip button." The PAs voice. She drops the towel on the bench and reaches into her sweats pocket removing the transmitter Rudy gave her. Flipping it open she presses the button. The timer stops at 12. Rudy created a 30-second delay before anything can be sent to the receiver. Pressing the button cancels the request entirely. Marie sits on the towel, connects her Portalock to communicator. A few strokes give a street view.

A blue car is almost stopped at the house next door to Marie's. Marie pushes three keys at once sending a "speed call" to her network. After two seconds Marie says, "Blue car outside 38 Jasmine. 'Transfer Cancel' activated." As she speaks, a man gets out of the passenger's side of the car and starts toward Marie's front door. Wessel's voice identifies the man, "That's Duke!" Rudy's says, "Double-lock and get out."

"Done. I'm in the fitness center."

"This is Security 23, ETA one minute."

Duke walks to the door with a keycard in his hand. The camera is switched to entryway.

He uses the card … nothing … and again. This time the card reader makes a disapproving "blaring sound" for 5 seconds. Duke kicks the wall.

Marie activates the outside speaker. "Not nice! If you have legitimate business, try the doorbell. Now put the keycard on the ground and walk back to the Security Officers who will take you and your friend in for questioning."

Running for the car, he reaches through the open window for an object. Security pod rounds the corner and officers are out of their vehicle. Marie shouts, "Weapon; it's *the* weapon."

Duke fires a shot—hitting the younger officer in the chest. No injury, no damage. Another blast is sent straight at his head. The shield snaps up and holds for a full 7 seconds. Appearing dismayed by the lack of carnage Duke straightens up enough for both officers to hit him with stunning shots. He is down. The car speeds away turning left at the corner on 3rd Street. Marie follows the car with cameras.

The vehicle is a rental. All rentals have a "stop control" built in so the rental service can deactivate an overdue car. A Security Coordinator can stop one as well. Stop control only works at specific intersections; Marie finds those in the area. The driver switches to Second Street at Lemon heading west.

Marie says, "Vehicle will be stopped at 2nd and Orchard."

Rudy says, "I'm a block away, should I take him?"

"Negative, we're two blocks," says Security 271.

"Vehicle disabled; suspect is running north on Orchard."

"I see him, and now he is headed for houses," Rudy says.

"Sectors Keeper is alerted," replies Marie.

"Doors are secure," says DK128.

Security pulls up, and two officers jump out. The driver, now on foot whirls around with something in his hand; no one is taking any chances. Two stunner blasts hit him simultaneously.

It's over. Marie asks, "Do I need to release the vehicle to free the intersection?" Security 23 says, "No, we'll tow it." There are now five Security Officers outside Marie's. The perpetrator, Duke, is placed in a detention pod. Detective 23 and his partner, head toward Orchard Street.

Noticing a chill, she realizes, *Oops, I've been sitting in plain view of Howard all this time. How gracious, Howard changed his position to give me privacy.*

"You are a *gentleman*," Marie says while putting on a robe.

"Oh, I got an "eye full." You are *gorgeous!*"

"Thanks for the compliment, but you need practice observing younger flesh."

"I'm here every day; please promise to come back."

"I'm off schedule this week, but I usually work out every other day, I think this is going to be the best time for me."

Back at her console, Marie checks on the arrests, Auto-Door admissions and sends messages to her contacts out of the area saying she was "never in danger."

It's 12:58. Wonder how Mother is getting along at the hospital. Allison Fulbright steps from a pod and starts toward the turquoise door but is intercepted by two officers. Using the outside speaker, Marie says, "Thank you, officers. I'm expecting her."

All the day's troubles melt when Allison Fulbright steps through the door.

At this moment, I'm happy. Howard's comments, saving some lives, moving the package on Monday, being taken off probation, and Dr. Norris's affirmation all contribute. And now Allison's here. All this sense of beauty and competence shows in Marie's smile as she greets her 'guest.'

Allison takes a mental picture of her daughter's radiance. "This is what I pray I'll see after I tell her what she must understand about herself." Stepping out of the entryway Allison unsnapping her SOG; daughter does the same as soon as the door is closed and double locked. A ritual observed by the two of them ever since Marie's father's death. Their arms reach around each other inside the open garments allowing skin touch. The practice initially allowed Allison to assess Marie's stress or anxiety. More recently, Marie checks for signs of aging in her mother. But most of all it allows each to be closer than anyone else. The ritual often opens a degree of conversation not enjoyed by many mothers and teenage daughters.

Allison speaks first as they embrace, "I'm so proud of you."

"Frightened?" Marie adds, knowing Allison would never say so first.

"Yes, I'm afraid. There are reasons. Thank God you are safe."

"You taught me well."

"Really? Recently I'm thinking; I didn't teach you the most important thing."

"What's that?"

"Later, not until after the inquests. Are they scheduled?"

"Today; one at 4:00 PM the other at 5:00. They are inquiries, not inquests."

"Of course, I'm too used to dealing with medical terminology."

Separating and reclosing their garments Marie issues the formal welcome to her home, and proudly shows her mother around, the small but efficient home. Allison examines the console, having never seen one. She suggests it resembles an airplane cockpit. Among other things, Allison is a pilot. Away from the console, and A. Fulbright meets "Friend," the Personal Assistant. They talk for several minutes.

Allison says, "Marie, she is marvelous. Where do I get one?"

"None exist like her. Phillip increased her capacity and taught her things. Friend, Private Conversation."

They reach the kitchen Marie shows off all the appliances, and unique storage system designed, built and patented by Phillip. Next, the counter material called "Liquid Lava." While there, they fix a tuna steak salad, of greens topped with raspberries, juice, and toast with Marie's new favorite bread.

At lunch, they talk about Phillip: how Marie and Wessel found him, and what they went through to get help for him. Allison says, "I'm 80% sure they will revive his body. The real question is how much brain damage? Not sure he'll remember anything."

At 1:20 Rudy, Harris and a vehicle robot arrive at Marie's and carry in boxes of electronic components. Rudy reports, "Two more shady characters are in custody; Security obtained the second weapon and the universal keycard. The lab is going over the rental car with a 'fine-toothed comb.'

"Now for the bad news: the keycard is not the one we expected. Somehow they've duplicated them. But having the actual card will help us be sure our 'lockout' will hold up.

"Also they found the computer he used to collect downloads. He had already picked up from two sites—neither listed by Cloud. So they have a second installer of spy equipment.

"The driver insists he's immune because he is carrying out the orders of the 'Select Tribunal' court. Either these guys think they can fool everyone or someone hoodwinked them.

"Anybody heard of the 'Center for the Study of Democracy in Unified Action?' The computer's history tells us collected data was forwarded to them. One of those 'non-think tanks' politicians use as fronts when they want to collect favorable information or to disseminate their latest fantasy version of reality. Their records are secret since they are not governmental. I have a pal in the CIA, recently retired, but said he'd send me the names."

Noticing a lull in the conversation Marie welcomes Harris and Rudy to her home. Drinks and food are offered and declined.

Marie asks, "Allison, how do you like the sofa?"

"Well...."

"Be honest."

"Hideous."

"It's being replaced this afternoon."

"Oh, thank goodness."

"They seem so out of place with the rest of Phillip's taste." Both men stop; glance at the furnishings, floors, walls, and ceiling; shrug and go back to assembling electronic components.

Marie continues, "I noticed Rudy did not check for electronics in the couches, so I thought I should before they're gone. I hit the jackpot; two memory chips, three old-style 'floppy disks' and three *unique* tools. The devices may relate to getting inside the PA cabinet." The finds are displayed. No one has seen anything like the "tools."

When glancing at the memory chips, Harris notes something Marie missed. "These are too big for today's computers. They fit previous generation devices, at least ten years old. The floppy disks likely work in coordination with other memory systems."

Marie tells them about meeting Howard at the fitness center. Plus her thought, "Perhaps the thing made to protect the PA is liquid lava, like the counter top."

"Should be easy enough to determine," Rudy says, "I did a density test to find bugs hidden behind the walls or under kitchen counters. Liquid lava is ultra-dense. Equivalent to a 26-inch solid concrete wall including metal rods." Rudy takes the monitor to the area in the bedroom and closet finding the same readings. He checks floor to ceiling, in every direction. Rudy also checks the floor, other walls, the glass doors leading to the hallway and courtyard.

Rudy says, "Marie, this room can withstand anything short of a direct nuclear strike." He mutters, "and I'm not sure about that. Here may be the safest spot on the planet. The glass is not glass—but a form of liquid lava."

"Should we stop what we are doing?" asks Harris.

"No, but it changes our objectives."

"Wait a minute," says Rudy as he goes back for a different test instrument. "When I checked for electrical wiring, I found it with this imager, but I did *not* adjust for density to trace them." Rudy "re-tests" with the same results.

"This is being driven by a very sophisticated computer."

Friend is reactivated, and Rudy asks, "Do you recognize when a sensor is checking on electrical supply routing in the apartment?"

"Yes."

"What makes you aware?"

"There is a minor decrease in the power level for a few milliseconds when a sensor is applied."

"If the sensor is on the outside of a Liquid Lave panel, how does it cause a drain on power?"

"The probing sensor causes fluctuation in the external grid of the Liquid Lava panel."

"Do you mean there's a constant electrical charge on the surface of Liquid Lava?"

"Correct; needed to detect when to liquefy for reshaping."

"What about a power failure? Will Liquid Lava stop being solid?"

"A backup system exists capable of serving for 100 days without external power. The system only requires .0041 volts for efficient operation."

"Friend, is this part of what Phillip taught you?"

"This is part of my instruction. He said I should share appropriate information with anyone asking about Liquid Lava, but not volunteer the information. There is more data in the protected subsection about Liquid Lava."

"Is there anything else you can tell us about Liquid Lava?"

"Yes, the invoice for its production and the proprietary control agreements, along with samples of Liquid Lava at various stages of production, are in a safe deposit box."

"Where is this box?"

"Unknown."

"Is it in Wichita?"

"No."

"What else can you tell us about Liquid Lava?"

"Nothing, until you give the password for the protected files."

"Anything *unrelated* to Liquid Lava?" asks Marie. One of her "flash visions" indicates her PA *can* share helpful information.

"Phillip created an electronic file regarding the 'Center for the Study of Democracy in Unified Action.' Part of the document is available, but a larger portion is on Phillip's Laptop."

"Where is that laptop located?"

"Unknown, but it is secure."

"Is it in this apartment?"

"Yes."

"How do you know it wasn't removed?"

"No one removed anything except Phillip's bed for replacement by one suitable for you."

"What about SOGS or other furniture?"

"Phillip's desk was the same style as yours. ID label was changed but nothing was removed from it. All his Outer Garments had been sent for cleaning, except the one he wore the day he was taken."

"Cleaning all his outer garments at the same time?"

"He was planning a trip."

"Do you know when or where the trip was to be?"

"Tuesday of this week. Destination and return date are unknown."

"Friend, how do you know nothing was removed while you were in Private Conversation? When Phillip was taken you went to active mode, but what about before?"

"There is a sensor at each door, so I detect any ID marked item entering or leaving."

"Is this standard for PA's?"

"No. An enhancement."

"Friend, please send the file on 'Center for the Study of Democracy in Unified Action' to my third screen printer."

"Affirmative."

Rudy says, "I'll call Wessel; there could be something in one of those SOG pockets."

It's 1:45 PM. Downtime for Marie starts at 2:00. She needs to leave then so the personal service workers can remove the ugly couch and replace it with the handsome one ordered yesterday. While Marie answers doors, Rudy and Harris work on some protection enhancement, occasionally referring to diagrams; Allison calls the University Medical Center and finds everything progressing as projected. Allison then turns to reading the partial file Phillip had compiled on 'Center for the Study of Democracy....' Between doors, Marie completes her latest report at 1:55.

The lengthy legal documents from Phillip again occupy Marie's attention. The room is like a library everyone engrossed in their work, with only a few whispers and the occasional turn of a page. In the midst Allison blurts out, "I forgot to tell you, Dr. Kim von Throne gave me the name of the 'other candidate:' Thornton Appleberry: he did one year of Door Facilitation School and flunked out. But the fabricated record shows him finishing with honors, without a school named.

Harris says, "Two of my guys are looking into him."

"Thanks," Rudy says both to Allison and Harris. "It feels like things are coming together. They overplayed their hand and failed to cover their tracks."

Marie asks her Personal Assistant to research the "Pacific Glamor Shop." Rudy wonders why. Marie says, "Phillip was suing them." They kept working this way until 2:03 PM.

Forty-One
Carlos C. Cotton

Today has been a disaster for Carlos Cotton, Senator Bluefoot's chief of everything. Being so close to the seat of power— provides a power of its own. Many fear Cotton's wrath, but he still answers to two men who will not like his news. He reflects:

"Most days it's exhilarating to be in the know; especially when I watch the oblivious fools all around me. The masses go on blindly believing their comfortable existence will continue forever; while we work to unravel everything.

"Today is different. Usually, I make things happen. Today things are not happening my way.

"When The General recruited me to manage Bluefoot, the process was laid out. As The General's surrogate BF chips away at the foundations of 'The Plan' in the public arena. But I do the real work—*behind the scenes—undermining the economic system and Programmed States*. As the Senator's 'Research Coordinator' I gain access to people and information. I use my findings to serve the General's agenda—which keeps changing. Originally he wanted to eliminate wealth restrictions; now the complete destruction of 'The Plan' is all he will accept. So we work on multiple fronts attacking the so-called Structured States.

"The General wanted me to have help: my twin brother. I thought it was a bad idea. Pete possesses neither the brains nor balls for this work.

"So now he's missing, perhaps arrested, and the weapon prototype is in 'unfriendly hands.' I give him one simple task. Go pick up information we already 'own.' OK, I should've explained what that thing could do, but he is squeamish about such things. Brother better keep his mouth shut. They'll think he is me—so why hasn't he pulled the *immunity* ploy and gotten free?

"The locals are stonewalling about getting the "vaporizer" back here. At least they'll never figure how it works. 'The shop' assures me no one, except possibly Cloud, can crack its secrets. We own Mr. Cloud.

"Now my 'A-team' isn't reporting. It's 2:00 PM Central, they're an hour overdue. What we need is at the Doorkeeper's house. *I'm sure of it.* So I sent Driver and Duke to retrieve the data. I said, 'Run into trouble, use the card and pull the disk from inside. Run into the new Keeper, take her or kill her.' So now they're not answering. I can't delay any longer. Better tell BF something, before he finds out some other way.

"There is still a chance we might learn something from the old door guy. Fat chance. The idea is lame at best: put him in a coma, wake him up and make him think he is reporting to "God." Wonder where the General found that Doctor?

$16 million in offshore accounts feels like too little for what I do. Of course, there will be more when "The Plan" falls—it's got to be soon.

I better face the music. I'll tell the Senator, "I need to go and fix it." If we can get through Monday's show, then we can come in and take the girl and that place apart. That's the strategy—damage control until Monday's past.

Forty-Two
Mother's Secrets

The requirement to leave one's home during services or deliveries is for personal safety and comfort. The policy applies if one expects to be alone when Central Service personnel arrive. Because others remain in Marie's apartment, she could stay during the couch delivery.

Marie wants to "get away" before the inquiries. She contacts her Doorkeeper indicating, "I'm leaving, but other friends will remain while I'm away." Jeremiah reminds Marie to return by 4:00 PM adding, "I'll send two pictures tomorrow given the strangeness of today."

I understand Jeremiah being subdued for now, but I hope things will be normal tomorrow. Perhaps someone noticed something I missed. Did I miss anything? Oh, stop obsessing.

Marie and Allison walk toward Lemon Park. Sensing her daughter's mood Allison says, "A penny for your thoughts."

"Oh, those inquiries."

"This is the first time someone died under your leadership. I remember my first; I played the 'what if' game thirty different ways. The waiting and self-questioning are hardest. Can I help?"

"I'm as ready as I can be for the inquiries. Glad they're today; I can't imagine having this hanging over me for a day.

Give me something else to occupy my mind. Earlier you said you had things to tell me."

"Are you sure you want to start this now?"

"Very sure."

"Is this all your sector we are walking through?"

"Yes...." They chat about the homes they are seeing and the general flavor of the area.

The park has distinctly marked areas for pets, children, picnics, and conversations. It contains flowers, shrubs, trees, winding paths, and even a fountain with jets operating a few times each hour.

Their "spot" picked, Allison asks to see Marie's Portalock.

Marie demonstrates how to hold and press the symbols functioning as keys.

"Phillip used this one?"

"Yes, it's keyed to the sector's console."

Turning it on edge Allison finds the symbol shaped something like a windmill. "Marie, do you know this one?"

"No, it's new to me."

"If the light comes on, call this number for instructions." Allison recites a 13-digit number from memory.

"Wait a minute that's not a 'phone number'—too many digits."

"Call from any computer or communicator."

"Please give me the number again."

Allison repeats it. Marie commits it to memory and recites it flawlessly.

"What is it for?"

"*Very extreme* emergency, I hope it never goes off. You will be told more soon, but not yet."

"Is that what you needed to tell me?"

Allison takes a deep breath; gazes deeply into Marie's eyes, "No." After two more deep breaths she continues, "Are you sure you want to start this now?"

"Yes."

Another hesitant breath "Let me ask you some questions. We hugged today, and I said, 'I'm so proud of you.' You added, 'and afraid…' A statement of fact—not a question; you were accurate, but *what made you aware* of my fear?"

"You ended our call Monday expressing pride in me. You didn't say, but I heard '… and afraid for you.' I can't say how … I just sense these things, and somehow they always seem to be right."

"I said those *exact words*, out loud *after* we disconnected. Do you experience this with others?"

"Yes, with Rudy … most of my professors … Wessel. I hadn't even met him, but I knew he was gay. I can't explain how—nothing he said tipped me off."

"What about seeing things? Any visions or dreams telling the future?"

"Visions: frequently. Dreams … I don't remember most dreams."

"Tell me about your visions?"

"Used to be one or so a month. More than a year ago, I was eating in the common's room one Sunday evening. A 'flash vision' came. Three young men from my year would be the next ones through the door: I never shared a class or study group with any of them. In the vision—I speak to them; they grunt and sit down at a table—backs toward me. One of them comes to ask me to a school dance the next Saturday. I agree. He's so convinced I'll say no he can't accept my 'yes.' He ends the conversation without even telling me his name. A few minutes later I go to their table and put my hands on his shoulders and ask where and when to meet. He's flustered, eventually, names a place and time. Three days before the dance he calls saying he is ill. The group never again comes to the commons room when I'm likely there. I saw all this in a 'flash.' Everything happened exactly that way."

"Are you sure you didn't modify your memory to match what happened?"

"I put it in my journal the same evening. I reviewed it after each thing happened."

"Have you experienced 'visions' recently—since coming here?"

"Every few hours. Ok first day: I *saw* a man being ill on the floor of his bathroom. It appeared on my screen, for an instant. Impossible: there are no cameras in bathrooms. Later the same day I *heard* an alarm that did not go off from a Personal Pleasure Service Worker. She requested supervision—meaning she questioned her safety with this client—everything seemed routine. About the time her client needed to return to work an alarm sounded. You know PPSW's get microchips installed in heel or elbow to sound an alarm?

"I'm aware of the practice."

"Well, she had no chips since she planned to start graduate school next years. I also '*saw*' her nailed to the back of the bathroom door; there was tape around her wrists and ankles, and the tape was nailed to the door. She was unconscious but breathing. Again *no cameras.*

"The next day I had a '*feeling*' I should check Sector 86 by camera. I checked everywhere else first. I found the problem on my street, at my home. It led Security to one of the three who took Phillip. When we went to pay respects at Central Viewing, I *felt* a living presence from Phillip. I needed something Wessel could notice. A *voice in my head* said 'the eyes.' I said to Wessel 'watch his eyes' we observed him squint as lights came up.

"Today, the weapon *did not* show up on infrared, but I *knew* it was there. I could tell it had been fashioned from a high-grade ceramic or something similar. Not possible—but it happened. Am I going crazy? Are these only lucky hunches? If so why are *they always right?*" Marie's eyes filled with tears.

"You are *not* going crazy. In fact, you may be the *sanest person* I know. What I tell you *will* help. I didn't know how to put this—and still don't. I planned to give you pieces over your Christmas break, spring break, and relocation month. But … you were thrust into this situation triggering your gifts, at the time they are maturing."

"I don't understand. Gifts, what gifts? What's reaching maturity?"

"Marie, please be patient for a few more minutes. Let me start at the beginning. This is not a bad thing. No need to fear."

Marie takes a deep cleansing breath. "Now. I'm ready to listen."

"You're aware I'm not your biological mother."

"Yes. You and Dad were 'choice parents.'"

"Correct. We chose to be parents. But Jamison Ward is—was your biological father."

"Oh, a *real secret.*"

"Yes, a real secret. All I tell you *now must remain a secret.* First, what do you know about the Human Mastery Project?"

"Nothing."

"Good. It's still secret. The military had a 'black operations project' to create a super soldier: increased endurance and strength, superior vision day and night, no emotion, and no questioning of orders. The project was never acknowledged. We believe it started in the 1990's. In the early 2020's some scientists began to work to develop the opposite: a super intelligent, super aware person with enhanced sensory abilities. In 2045 your father and I married. In '46 we moved to Canada to work on the HMP staying for about five years. We kept ties with the founders for years; I still maintain a few contacts.

"This approach sought to identify people with unusual gifts in one of the three areas: intellect, awareness, and sensory ability. We developed objective testing to score individuals in each category."

Allison explains definitions, parameters, and methodology. They found particular "gifts" present yet often dormant in some adults. Success in "turning on the gift" increased when working with young people about 5 to 9 years after the onset of puberty. The development proceeded more often in girls than boys.

"We developed five degrees: Low, Average, Above Average, High and Super High. Your father scored Super High on Intellect, and Above Average on the other two. Once we found people demonstrating particular qualities as measured by our studies, we tried to match them with those enhanced in other measures. The offspring might take a step up the evolutionary ladder. That caused controversy. Powerful groups raised 'moral question' about this work. The project could not risk working in the U.S. or openly in Canada.

"When we joined HMP they had nine women in childbearing years who tested high or Super High on at least two of the three areas. They all agreed to be recipients of donated sperm. Our task involved supporting them through their pregnancies with testing throughout to predict the characteristics the child might possess.

"The Human Mastery Project leadership used one small team to work with each person. Your grandmother's included Jamison, Bulla and me. Researchers plus several of the women and children lived at the center. We interacted with both of them every day.

"There is limited knowledge about your biological grand-mother: Rose Plum Cranton scored High on Intellect, High on Awareness, and Super High on Sensory. Born in '27, some-where in Canada. Your Mother, Rose Cranberry Cranton, was born March 18, 2046 – two years and three days after we joined HMP.

"The half-century mark found many positive things hap-pening in the US. Earldrige and The Plan for the Future took center stage. Resistance was building as well. Some conserva-tive members of the Canadian parliament learned HMP might be in Canada. They had nothing specific. But no one was tak-ing chances. We dispersed to different locations. Some of the nine went as far away as Brazil and Switzerland.

"They moved often. About this time we started reinte-grating the nine into society. We needed to get away from the perception of being a 'lab rat.' Don't misunderstand: no one ever sat around being poked and prodded. All had jobs. Many worked in home-based jobs: computer-based tutoring, cloth-ing design, interior decorators and similar activities.

"Rose was a chef. Running hotel or convention center food services. We lost track of them for a few years. The women agreed to contact us every six months for some data updates, and once a year for a larger study. More frequent contacts any-time a problem arose.

"We got into our Cyclops complex in '53. In '58, when your mother turned 10-years old, your grandmother called asking us to take 'Berry' while she relocated.

"Rose believed people followed her. Rudy's friends inves-tigated and found nothing definite. Some suspicious situations were addressed. In one of them, Rose's communicator was stolen, in a 'shove and grab.' A Not a Dozen operative appre-hended the mugger before he got a block away. So we started the practice of never putting key numbers in phone memories.

"I digress. Berry stayed for over a year. She added light and energy to the center and loved 'helping.' We homeschooled her, rather than risk her safety outside. Berry seemed a well-adjusted, happy child. When Rose came to get her, we noted disturbing changes in Rose. All the regular contacts and evaluations had been kept, and no concerns surfaced. Four months after Rose's last assessment there was noticeable deterioration. We encouraged Rose to stay for a while, but she couldn't. She agreed to contact HMP so they could send someone for her support. By then we were only consultants.

That all happened in 2060. Seven years later Berry called to say Rose was dying. She needed contact information for HMP to do a postmortem (one of the original agreements). Berry was 19 when her mother died. She stayed with us for several months deciding to dedicate her life to the Project. We talked about how she could contribute; lack of funding and political opposition took a toll on the program. Berry wanted a child to pass on the line in honor of her mother.

"She worked with our former colleagues still in Canada; the sperm bank and donor profiles were intact. Later we learned Berry gave birth to a boy in '69, and a girl in '72. Her caseworkers believed the children would benefit by having others raise them. Your Berry agreed but soon regretted her decision. She convinced them to permit her a third child ... you."

Marie focused on a spot six inches in front of her shoes during Allison's recitation. Allison who can see only the profile of Marie's face thinks, *Marie will insist on learning the whole story. She will want my conclusions only* after *hearing details. She's taking it all in and will interrupt if necessary.* Marie interrupts for the first time.

"Where is my moth...? Where is Berry now?"

"I'm getting to that. What do you think happened?"

"She's no longer alive, and *I'm to blame.*"

"*It is not* your fault; she wanted you *more than anything in the world.* You will understand … when you hear the rest. Should I go on?"

With tears in her eyes, and shaking in her voice, "Yes. I know the worst."

"Berry's pregnancies were artificially inseminated. After confirming her third pregnancy, Berry called on Christmas Eve 2074. She asked to visit, of course, I said, 'yes.' Arriving the day after Christmas, Berry requested staying for a while; she needed a break and would do anything for the Institute. Nearly as excited and inquisitive as her 10-year-old self—Berry again added life to Cyclops.

"After two weeks, I asked her, 'why are you *really* here?' She told me how her heart ached for two children she would never see. She begged me, 'don't tell HMP I'm here. If they find out—don't let them take me back. I lied to them. I got them to give me one more baby. They said this one would *be the highest* of all rating wise. I told me I wanted to travel before they confined me; gave a fake itinerary without Cyclops. If you tell them, they'll make me give the baby up. I can't do that again.'"

"I said, 'something will work out.' She tested poorly to be a parent, unmated, with no prospects. *Then she changed my life forever.* Rose Cranberry Cranton, your biological mother said. 'I want you to help me raise my baby, and if something happens to me, I want you to keep her. Between your influence and my genes, we can create the Mature Human. You tested high as a mother, and Jamison will be an outstanding father.'

"I agreed and promised you would always have a home with us. Berry began working as an assistant researcher. Her perceptions were like you have been experiencing. She helped us avoid several pitfalls in research by suggesting one direction would not be productive. We would pursue the path far enough to confirm Berry's assessment. But the one's she identified as positive would lead us to new understandings. Everything seemed fine till one morning in mid-June. I observed sadness I'd never seen in her. Asking her what happened, she told me of a dream. Rose Plum spoke to Berry telling her they would soon be together. She protested, 'I have a baby to raise.' Rose said, 'you'll have a week with her. Cherish every moment.'

"We examined her, did blood work, checked your health and tried to talk her out of the dream's message. We even used the 'Ghost of Christmas to Come' these things don't have to be. She said she would enjoy every minute of life left with you inside her and in her arms. She did. Berry never uttered another word about it, and she fully lived every day. She spoke of all the things she appreciated about each of us, her time with us. She shared memories of her mother.

"You were an easy birth. Less than six hours labor. She reluctantly let us clean you up and examine you before taking you back. You slept in her arms or by her side all week. Berry was up and around, almost like she'd never been pregnant. We examined her and found her healthy. She recovered quickly, and when not holding or feeding you, she let us know her hopes for you.

"On your eighth day of life, Berry died. She nursed you and laid you down, but you would not go to sleep. The time came for your next feeding. Berry told *me* to nurse you. I said, 'I have no milk.' She said, 'yes, you do.' I did … you nursed to your fill.

"Berry took you back one more time. She got weaker by the minute, and we didn't understand why. We monitored her vitals constantly—everything slowed down, but we found no physical reason. Berry didn't take her eyes off of you and said, 'I'll miss you, Marie. I'm glad we met. Allison is your mom now. So now you need to save the world, I couldn't do it.' A tear fell on your hand, and you reached up and touched her lips. She handed you to me. I tried to hold you so you could see Berry, but you turned your face toward me and went to sleep. While putting you down in the next room, she slipped away.

"Bulla and Jamison were by her bed. Berry watched us leave the room. She glanced at everyone and smiled. She said, 'my liver held the poison until now; I couldn't keep it in any longer. Poison reached my milk. But this is good. Thank you all. I had a wonderful life. Let Marie's life be exciting.' She took a deep breath and was gone. All the monitors went flat."

Both women have tear stained faces. Marie speaks, "It must be hard for you to tell me this."

"Yes, it is. I'm sorry I waited so long."

"I wish I'd known, but I'm glad I didn't. Makes no sense, but it's how I *feel*." Marie turns; lifts her eyes to Allison's. "There is more isn't there?"

"Yes, one more thing. Your mother gave Jamison two envelopes earlier that day; she made him promise to keep them 'until I'm gone.' One addressed to us: me, Jamison and Bulla to be opened on your first birthday. The second addressed to you, for your 20th. But I think you may need it now."

"Where is the letter?"

Allison slips a fat envelope out of a pocket in her Outer Garment.

"Have you read it?"

"No, it's yours."

Marie takes the envelope into her hands like one would hold a satin pillow with mating rings. An ivory colored business size envelope has beautiful script handwriting: *"Marie"* below in neat hand printing *"For Your 20th Birthday."* Marie holds it for a moment; smells it; rubs the outside against each cheek.

Putting the envelope in her lap Marie says, "Not now. In 20 minutes, I need to be back at my console. I want the time to absorb and give this my full attention. Please keep it until later?"

"Of course … can you forgive me for not telling you earlier?"

"*You* are my mother. I'm *connected* somehow to the writer of this letter. I want to understand the connection, but you are my parent." Marie stares at Allison's face, "You have given me an Immense *gift* today: you told me reasons exist for the things I've experienced. I'm *not* delusional nor possessed by an outside force I can't control. That's a real *gift*.

"Am I angry? Of course. *You had no right* to keep this from me*!* My life has been upside down, and there's a reason that's been kept from me. *How dare you?* So say my emotions.

"But my mind says: imagine how dysfunctional I would be now—my priorities would be different. Obsessing about developing the gift, I would likely have forced it before I could manage the outcomes. I would wonder why my 'visions' happen with some people and not others. It would have distracted me from learning.

"So don't ask me to forgive you. You carried this burden for me all this time. If you told me too soon, and I messed up—you would've blamed yourself. You gave me the gift of my education without this distraction. *Now* I'm a Doorkeeper, too busy to let this new awareness consume my life—work comes first.

"The gift helped me do things—even before I realized it existed. Now, I think, I can partner with the gift, relying on it when helpful but using my training foremost.

"I still need to absorb all this. Please take the letter; I don't want to touch it again until I'm ready to read it."

Allison picks up the envelope as gently as Marie handled it. Glancing at the cover while placing it in an inside SOG pocket. "Your handwriting is a lot like Berry's.

"I thought the same thing. What did she look like?"

"Like you. I have a picture of her at 19 to give you when you ask."

They stand and embrace for a long moment; both have tears running down their faces. They turn and walk to 36 Jasmine arm in arm. Not another word.

Forty-Three
Inquiries

Seeing the delivery vehicle in front of her house, Marie quickens her pace. "My new couch is here!" Allison is beside her as they pass the old, stained, shabby and faded sofa being loaded into the van.

Marie's excitement rivals a child's racing to the Christmas tree. There is an elegant dark-red sleeper-sofa, exactly as Marie specified the day before. Allison speaks first, "It's gorgeous; it fits with the all the wood: console, table, and window frames. This ties everything together." Marie points out it makes into a queen-sized bed. She touches a button at the back of the arm-rest, and it swings up and opens. Even Rudy and Harris stop to admire the technical smoothness.

A second touch and it returns to its couch shape. Both women are pleased; the guys are back to work—testing components.

The Inquiry Team needs to review transcripts, audio/video of the event, as well as written reports from Marie and Supervisor Kim Sam Rea. Meanwhile, Marie examines the Keeper-to-Keeper results about unauthorized entrance attempts.

Total responses: 114. After eliminating the easily explained attempts (ex-mates, or a parent seeking their child at other than negotiated times), nine entries remain.

One questionable Auto-Door entry, while the residents were on vacation. Plus three sectors noted a total of 8 entries detected by Doorkeepers or Security after the fact. Checking occupations of targeted home residents: seven had one person in the Financial Sector the other two—Security Officers.

Seven entries used "stolen keycards." Two entries denied because a family member was home. Six of the entries took less than ten minutes. In one case the residence was occupied for more than an hour. Adding the Sector 86 numbers makes 11 attempts in two weeks. Marie confirms the report has been sent to Supervisors, Security 23, and Mr. James Calhoun. Rudy, Harris, and Allison are handed paper copies.

The signal comes indicating they are ready for Marie. Dr. Norris, Head Supervisor, identifies who is on the line; the purpose of the inquiry; all that has been read and viewed. Supervisor Kim Sam Rea completed his interview before contacting Marie. Dr. Norris asks, "Marie would you like to make a statement or add anything to your formal report?"

I didn't expect this question. I'm aware of my right to make a statement but didn't expect it to be the first order of business. She says, "Yes … I want to express my sorrow at the loss of life. I hope to learn what I can do to prevent similar situations in the future. I may desire to add something later, but at the moment I believe the written report is my best recollection."

Dr. Kim von Throne asks, "What caused you to search for an intruder?"

"Mr. Burns' wife had reported seeing someone staring in their window from the courtyard before her seizure started. Even though he saw no one, I felt compelled to investigate."

Jeremiah chimes in, "You insistently told the Officers the person in the closet had a weapon. What made you think he had a weapon?"

"He was an intruder, sitting on the closet floor; there was something in his hands extending maybe three to four inches beyond his body. I was unable to identify the object, but an object for defense seemed the best explanation."

"Your classifying him as 'armed and dangerous' surprised us." Added Dr. Norris, "you read his intentions."

I better be careful. I don't want to leave the impression I used anything but my training. "Well, I knew of the existence of stolen, or improper keycards. One had been used to enter the home I now occupy enabling the kidnapping of my predecessor. An unauthorized attempted entry occurred yesterday in Sector 86 using such a card. An entry also occurred yesterday at 36 Jasmine. I found someone inside Mr. Ford's home with his door ajar. I believed the invader entered the courtyard using that keycard. The intruder appeared to be waiting for Mr. Ford's return with a weapon. I drew conclusions from the facts."

Dr. Norris follows up, "We all viewed the video of the incident, and none of us can identify an armament from the infrared images. So again, how were you so sure about the weapon?"

So that's it. I saw more than possible, so they wonder how. "Well, I saw it only for an instant as the infrared imager found him. Only a glimpse of some object, not part of his clothing, or anything in the closet. I *inferred* it to be a weapon. A Doorkeeper principle is: 'Always err on the side of more preparedness rather than less.' Had there been no weapon, laughter at my over-reaction would have followed. I wish that had been the case."

"Thank you, Marie. Any further questions?"

Both Dr. Throne and Jeremiah say "No." Dr. Norris declares the inquiry completed signaling the recorder, a device not a person, to stop recording.

"The preliminary report will be filed this evening, and the final in two weeks or less. Marie, I suspect this has been an ordeal for you. I understand you made a counseling appointment."

"Yes, sir. I believe it'll be fruitful."

"Well," says Dr. Norris, "It may be comforting to know we have nothing but admiration for your compassionate, professional conduct since arriving in Wichita. This incident is no different."

"Thank you, that is reassuring." *I hope the Security forces make a similar statement.*

Dr. Throne says, "Due to the formality I could not say earlier, it's refreshing to hear your voice again. You are an excellent choice, but I now realize you were *sent* to us for a time like this."

Jeremiah adds, "I hope my clowning around did not cause you to think I disrespect you or your abilities."

"I missed your 'clowning around' as you call it today."

"Don't worry it'll be back tomorrow."

I may never have a better chance to find out about my selection. "Dr. Kim von Throne, may I ask a question?"

"As long as it's not about this case."

"Something else. I wonder why you called me for this position? No other TA's were interviewed, and as far as I can find, no one has ever been taken out of TA role to accept an assignment. Why me? I'm not seeking compliments. I acknowledge my abilities, but there are many good Doorkeepers."

"Do you believe in the mysteries of the Spirit; the working of God?"

"Still trying to understand them—but yes, I believe."

"That's why you were called. We completed a series of meetings. We learned of several missing Doorkeepers as the meetings ended. I identified people who could be moved to fill rolls, and temporary Doorkeeper to fill others until the October rotation of the second year TA's moved into service. We came up one person short. No one felt right for Wichita 86.

"Dr. Stanley was helping me with logistics. I said, 'I still need one more; someone extremely qualified. Is there a TA who can take the role tomorrow?' He said, 'One. I would hate to lose her; she is the best TA I ever supervised.' Of course, he'll deny saying such a thing.

"We checked with all your instructors, available on Sunday afternoon, before calling you. During that time, I got an application from someone who appeared perfect … too perfect. Well, the rest is history, we interviewed you, found you to be the real deal, and he wasn't."

"Thank you, I was wondering. I love my work, but sometimes it seems like a dream."

"Or a nightmare?" suggests Jeremiah.

"Well, this one guy who calls himself 'Super Door.'"

"Watch it, remember the report's incomplete."

With a laugh, everyone signs off. The clock says 4:50. *Only 10 minutes until the next inquiry starts. I'll be up first and then leave the discussion to others. The Door inquiry did not interview Dr. Rea and me together. I thought they would. Someone changed his or her mind, for some reason.*

Marie steps away from the console for a drink of water. Allison says, "You appear ok."

"I think so. I found out why I got this job rather than someone more experienced. Rudy, Harris, and Allison stop to learn what Dr. Throne said. After a few comments, it's time for the next inquiry.

At exactly 5:00 PM the call comes. Marie answers and the first voice is the Inquiry leader.

"I'm Security 1, responsible for the conduct of all the Officers throughout the state, plus some counties in Nebraska,

Missouri, and Oklahoma. We are here to convene an inquiry into events leading up to the death in the line of duty of a Security Officer. This is the first such occurrence under my command, and *we will* get to the bottom of this." He goes on to identify the other people present and indicate the case number. Marie is surprised when he adds, "listening, but not participating, is Doorkeeper Supervisor, Dr. Norris, chair of the Doorkeeper Inquiry. Both Inquiry panels will work independently, but will coordinate to produce compatible results."

The Grand Chief identifies the reports, records, recordings, and service records of the officers involved that have been reviewed by each team member. "There is only one question for you Marie. What made you think you had the authority to tell Security Personnel how to do their jobs and as you said, 'outranked them?'"

The belligerent tone is not setting well with Security 53. James, the DK-SC, is waiting to see how I respond. I'm picking up their emotions over an electronic line. I get only one chance to impress them.

"I became Doorkeeper of Sector 86 at 5:00 AM Monday morning, two days, 13 hours and 6 minutes ago. I studied for more than four years to become a competent Doorkeeper. Upon my arrival, I learned I was also Sector Security Coordinator. I had no instruction for that role, so in my spare time between door openings, I read the Manual and Guidelines for this position. The manual states 'in the absence of a ranking Officer where human life is in danger, the person with the most complete information assumes command.' Human life was in jeopardy, and I had more information than the Officers. There was no ranking officer at the Security Center, or monitoring the situation since a superior officer would have taken charge."

"Why didn't you give way to your supervisor, when he joined the communication? If I had an officer on probation who kept the reins after Supervisor stepped in; they would be washed out or back in school." *The anger tone in Security 1s voice makes it clear he thinks I'm insubordinate.*

"I contacted my Supervisor for assistance in managing the situation. Since you listened to the transcript, you know Supervisor took charge of getting Medical and other Security Personnel into the event, while I sought to distract the intruder. I understand your concern about one under probation taking such actions, but I'm no longer on probation."

"What! You're on the job three days and off probation? Unusually lax supervision don't you think?"

Security 53 jumps in. "I'll answer that Chief. Marie proved herself long before she came to us. She functions like a Doorkeeper Security Coordinator with ten years experience. She was released from probation in the first eight hours of her work, because she knows it all, and she does it all. She saved eight lives this week, including two of my best Security Officers. Marie is responsible for the arrest of now three law-breakers. Also, she uncovered a scam which may lead to more arrests, relating to a kidnapping."

Now James, Doorkeeper from St. Louis adds, "I've been a Doorkeeper for 11 years and DK-SC for the last seven years. Six emergencies with three lives saved are all I can claim, and I'm typical of Keepers. I wish I could count eight lives saved in 11 years. Marie has read the Manual more recently than I, but for the record, a Doorkeeper's first responsibility is to the safety of her residents, second to any visitor, and third to other services working the sector."

Security 1 responds. "Well, I came on strong because I wanted to convey the criticism I'm getting from my superiors in Washington. I was unaware the Doorkeeper had completed probation. That changes the complexion of the Supervisor's participation."

Three things I learned from Security 1's statement. 1. The people in Washington must be connected to Senator Bluefoot. 2. This Chief is not to be trusted. 3. His anger is because he thinks I was responding to the officers' putdowns.

Fifty-three says, "This may not be the proper time, but I want to add for the record, I talked with Security 107 the injured officer. He was awakened for a few moments while they switched something about his treatment. I asked what he remembered. He repeatedly said, 'We should have listened.' I asked to whom? He said, 'the girl, she knew. We made fun of her; we should have listened.'"

Marie adds before anyone else could speak, "I'm pleased he is improving."

James says, "One other question Marie, did you think about not opening the door to these officers?"

He's giving me an opening to make a point about the Security Coordinator's work. "I take my role very seriously. I believe in following procedures and policies. I did not overstep my authority as SC when I ordered them to take out their stunners, but refusing to open the door would exceed my authority. They're trained Security Officers, and this situation needed them. I believed they would act based on their training once they faced the situation. Their actions were not quick enough."

Security 53 adds. "They treated you with disrespect. Did that enter into your decision?"

"Yes, it did. My decision to call Supervisor was based on their attitude. I feared for their safety and that of my residents. It's standard procedure for a Doorkeeper to request Supervisor's assistance when needed."

James says, "The question on everyone's mind: was your decision to order them to draw their stunners an attempt to 'get even' for their treatment of you?"

"NO!! 'A Doorkeeper does not need to be liked to be effective.' 'When choosing between being liked and being respected always choose respect.' 'The action of a Doorkeeper is about *Service, not Status.'* Last week I was teaching those basic principles to new Door Facilitation Students. I *believe* them, and attempt to *live* them."

Number 1 wants to move on. He invites Kim Sam Rea to join for the joint interview; repeats the details of who is on the call, what has been read, viewed, heard, etc. "Doorkeeper already responded to our questions. Now it is time to clarify any differences in the two accounts. What differences were noted from the written accounts?"

No inconsistencies were noted. James and 53 agree it's impossible to listen to everything the other is doing when engaged fully in a related task.

Supervisor Rea states. "I joined the situation at the Keeper's request. I quickly realized the officers failed to grasp the seriousness of the situation. They did not honor the information being shared. When one referred to 'moseying' over to the sector, I jumped on them for their lax attitude. *In hindsight, I should have called for backup immediately.* I thought they were a couple of guys having fun with the 'the new kid in town.' I believed they would address the task professionally if only to impress the 'pretty girl,' as they referred to Marie on their way to the scene.

"Any fault for lack of action should fall to me—not Marie. She was in charge, but I could have aided her more effectively. None of us knew the weapon's destructive potential. The officers' attitudes foreshadowed a problem."

A few more questions are asked and answered. They give Marie a chance to say more. She thanks, Kim Sam Rea for his comments, and indicates her high respect for the Security Officers who are "facing what I only view." Finally, she says,

"The scene of Security 88 being blasted backward will stay with me the rest of my life."

Marie is asked to sign off, and they will continue, preliminary findings will be posted by 8:00 PM, etc. *They will ask Kim Sam Rea about letting me off Probation so soon. I also know how he will answer.*

This afternoon I have depended much more on the gift or talent than ever before. I wonder how others coped with learning of their gifts? Perhaps Berry's letter will tell me some of what she experienced. That will have to wait. I need to check on Auto-Door, but first I need a break.

Marie steps out from behind the console. *My friends and Allison will want to learn how it went. The dead zone prevents them from overhearing.*

Only Allison remains. Without Marie's notice, Rudy and Harris had departed for other business. The dining table is clear of electronic devices except for two identical components. Marie asks, "Where are the guys?"

"They left to fix a few other problems. Said they'll be back for supper 7ish."

"I better start."

"No, I'm cooking, salad is ready. How are *you*?"

"I don't think they are going to can me." *Why did I say that? I must have been more worried about the Inquiries than I admitted.*

Marie recounts every question, response, who came to her support, and who remained critical. They speculate on who in Washington might be putting pressure on the Grand Chief about Marie. They come to the same conclusion—Senator Bluefoot.

Marie checks and corrects Auto-Door entries while Allison fixes the evening meal. Rudy and Harris return at 7:00.

The Medical Center calls to request Allison's return about 9:30 for a critical juncture in the treatment. Allison agrees. Rudy and Marie exchange a quick glance, knowing that might be a problem. Problem averted: Marie receives a call from Dr. Norris, "May I come to share some observations about the Inquiries?"

"Have you eaten?"

"No."

"We are sitting down now, why not join us?"

"Thank you, I would gladly join you, but don't wait for me." Dinner consists of baked salmon, green salad, corn on the cob, green beans, drinks of choice, and a fresh fruit dessert.

Rudy tells Marie about the security enhancements in her apartment and how to use them. He is nearly finished when Dr. Norris arrives.

Supervisor is welcomed and reintroduced to Rudy. Harris is also introduced as "A colleague and former partner of Rudy's." The two men acknowledge each other and shake hands.

"And I think you are acquainted with my other house guest...."

Dr. Norris has not taken his eyes from Allison since he entered, except to be polite to the others during introductions. Allison makes the connection. An instant smile lights her face and eyes making one think 15 years have melted away. People usually guess Allison's age at 55; not her actual 72 but at the moment she appears barely 40. "Why, Abe Norris, when did you get *old*?"

"Allison Ward, the belle of the ball, how did *you* stay so *young*."

"I haven't been to a ball since Oxford."

"I can't understand how you could give up all this and dancing."

"Nor can I. You were a catch. I always went for the brainy type … and now look at you. Supervisor of…. Supervisor of the most significant person in the world—to me."

"*She's* amazing, *isn't* she?"

"I think so."

No business talk during the meal. The others marvel at the easy way the couple catches up. It's like Abraham Norris has been in the next room for 50 years or so, and just stepped back in. Allison's life is somewhat public. In contrast, Norris stays out of the limelight. Yes, he is often the voice of Doorkeepers and their work, but usually, he addresses specific situations and threats, not publicized in mass communication.

As the meal is winding down, Rudy and Harris prepare to leave for other work. So Norris says, "Before anyone leaves, this is of interest to all. Our friend Fenton J set up a sting operation to catch whoever put Phillip in the coma in the Hole of Completion Center. He replaced our friend with a student. Well, Cremations Service came to get the body. They transported him to the Cremation Center outside the sheltered city. One of the people working at the center was being blackmailed into cooperating by turning him over to the van we located yesterday. Three men were in the van. All now in custody and the van is being searched meticulously.

"The other thing I want to say is Marie handles herself most professionally, even when challenged by the Grand Chief." Handing Marie a copy of the report he continues, "We all need to be aware, especially Marie—Security 1 is an enemy. He is obviously in sympathy with those who would diminish our role. However, the local Chief is a champion of DKs in general and Marie in particular."

Harris says, "I'll see what I can learn about his connections to 'Jerkhead.' We'll know how often he sneezes by this time tomorrow." He uses his communicator to contact colleagues who will start pulling data. No one in the room doubts that if a connection exists; it will be found.

Marie glances over the six-page report for Doorkeeper Inquiry. It contains lots of references to specific actions taken by Marie and Kim Sam Rea.

Dr. Norris reads the last section for all to hear. "'*Conclusions*: Marie did everything according to procedures, did not exceed authority, and exercised extra caution with Personnel on temporary assignment. Supervisor and Doorkeeper had 'reasonable expectations' of Security Officers acting professionally. *Recommendations:* Security Personnel in-service training on the role and authority of the Doorkeeper in emergency situations.' Overall the report is a clear affirmation of Marie and Dr. Rea."

Everyone is leaving. Marie asks, "Allison may I have the letter? I'm ready to read it now."

Handing her the letter Allison asks, "Should I stay?"

"Go help Phillip. I'll call you if needed."

Forty-Four
The Letter

"*June 18, 2075*

"*My Dearest Marie,*

"*You are expected to arrive in early August. I will only be with you a few days after your birth. So much to say. By the time you read this, you will be ready to start your first job. I know little about Doorkeepers, your first job, but you will be a fine one. I'll say more about this knowledge later.*

"*Shortly you will be 20 unless Allison gives this to you earlier because you need it. She will do what's right.*

"*Where can I start? Allison told you about HMP and me. Please don't be hard on her for keeping this from you. She is following my request to keep this until you are moving into the workforce. You will come to understand 'not knowing' as a gift. 'Knowing' would have distracted from your regular studies. You will need everything you can learn.*

"*Allison Ward, your actual mother, may be the smartest person alive. She knows as much as anyone about your special abilities; what causes them to function; how to duplicate them;*

how to measure them, etc. She understands a lot about what she calls your gifts. I call them 'talents.' Allison is like the music theorist's knowledge of the concerto, but you are the violinist who must play the music before ever increasing crowds. She does not possess the talent, <u>you do</u>.

"I was fortunate when my abilities began to show up; I had a mother with similar experiences. I also had a community to help me understand, and guide me as I discovered, developed and learned to use—but not abuse my talent. You lack such a mother and community. But this letter is yours. I'll try to tell you what I've learned, and where I made mistakes.

"One request, Dearest Marie, let the talent develop naturally. It's already growing and developing. At times expressing itself in unexpected ways. So here's knowledge. You are not making it up. You are not losing your mind. You are not a freak.

"Now you could be tempted to spend time thinking about your talent and what else it might do. Or remembering things you've already been shown. Dear Daughter, I beg you DON'T DO THAT. Your grandmother, my mother, obsessed about her talent. It almost wrecked her life.

"The talent will grow—let it. Your gift will not replace your knowledge. It will come when needed. Don't push your ability to use it and it won't get ahead of you. You are in charge of the talent, not the other way around.

"Like when you learned the electronics of the console. That happened over time and did not prevent you from learning the other things in your curriculum. Now you have a tool to use when needed. Approach your gift–talent the same way. The only difference is –no curriculum or textbook; the talent itself will be

the teacher and classroom. You must decide when to step inside the classroom and when to stay away.

"Well, that was heavier than I planned for a beginning. Now, let's turn to some lighter stuff. I think it's the way you function – get the heavy, hard stuff done first so you can relax. I probably passed that style on to you.

"Where do I start? How about your name? Marie is not a family name: so why Marie? It is the name I insisted on, but Allison never knew why.

"Your grandmother, my mother, was Rose Plum Cranton, born February 8, 2027. She had a gift. Not much is known about her early life, but from what I heard it was grim. Born in Portland, Oregon, delivered by a licensed midwife who issued a valid birth certificate. At five weeks old she was brought to a hospital under the 'safe haven program.' Neither of her parents brought her but a social worker. The social worker's report stated she met with the baby's mother only once, in a neutral location, after a phone call to the social worker at her home. The mother said she was desperate. The father of the baby died in an accident weeks before the birth. She could not let the social worker come to her home because her father did not know, and 'he will kill the baby and me if he finds out.' When I was a disobedient 13-year-old going through mom's things without permission, I saw the report. Along with her foster care records, and birth certificate. I read the social worker's report. It said something like, 'The mother tried to appear 'destitute' by wearing old and torn clothing, and putting some smudges on her face. Her flawlessly cut hair—messed up for effect, 'dirty' designer running shoes, and top-of-the-line nursing bra—all belied her *poverty. I confronted her about her deception. The mother started crying and said I had to help her. I said I needed the truth.'"*

Those are the same words I used Monday with Ann: 'I need the truth.' Was I channeling the social worker from 67 years ago? How did Berry know I would be a Doorkeeper and learn electronics? I hope she tells more about how she saw my future. Maybe this explains something about those dreams ... about the future. Ok, I need to read more.

"'Here's the truth,' the mother said, and the social worker believed her. 'The baby is my uncle's. He was an engineer working with an international architectural firm. He worked on a skyscraper in Japan. Something about testing stresses on beams, he fell to his death.' Her father was a great 'right to life supporter,' denouncing abortions. His pregnant daughter, however, was sent to Europe for an abortion. The abortion doctor was bribed to say she did it. The doctor discovered who the daughter was and blackmailed her.

'The social worker's report included some medical information from the mother plus as much as she could tell about the father's. Your grandmother was taken to the hospital the social worker used: Saint something hospital. In '61 when I read mother's papers without permission the hospital no longer existed. I found out the hospital burned two years after mother arrived. The patient records were all digitalized, but by law, details of safe-haven babies were never computerized. You guessed it; the paper records all destroyed. The social worker's name: Marie.

"Mom's copies also showed a hospital official had tried to contact the midwife, the day after admission. Oh, I forgot, Rose

Plum went to the hospital on March 18, 2027 she was five weeks and three days old. My birth was March 18, 2048. Coincidence? Maybe.

"Where was I? On March 19ᵗʰ they tried to reach the midwife, for more details. She was comatose; diagnosis was a rare nerve disorder. Never recovered. The hospital sent someone to the midwife's home to check her records. All such files are by date. February 8ᵗʰ was missing. Whoever took it didn't bother closing the cabinet drawer. The folders for the day before and after were a bit askew, as you would expect if the one in between had been removed. There's a picture of how they found it.

"I thought whoever stole the file found Mother's name, and therefore mine. I checked and found midwives did not keep a copy of the Birth Certificate Application. The registrar's offices accept only original forms. Usually, the midwife only confirmed the date of birth, signed and affixed her seal, leaving the form with the parents to complete and return to records. Okay, could whoever stole the file get the birth record from that office? I checked. Due to some identity theft laws, those offices must use the last name only with no cross-reference to birth dates. Then I figured out why her mother chose such an unusual name. Cranton would be an unlikely guess. We may be the only ones.

"The social worker turned the birth certificate for the baby over to the hospital with the baby. The hospital obtained the application because they possessed the last name. They checked out the address the mother provided. It was a rented postal box from a package service. Rented for one month, paid for with cash.

"Well, I said Mother's first years were unpleasant. Problems started as soon as Rose reached the hospital. They sent her to

a foster care family specializing in infants. The woman had been nursing babies for years; she cried for 11 hours straight; she would not nurse, take water or sleep. They took her back to the hospital where she was sedated and given I.V. fluids. Any time they let the sedative wear off she started crying again. They found a low-level sedative and kept her on it continuously until she was four.

"A family wanted to adopt my mother at about that age. The adoptive agency had listed her as mentally deficient; no one had heard her speak, laugh or smile. Rose only cried, grunted and threw things. They told the family she was difficult. Somehow this family was drawn to her. They put her in a highchair, and whatever was put in front of Rose she pushed on the floor. The would-be adoptive mother created a game. Rose pushed an empty bowl off, the woman caught it and put it on Rose's head. She reached for the bowl; the woman put it back on the tray; Rose pushed it off again, and the mother caught it and put it on her own head. Rose laughed. The hospital staff was amazed. This child never laughed.

"They began to walk around the hospital wing. The parents talked to Rose and asked about different objects, colors, lights, floor, ceiling and stuff like that. Rose named them all. They came to the nursery for newborns and picked her up to look through the glass, and Rose said, 'The preemies are in there.' At four years none of the hospital staff knew she spoke. Long story shortened they took Rose home and kept her until she was seven. The mother became ill and died suddenly right before the adoption was to be completed. The mother's name was Marie. The father, Mark, decided he could not care for the child alone. She was placed in an orphanage specializing in working with children who lost a parent by death. Mark came to see Rose every month, but she reminded him too much of the loss of his wife.

"The years with Mark and Marie were her happiest. So Mark's visits in the orphanage were her best times there. Each time she thought he would take her home; each time he left without her Rose convinced herself it would be next time.

"At the orphanage, she was considered a troublemaker. She would run away—never planning to stay away, only to be out in the world. She would come back when ready. She had to return. If she wasn't there how would Mark be able to take her home?

"Rose visited strange places. One story mother told was about a poster for a lost dog, picture, and a phone number. She said the 'dog told her' (I guess from the picture) 'I am at the dog pound, and they will kill me at 5:00 pm if no one comes.' She got to the dog pound on the other side of town and went to the cage where the dog was being kept. The dog's name was 'Rosie.' An attendant asked if she would like to adopt the dog. She said 'I can't keep a dog where I live. Her people want her back. They put up flyers all over town.' The attendant told her they weren't allowed to read them. Anyone could put one up. So your grandmother said, 'So you can call,' and she rattled off the phone number.

"The attendant called, catching the woman of the house leaving for a doctor's appointment. She explained she could not get there before 5 pm. The attendant asked if she could send someone else, before 5? No one. While the attendant explained the rules he had to follow, Rose went to the cage, picked the lock, took the dog and left by a different entrance. They got on a bus, borrowed a passenger's cell phone and called the number.

"This time a babysitter answered. Rose told the sitter she had 'found her dog' but needed the address to bring it back to them. She got the address, checked the map in the bus, negotiated the bus system and delivered the dog to its owner.

"She dropped the dog off at 5:20 pm. Supper at the orphanage was served at 5:30. She was scolded for being late and for leaving without permission. She replied, 'I couldn't let the little dog die.'

"The last time Rose left the orphanage she went to the University for a fundraising presentation about some of the early work of the HMP. The name was something like Intellectual Capacity Study. She slipped in the back; listened to the presentation. They outlined the core principles. Their illustrations came from children who 'know things they cannot possibly know.' They were getting to the appeal for money. Rose walked down the aisle to the stage. There were three adults on stage, two women, and a man. One of the women came over to her and asked what she wanted. Mother said, 'I think I'm one of them.' The woman, not believing her asked for an example. She said, 'Well, the man in the fifth row, fourth seat from the aisle is your mate; that's not his real hair,' pointing to the male member of the group. The woman said she had no mate, but the man in the fifth row turned out to be her ex-mate, who came hoping they 'could talk afterward.' The presenter wore a hairpiece due to recent surgery on his head. The two seemed a bit impressed, still not convinced.

"The other woman got down off the stage and came to Rose and asked, 'Is there anything you can say about me?' Mother said, 'Your name is Marie.' The woman asked why she thought so? 'The only people who believe me are named Marie, and it's your name.' The other woman still on stage said, 'Well her name is Judy.' She was told, 'My name is Judith Marie Clayton.'

"Judith Marie took Rose under her wing, found the orphanage, retrieved her things and transferred her custody to the Project—sometime in 2032. Mother was seven. Judith Marie became her advocate and researcher.

"Judith Marie remained with HMP until Allison and Jamison Ward joined. There may have been some overlap, but Allison said she wasn't sure.

"Rose took an immediate liking to Allison, and it seemed to be mutual. Allison became mother's researcher, and for some time they occupied the same location. Allison delivered me March 18, 2048. My name is Rose Cranberry Cranton. They began calling me 'Berry' and the nickname stuck. Mother was always 'Plum.' Nicknames made it harder to trace us.

"Sorry, I'm getting ahead of myself, back to your name. First, three women who helped your grandmother had Marie as part of their name. Second, on one of those rare times when my mother talked about herself, she said I should name the 'best child' Marie. She told me I would have three children: girl, boy, and girl. She said the 'best one' meaning the child closest to the ideals of the HMP would be my last child—you. You are our hope. Sorry, I didn't want to place a heavy load on your shoulders. But you will likely make a greater difference in the world *than anyone else in this century, except perhaps James Earldrige and Allison Ward.*

"I'll say more about your grandmother, you and me later. First I need to tell you some of what the Human Mastery Project learned. I hope you will let Allison read these pages. She may disagree with some of my conclusions, but she will eventually come to understand things this way.

"Allison has probably told you about the genetic side of the work: identifying genes in other species which humans also possess that can be 'turned on' to increase our sensory ability. This work is vital. Success at this level makes possible what I mention next.

"We think of people, animals, plants, bacteria and the like as having a physical body. Physical matter is composed of organized energy. Around each identifiable physical body, is a swirling mass of energy creating another 'body.' Both the material and energy bodies interact with the world and each other. Normally those encounters are routine and fit our experiences. Such as someone comes into a room; you notice them visually; they register as someone you know; you speak; calling them by name; they respond and leave the room by a different door. In this scenario neither are close enough to touch; neither modify their basic course of action; no intellectual information is exchanged, and nothing about the room is changed. However, at least seven major energy patterns shifted during those few seconds.

"1. You stopped your activity because of an 'intrusion' or 'interruption' by the entrance of another 'energy field' into your 'space.' (The disruption is minimal, but it changes your focus).

"2. You used visual and auditory energy to determine the source of the new entrant. (You received data coming toward you from the new field).

"3. You redirected the data to your memory finding: first, the interruption is a person; second, the person is no threat; third, you recognize the person; fourth, you have a name to go with this energy field. (This may seem like 'splitting hairs' but if any of the steps are missing the response will be off target).

"4. Next, you brought up internal energy to greet the person verbally, and your auditory sensors are turned on anticipating a response.

"5. The person responded to your greeting in like manner. (Most of the same internal process occurred within the other person, but we're only looking at it from your perspective).

"6. You analyzed the response as requiring no other action; you settle back toward what you were doing before the interruption. (Your energy distracted by other activities is now returning to its previous focus. About the same amount of energy had been expended and received, so there is no real sense of draining.)

"7. The other person departs, leaving behind an energy trail. (The trail would exist even if you had been in the room).

"I've given more detail than needed, partly to point out how easy it is to become sidetracked in analysis. Each interaction impacts what happens to us. However, my primary concern is the energy trail. In attempting to figure out how some of us 'know things not possible to know' I always come back to energy trails.

"Here is how it works. Suppose you walk around in your home, and you are worried about something. Of course, you don't do that but play along for illustration's sake. Worry is one of the higher energy users. Say as you fret you pace from room to room leaving behind an energy trail concentrated with your concerns on the issue. Now let's say another person <u>with your talent</u> enters the room. Regardless of how welcoming, pleasant, or how well you put the issue out of your mind; when the other person arrives he or she will 'perceive' your worry and the subject. They pick up the trail you leave behind.

"Some people could do this to a greater or lesser degree, from the beginning of time. We called them intuitive, psychic, sages, or prophet. They touched the energy trails and found information. Ordinarily, it starts as a 'feeling' or 'emotion' that then turns more cognitive so it can be verbalized.

"Disruptive emotions are the easiest to tap into. When an energy trail contains: fear, worry, anger, hate or some of the lesser forms of hatred — hostility, envy, and dislike. Others easy to pick up: deception, plotting, conniving, jealousy. People with hidden agendas who are saying one thing but meaning something else stand out like a red flag. Many of these emotions can be read from the energy trails as we move through any space.

"Some positive emotions can be read as well, but they tend to be closer to the present moment: for example when someone doubts you or what you say, then something convinces them you are correct. You sense the sudden change; you also recognize when they are still unaccepting. As I write this, I get the clear impression your recent experiences will confirm what I'm saying.

"Back to the energy trails. I attempted to learn more about what a Doorkeeper does. One thing you handle is any change in the daily routine someone needs to make. Suppose someone tells you to change their routine because of a meeting later in the evening, but instead they plan a clandestine meeting. When your client gives you the alibi —he/she thinks of the real reason. The communication is electronic (even wireless). They are physically isolated from you. However, I bet you 'hear' the real reason, as well as the false one. Some of the emotion from the individual comes through even electronically. You connect with the person energy. Both the intended (words) and the hidden (emotions) come through.

"Once you have connected to an energy trail, you may be able to follow him or her to their present or previous location."

Marie stops reading again. *This is a lot to take in. Berry wrote all this over 19 years ago before I was born. Berry is right. When Candy was in distress, the 'alarm' happened because I tapped her energy trail—especially the fear of the unknown client. So can I follow a trail forward as well as backward from where I touch it? Can I see the future? It makes sense that if I "follow" an energy trail to where it is now it will be present—not the future. Then how does Berry perceive so much detail about my life: my career path, my attitude of getting the hard stuff done first, even that this might be given to me before my 20th birthday? I wonder how much of this theory Allison will dispute?*

I need a cup of tea. There have been many people this apartment during the last 24 hours. So many energy trails. Can I tap into one at will? Rudy spent a lot of time in one area of the dining table assembling components. What if I go to his spot and see what happens?

Marie steps to the end of the table and sits. *Ok, here I am ... nothing happening. I'll close my eyes and take a few cleansing breaths....*

After a few seconds, Rudy's thoughts and presence wash over her like a wave.

This is the Rudy I know—confident, organized, focused, methodical and self-assured. But I sense something else. Here's an anxious emotion. Quite out of character for Rudy.

She focuses on the emotional "outlier." *Rudy is suspicious of a new hire at Cyclops—a young woman who "forgot" to mention a live-in boyfriend. How does that connect? While listening to the interview with Cloud, Rudy learned about an "insider" feeding information to Bluefoot's people. He immediately suspected this young woman and her boyfriend. He plans to talk to Allison but hasn't done so yet. Rudy's not confided this to anyone. If my impressions are right this is proof: energy trails exist, and I can tap into them.*

She takes another deep breath and focuses. *Where is Rudy now and what is he doing? He and Harris are at the Door Service Supervisor Center installing protective equipment.* Marie notes the time and her observations with her PA, to hold for recital when requested. *Enough confirmation, for now, I'm ready to read more.*

"I say you 'may be able' to follow a person to the present and find where they are because that has not always been the case with me. When I try to find someone in the present I often fail. I believe this is because the energy trail is strongest when there is some intense or unusual emotion. The emotions can be either positive, (surprise, honor, love) or negative (fear, confusion,

anger). The stronger the emotion, the more likely we are to be aware of or tap into the trail.

"After noticing a feeling, I let it wash over me; 'live with it' for a few seconds. A meditative state makes it easier. Always stay grounded. Don't let the emotion 'carry you away.' Follow with your mind, but never leave your safe space especially if the energy you tapped into is violent or self-destructive. DO NOT try to anticipate what might come next. Your grandmother did. It messed with her sense of reality. Rose Plum often could not let go, even after the person was safe and protected.

"One more thing about the trails. How long does an energy trail stay intact enough to be read? It depends. Some things make the trails last longer. I think three things make the trail more stable. 1. The intensity of the emotion (more intense =longer lasting). 2. Detail of the thoughts/emotions (a specific plan lasts longer). 3. Emotional closeness to the person (you can more easily tap into Allison's than those of someone you just met; likewise the stranger's will weaken sooner than the trail of someone you feel attached to).

"If an emotionally charged trail passes through an area containing an active but 'lower' emotion trail; the older one is harder to identify—but not impossible. If a trail is not 'renewed' by the person coming back into contact, it likely diminishes in 3 to 5 days. The trails seem unaffected by wind, temperature, sleep, leaving the area, or others passing through (except as noted above).

"I think you will be reading this letter in sections. So I'll cue you – change of subject coming up next."

By prior arrangement Marie is sleeping on the couch, so her guest can sleep later. When Allison returns, she realizes her daughter is not asleep. Allison says, "Phillip is alive, breathing on his own, temperature near normal, and other bodily functions returning. Preliminary workup puts him in the same category with a severe stroke victim."

"Heard from Rudy?"

"Yes, he will be by in the morning to finish showing you the extra protection he installed and how to use them. He and Fenton got some information from the guys in the white panel truck. They said they work for a court, but they couldn't name a contact only a "set up guy." He's in custody as well. Fenton said it's the guy Wessel suspected in the explosion at the rail entry area."

"What a day. I didn't get to the clinic to visit my people. I'm amazed at how quickly they became 'my people.' If they are injured under my watch, they are *my responsibility*. I care what happens to them."

"Dr. Kildare wanted an update on Phillip. She said the young officer is recovering better than expected, and he is talking up a blue streak about how you warned them, and they ignored you. They ridiculed your concerns. His partner believed they'd find some kid hiding from a parent. They were sure the 'weapon' was a baseball bat or water gun."

"I'll see him tomorrow."

"Have you read the letter?"

"Some. Too much to do all in one sitting."

"How are you doing?"

"I'm calm about realizing *I'm different* from some others. I understand more than ever how much you love me. I'm glad you didn't tell me until now. Thanks for being here to help me sort it out. No, I'm not mad at you … well not much. I would like you to read the part of the letter I have read."

"I'll do it tonight."

"Aren't you exhausted?"

"Are you?"

"Well, no, but I'm running on adrenalin, my first job, all the new experiences, having you here and—you know."

"Understood. I'm very high too. Seeing you doing so well. All my concerns are vanishing."

"And ... Dr. Norris ... come on ... no secrets between us."

"OK, yes, it's wonderful seeing him again. I don't *understand* how I feel—but *if* romance *were* in my future ... I would enjoy a swing at it with him. Got no time for romance, but I like having an ally who understands my work."

"The emotions don't *care* whether you have enough time or not."

"Oh, quit meddling and go to sleep. I would like to read Berry's letter, as much as are done with."

Marie hands Allison the pages she has finished. "You can sleep in, but I warn you a Keeper's house is a way-station for early morning joggers. There is runner I would like you to meet if she is out tomorrow."

"What time?"

"Close to 6 AM."

"I better read and let you sleep."

"Goodnight, Mother."

"Goodnight, Marie."

Forty-Five
Counseling

"Good morning, Marie. I am waking you in the living area as requested. Since you are not sleeping in a sensor-activated bed, I'm unable to determine when you are up. Please indicate if you desire a second wake-up call."

"OK, Friend, I'm up."

Marie dresses, prepares coffee, tea, and two water pitchers, for the joggers who will appear soon. She asks, "Friend, anything I need to know?"

"Tornados damaged some wind farms in western Kansas and southwestern Nebraska. Today is an unusually cloudy day. Therefore electric production will be 7% below the maximum for the next 48 hours. Individuals are requested to limit non-essential electrical use. The power consumption in this location is consistently 14% to 19% below projections."

"Are there any non-essentials we can reduce today?"

"None. All consumption is minimum. Your console automatically goes to power saving when not in use."

"Thanks. Is there anything else for today?"

"People are disappointed in the lack of new angel sightings. The injured Security Officer's family said, '… an angel saved him….' An incoming call from Franklin A."

339

"I'll take it." Answering she says, "Morning Mr. A. How may I help you?"

"How soon can I come by? Is your guest up?"

"No, she was reading late. An hour or so." The bedroom door opens, and a yawning Allison heads for the bathroom. "Oops, here she is."

"Is it R?"

"Yes."

"Give me 30 minutes, and I'll start breakfast."

Marie asks Rudy, "Did you hear her?"

"No."

"Well of course not. You repaired the console dead zone. My guest says she will begin breakfast in about 30 minutes."

"By the way, the open part of the dead zone only works for your voice and ears; a substitute will experience a standard—sound free dead zone. I'll show you some switches. Be there in about 40 minutes."

"Harris too?"

"On another task. It'll be 9:00 before he's free."

The conversation is relayed to Allison as she heads to the bedroom. Marie adds, "You should get water for today's shower, and we are under an energy conservation request."

It's almost 5:00 AM. Ava is ready to leave for work; she is told about the energy conservation.

"We use minimal energy in our offices. Are we still on for 10:00?"

"Yes, unless you need me to reschedule. I'm free until 4:00."

"No need, I'll expect you at 10:00."

"Looking forward to it. Your door is activated. May your day be pleasant and calm."

"Thanks, Marie."

There are some stores along 4th Street. Retired people often operate small sideline businesses: craft shops, photography, pottery, calligraphy and the like. They enjoy the activity and passing on their knowledge giving lessons, and selling supplies. I'll contact them about the energy conservation request.

Their Doorkeeper sends energy conversation requests to retired people. Personal Assistants will inform their residents (most people in the workforce). Others receive a communication marked "important." Opening the message sends a response to the originator. All standard procedures learned in Door Facilitation studies. *Doing something normal feels affirming. I'm surprised at how quickly responses started arriving from retired people. All 92 retired persons have received the message by 5:30.*

Marie opens her door to early morning runners. Allison is in the kitchen fixing a casserole with a pleasant aroma. The first two runners are men. They are told about the energy limits.

Vivi is next. Marie introduces Vivi, "Allison, this is my first real friend in Wichita, Vivi, who works in financial services. Vivi, this is Allison Fulbright, the person who understands me best."

"A pleasure to meet you. How do you know Marie?"

"She is like a daughter to me. Before her mother died, she asked me to watch over her."

The two of them go into the kitchen where breakfast is almost ready. Mother and Vivi talk cordially while their host works.

Franklin A. arrives as Vivi is leaving.

Rudy shows Marie some unorthodox switches he installed on her console. Breakfast is on the table. Rudy is ready to update his boss, but Marie interrupts.

"There are a few quiet moments, long enough for something I need the two of you to hear. It's important." She has their undivided attention. *I seem to possess some new power.*

"Allison, you read what Berry said about 'energy trails'?"

"Yes, I did. Her theory can't be easily disproved. But I can't think of a way to verify it either."

"Maybe I can." Giving the code, Marie asks her Personal Assistant to play the note she recorded last evening.

The recording, in her voice, details how Marie searched for and found Rudy's "energy trail;" followed him to where he was at that moment (9:58 PM); and identified the higher emotion of his concern about a possible spy at Cyclops.

The recording concludes: "Now if this information is correct I tapped into Rudy's energy trail for there is no other way I could know these things. If only part is accurate, then more work must be done to understand the process. If I'm completely off base, we start over."

The PA says, "End of recording."

Allison and Rudy stare at Marie with amazement. Allison turns to Rudy, "Well?"

"She is entirely accurate. The spy was the first thing on my agenda with Allison this morning. We need an action plan. No one else knew about my concern; not Fenton, Harris, or Marie."

Rudy turns to Marie. "I'm intimidated by your awareness. What else do you know about me?"

"Last night is the first time I tried to enter a trail to test the theory. You've heard everything I gleaned. So far clear details come only with high emotion."

Allison questions, "But perhaps you unintentionally tapped into trails before?"

"It would explain what I experience when seeing or hearing the impossible; like the PPSW with no 'signal chip' and my 'seeing' her taped to the back door in a room with no camera access. Other times I understand another's thoughts if they are lying to me."

"Ok, this is valid evidence. What we can do is try to measure Marie's brain waves as she experiences an energy trail? Does Berry say anything about the unbidden experiences?"

"I haven't read more."

Rudy says, "I've always known you are smart. So now I must add your ability to read minds."

"No, I can't interpret your thoughts. Glimpses of what you are thinking come through attached to the emotion."

Allison is switching to her scientific investigative mode. "Can you tap into a person's past when you are with them?"

"When in their presence I'm focusing on what is happening now. One variable seems to be an *unexpressed* emotion: like when the guy asked me on a date but was convinced I would refuse. That's the most sense I can make of it now. I hope the rest of Berry's letter will tell me more."

"Ok," Allison says, "This is all new information we need to work with. We must keep it quiet. We need to remember Marie is the latest in a long line of intuitive people. She may be what the founders of HMP envisioned decades ago: aware, compassionate, capable, and discerning. They *never* envisioned tapping into other's *energy patterns* to find things in the past to explain current behavior, but it seems to be happening. Frankly, if anyone but Marie said this, I would question her veracity. But the evidence is indisputable. We need a scientific verification. One more thing, Marie, are you in control of this process, or is it controlling you?"

"I'm in control of how, or if, I use energy trails, and for what purpose. Before exploring the trails further, I need to clarify my ethical perspective. Remember you taught me to be a scientist but first to be an ethicist."

Allison says, "I'm ready to leave the subject."

"Rudy, are you alright? You seemed disturbed by what I told you and maybe how I responded. Are *we* OK?"

"It's a lot to take in; must be more for you. If someone gets to visit my past, I'd rather it be you than anyone else. *We are ok.* I need to adjust to being vulnerable; my persona is built around being invincible. This is a new for me."

Marie handles doors; Rudy and Allison discuss Missy Calendar who may be spying on Cyclops. They strategize next steps emphasizing that no one mention Marie, or where Allison and Rudy are.

At almost 8:00 AM: all the retired people in sector 86 are up and have received the message about energy usage. *When I retire I'll not be up at 5:00, 6:00 or 7:00 on ordinary days.*

More doors. Another break comes about 9:10.

Her pod to the counseling sector is due shortly as she contacts Supervisor to remind the office of her departure. She is instructed to return by 5:00 PM. She and Allison plan lunch at a sidewalk café near the Med Center.

She contacts "Super-Door" to tell him she is leaving. He sends her another picture: this one is Mickey Mouse's sidekick, "Goofy."

"You are 'goofy,' but I don't think you look like him."

At 9:52 Marie checks in for her appointment, and is at the office door at 9:59. Ava greets her warmly. The drapes are open, and a small lamp is on a table with a cluster of 3 chairs. A medium sized dark mahogany desk, without paper, work pad, or computer. Off to the left is another small room with a couch and some comfortable chairs.

Marie's hostess is skilled in making newcomers comfortable. A woman in her early 40's, dark brown hair done up in a small bun, kind brown eyes, and one small blemish on her left cheek, maybe a scar. Her SOG is the light blue with dark forest green accents standard for fully qualified counselors. The green is like waves near the hem of the garment, and on her sleeves. Her shoes are modest heels in a matching green. Marie realizes Ava is a real beauty. But knowing most of her clients are women with "mating issues" Ava wisely softens her features favoring a more welcoming appearance.

The guest is given the choice of sitting at the desk, or in the small cluster of chairs. "Anything but a desk please." A seat is chosen based on its size and dark blue color. While Marie sizes up Ava and the office, the same is happening in reverse.

Ava chooses a chair putting her slightly to Marie's left allowing the counselor light on the client's profile. If Marie turns to look at Ava, the slight glare from the window will obscure Ava's facial expressions. *Nicely played. Ava realizes I'm an introvert, and not being face-to-face may enhance my comfort level.*

Ava begins, "Welcome Marie … anything, in particular, you would like to discuss?"

"No," *What might I have done differently to avoid the death. Nothing will change what happened, but if there is anything to learn I want to learn it.*

Ava asks, " The Inquiries?"

"Yesterday. The most significant conclusion is the need for clearer understanding by Security forces of the role and authority of a Doorkeeper in emergency situations."

Marie details the events, her reports, inquiries and the emotions expressed by others. She demonstrates her extraordinary capacity for recall.

"The security inquiry group was concerned about my being off probation so soon. Security One implied I was not ready. My Supervisors defended their action after I left the call."

Ava asks, "What did you fear most from the inquiries?"

"Learning I had made a grave mistake or did not do something obviously needed."

"On a scale of 1 to 10 how high was your fear?"

"One. I know my job."

"Has this changed your feelings about working with Security?"

"Not at all. Most of the Security people are excellent. We are on the same side."

"Do you fear repercussions?"

"No. People are telling me, 'You did all you could.' I believe them."

They talk about death in general. The obligatory questions about depression, disillusion with her job, and fear about future situations are asked. Marie's responses raise no concerns. Counselors pay attention to inconsistencies between words and body language. None noted.

Ava says, "Marie, you are a strong introvert and intuitive. You scored higher on the expanded intuitive scale than anyone I've ever worked with. How does that square with a job requiring a lot of people contact?"

"I trust my intuition. Feelings guide me. My contacts with people come by voice and, when needed, visuals. Following my training I help meet peoples needs; feel accomplishment and move on to the next task. Very different when someone *needs* something, and I can help."

"So what happens when your intuition fails you?"

"I resort to what I learned for answers. For example, my first morning I had a door out of routine. Audio was disabled. My intuition told me he was ill, and in the bathroom, where no visual is possible. Protocol dictated I visually check every room until only the bathroom remained. Supervisor overrode the audio lockout, and I talked to him, confirming my intuition. Either way, I fall back to my training when the situation becomes clear."

"So you are not relying solely on your intuition?"

"Never. Intuition supplements what I know. Logic lets me choose one action over another."

They talk a bit more about life, and what it was like being yanked out of one role for an "emergency relocation." They set their next counseling session for Saturday, August 28th at 9:00 AM. An invitation is extended by Ava to call anytime to talk.

They embrace, for longer than necessary. Ava whispers, "You are a healthy person, but you don't need to do this alone."

"I'm not. Thank you. Next time I'll tell you about the support I have." *Talking with Ava helped. I have more energy. There's time for a quick trip to the clinic before lunch.*

All the patients she planned to visit, except Chester L and Security 107, Tommy, had been dismissed. Tommy's mate confides, "he's so impressed with your abilities that he now wants to become a Doorkeeper." Tammy also talks about their massive debt. Marie gives her contact information for Vivi. "Financial counseling is not her area, but she will tell you who can help."

Never before have I met someone in a Structured State with debt. Can't help but wonder how Tommy's income dropped so low.

She found Chester L depressed, remorseful, and self-recriminating. Without intending to, Marie taps into Chester's energy trail and helps him address his worst fears. She suggests, "Explain how much you miss what you experienced with your mate. You thought the drug would help recover those feelings."

That's the key. Chester never identified his loss of intimacy as the driving force behind his actions.

Marie indicates to Dr. K, "Chester L may be open to some suggestions for his recovery."

Lunch is at the "Sidewalk Café number 4" noted for its seafood. There is a series of Sidewalk Cafés, all managed by Central Services.

The conversation remains light. The counseling session and Phillip's progress are the weightiest subjects broached. He will be transferred to a stroke treatment center in Seattle. Allison can keep tabs on him. The move by medical service plane will likely be Monday. Allison will accompany him on the "med plane."

"We want to keep his identity under wraps, so we are creating a whole new person. It's harder than when we made up 'Margaret' because we must create an entire life including financial records."

"Phillip's records are available to me: past activities, job applications, financial reports. Would that help?"

"In addition to what you gave us?"

"Yes. It comes from Records and Inquiries. As his colleague I have access."

Marie contacts PA instructing "her" to obtain the information and print it at her third screen.

Allison talks more about her memories of "Abe."

"We had a pleasant friendship, with romantic potential, but both of us were committed to our educations. Abe's memory is that as soon as I met Jamison, he was out of the picture. My memory is Abe got wrapped up in his studies and disappeared. The reality is somewhere in-between."

Allison says, "Changing the subject; you're aware I need to tell you more. You will want to finish Berry's letter first. Correct?"

"Yes, unless we run short of time for what you need to tell. I should have Saturday and most of Sunday. Is that enough time?"

"Should be."

Allison shares her conversation with Vivi. Part of her work deals with the political opposition to disclosing the manipulation of the system. Vivi wants to talk more tomorrow.

"Perhaps I can join you."

They stroll down the street, observing the small shops, shoes, beachwear, jewelry, office supplies and stationery. The stores fascinate Allison. She wonders if Central Supply operates all these stories?

They find the Public In City stop and indicate their destination on the kiosk. It's 1:15 PM. Four of the five passengers on the pic pod greet Marie and Allison as they enter. The 5th sits with her mouth open. Marie recognizes Thelma, the one spreading the rumors about Marie being an angel.

"You're her! She's the angel."

"Hello, Thelma. I missed you yesterday. It was such a busy day. How is the medicine working for you?"

"Dr. K said I had *the wrong* medicine, I needed something different, and she gave it to me. I feel fantastic. You angels do such wonderful work." Turning toward the passenger next to her, Thelma says, "Dr. K is an angel too; she told me," indicating Marie.

Allison whispers, "How long's this been going on?"

"Started Monday, she was on the pic pod when I rescued the PPSW. She witnessed everything: the drug, saving her from the door ax, and chasing down the client."

In a moment of inspiration Allison says loud enough for everyone, "Well, there is no choice."

Marie is surprised but ready to play along; it was old times again playing follow the leader. "What should we do?"

"We must make her one of us."

(Sigh) "Well, I guess you are right. You want the front or the back?" Now Marie is leading.

"You are so much better at the front; I'll take the back."

"Well thank you, I do enjoy it more. OK, Thelma, here is what will happen. We will make an A sandwich. You are the filling. My superior will stand behind you and reach her arms around you toward me. You rest your arms on hers. I'll stand in front, and you will encircle me. Touching your cheeks and your temples I'll give the oath. But first, do you want to be one of us?"

"Will it hurt?"

"Of course not, the other guys bring pain."

"Yes, I want to be an angel. Do I have to die?"

"No, angels are messengers of the eternal. What use is a *dead* messenger?"

Thelma seems satisfied. Marie and Allison with a remarkable degree of composure go to Thelma's seat, and she stands. Allison, behind her, reaches around her and below her armpits so Thelma can rest her arms on Allison's. Marie steps in front; Allison places her hands on Marie's shoulders. Marie touches Thelma's cheek and says, "Angels are messengers of the spirit working for health. Our task: find good in action and help it; find bad things and stand-up to them. Our only power is our belief, and what others believe about us. Real power comes from within because the eternal Spirit touches our core. Angels are and always will be." Moving her fingers from cheek to temple, both together and individually, she, gently touching Thelma, while speaking.

Thelma sits. Marie says; "Now you are one of us. Remember, you can never tell anyone you are an Angel. It must be a secret. You try to find helpful things and aid them when you can. If someone rejects your offer—silently pray for him or her. When you find someone ill—call a clinic or doctor. Someone has a stressful day you talk to them; listen; don't pry they *will tell you what they need* to make it a better day. Most important when you find something wrong, first ask, who can help: Security, Medical, or a friend. *Never take on bad things by yourself.* Remember when I 'helped the girl,' I had all kinds of help, Medical, doctors, Security, and Transportation. Never take on bad without help. All these people will forget everything as soon as they leave the pod, right?" Most of the people are having trouble keeping from laughing, but they all nod.

Allison shakes Thelma's hand and says, "Welcome, but remember it's a secret."

"Oh I will, I will. Thank you so much. Do I still need to eat?"

"You certainly do, and take your medications, drink plenty of water and keep your doctor's appointments, and walk and pray every day."

"Always ask for help when you need it," Marie adds.

The pod doors are open waiting for Marie and Allison to step off. Marie whispers, "Don't laugh until they're out of sight." They start walking the two blocks toward Marie's home. The pod turns the next corner; both women double over in laughter.

Allison says, "I haven't had so much fun since you went to college."

"But we did a positive thing. Now she can stop talking about angels and help people. And take better care of herself."

"I hope she doesn't try to walk through a wall or something."

"She'll only try it once."

"You must tell me the rest of the story."

So Marie fills in the missing details about her first "angel situation," and the "necked" man (who became several men in the retelling) running away and jumping fences. Also being identified as the angel when going to the clinic to visit the injured. Finally, they plan, to get on the same pod a year later to check on how the story has changed. Both are laughing like 5th graders when they reach the door.

It's 1:35 PM and Rudy is there. Harris is back at the hotel doing some investigation on the newest guests of Security, and Rudy is getting his equipment ready for transport.

Rudy plans to leave Wichita Friday morning. "Called Bulla about Missy and her boyfriend. Bulla already caught her trying to make an outside call. She read her the riot act and told her 'this is your only infraction. Next time you're gone.' I shared our suspicions. Bulla responded 'I'll kill her.' Told her we want to send some misinformation by Missy. Bulla said, 'OK. Then I kill her.'

"Talked to Carter. He said she had made a call the day before. I heard the call. It was about not seeing Allison and being told 'she goes into deep research mode and isn't seen for days.' Missy is not innocent. They are working together.

"So I'm going back tomorrow—8:10 AM flight. Harris will stay and return with Allison."

Allison says, "We'll know in the morning if I'm going on the plane with Phillip. If so Harris need not stay."

"True. We'll check that out when we know more."

Marie hands Allison and Rudy a ream of nearly 300 pages. "Here is the Records and Information file about Phillip. As his successor I get access. It might be helpful as you create the identity replacing him."

Rudy flips through the pages. "This saves us a hundred hours of research. This lets us put funds in the replacement's name without raising red flags."

"I wonder how you and Allison use multiple identities without getting double compensation."

"Our additional identities 'reside' in non-programmed states, so the economy does not pay us anything unless we 'perform services' like Franklin A. this week. Mostly it covers Franklin's travel, meals, lodging, etc. Anything left over is given to non-profits. Our real selves are 'on vacation' so there is no overlap in compensation. Funds never leave the economy, and there is no 'double dipping.' Financial Services looks for double dipping—raising red flags—then everything gets investigated."

"I assumed you acted ethically. Only wondered how."

Rudy shows Marie the latest security enhancements made to her quarters. Allison is busy on her laptop, work-pads, and communicator. *Two and one-half hours before I go back on duty. I want to get back to Berry's letter.*

Forty-Six
More Letter

"*I promised to tell you more about your grandmother, and me. My mother was one of the first who had natural talent, scoring high in several categories. They tested her and encouraged her talents from an early age. That approach seems flawed. By the time I came along the best minds believed right after puberty to be a natural time for developing talents.*

"*Starting so early distorted Rose's perceptions. Assuming her stories are true (most are), she used 'her gift' before finding HMP. Being lonely she dwelled on her abilities. Any positive relationship became an obsession—like Mark and Marie. She was confused about what she could do because of her talent, and what would be normal. She developed unreasonable fears and bouts of deep depression. Rose learned to use energy trails before we could name them.*

"*Moving to avoid detection was hard on Mother. She was grateful to HMP for saving her but resented their control. It was easier for me—partly because I was 14 before HMP began encouraging my talents. I had experienced a few things, like knowing we were going to move before they told us. Mostly I loved my childhood. Except for a moody mom, it was relatively stress-free.*

Homeschooling was the best choice until I reached Secondary level. Relationships are hard for me, especially with those my age. I could tell who thought me weird or would ignore me, so I did not try with them or any of their friends. Finding a few 'loners' made high school bearable. Like me, they moved a lot.

"Mother was wrong about the order of my children: she said – girl, boy, girl. The boy came first. While waiting to become pregnant with you, I had access to files, including those concerning my children. No names, but they used an adoption agency in Edmonton. By the time I was searching, it had closed, but I located the repository of their records. I traveled to the recorder's office in Edmonton before coming to Cyclops.

"Your brother was born October 9, 2069; adopted by an American family. Both college professors: the woman taught child psychology, and the man was a full professor of mathematics. They were in Chicago at the time of the adoption. I think they taught at two different Universities. His last name was Trenton. Dr. Andrew Trenton got his Ph. D. from Harvard was a professor of math at the University of Chicago. His mate did not use the same last name—probably for professional reasons. Dr. Andrew Trenton left the University of Chicago in 2073 without a trace.

"Your sister was born September 8, 2072. Her adoptive parents were named Fleming (at least one of them—I think they were both women). Behavioral science was their field—working for years with gorillas in Africa. They had returned to Canada on furlough for two years. Don't know if they returned to Africa. There was one news report saying they planned to work in the rainforests of South America. I found nothing more about either. Wish I could say more about your siblings."

Allison and Rudy will want this.

"Do you know anything about my brother and sister?"

"Only that they exist and the years of their birth. We are not sure which is older. The records at HMP were all but destroyed, when the center was threatened. Everyone involved tried to recover files from memory, but there are a lot of holes."

"This might fill part of one," Marie says as she hands the sheets to Allison who slides them over so Rudy can both read them. After a moment Allison says, "Berry had the adoptive parents names. Why didn't she tell us, we could have tracked them?"

Marie returns to Berry's letter.

"When you give these pages to Allison, she will ask, 'Why didn't she tell us, we could track them?'

"Here's why: 1. I'm not sure about the accuracy. I passed myself off as a lawyer looking for these kids to give them an inheritance. I was unsure the clerk believed me, so she may not have given me the correct information (never got close enough to "interpret" her energy). The documents are incomplete. So were many adoption papers from that era. 2. If Allison had known, she or Rudy would have found them. Then what? Would you ask to take the children so they can be with their sister? I don't think the adoptive parents knew about their specialness. HMP was under attack, and I feared for their safety, as well as others including Allison, Jamison and you. 3. Allison would be extremely busy, and under a lot of pressure in her work between the time of your birth and now. In fact, this will continue for several more years beyond when you are reading this. I selfishly

wanted them to give their attention to you. Also, I hoped to save the Wards one more stress.

"The 'children' are now adults. I think you owe it to yourself to try to find them. Rudy can probably trace them down, and then you decide how to approach them. If their parents did not understand their talents and they developed naturally, then they may welcome someone who can help explain what happened to them.

"I would suggest finding them, observing them before coming out to ask them about their talent or unexplained experiences. You and Allison will do what is right."

Marie reads these paragraphs out loud to Allison and Rudy. Everyone is quiet.

Allison speaks first, "Berry knew me well, maybe, too well? OK, we follow-up now. So where do we start?"

"*I start* when I return to Cyclops with a friend in the Canadian Services. *You* keep doing what you are doing. *I'll find them.* Then *we*'ll decide what to do."

"Don't I get a vote?" asks Marie.

"Of course you do—after the *grown-ups* figure out what to do."

Marie steps into the kitchen; picks up a small cooking pot; steps back in the room; throws it at Rudy's head, if he had not ducked it could've hit him in the temple. All but Marie laugh, as the pot hits the wall and bounces away. Without cracking a smile, she says, "I was 'grown up' at 13, and *you* know it."

Rudy said that to get a rise out of me. A little surprise might do him some good. I better be careful with this new spontaneity; it would be horrible if I had hurt him. The shield would've protected him.

They laugh as Rudy says, "Of course, you'll be involved. I was joking."

Marie returns to the letter.

"One more point before I change the subject. My last day at the HMP headquarters I found the list of specific mother/child matches and their coded donors. The coded list of the donor specimens was in a second building, and a list of donors with abbreviated 'contribution' codes was in a third location. So I memorized two complete lists of 45 individuals with an 8-digit code for each. Then I compared the third list; it was worth it. I found the donors for my children. Your father is Jamison Ward; your older brother's donor father is James Callahan, one of the founders of HMP. He died in 2069 before my son was born. Your sister's biological father was Gene Benjamin, a genius recruited as a donor by the Wards.

"Now let me turn to something none of the scientists of HMP understood: predicting the future. Mother told me I would have three offspring; she would die before I reached adulthood and I would not see my children grow up. When she said these things, I asked how she knew. Her answer put me searching for the next development of Human Maturity.

"Mother said it was because of her high scores on all three HMP markers for Maturity. She said we see some aspects of what lies ahead. I was 17 when she told me she would die in 2 years. She was in good physical health, so I dismissed that claim. She told me all my children would make a contribution to knowing more about life as a Mature Person. She also said the third would be a girl, and she would be the 'ultimate regarding

what our line can develop'— her exact words. *I asked about other 'lines' producing a more Mature Human. She said not for a century or more, and they will be connected somehow to our line, but she wasn't sure how.*

"I'm not a scientist but here is what I understand about 'future seeing.' It relates to energy trails and high markers. The prediction may not be correct in every detail. Mother got the order of my children wrong. She was right about the total number of children and the gender balance. So some of the things I say may not be entirely correct, but if they turn out to be wrong in only one detail don't dismiss the relevant data.

"The only way to confirm semi-scientifically the prediction quality is for me to make predictions that come true after my death. You will be able to judge the accuracy of my predictions.

"Let me start with what I'm most sure of. By the time you read this Allison Ward will be the holder of a second Nobel Prize. I believe this one will be for work she and Cyclops and eight other research centers around the world did to prevent a virus causing blindness from attacking humans. Allison Ward will also receive a third Nobel Prize – this one for her work to stop a series of organisms the researchers call 'clambering viruses.' I'm not sure why that name but if this work fails most plant and animal life on earth will cease in a matter of decades.

"This writing has been over a series of days. Each evening as I go to sleep I pray for more clarity, of what to share with you. It's obvious to me now you will have this letter before your 20ᵗʰ birthday. In fact, you are barely 19.

"Jamison Ward dies in September 2082. It will be ruled an accident, but it was not. Allison and Rudy can tell you more.

"Rudy will become in many ways your substitute father. He will teach you things. They will keep you safe for many years, and he will extend the security of Cyclops to you, wherever you are.

"Allison will be your rock for most of your life. She will live into her late 90's; maybe even 100. She will work and be healthy until about a month before her death.

"Marie, you are smart, aware and compassionate. Few real friends. In school, everyone wanted to be in your study group, but no one felt close to you. Your resourcefulness intimidates them. Your Instructors are impressed by your insights and mastery. None of this surprises you.

"You will teach, not only as a Teaching Assistant, which will be cut short for you to be where you are. You will be on leave of absence for a year or more to lecture and travel, returning to Door work. Later you will again teach while working on some other projects.

"A name of a person who is important to you keeps coming to mind, but I think you have little contact with him. His name is Phillip. He was HMP, a natural like your grandmother. He tested high on all three markers and understands energy trails. He is working on a project to identify and measure them if he lives to complete it, which is questionable. What he learned will benefit you, and you will take it to a new level.

"Now I get it. Something happened to Phillip. He is disabled but alive, and you were brought to finish and protect his work. No one else seemed right. So they got the best Door student ever—you.

"Another ally is someone named Norris. I don't think he was one of your teachers, but you will learn a lot from him.

"One more thing I'm sure of. There are enemies. Some are Allison's, but soon they will be after you as well. One has lots of stooges. His name is a color and a body part. I think it's Bluetoe. Not sure about the body part, but the color is blue. No matter it is not his real name. He was the last of the Military's super soldier project to create the fearless, heartless fighter: without emotion, soul or remorse. Bluewhatever is the last of them; he is pure evil. Be careful of him. About the time you receive this is when he becomes desperate to bring down Allison's research.

"Now we are getting into things I'm less sure about, but it may make sense to you, Allison, or Rudy. First, you are where you are partly to facilitate the movement of some "packages" Allison's researchers need. Blueguy is doing everything he can to find and destroy them. Somehow you are involved in getting the last ones to the right place.

"There is also something about a group. A black bird is somehow involved with it, crow or maybe a raven? All that comes clear is you will be safe there, and they need you.

"Not sure I should tell you these next things? You will receive a Nobel Prize.

"You will also be in the public eye, soon and for the rest of your life. There will be supporters and admirers of your work.

"One more thing about your personal life: you may wonder if you will ever experience a sexual and emotional intimacy. You do. Can't say if you ever mate—could go either way. Unsure *about children. Perhaps you have offspring using a surrogate—very unclear.*

"*My mother died unsure of her purpose; why she had all these abilities and how little she accomplished with them. She was deeply depressed.*

"*My purpose among other things is to bring you into the world. You are our hope. Allison will do her part to save life on earth. You will save the planet with ideas, faith, and compassion. Millions will trust you.*

"*This is your life as I see it. It will unfold, as needed, everything in its proper time. You will receive the talent, gifts, and knowledge to address whatever comes to you. You do not need to go out seeking the place to make a difference. Opportunities will come at the proper time, and you will be ready. Along the way, there will be lots of fun, because you understand it's not all up to you. You possess the gift of not taking yourself too seriously and letting the spirit lead you.*

"*An eternal energy transcending our limited time on earth must be a reality. Watch for spirituality both inside and outside organized religion.*

"*Seek the companionship of others working for peace, personal and global. You will need people who are open-minded about the empowerment coming their way.*

"*Meditation and mindfulness provide direction. Listen to the voices from the past, the present and in particular the voice from within. Meditation: with and without mantra, focusing and claiming the moment helped me find purpose. The practice grounds me and brings me back when I start losing my way. That is why Faith is a pillar of The Plan. That's your pillar.*

"Earlier I said I was fortunate. I had a mother who had lived with the concert I was learning to play. I learned early about meditation and pulling the resources from within and without to keep me safe.

"The Spirit is driving you. Despite the pollution, greed, arrogance, and lack of unity almost everywhere there is kindness, compassion, and a driving force. The Plan for the Future is working. Some want to undo all its good for their self-interest. You, Allison, Rudy, Phillip, Norris, Bulla, and everyone working with you are the front lines in a battle for survival of the planet.

"So my final words of advice—don't give up on what we don't understand. Meditate—find what works for you, connect with others who are searching. Even those who say they do not believe are sources of life and ideas. Surround yourself with people who will accept you. Beware of those who do things 'in the name of God' because they often put an idol in God's place.

"Now I must concentrate on keeping the toxins from reaching you. I recently realized when it happened. Rudy will remember the time just after I got back from Canada. We had an errand downtown and found ourselves on a crowded sidewalk, trying to return to our vehicle. There was some protest group, and a man came up behind me with a hypo of something aiming for my neck. My outer garment had no face shield. Rudy decked him, and syringe broke spilling on the sidewalk. The guy grabbed the broken parts and ran. Only a scratch on my neck treated with

alcohol and antibiotic cream, as soon as we got to the car. Rudy
called Allison for instructions. She said to apply a cold pack and
get back as soon as possible.

"They ran all kinds of test and found nothing. They still
run tests—nothing. In meditation, I learned my liver is storing
the slow acting toxin keeping it out of my system. It told me
foods to avoid. You will be born in less than a week; I must
protect you.

"You were born today, and I held you and nursed you.
Marie, you are beautiful and perfect in every way. Your eyes
reveal a wise soul. I have a few days with you. I want to give
you as much of me as I can in these days.

"I'm not sad to die. I fulfilled my purpose: giving you life
and finding the people who will provide you the best start.

"God bless you, my love.

"Cranberry, they call me Berry, I hope that is what you will
call me."

Then it was over. Marie's eyes fill with tears. Sobbing, she
clutches the letter to her breast. Allison stops setting out supper to put an arm around her daughter's shoulders. Rudy, never
one to intrude on another's privacy, sits at the table with his
head bowed and eyes closed. Glimpsing him Allison wonders,
is he praying?

After a long moment, Marie buries her face in a familiar
bosom. The uncertainties and anxieties of the last five days all
come pouring out. At this time, it's all too much. After three
minutes Allison persuades Marie to leave the console and go
to the couch, where they hold each other.

Seeing Marie in pain hurts Allison. *I can't take the pain away, but I can be here.*

Marie finally speaks, "I felt like I was just getting to know her, and she's gone." Allison says, "The letter is yours; you can visit her anytime. She lives in you. We are here to help."

Outside call rings from the console; Rudy checks on the call. "It's from Wessel," he says as he answers it. "Hello Wessel, this is Rudy, Marie is not available. May I give her a message?"

"Phillip's old couch Marie traded in. When removing the padding and cover, we found a slot containing a memory chip. But it does not fit the current computers. I would like to bring it by if it's ok."

"Let me check." Rudy steps away from the console and summarizes. "I can put him off, or I can pick it up."

"No, it's ok. I've had my 'life isn't fair cry,' and I need to pull myself back together."

Allison says, "You don't have to."

"Of course I don't, but Berry said Phillip would be an important person in my life. The chip is his. I need it."

"How did she know about Phillip?"

"How does she know any of the stuff you'll read about?"

Wessel delivers the memory device and stays for dinner. Rudy keeps an older computer in his electronic repair kits. After checking the chip, Rudy says, "Only one computer can read this one." Everyone surmises it's locked away with the Personal Assistant electronics.

They talk a bit about Phillip. Allison receives confirmation a medical transport plane will be at Eisenhower Airport, Monday, ready for passengers at 10:00 AM. Allison will ride along to care for him; therefore, Harris can return with Rudy tomorrow.

Wessel thanks everyone for the break, hugs Allison, and says, "Well, I'll see you before you leave." He hugs Marie who instantly knows about the surprise Wessel, and Allison cooked up. *I slipped into his energy trail without even trying.* Wessel and Rudy shake hands. No one hugs Rudy except Allison or Marie.

As Marie smooth's the crumpled papers, she finds three additional sheets. In the top margin of the first a handwritten note, "Reconstructed from Memory."

The page contains seven columns: the sperm donor name, code for vials administered, name of the recipient, code for offspring, name, gender, and birth date when available. Only about 20% contain a birthdate or child's name. Marie notices a second baby "fathered" by Jamison Ward in 2051. The potential mother is "Brenda L." No other details are available, not even the gender.

There may be a half sister or half brother somewhere in addition to Berry's two other children.

Marie says, "Jamison Ward's sperm was used in 2051 to create a child with Brenda L."

"None of the donors ever knew about offspring. None of us did. We thought it made for better focus for all concerned. Now I remember... Brenda L. was in another center; Bulla may remember her, I'll ask."

Handing the page to Allison, Marie glances at the remaining partially completed adoption applications. A sticky note in Berry's handwriting says, "This is what I got from the office in Edmonton."

One is written in longhand, and the other printed.

Allison is overjoyed with what she finds. "This is wonderful! We thought all this was lost. A 'purist' group raided the HMP center. Everything was destroyed including the sperm bank. Afterward, four of us tried to reconstruct what we remembered. We didn't come up with a third as much. This is a godsend."

Marie hands the other two sheets to Rudy, who peruses the note and the papers. "There's a handwriting expert we use; I'll see what she makes of these."

Marie hands the pages that had upset her so to Allison. "Treat them with care. There is a lot here you will want to know."

"I will. They'll never leave this house—thank you for sharing them with me." Both women are weepy as they hug. Marie goes back to the doors, and Allison to Berry's words.

Allison asks, "Marie, is it ok to share these with Rudy? They seem rather private."

"It's all private … I trust you and Rudy with everything. You nurtured and protected me. Even when pissed off—I'm still grateful for all your sacrifices. I don't say *thanks* often enough."

During the silence, each person reads. They are soon lost in their emotional landscape—searching for places to put these new constructs. All three end up reflecting on the foundational beliefs that sustain them.

Allison asks Rudy, "After all these years I feel foolish asking but are you a person of belief? Do you communicate with a higher power?"

Rudy affirms his support of Faith as part of the Emotional Foundations for The Plan. "I used to believe in the 'America Ideals.' But now I understand that no nation or government possesses all the answers." He talks about how Jamison Ward taught him "awareness," and the value he finds in that practice.

"God is the only explanation I have for why I get to work with the most righteous people on earth. It fortifies my moral compass to be in the same room with you all ... I don't mean only at Cyclops," he says looking directly at Marie.

"I know you hold me in high regard." Marie responds, "I have similar respect for you—my teacher, protector, and friend."

Forty-Seven
Friday

Mother and daughter find themselves on an emotional rollercoaster after reading Berry's letter: grateful for the new learning. Sill—grieving their loss. They hold each other until falling asleep. During the night Allison moves to the couch.

After waking but before leaving her bed, Marie takes a few moments for self-talk and reflection. A daily ritual—temporarily lost during her transition to a new job, home, and obligations. *OK, what have I learned? Faced the worst: death on my watch, and two inquiries. I followed the rules, wrote the reports and answered the questions. Anxious? Discouraged? Fearing repercussions? A little. Emotions were sorted and addressed.*

Marie: Doorkeeper. Trained for this: crises, rapid decisions, even bending some rules for the Common Good. Anything I wish different? Of course, no one dies.

Otherwise, no—all this is part of my chosen profession.

In last 48 hours, I've learned about me. So who am I? Marie Ward? Marie Cranton? No, Marie Cranton Ward. I'll never stop being a Ward—Jamison was my father, and Allison, a true mother.

I now have clues about the unexplainable things I've experienced. I believe I'm becoming the person I was created to be. I'm ready for a new day.

What new things for today? I love learning. Much of what I expect today will come from inside—my mind and spirit. I'll try to heed Berry's advice not to force the talent.

The Personal Assistant reports on Marie's sleep time and related health data.

Allison shares a message from Rudy indicating that Harris is on the flight back to Cyclops. The two women eat a leisurely breakfast concluding at 4:50.

Ava is ready for work asks, "How are you coping?"

"I'm fine. Thanks in part to your help. I also learned some things about myself these last two days. I'm clear headed about so many little things—I'll tell you when we meet. Changing the subject is your mate coming home today."

"No, not until tomorrow morning. His flight was canceled due to storms."

"What is his work?"

"He teaches in the Psychology Department." What Ava does not say, but Marie instantly knows: Eva's mate is Dr. Randolph Cliff. He will be heading the Department starting in March when the current chair becomes University President. The conference he attended this week dealt with balancing administrative and teaching duties.

"Ava, have a fulfilling day bringing understanding to others."

I used my talent, without trying. Is Rudy right? Can I read people's minds? It seems strange. Ava is under my door authority, but I'm sharing my most intimate thoughts with her; maybe that's part of maturity—possessing authority while being under authority.

Friend says, "Do you desire your daily news summary at this time?"

"Yes."

"In local news, the University's Central Hall will host an information gathering, Monday at 9:00 PM. Topic: proposed changes to the Programmed States governance, representation and legal system. The Central Program States Updating Initiative is conducting the session seeking responses from those present. Registration is not necessary but encouraged.

"The repair work on the south shelter entrance continues and is expected to be completed before the weekend. Repairs restore full use of the rail access returning the area's pod traffic patterns to standard. The transportation sector thanks the public for their patience during the time of altered routes.

"In angel sighting news. An angel and her supervisor were on a tram yesterday recruiting other angels. According to one anonymous source, they are actively seeking recruits who will listen, help others and confront evil.

"Another rider on a pod reports seeing an angel inducted into 'angelhood.' The angels were in such a hurry to get on with their work they forget to erase the memories of all the people on the pod."

Allison is laughing, "They left out the A sandwich."

Marie adds, "Now you see what I have to put with—*incompetent reporting*."

"But they got most of it right."

"Didn't think she could keep quiet."

"Perhaps we should send her 'The Handbook?'"

"You work on that Mother. Whoops." Realizing she said something never intended for her PA's ears.

Friend responds, "Did you identify your house guest as your mother?"

"Yes. I did not want you to learn that. No one else *can ever know*."

"This is the same A. Fulbright, who later became Dr. Allison Ward, head of Cyclops Institute, holder of two Nobel Prizes?"

"Yes, it is. But how did you find her name?"

"Part of my additional programming is to check the identity of individuals who enter by sleeve scan. A. Fulbright is also Allison Ward. So I checked her biographical details."

"Is this something all PAs do?"

"No. It's an enhancement. Dr. Ward is my first from out of the area."

"What about Franklin A.?"

"He never used the ID strip."

Allison says, "I used it after returning from my outing with Abe, and then remembered the keycard in my pocket. Living in a city is strange to me."

Allison explains to Marie's PA why it's essential no one learn the relationship between them. "Some people would endanger Marie to get an advantage over me; the same ones who threaten to dismantle you."

While Allison and Friend are conversing, Marie handles some routine doors. Skimming the *Wichita Eagle,* she finds nothing about the Monday meeting. "Friend, please send details of Monday's Informational Meeting to my third screen."

"On the way."

Let's find out about "The Central Program States Updating Initiative." It's probably bogus—like that court. Here it is.

Summarizing out-loud, ''The Central Program States Updating Initiative' was proposed by the Grog Foundation.... The proposal went nowhere, except talk shows, and the 'backlash' print media.... Their position is, 'The people living in the Programmed States must understand the severe loss of freedoms imposed upon them before the 2099 referendum.' So far it sounds *constructive* doesn't it?"

"Sarcasm has always been a reliable communication tool for you, but someone might miss your intent."

"Thanks for the reminder ... okay. They want to hold 3 to 6 public forums each year in each state until the vote. The *stated* purposes of the forums are three-fold:

1. Listen to the people.

2. Inform citizens of the changes to be imposed *after* the referendum.

3. To outline the evolving vision for an alternative structure.

What's the alternative structure?

Oh here we are. Their principles and rational

A. Eliminate Doorkeepers. Rational: an unnecessary inconvenience.

B. Eliminate Central Services. Rational: restore the joy of shopping, increase competition and reduce costs.

C. Restore private property ownership. Rational: freedom of choice and increase options.

D. Give property ownership back to individuals. Rational: citizens are being cheated when they downsize later in life.

E. Restrict medical care based on need. Rational: younger people are paying for medical services they never use.

F. Remove requirement for counseling. Rational: individuals should determine their need and pay accordingly.

G. Eliminate Financial Sector's control of funds. Rational: all funds should be at the disposal of individuals.

H. Eliminate dietary restrictions. Rational: allow people to eat what they want.

I. Eliminate cleaning and laundry services. Rational: return responsibility to individuals and families.

J. Return commerce to a system of free enterprise which has stood the test of time."

Allison says, "About all they leave out is tearing down the sheltered cities, and go back to polluting vehicles and weapons."

"Oh, here's something in the 'freedoms we have lost' section, and 'Police are at risk because they cannot carry guns.'"

Marie contacts Supervisor. The 44-year-old male voice is unknown to her.

"Supervisor, how may I help you?"

"This is Marie, Sector 86. You must be recently returning from vacation. Welcome back."

"I'm Supervisor 779 back this morning. This is your first week, welcome to Wichita."

"Thank you. I wondered if supervisors are aware of the session scheduled for 9:00 PM next Monday, August 23rd at the University? Promoted as an information forum by 'The Central Program States Updating Initiative.' In their proposed 'adjustments' to The Plan; Doorkeepers, Central Services, and Financial Services are to be eliminated."

Dr. Norris joins the conversation. After several minutes he declares, "Any DK desiring to attend, will be granted the time, no questions asked—set Auto-Door. I'll contact Wessel and Mr. James Calhoun, so their people are aware. Thanks, we'll get the word out."

Vivi stops by for water and a long conversation with Allison. Vivi leaves about 8:00 promising to contact her supervisor about the Monday meeting.

At 10:30 AM Marie and Allison change into workout clothes also taking bathing suits for the hot tub; explaining the incident with Howard two days earlier. "You remember how I get in emergencies. I ignore everything around me. Poor Howard was stuck watching my nude body turn blue while I saved the world."

"I doubt Howard considered himself 'poor.'"

After a moderate workout on the upper level, they go downstairs to find Howard in the hot tub. Marie introduces her houseguest, A. Fulbright.

Howard being a gentleman does not mention the first time they met. Both women notice his attention to all the skin not covered by their string bikinis. He is admiring and respectful. His appreciation and tender caressing with his eyes are not unnoticed. For some reason both women feel a bit more beautiful the rest of the day—it must be the workout.

After lunch, they get clearance from "Super-Door" and leave for a walk in the park. On the way, Allison, tells about her conversation with Vivi. "Did you know Brenda who left from Ann's house going to Europe, also had a package?"

"I suspected something because Ann was so attentive when Brenda was leaving—but I didn't 'know' until now."

"Vivi served as Phillip's backup. Only two packages remain. We're unsure where they are. They should have reached Phillip on the afternoon *before* he was kidnapped."

The packages are somewhere in the apartment. How do I know this—not from energy trails—or is it?

Stopping she turns to Allison, "Did she say when Phillip told her about the other two packages?"

"Yes, just before he was taken."

"Same day?"

"No, the evening before. Phillip messaged Vivi a package would appear on her desk, at the time of her next servicing. And he said two more would arrive the following day. Her service date is Friday, but Vivi was away until Sunday afternoon. Seeing the package, she assumed she could not touch it. Vivi worked out a plan and contacted Ann Sunday."

They start walking again. Marie wears her camera sensing glasses. Aware that Security 1 is not a fan makes extra precautions her norm.

Phillip was already missing by the time Vivi found the package. The kidnappers did not remove the other two packages, so they must be in the apartment. But where?

They reach the park. Others, mostly older folk, are walking. A father and daughter are doing the seesaw, and an older woman is coming straight toward them. It's Thelma, the newest Angel. "Oh, this should be fun."

Marie says, "Hi Thelma."

"I thought I would find you here. When you got off the bus I watched you head that way," Thelma gestures with her hands in the general direction of Marie's home.

"I live there; I'm the Doorkeeper for sector 86."

"Angels do jobs too?"

"Of course."

Thelma says, "Well, I have been observant, like you said, and I think I spotted an evil person. He was standing on the next corner (pointing west). He seemed to be watching a storefront across the street. He looks away like he doesn't want to attract attention. But *I saw him*."

"Which store front?" Marie asks trying to be casual.

"The one where they make pottery and things."

After attaching portalock and communicator, Marie has a live video of the man, loitering. "Is this the man?"

"Yes, that's him, doesn't he seem shifty to you?"

He seems rather impatient. Marie switches camera angles to what he is watching. It's the pottery shop. Apparently, a class is letting out. Marie uses scanning function and finds the identity of the man. "C Leadfoot is from Chicago. Arrived this morning. His flight was delayed by storms, or he would have been here yesterday. He's an 'investigator' for the Select Tribunal for the Central Program States.'"

A class, about 15 people, is leaving a few at a time. Marie spots the target: Charles, her first emergency, who is taking the class for stress management.

Charles is with several others walking to a PIC stop. Leadfoot crosses the street. This surveillance camera includes audio capability.

Marie is listening as "the investigator" reaches Charles, flashes an "ID" and says, "We need to talk."

Charles responds, "I told you, people, I have nothing to say. My work is confidential. Contact my superiors for details." The stranger takes Charles by the arm moving away from the stop. One of the other people from the class says, "Hey mister, leave him alone."

Leadfoot responds, "Shut up Four Eyes, or I'll give you two more."

Security is called. "Situation at the corner of Kingsway and 4th: Charles from 16 Kingsway is being accosted by C. Leadfoot who arrived this morning from Chicago. Perpetrator is attempting to 'drag' Charles from the street to a van parked around the corner on Kingsway. Charles is an employee of Financial Sector, currently on leave."

"Security 23, ETA one minute. Can you disable the vehicle?"

"Attempting to do so. I'm not sure if it's close enough to the intersection, but the block is active. Other people at the PIC stop are arguing with the outsider who is leaving empty handed … he enters on the passenger side. It starts up, but only moves a couple of feet and dies. Oh, I see you are at the scene, be careful there are at least two people inside, probably more. I forgot to mention Leadfoot is an investigator for Central Program States Tribunal."

"Thanks, we have a new stunning cannon I'm kind of anxious to use—*only* if needed of course." *What makes a stunner into a "cannon?" I'm sure he'll tell me.*

No need to ask the difference—it's soon demonstrated. The two in the front seat fire stunners at 23's head; his shield protects him. A single blast from the cannon hits the side of the van rocking it as at least four people inside scream. Medical is contacted, "six people, maybe more stunned by Security." Fenton J. puts on thick insulated gloves that accompany the cannon, opens the passenger door and the side door. He pulls the two from the front seat and carefully places them on the ground. The Security Officer then places a yellow square on the cheek of each man. *Those squares must somehow neutralize the effects of the stun.*

The officer opens the panel door, and four people stumble out, falling on top of one another in a wriggling pile, unable to control their movements. Again Fenton drags each one to a spot on the pavement and applies a yellow patch. When everyone is removed, yellow and blue energy arcs can be seen jumping from van floor and wall to any other metal object. One of the six is a woman. They all appear dressed in SOGS, mostly white with patches of green on the sleeves and legs indicating medical assistant. As the last one is dragged to a safe spot, Security 93, Fenton's Apprentice Detective arrives.

"Don't touch the vehicle," Fenton instructs.

Security 93, Lisa, glances, "That's some powerful hotspot." She steps to the cannon and opens the handle removing a four-foot long cable. One end spreads out with flat quarter-sized magnetic disks. The other end is shaped differently; right angle to the main cable.

Lisa asks, "Ground first?"

"Yes. The pavement will do fine."

Lisa sets the ground end on the pavement, tosses the magnet end into the van, and jumps back three feet. There are sounds like bacon frying, as well as smoke, coming from the cable at the pavement. After 20 seconds it stops.

Fenton had been checking each person's vitals using a telescoping probe to touch the yellow squares. "One of our guests is female, would you do her vitals?"

Lisa takes the device and checks on the woman. Meanwhile, Fenton talks to those waiting at the PIC stop, especially Charles who seemed to be the intended target. Medical arrives, and Lisa is taking charge of their identifications and readying them for transport.

Marie disconnects. Both Allison and Thelma have been watching. Turning to Thelma Marie says, "You did an *excellent* thing today. You remember the man talking to the Security Officer at the end?"

"Yes."

"You probably saved his life. You can be proud of your work. Thelma will be honored for her vigilance."

"I did right?"

"You did exactly right. You asked for help and corrected a wrong." Allison says, "Keep up the good work."

Thelma stands taller and appears ten years younger. Allison says, "Don't overdo it, rest when you need to, and remember to eat and take your medicines. Go about your regular activities. When you see problems, ask for help."

Thelma leaves likely looking for her friends.

Knowing Central Services are still servicing her home, Marie says, "Mother, there was something else you started to tell me the other day—something personal?"

Allison's eyes fill with tears. Taking her hand Marie puts an arm around in a side hug.

Allison says, "You remember we said your father died in an accident? And Berry's letter says it was not."

"Yes."

"Well she's right; he was murdered."

"What makes you think so?"

379

"Jamison was a safe driver. He was in Italy; called Rudy to say he was being followed. Rudy told him how to lose his tail. Later he said he had lost the tail and was going to a mountain village that afternoon. His car went over a cliff crashed and burned. Rudy took a crash analysis expert to the spot. They found a device attached to the brake line to cut it by a remote signal. So someone followed his car going up the mountain, then, at the right place, cut the line.

"You need to know because, unless he died, the person is still out there. We think we saw the murderer once. He was tailing us after the funeral. The man was in his late 20's." Passing Marie a photo she says, "Remember this was 12 years ago."

"I've seen him."

Allison freezes, "You mean here?"

"No, he's a DK. He was at the sectional meeting held in Kansas City, two years ago. Everyone in training was told about the meeting. There were two open lectures at the Hotel Ecuador, a few blocks from the University. He attended one of them."

Allison uses her communicator to contact Rudy then Dr. Kim von Throne, to get a line on this guy. After her short calls, Allison asks Marie, "Do you remember everybody you see?"

"No, but I remember him because he was particularly intense with everyone he spoke to. He seemed to be selective— trying to reach particular people with his 'point of view.'"

"We will find out who this guy is and keep him far from you."

"And you," Marie adds. "He's killing scientist, not Keepers."

"I should have told you sooner."

"I understand. Are there any more *surprises* from the past?"

"If so, they'll be a surprise to me as well."

Marie's PA texts: "Central Services delivered clothing, food, and two chairs."

As they walk, Marie asks, "Why would Jamison Ward be targeted?"

"He was close to developing a natural substance based medication to replace 5 of the best selling pharmaceuticals in the U.S. and Europe."

"So that would cause a revenue loss for the makers?"

"Yes, and they all operated outside of the parameters of 'The Plan.' Two have since gone bankrupt, and the other three merged into one.'"

"I thought with 'The Plan' all pharmaceuticals are collaborative for research and its innovations."

"International companies doing business in 'non-plan countries' are the exception. They can avoid losing their profitable products as long as the research is unfinished."

"So is the research dead, with Daddy?"

"On hold until our other crises are out of the way. When this is over, we'll be in a position to pick up where Jamison left off."

"Is it still needed?"

"More than ever. Two weeks after Jamison's death the price increased in three of the five medications. With no competitors, the prices are now triple. I asked Vivi about these companies. She said they are a major part of the problem that she and her team are tracking. All their medications are overpriced, so the makers of these products are getting profit from everyone who uses them. Since there are no generics or alternatives, they have patients over a barrel."

"So would competition in this arena be a positive thing?"

"No. Vivi says it would be disastrous putting us back on the slide to the so-called 'free market.' It would mean duplicating manufacturing facilities, inspections, distribution systems, thus keeping the prices from coming down. The whole problem with the free market of the past—none of it was free—and everything anyone bought carried extra costs of competition. Only the collapse of the economic justice system would put us back there. Of course, Bluefoot and his cronies are working to make that happen."

"Remember, I've only read about the free market. It sounds chaotic. One statistic I remember: 42% of every consumer dollar spent was the result of duplication, advertising, and regulatory oversight."

"Many companies succeeded at being 'competitive' through inferior products and quality. And, don't forget the wealthy stockholders who made money never contributing a thing to the actual product."

Forty-Eight
A Quiet Supper

The conversation stops as they reach Marie's. They admire the two new chairs deep blue chairs next to the dark red sofa. They stare for a long moment. Finally, Allison says, "All I can say is 'Wow.'"

Buyer's guilt is beginning to wash over Marie. "I feel selfish. Beautiful luxuries. The couch is enough. And I have 7 SOGS; three is all I *need*. It seems self-indulgent."

"You're always frugal. A few extra things are not extravagant. Not needing them you say? Aren't Doorkeepers expected to entertain? When you travel, you'll need all those Outer Garments."

"You're the 2nd person to say something about my traveling. I'm expecting to be here most of the time for years."

"Who was the other person?"

"Dr. Norris."

"I thought as much. Marie, you are the best. Why do you think they brought you to this sector? It's critical to what is happening in Wichita, and our research to save millions of lives. You will be invited to speak, teach as a guest lecturer, serve on screening committees, and probably much more. *You're a bright star*—the 'poster child' for Doorkeeper recruitment."

"What if I'm not up to it? What if I don't do the right thing?"

"Don't be silly. Be yourself—that compassionate, insightful, knowledgeable, self-effacing self."

They embrace, and as they do Allison whispers, "You don't understand how skilled you are, do you?"

"You're prejudiced. You love me."

"Dr. Norris isn't, nor are your instructors. They all say glowing things about your abilities."

"You read my transcript?"

"A guardian has access—you signed for me remember? After you said your TA role was shortened, I read your transcript. No seasoned Keeper with 20 years' experience would do better. Don't be afraid—be careful."

"Thanks, Mother, I needed that."

Taking a seat at her console, the chair squeaks. *I remember that sound. PA recorded it when Phillip opened the PA cabinet. Personal Services must've moved the chair putting it back different. Wait. One of the five legs is marked with a small blue dot. Squeak happens when the dot is pointed toward the console kneehole. So, when I figure out the clicking sounds, I can open the compartment.*

Two messages are waiting—one from Wessel: "Rudy asked me to check Phillip's SOGS. All are Doorkeeper's. I also checked pockets—nothing." The second message is from Records Assistant 186, suggesting lunch next week. A time and place are agreed upon.

Marie writes her report. *I'm becoming efficient at writing incident reports: from blank form to complete in 12 minutes.* Next, she sends the news gathering site an "item," noting how an alert citizen prevented an attempted abduction by calling the authorities. Others are also recognized for aiding the intended victim's resistance."

Marie greets Dr. Norris who brings a bottle of wine. Dr. Norris apparently changed into his most formal SOG: nearly solid black in front with three crescent-shaped one-inch wide stripes of the Doorkeeper colors on each sleeve. *What an elegant gentleman. Allison always appreciates the extra effort. I wonder if he remembers that from their history?*

"Before I become engrossed in this wonderful meal," begins Dr. Norris, "there is a matter of business to cover later. Marie, I need you to manage the transfer of our friends to the plane Monday."

Allison says, "I leave here Monday about 6:00 AM and go to the University Hospital. Can you cover my tracks, so no one is aware of that trip?"

After discussing several options, they decide Marie will utilize an out of service pod to take Allison to the Medical Center.

"The University staff will prepare Phillip for transport. They will put him on a transport van similar to a morgue unit. The van will pick up a pass at the transfer station on the southwest side. The pass allows direct entrance to the med-plane at the airport."

As Security Coordinator, Marie will monitor the entire trip using cameras, and satellite views. Both she and Rudy will oversee the flight once airborne.

"This leaves only one issue," says Dr. Norris. "We still need to get the visiting A. Fulbright back to the airport."

"We need to make it appear that she used her return ticket. The best way would be to put her on a flight that's already been completed, but then we must adjust the 'ticket' to confirm her arrival."

"I could do that, but I can't access the reservation system without leaving a trail."

"I can help." Abe Norris consults his communicator. "This is *top secret*. Head Supervisors possess the codes for all areas of society. The thinking is: if there's an attack or catastrophic failure in one system, other's can access essential information and pass it on. So an enemy attacking one sector would need to bring them all down simultaneously. The code list is at each center, in a safe place; but I travel so much I put them on my PCD." He writes down a nine-digit alphanumeric code and hands it to Marie.

"So every center can access this information?"

"Yes, but only the Head at each center has access. We can instruct other supervisors where to locate the information."

The planning is finished, along with a backup in case no flight completes during morning hours.

"One more thing," Marie adds, "should Auto-Door handle my routine work while doing the other?"

"Oh, glad you asked. You are on 'special assignment,' Monday morning, and part of the afternoon. That means a Supervisor covers your work. Kim Sam Rea likes you and will ask no questions."

"Thank you."

Dinner is one of Allison's salads: tuna, salmon, cod, and shark on a bed of spinach pineapple, mango, mandarin orange slices, and kiwi quarters. Dressed with yogurt dressing made with juices from the fruits plus lemon. "I usually use swordfish instead of shark, but Wessel couldn't find it on short notice."

They enjoy the meal with pleasant conversation. Abe Norris and Allison decide to take an evening stroll. It is 8:22. They are old friends who found little private time this week.

There might be a budding romance here. Why not, they deserve some pleasure in their lives.

My guest is out. I discovered a false bottom in the center desk drawer, just like the one I had in KC. In it is an envelope from Phillip. I'll read it before Allison leaves but not tonight. Tomorrow is a day off. We plan to explore several museums and the city.

By prior arrangement, she takes the bed; Allison will take the couch when returning. Marie asks her PA to wake her when her guest returns.

Marie is asleep in a minute. The PA wakes her slightly after 1:00 AM. Marie calls, "Good night, Mother" from the bedroom. Allison responds, "We enjoyed ourselves. Made some plans, will talk about them tomorrow and did not have sex."

"I wasn't *going* to ask. It's none of my business. You are both adults. I want to hear about your plans, but not now."

"Sleep well."

Thus ends Marie's first workweek as Doorkeeper. Tomorrow is a day off.

Forty-Nine
Phillip's Secrets

The Automated Personal Assistant is not to wake Marie until 7:00 am on Saturday. She is at her desk in the bedroom before 5:00. *I'll let Mother sleep. I can satisfy my curiosity about Phillip's letter. It's hand printed.*

If you are reading this, either I'm dead or incapacitated. If you work for Bluefoot, or his cronies and hope to find information here, you could not obtain while I lived—you are out of luck.

Assuming you are my successor I share information with you. Congratulations. Be extremely careful. Know the people you trust and listen to your inner voice. Err by saying too little, rather than too much. Despite the "Truthfulness at All Costs," command of your job there will be times when the situation will dictate what is true.

1. I prepared a will. My attorney is in Maryland. A Doorkeeper will be able to find my lawyer. Documents will only be given to specific individuals in person.

2. The will covers my patents, the distribution of funds derived from their production and use and distribution of my assets to non-profit groups.

3. The attorney possesses other documents relating to my particular duties as a Doorkeeper. These documents while non-essential will be helpful for the leaders of Door Services.

4. My successor no doubt is acquainted with my child. She is as near artificial intelligence as we humans dare attempt at this stage of our development as a species.

5. I sought to protect my child by making it nearly impossible for some ignorant one to access her. Only a Keeper will be able to gain access. Indeed only the most extraordinary Doorkeeper can find the key.

I leave no living family. So you, my friend and my "child" are all the family I can claim. I pray you will find it in your heart to forgive my mistakes. Of one thing I am sure. The future of all life on this planet depends on work I had some small part in moving forward. I regret burdening you with the task of completing the work.

Another thing I know. The structured states are critical to allowing all life to be productive. And you, my friend, will be responsible more *than any other person alive for seeing that those states remain viable.*

Best luck. May God protect you. May your friends be loyal; your training and wisdom sustain you.

Two unsigned handwritten pages with a smudge at the bottom. I'll deal with it later. Three more pages: all diagrams. The first I recognize ... sort of. It's something like the kitchen, but everything is off, out of shape. Upside down doesn't help. What about mirror image? Here's a mirror. Better. Apparently the kitchen: counters, sink, and outlines for the stored appliances. Appears to me some of the devices are missing from the diagram. I'll check that theory out after Mother awakens.

The second diagram is ... what? Maybe a closet? Tall, narrow, similar to the cabinets we used during electronics courses. Perhaps how the PA's area will appear.

The final page is a lot of symbols—seemingly random. Similar to a game we used to play. I bet this will overlay on a map or picture. Some progression of markings will make sense. When the two of us played, we would be given the overlay plus a clue like "we were looking at this last week after supper." Then I would need to find the picture or map and go to the last place in the progression to meet Mother. She did one when we were going to a movie, and I made some so we could meet at a museum or park.

If it's that kind of diagram, I'll need the key before interpreting. The key is in the PA's closet. Phillip would have protected it.

What am I overlooking? Only a Doorkeeper ... *I better reread it. Phillip misquoted the mantra. Not "Truthfulness at all costs;" but "Truthfulness at all times."*

Marie begins turning the letters into numbers. The incorrect statement comes out 183, 21, 25, and 76 totaling 305. The standard wording "Truthfulness at all times" produces 183, 21, 25, and 66 totaling 295. *Now I need a device to enter the numbers.*

Marie has a flash of inspiration. She decides to check out her hunch.

"Morning Friend."

"Good Morning Marie, you asked me not to wake you until 7:00 AM. Do you desire your morning briefing at this time?"

"Not yet." A question first, I asked about sounds you heard before Phillip installed or modified components in your circuits. Was anything omitted, like silences, when you played the sounds before?"

"Yes. You asked for sounds."

"Please play those sounds again for me, this time with the silences left in place."

"Acknowledged." The Personal Assistant plays the sounds. *The squeak made by the console chair. I'll time the silence. The first silence is 29 seconds, next a "click." 28 seconds more of silence followed by a second click. Then 19 seconds, followed by the third click and immediately the swooshing sound. 10 seconds more of silence then a faint humming sound. I missed the hum before.*

"Sound replay complete."

"I'm ready for the daily summary." Allison is up and leaning on the bedroom doorframe as the PA begins. Friend is unaware of Allison's presence while detailing hours and percentages of sleep, temperatures for the day, absence of storm warnings/watches and no job or responsibility changes.

"In work related news: Doorkeeper Head Supervisor issued a call for a significant presence at the Monday evening session. The focus is on changes to the overall plan for

Structured States. Any Keepers on duty will be released from work time to attend." The PA turns to international news: worsening food shortages in northern Africa and the international responses. *Still missing is any direct support from US strategic food supplies.*

"Local news contains numerous reports of angels and local citizens coming to the aid of a resident who was being threatened by a stranger. The stranger is in custody."

Allison says, "Despite the emergencies, I'm enjoying myself. I almost forgot how to laugh. It's a joy to see you doing your job so well."

"I'm glad you are up. Here is something you need to read." Handing her the two pages, Marie heads to the kitchen and soon locates the 'missing' appliances using the laser imager. *Two are missing: a bread maker and something I cannot identify.* First the bread machine—after a thorough examination she finds nothing out of the ordinary. The other object is spherical and sits in a holder similar to ones used to display a basketball in a trophy case. The sphere is 24 inches in diameter, containing no visible power source.

After reading the message, Allison asks, "Where did you get this?"

"In a false drawer like I had in KC along with another chip for an old style computer, and a few playing cards, not a whole deck."

"Only a Doorkeeper can access?"

"I'm trying to figure it out. I think I understand part of it, but I need more. We have three pages of diagrams: one is of this kitchen with at least two appliances missing. These two."

"What is that?" Allison indicates the strange object.

"I was hoping you could tell me."

"It resembles the 'Death Star' from the Star Wars movies we used to watch. The Death Star had a fatal flaw right along that groove."

Picking up the object Marie finds it heavier than expected. There is a little projection where Luke Skywalker dropped an explosive device. This one is a lever causing the sphere to separate into three pieces, two half spheres, and a center slice about an inch thick. Marie quickly perceives how to reassemble the object in a different shape. The inch thick disk is the base; the bottom is nearly smooth. The other side is concave with notches. *Ok, this half-sphere will nest comfortably.*

"As soon as I positioned this half, it locked into the base—held magnetically I think. Three lights came on inside this carved out sphere portion. I hope that is a positive sign. Now the other half-sphere should easily nest here."

When the lights match up with three small bulges on the outside of the remaining half sphere, it locks into place. The outer rim of the second half sphere is a perfect circle. Lights come on showing numbers and marks around the flat outer edge. It's 360-degrees with numbers every 10 degrees. There is a small curved lever connected to the bottom-center under some electronic circuits; the top of the lever almost reaches the outer rim with a pointer. When moved along the inside, the degree number or mark lights up brighter.

"Three clicks. I think I understand how to make the first two, but where is the third one?" Holding the diagram page at arm's length, she waits for inspiration. "There's a watermark on the paper."

She takes the pages to her console for a stronger light. The watermark is a number 2071. The other two pages reveal "February" and "Think."

"Think February 2071."

"What happened then that only Keepers know about?" asks Allison.

"Got it," Marie says. "They tried to use Auto-Door for all but emergencies. In the trial project, the automated system delivered a pod full of students with one professor to an unattended Agricultural Transfer Station outside the shelter in subzero temperatures. The key was the Door Student remembering the code to open the shelter door—Z50, or 26, 50. The third click?"

Allison is confused. Marie says, "It's easier to try it than explain."

After moving the console chair next to the cabinet housing the Personal Assistant electronics, Marie sits in it: they hear the squeak. With the strange instrument in her lap, she begins moving the pointer clockwise to 183 pausing for 2 seconds, counterclockwise to 21, clockwise to 25, counterclockwise to 76, and clockwise to 305. They hear a click, and the pointer moves back to "0." The next sequence is 183, 21, 25, 66, and 295. Click, and the lever swings back to 0. Now Marie enters the third series: 26 and 50. Nothing happens. *I left out the total.* She turns to 76; followed by a 2 seconds pause brings the click and a swooshing sound.

The exterior wall below the PA panel remains unchanged. But an 18 by 24-inch opening appears in the closet floor. On her hands and knees, Marie finds and removes a one-inch thick document with a blank cover plus a bound volume: a yearbook of University of California, Berkley 2048. Nothing else except a toggle switch hidden up under a ledge.

Marie flips the switch. A six-foot, by four-foot panel in the closet wall behind the PA controls, opens revealing a view similar to Phillip's second diagram. However, the electronic cabinets cannot be opened manually. There are no handles, latches, switches or locks. Nothing.

Back to the pages ... the 'smudge' is the only thing left.
Marie uses several lights and glasses to examine it before an ultraviolet light exposes an 18 digit alphanumeric code. Allison writes it down as Marie reads it off.

"So where do we enter this? I can't think of a way to turn it into a 360-degree code."

"Me either. Perhaps something in one of these books ..." Allison suggests. "This one is a yearbook from when Phillip finished his Ph. D. in Economics. In the back where fellow students enter notes here's one, in particular, saying 'you will make a great economist Phillip. But I'm off to law school. Please keep in touch. You are my best friend. I need your sober wisdom.' Signed, 'Sheryl.' The only class member with that name is Sheryl Tillison. My PCD found an S. Tillison, Attorney at Law in Baltimore. I think we've found Phillip's will."

"Excellent, I have an idea about this step." Marie looks at the piece that started as a sphere and now resembles two satellite dishes spooning. Only one amber light near the 360-degree mark remains visible. Marie touches the light, and the top half-sphere separates from the section below. The remaining piece now morphs into a familiar shape. Marie says, "'Only a Doorkeeper...' we have a portalock, I can enter the code." Marie enters the code from memory. With each digit, various colored lights flash on and off all around the device. The final entry turns off all lights. The base separates from the remaining half sphere. All three pieces are now inert oddly shaped pieces of art. The hum from the closet is barely audible.

Back in the closet, the floor opening has changed. *What I thought was a sealed opening has dropped 3 inches. There is a tray I can lift out using the handle that just appeared.*

When the container is removed, a much larger area is revealed. The first item is a large manila envelope tied with string. Marie gently places it on the floor outside the closet.

"Package!!" Allison shouts. Marie understands *this is part of the missing research.*

"Private Conversation."

"Someone is approaching your door. Private Conversation acknowledged," says the PA.

Marie begins to reassemble the closet. *No time to explore the rest of this opening.* As she replaces the package, her hand brushes against three business-sized envelopes taped to the side of the larger opening. She removes them. Replacing the pan to its original location starts everything closing up. *There must be a pressure switch where the tray sits.*

Marie and Allison are still in their sleepwear. Marie slips a SOG over her nightclothes and steps into her shoes. Allison closes the sleeper, grabs her clothes and goes to the bedroom.

Allison says, "Probably Vivi, I invited her to stop by this morning to finish our conversation." Marie slides the three sections of the sphere out of sight, opens the door to Vivi who jogs to the restroom. Only then does Marie realize the three letters are still in her hand.

"Oh, Marie, this must be your day off, I'm sorry."

"Don't be silly, we made plans, we need to be up anyway."

"But I could come later; I don't go in until one on Saturdays."

Marie places the envelopes on the kitchen counter and starts the coffee. She glances at the names on them:

Vivi

Wessel

My Successor

Should I give Vivi hers now or after the conversation? If the tables were reversed and Vivi had a message for me, I would want it now.

Allison reads the names as Vivi steps into the kitchen, for water. Marie hands Vivi hers. Recognition comes over Vivi's face when she sees the handwriting and clasps one hand over her mouth as tears well up. Marie says, "This was well hidden in the apartment, I found them only moments ago. I saw the names while you were occupied."

"There are others?"

"Yes. For Wessel and me."

Vivi accepts the envelope and turns it over, "It's not been tampered with." *Phillip used wax on the edges. All three appear unopened.*

Vivi staggers to a chair at the table and sits. Marie hands her a small letter-opener. Vivi opens hers handing the letter knife back. At her console, Marie slices her envelope. Allison brings water to each of the younger women as they become absorbed in their respective epistles. Neither answers a question about coffee. Allison prepares breakfast for the three of them, eggs, wheat toast, and pomegranate juice.

Vivi speaks first with tears in her eyes and voice, "That dear man. He wanted to be certain I didn't feel guilty about his disappearance. His letter astonishes me.

"He says, *'Don't blame yourself. The man in Chicago calling himself 'Andrews' (his real name is Cotton) works for Bluefoot. His interest was getting information about the network. No one you know is a problem, but they may be in danger. Never contact them again, and they will not contact you.*

'The plant, who I believe betrayed part of the network, is a person separated from you by two levels. He made no interception until the word came down: six packages remain. He betrayed

several members of the network, including me. He, or his handlers, raided the upper tracks, hoping to find packages. No luck, I was his last chance.

'Why didn't I protect myself? Call Security? Double lock my door? I thought about it. It all happened in less than 48 hours, so no time to try warning others. Besides, I might be "warning" someone who was already taken, giving the thugs more to go on. But I could protect those unknown to him. So I let myself be taken, believing they will get nothing from me.

'Now the future: you must be protected. Do not step in to replace me. First, I kept information from you, so you cannot take over. Second, by the time you read this everything should be done, well almost, and the network will close. Keep up the work you are doing. The Structured States must continue. Your work is essential to that task.

'I believe my successor will be female, young, whose name starts with M. If so, you two should become friends. You can trust her. You will need each other and likely will support each other in trying times.

'If my successor is anyone else, be guarded with that one and assume they read this note.'

"How could he know?"

Calling her mother over, to read over her shoulder Marie says, "I think mine gives some clues."

"He wrote, *'I have a strong feeling you are young, female, and your TA role was cut short for this position. If I'm wrong, the rest of this will not interest you.*

'If I'm right, you wonder how I know you. Faculty from other schools reviews all Door Service student work. Outside readers are sought to assist with those reviews. I encountered all your work. Understanding your capacity, and dedication I planted the idea that you take this sector. I expected you to be able to complete your TA year. Then I would return to Supervisor's role. But things moved too quickly.

'There are three people you can trust completely: A supervisor named Norris—Head Supervisor—sounds gruff. But you can depend on him. Second, the Head of Central Services: Wessel. He needs self-esteem built up at times, but is reliable and loyal. Third, is one of your doors, Vivi. You share the same values. I predict you will become friends.'

"It's like reading all my work he climbed inside my mind. He understood you well enough to predict we would hit it off."

"Phillip knew we would need each other but not how soon."

Part of Phillip's writing was skipped in the reading. It indicated Phillip had been a sperm donor for a "project. While waiting in Canada, he spent some time with a woman named Cranberry. She taught Phillip how to read "energy trails." That was how he found the traitor in the network, but too late to warn others.

At breakfast they talk about Phillip. Each expresses sadness at the loss.

Then the conversation turns back to how non-profits including research are funded. Non-profits include the arts, symphonies, museums, cultural centers, zoos, botanical gardens, religious organizations, relief efforts, and research. Support for such groups is encouraged. Individuals with income levels of three or higher are *expected* to give. Anyone at level five who fails to contribute at least the recommended portion to non-profits will be denied further increases.

Vivi credits President Earldrige with securing the financial foundation for non-profits. He said, "We eliminate *greed* by removing the profit motive, but we also must invigorate *generosity*. This nation became strong not primarily because of capitalism, democracy, industrialization or the technological revolution—though each played a role—our strength and greatness come from *people helping other people*. The faiths that drive us all call for compassion and love which comes alive through volunteering and giving."

Marie later summarizes in her journal what she learned about how research became a non-profit:

1. One proposal for The Plan was to make the government responsible for funding all research. Rejected – because elected non-scientists or their staffs would be passing judgment on activities they do not understand.

2. Initial agreement: government will contribute to research starting at 3% of all tax revenue decreasing

to 1% over a decade. All designed to ease the transition from business/grant-based models to volunteer contributions.

3. Government contribution to research never happened. Still, the federal government maintains a Research Oversight Board, ROB for short. When it functions, the goal is finding fault so they can "confiscate" the results they don't like.

4. Vivi is gathering evidence, but no definitive proof (yet) of government funds being channeled to for-profit research groups in Unstructured States.

5. Each non-profit sector has oversight/guidance committees (or boards) responsible for efficient management of resources. They have guidance boards for each sub-discipline—one for medical research, another for pharmacological, etc.

6. The financial sector also audits the use of funds, to prevent waste and to help determine how products or new knowledge may be integrated into the economy. Within research, a collaborative spirit exists.

7. An organization must be listed as a "recognized" NPO to receive contributions. Groups are removed from this list for mismanagement or outright fraud. No organization has been disqualified in the last two decades.

We talked about the "presentation" next Monday evening. Vivi indicated her group is being asked to keep a low profile. Vivi's boss does not want anyone from her department attending."

Dr. Norris will be speaking on behalf of Door Services. He will take them on. We need a proactive strategy, not merely reacting to what they bring up. We need to support Structured States and The Plan.

Allison said, "The Research Coordinating Council is addressing this. No strategy yet."

At 9:00 AM Vivi leaves to wake up her two nephews who live with her while in college. They have a field trip later today, and she goes to work at 1:00.

Allison and Marie decide to stay with their original plan: a day of museums. After10 minutes at the Native American Museum they both realize a man in his mid 60's is following them. Marie and Allison head down a hallway toward the restrooms and flatten themselves against the wall. In a few seconds, he rounds the corner. Allison grabs him from behind pinning his arms and puts him in a chokehold. Marie in her most menacing tone growls, "You get one sentence to tell us who you are and why you're following us before you take a nap."

"Uh, I'm Goshen, most folks call me 'Glub.' A fellow named Rudy called yesterday and said I should follow you two to be sure nothing happens to you."

Allison loosens her grip on the man and asks, "So *you're* our bodyguard?"

"I told Rudy I couldn't do this stuff, but he said it didn't matter; you two would spot the best. So he said 'if someone messes with you I should call him.'"

"Suppose we'd split up?"

"I should stay with the older one, and call him. He said if I made it 30 minutes before you spotted me, he would buy me a steak dinner."

"Well, we'll get you a ham sandwich for lunch."

"I tried hard. Will you tell me what gave me away?"

Marie and Allison glance at each other, communicating with their eyes to let him down gently. "Well...your SOG colors indicate a maintenance worker, and you are doing no maintenance."

"Secondly," adds Marie, "each time we glance in your direction, you turned away, but back again in a moment. We could see your reflection in the window."

They made arrangements for Glub to keep track of them adding, "If someone accosts us, you'll hear it. We would not go quietly."

"I believe that," he says rubbing his neck.

The rest of the day is uneventful. They have lunch at a corner deli and provide a sandwich for their guard.

They are back at Marie's at 4:35 PM. Both are proud of themselves for not changing their plans after the morning's discovery. Marie goes through the opening sequence again, removing the items from the tray, then the tray itself to get to the packages below. Allison uses a light designed to read "invisible ink" on envelopes or pages. She says, "This is from Central America. They found an herb showing promise." Marie pulls out a second package, not seen before, also in an envelope. Not as thick as the first, but quickly confirmed as the remaining data. The data collection is complete. Allison is ecstatic.

Marie is pleased for another reason; underneath the two documents is an older laptop. *Now I can read those memory chips.* Marie takes the laptop out; under it is a small thin "notebook." *This might contain instructions or codes for the laptop.*

Allison says, "I don't dare take these on the plane Monday. I will contact Rudy. May I use your laptop?"

"Of course."

Allison opens the laptop, plugs in the scrambler, sends codes, and soon Rudy's voice answers. "What's up friend?"

"First, how are things where you are?"

"Oh ... not bad. You remember the woman who wanted to see her boyfriend?"

"Yes."

"Well, she insisted she had to go, and her boss said, 'Go, and you're fired. Stay, and we'll see if you can be useful.'"

"What did she do?"

"She stayed and is sulking. Tried to get me to take her side. I said, 'Listen, sister, I haven't seen my girlfriend in years. You can wait a few more months.' She nearly had a coronary when I said *months*. Everyone's got her number now."

"You're *so* diplomatic."

"Of course, you rang madam?" Rudy says in an exaggerated British Butler's tone.

Allison responds in like manner, "Well, you remember those two pairs of shoes I so wanted to find. Seems they were here all along, don't you know. But the airlines are so unaccommodating about extra luggage. I simply can't bring them on the plane."

"Leave it to me, madam. Will they be a bother to your companion until I can make arrangements?"

"Oh, of course not, she is most gracious…."

"Very well, Madam. Well, if there is nothing else, I'll return to my duties."

"Nothing of note. There was this strange fellow, who said he needed a steak dinner. He settled for a ham sandwich—it is meat."

"I suspected as much. Was he a bother?"

"On the contrary, he was quite charming—when he could breathe, that is."

Rudy tries unsuccessfully to stifle a guffaw but manages, "Well, I'll let you get back to your fun."

"Thank you." They both sign off.

Marie realizes, *what appears a notebook is a map of part of Wichita. This must be the key for the diagram in the letter. I'll work this out later. Not critical for my limited time with Allison. How do I know* this *can wait?*

Marie responds, "Changing the subject; I need to tell Wessel about his note."

"We'll see him at supper."

"You invited him for dinner?"

"No, I made reservations through Wessel. He'll probably drop by."

"Ok, I'll take Wessel's with me. What time is our reservation?"

"Seven."

"Where?"

"I'm unsure of the address."

"The name of the restaurant?"

"The Prince's Feast."

Marie finds the address on her communicator.

"Map says it's about 10 minutes away. I'll order a pod for 6:45."

"There is so much I don't know about living in a city. How do you request a pod?"

"Just change or enter a routine. You had to do it when we were in apartments."

"I always had the Doorkeeper do it."

Marie steps to her console to use the larger screen. She shows Allison how to bring up daily routine and make transportation requests including time, destination and number of passengers. They also talk about how to prevent A. Fulbright from being scanned as Allison Ward.

Rudy has a system allowing him to assume other identities. I must ask him how he does that. It sounds like something I'll need. Now, why do I think that?

405

Fifty
A Celebration

Allison needs to check with her colleague at the Medical Center. Marie is ready for the evening having changed into her most festive SOG (one with a swirl pattern on the back).

There is some time, so I'll return to exploring the closet's contents

Marie opens the PA cabinet removing the older laptop. *What's this under the computer? More memory chips, same size, and color as the others. Thirteen all total. No markings, or ID of any sort, even with various scanning lights and glasses. Wait, some small bumps on top edge. Rises the size of an individual dot used to construct a Braille letter.*

Must put these in some order. So how are they identified? Standard left to right yields nothing useful—too much space at the front. The other way – right to left is more productive. Binary numbers. A dot indicates 1; a blank is zero.

Marie starts jotting down numbers for each one. *Some are missing and some high numbers: 41 being the highest. What can be the pattern? Of course—they are all prime numbers. Here's a possibility: 1, 2, 3, 5, 7, 11, 13, 17, 19, 23, 31, 37, and 41.*

Only eight chip ports are available on this style computer. So how do I deal with 13 chips? Phillip would use a pattern. Maybe this will work: put them in sequence, until there is a gap—like between 3 and 5. Skip the next number—5. That makes the distribution 1, 2, 3, 7, 13, 19, 31, and 41. Something will tell me when to use others.

When Marie connects the 8th chip; the screen fills with a list of "file names." *These names are strange: one to three words. They are portions of Doorkeeper mantras; however, one or more words are wrong. "A Doorkeeper is deliberate, diligent and discrete," is correct. But the word "definite" replaced "diligent" in these versions.*

Marie ponders other combinations until she finds six possible mantra phrases—each with a similar error. They would likely go unnoticed, except by a Doorkeeper. One phrase is a "general mantra:" "All work is dignified, and all workers are to be honored." By combining five file names in the right order, the phrase is error free.

Again the display changes, and she hears small motor sounds from the PA closet. The electronic cabinets that previously blocked access are moving up and to the right, leaving an open space in the center and left.

In the bottom of the electronics cabinet is another laptop—like this one. Also an outer garment, mostly black as a supervisor would wear. This must be what Phillip used to change identities. The SOG is open. I'll check the inside pockets. A sealed envelope with no name, a small folded piece of paper with what appears to be a hand-drawn map; on the back—letters separated by equal signs. I'll deal with those later, first the other computer.

Opening the laptop she finds three memory slots are already occupied. A quick check identifies their numbers: 51, 47, and 43 all prime numbers. Descending order. *So the remaining five must also be descending: 37 ... 23 ... 17 ... 11 ... now 5.* As the last connection is made, both screens light up with rapidly changing color backgrounds behind the word CONNECTING in large white letters. In 10 seconds the flashing stops and the first has a questionnaire.

Should I fill this out as Phillip? No, he wouldn't go through this process each time. This is for me. The computers are connected; each time I enter a letter the other's display changes color. It's drawing an outline. Most questions are standard: birth date, birthplace, schools what years and locations, etc. Some questions only I can answer: What time was your first Doorkeeper's Class? Who was the instructor? Name the members of your study group second term college.

More questions: Are you a Citizen of the United States? Yes. Any Other Country?" Wait a minute. Why do I think "No" might be wrong?

"Allison, could you come here a moment?"

Seeing two laptops on Marie's desk, Allison asks, "Where did those come from?"

"They were Phillip's in the closet hidey hole, along with a SOG Phillip used when taking on a different name. The machine is asking questions to determine my identity. I hesitated on one question. Not sure why."

"What is the question?"

"It asks about citizenship—U.S. and any other country. Yes to the first, but why am I hesitating about saying no to the second?"

Allison Ward covers her face with her hands. "Oh, Marie, I never told you. I forgot. We don't talk about it much. Lot's of people don't know but you should."

"Mother, you are rambling, is this another big secret?"

"Well … a secret, sort of … I just never thought to tell you…. OK, I forgot—you can forgive me can't you?"

"Probably, but what did you forget? Am I Russian or something?"

"No, you are not ... well yes, you sort of ... let me explain. You are a citizen of the U.S. Your biological mother was a U.S. citizen. You were born at Cyclops Institute. What I never told you is—Cyclops is a United Nations protectorate. Thirty-eight research centers worldwide are under the United Nations Cooperative Medical and Health Research Treaty of 2055. Anyone born within the boundaries of one of those centers is a UN citizen, and therefore all nations that are part of the United Nations. You own both US and UN passports. I'm sorry ... I should've told you." Allison's brow wrinkles as she watches intently for Marie's reaction.

"Well, I'll be damned. I always felt like being human was most important. But I really *am a global resident.* I sure hope I don't wake up in 10 minutes and discover this whole week is a dream and I'm expected to teach a class in an hour."

Allison laughs with tears in her eyes, "It's not a dream—I love you so much."

"I know." They embrace for a moment. Marie says, "So I answer 'Yes.'" Clicking the "yes" causes one computer to begin quickly changing numbers and symbols; the second device fills in a picture. After a half-minute, background flashing stops. The picture is Marie's Photo ID from Door Facilitation School. The other's screen has a message: "WELCOME Marie Cranton Ward."

A deep male voice speaks from the computer. "Hello, Marie. You are the one I expected to take my place. If you hear this, I'm incapacitated or dead. You reached the inner-most level of security. Only an extraordinary Doorkeeper could manage the levels of protection. Only *you* can answer the final questions.

"At your disposal is the most sophisticated Personal Assistant in the world. I say that with as much modesty as I can muster because I created her. I call her 'Babe' because she is my child. Someone overhearing me would think I'm a dirty old man, not a guy building a supercomputer in the closet. To verify who you are, these laptops and the Assistant tapped into your school, health and travel records. She can also monitor governmental activities, airline information, travel information for all flights as well as daily routines for *anyone*. Babe can use satellite, infrared, security cameras, and Door Service visual even in another country. You must function as a Security Coordinator to become familiar with the workings, and so it'll be unquestioned when others note you're using those systems.

"From the moment of your arrival, the PA has protected you. She looks for intruders, listens for your name or position used by anyone in electronic or media communication anywhere. Just as you can follow an individual with security cameras, this machine can follow and listen in on any person using your name.

"Babe will not bother you with details unless a threat exists. You can ask her at any time about threats. Her answer is guaranteed truthful *only* if you are alone.

"You may wonder if she is so sophisticated how did I get caught. Learning I had been pegged as a network organizer, with only 48 hours to prepare. They would obtain no information from me. Others were more vulnerable. Two people 'disappeared' before the enemy reached them. In an inside pocket of my extra SOG, you will find a note with code for the two I helped. The reverse side contains a list of those who 'got out' before they were 'removed.' The enemy got four plus me, but not the higher number some may assume due to the absences."
Marie hands the paper to Allison, as the recording continues.

"You are aware of two people I'll call A. & R. They can interpret the codes.

"The last two packages are in your possession. You helped facilitate two on your first day. One traveled with a student who left for Europe, packed in the wall of her trunk. The other one related to Vivi. I realized too late Vivi could not touch the one she got. I managed to get word to her to seek assistance. It must've worked, or you would not hear this. For these last two: A & R can handle them.

"You need to put your ID on the computer system and PA. Here is what you do: Choose a finger from your left hand; place an imprint of your finger on the last chip on the device with your picture. When you want access to the closet or floor safe, simply wave the finger in front of the keypad; key-in or speak your code. All will open. You can open one or the other by setting up different codes.

"You know about my will. You can find my attorney by looking at the yearbook in the floor safe. To receive the will, you need to go to that office and give the attorney the sealed envelope in the inside pocket of my 'spare SOG.' Take extra security. You must appear in person wearing that garment. How do you close and open the garment? In the bottom left inside pocket find two artificial 'thumbs.' They contain thumb microchips. When you use this SOG, you are C. F. Fields of 1111 Fielding Road, Wichita. Your birthdate is January 10, 2064. The C. F. stands for Carter Francis. You seem young to be a supervisor, but no one will dare question you as long as you act the role. You will likely be one soon enough.

"The welcome displays your full name. You may wonder if others can find the same connections. No. I had the advantage of knowing some things about you through your mothers. Previously mentioned is my acquaintance with the project. I learned only the initials HMP. The document in the top section of the floor safe is a history of all I put together about HMP. You will notice the pages are coded. Here is how you read them."

He goes on to give a detailed explanation of how to use the spherical object to create a device to decode the document. Also by using the "extra tools" found in the couch, a chip converter can be made. This allows conversion of data to be transferred to current devices. Included is a way the Personal Assistant can to be in touch with Marie anywhere.

"By now you may be wondering about your importance to the future. Remember the old saying 'Some are born to greatness; others have greatness thrust upon them.' In your case, both apply. You are discovering part of your capability—you possess what is essential to thrive in the role being thrust upon you. You will need to step forward and help make things happen. The Structured States are under attack. I never uncovered the identity of the one bankrolling and controlling Bluefoot. Greed is the primary motivation for breaking The Plan.

"I recently figured out what's behind the opposition to the research Cyclops and others. They don't want the research to *fail*; they only want it to be *delayed*. Suppose the pandemic starts before the vote in 2099. People turn their attention away from the issues of The Plan versus No Plan and will listen to the opposition's lies and dire predictions. If The Plan goes down, they take credit for the solution.

"Manipulating the economy is another strategy. The enemy hopes to leave the Structured States with heavy losses causing ultimate collapse. Then the 'free market' advocates will rush in saying 'We told you so' while stashing away big money in 'offshore accounts.' Sorry to lay one more thing on you—but you need to be able to speak authoritatively about Planned versus free-market economics, and why the latter will only fail again."

"I need to wrap up. You have friends and knowledge. All I finished and everything I'm still working on is yours—Babe will tell you how to open those files. You possess wisdom, compassion, and exceptional gifts—use them.

"Good luck Marie. May God bless and protect you."

The voice stops. Printed on one computer is the question: "What do you wish to do?"

Marie types, "Can I hear this message later?"

PA says, "Yes, ask for Phillip's welcome message."

"Friend, you heard everything?"

"Yes, you are now at the highest level of clearance with my systems and subsystems. Now I can show you my full capacity. Phillip warned me not to seem 'too advanced' over other Automated Personal Assistants until you cracked the codes."

"Are there any threats?"

"No immediate threats to your safety, your guests, or any of the other 217 people I now monitor as your close or connected associates."

"Define 'immediate.'"

"Strictly it means no threat is actively being planned that could impact you in 48 hours or less. At this moment there are no threats within a 5-day window. I currently project five days."

"Is there anything I should be aware of?"

"Phillip did not mention the 78 files on members of the immediate community, compiled over the last two years. They include Wessel and Security 1: two people you had questions about."

"You pick up on my concerns—how?"

"Tone of voice analysis."

"Rudy thinks Wessel is genuine and loyal. Is he right, or should I be concerned?"

"Nothing in Phillip's record indicates disloyalty. He will not betray you, the network, or what he knows of me."

"What does he understand about you?"

"Only that I'm 'enhanced' and no-one can reach my circuits without Phillip, or now you telling them how. He does not know you cracked the codes."

"Is it just me or is your voice lower and you used contractions?"

"When connected to the data on the 'laptop extensions' my vocalization drops one eighth an octave. Phillip referred to it as my serious voice. I use contraction when in this mode."

"I see. How do I close this up?"

"Close the laptops and replace them in their proper holding places. I do the rest. I suggest replacing the HMP book also."

"I would like to place some of my back-ups in here as well."

"They all belong to you now; add anything that will fit. You can open it anytime."

Friend adds, "By the way, I'm pleased to work with you. Your intelligence and persistence are assets in our fight against corruption. Phillip thought you would need two weeks to reach this point."

Codes for floor only and complete access are set. Once the laptops and books are in place, everything closes up.

Allison and Marie have only 10 minutes to process what they have learned before the pod arrives to take them to dinner. There are loose ends. Where are the network members who "disappeared?" At least, they *may* be safe. With this news, Rudy and his team can begin locating the survivors. They remain confused about Phillip's willingness to become the sacrifice to protect others. It's a lot to take in, but first dinner.

Allison could not keep the evening a complete secret. Marie is aware of reservations at an elegant restaurant, and that others will be joining them.

They arrive at the Prince's Feast at 6:57 PM. They are greeted by a young man Marie remembers, "Aren't you one of Maurice's assistants?"

"Oui Mademoiselle, we have additional duties in the evening. May I show you to your private dining room?"

"Thank you. Is it possible to get a glimpse of Maurice this evening."

"Oui, Mademoiselle, 'the hat' has arrived."

Marie turns to Allison, "You must see this chef's hat—it's amazing, and his cooking—well we've been eating the leftovers all week."

Allison says, "But this is a British restaurant, what's a French Chef doing here?"

"He is – as he says – 'slumming' this evening, Madame."

They know Maurice and Wessel are the same person, but pretending adds to the fun. They reach the room and the assistant flings open the door announcing, "You are the last to arrive."

On the left side of the room is a buffet table, with far too much food. At the far end of the table stands Maurice wearing his oversized chef's hat. The other side of the room is prepared for a party of six. Marie notices the same china and silverware used for her on Monday.

Standing at the end of the room is a cluster of three people. Marie immediately recognizes Dr. Norris and Vivi, but the third person is hidden from her view. Allison begins giggling uncontrollably at Maurice's outrageous hat, which looks to Marie even taller since he stands erect owing to a higher ceiling.

Maurice says, "You find zee presence of a French Chef at a British Restaurant amusing. I assure vou, I would not be here except for my concern for zee culinary health of the zee beautiful one, and her guests. Of course, the cuisine is most disgusting. It is not prepared in the approved French style. You should eat it since it's so much better than the 'American stuff.'" Maurice continues in his condescending manner to describe each dish and why the French version is superior. Finally, he asks them to"... serve yourselves. I vill carve the prime rib."

As they get in line, Marie finally sees the third person in the little cluster: Dr. Kim Von Throne. Marie's jaw drops.

"Close your mouth dear; we wouldn't anybody to think we choose someone who can't hold her liquor." Marie laughs saying, "I didn't think I would see you again for years. I'm honored."

"The pleasure is mine. I need to be here tomorrow so I came a few hours early. Happy to see you again."

They are served and begin eating. Maurice excuses himself saying, "I must return to French aromas before I become nauseous."

Dr. von Throne is unable to stay for the Monday evening session. However, she asks. "How did your PA find that announcement?"

"Phillip instructed her to search various news and information sites looking for keywords. She has the program in a subroutine, and is scouring the data 24/7."

"Can it be copied and installed in other places, *like my center*. We need awareness of these 'events' so we can respond. About a dozen have been held in the last few months."

Marie sends a message by communicator to Friend requesting a copy of the subroutine be prepared for Dr. Throne.

The Assistant replies by text: "The data sent to your third screen for downloading to a memory device may also be sent electronically to any location."

Dr. Throne gives an address, and the program is sent to her office. Marie will copy the program to a chip for Dr. Norris.

Wessel "arrives" apologizing for his tardiness. Marie gives him his envelope from Phillip, with a word of explanation. It was a pleasant evening. At almost 10:00 PM the evening concludes.

Back at 36 Jamison Court, PA indicates an audio message from Rudy. "I will personally pick up the shoes on Monday afternoon. Keep them until then. Details later."

Marie texts, "Message received."

Allison says, "Bet he's secured a plane."

While preparing for sleep, Marie reviews her week. *I'm truly grateful for all the help I've received this week. I need to resume practices that feed my spirit: journaling, worship and learning new things. My goal is to restore stability to my life—starting tomorrow with journaling then church.*

Fifty-One
Stability

After her daily "self-talk wake-up" ritual, Marie is out of bed, at her desk, computer open and ready to "Journal." Hers is organized into several sections; grouping related topics. After filling in some details in the "Events and Happenings" section, she stops.

This is not where my energy is taking me. What section do I need? I'll start a new one: "What I'm Learning About Myself."

The last week has been a smorgasbord of emotions: anxiety, relief, confusion, disbelief, and responsibility. After a half hour of reflection, she stops again.

I need another new section: "Questions and Ponderings."

Questions

Major question: How do I use and develop my "talents" without violating other's privacy? Ethics must be defined.

What else may I be able to do, or learn? How do I balance talents against what I learned in school? To keep

418

from needing to explain my different perceptions, I've altered reports. (Sound for PPSW emergency).

Another question: If other people find out what I can do—what might they try to force me do?

So who else "suspects" my talents?
Allison
Rudy
Phillip practiced energy trails with Berry.

Dr. Norris – how much does he know?

Dr. von Throne? Not sure. Allison and Dr. Throne are friends.

Bulla worked with HMP, present at my birth. She knows, but how much?

No one else? No one knew about Berry's pregnancy?

I trust them all.

We need to learn what Phillip recovered regarding records. Why was Berry attacked? Did the attacker know about a baby?

Another MAJOR question: why do people keep saying I'll make such a difference in the world? Berry even says I'll receive a Nobel Prize: for what? I'm not a scientist, engineer, artist or writer. If they give a prize for befuddlement, I'm in.

Marie reads through her new journal sections. *Typing my entries makes it easier to search and more legible to whomever I let read them. At the moment not even Allison can read my journal. I need to decide if that's wise—later not now.*

Marie adds details in "Events" and "Plans" sections. Adding more security. She notes the time: 5:30 AM. Quietly opening the bedroom door, she finds Allison is up, dressed, coffee in one hand—communicator in the other.

"Rudy is asking if he can stay here," Allison says.

"Of course."

"Can you get him an 'out of service pod' to pick him up at the airport. He's traveling under his name. Wants to keep his footprint as light as possible."

"Pods do not operate outside the shelter. What I can do is rent a car in my name, and leave it in the parking lot. In fact, we should rent one today and do some exploring before my evening shift."

"What about electronic locator signal on the car?"

"I'll turn it off."

"You can do that?"

"Sure, Rudy taught me years ago."

"OK, But how will Rudy get a key. Shouldn't leave it with an agent for pick up?"

"No. The key is electronic; it's put on your PCD. I'll send a copy when he's on the ground."

"How will you return from the Airport after leaving the car?"

"Take a shuttle. It'll drop me at a PIC line stop. They don't scan ID's on Shuttles, and my being on a PIC line is not a problem."

"Rudy says fine. He is supposed to be here at 2:20 PM Monday afternoon."

Allison and Marie eat a light breakfast. They chat like people without a care in the world.

"Friend" reports the news of the day. No major weather systems will impact the area until Wednesday. Chances of storms, high winds, and heavy rain are near 100% Thursday through Saturday. Marie is reminded, "The Activation Specialist will arrive Monday at 4:00 AM for reactivation. You are on Special Assignment Monday from 5:00 AM to Noon."

"Thank you." Thus begins a pleasant day.

Fifty-Two
Faith

President Earldrige said, "If our nation lacks greatness *today* it's because we ignored one or more of the [five foundational] pillars *yesterday*."

Central among The Plan's five foundational principles is *Faith*. It provides the backdrop necessary to keep the other four in balance.

The success of The Plan required *reweaving the fabric of society*. Community, Vigilance, Faith, Respect and the Common Good are the *fibers* of that fabric.

These concepts became the philosophical and emotional foundation for renewal. After being identified as the basis for renewal, they were discussed in the media, coffee shops, book clubs, the halls of Congress, state legislatures, places of learning and boardrooms. Every *cultural value* was examined in light of these five standards.

Refusing to allow others to define The Plan Earldrige took to the airways and electronic media. Dubbing his role "Teacher-in-Chief" he said, "When all five [principles] function, no room remains for greed, abuse, prejudice, or superiority. That's the culture we *want*; the society we *need*; and our real 'Manifest Destiny.'"

In the 50s and 60s, a resurgence in belief coincided with the public discussion of the Foundational Pillars. "Faith" is intentionally located at the center of the Five. Belief in one's *self*, *others*, human *decency* and a *creative spirit* strengthens commitment to Community, Vigilance, Respect and the Common Good.

Detractors bemoaned the absence of "Freedom" and "Liberty" from the list. Proponents responded: "Those terms are devoid of meaning from overuse and vagueness. *Freedom* has been used to justify stockpiling weapons, keeping others in economic slavery, and perpetuating injustice. Often those who insist on exercising their *liberties* do so at the physical, financial and emotional detriment of others.

More inclusive belief systems fueled the resurgence. In census records from 2060: 88% expressed a belief in "a higher being" (up from 40% in 2040). Most considered themselves "Spiritual-but-not-Religious."

"Spirit" is understood as the force (internal, external or both) driving us to make positive contributions while directing us away from selfishness, bigotry, envy, violence, and abuse.

Faith communities give people places to share their journey. What one *needs* for this stage of life's journey informs the type of supportive community sought. The "Gathered Experience" (often called worship) focuses on increasing understanding, compassion, ethics, and supporting one another. Many congregations draw from Judeo-Christian, Islamic, Hindu, Buddhist, Confucian, Native American, and other teachings. Believing all expressions of faithfulness come from the same originating Source opens one to insight regardless of its origin.

Interests in matters of the spirit were spurred on by scientific studies. One large study concluded meditation, prayer, and similar practices are as effective, often superior, to traditional medical/psychological approaches for many chronic situations. Science is beginning to learn about "energy flow" within and around living organisms. The mind's ability to shape, support, modify and heal our bodies is being researched. All world religious traditions have proclaimed similar awareness *for centuries.* So interest in and acceptance of religious principles continues to rise.

Vivi had invited Allison and Marie to "her church:" Wichita Protestant 186, which meets in the lobby of a counseling sector building. From Vivi's description, it seems like an appropriate group for them.

Checking the public listings, they find worship is Judeo-Christian also draws from other traditions. Resources include weekly Bible Study, Current Events Studies, fellowship, work projects and Spiritual Care.

The group's leader is seminary-trained and certified as a spiritual coach. He teaches philosophy and ethics in Secondary School and works 12 hours weekly for the congregation.

When the pod draws up to 36 Jamison, Marie and Allison are greeted by Vivi and four others on their way to the same place. Arriving 15 minutes before worship is to start, they find about 80 people gathered. An active discussion about an upcoming work project in Arkansas is taking place in one corner. The congregation is part of a network attempting to repair or build suitable housing for about 1500 folks including 500 children. The trip will be the last two weeks in September. Most will stay only a week, but some of the group will be there until the issues are resolved.

I'm reading energy trails. But this is different; these people are happy, confident, calm, and healthy. Perhaps having so many to read is leading me to another level—positive energy?

Vivi introduces Marie to Dr. Samuel, the Pastor. When he learns she is the new Doorkeeper for sector 86, he asks about Phillip. The official version is recited. He's not buying it but says nothing.

Marie asks, "How well did you know Phillip?"

"He was a regular. We would talk about the merits of the economic justice principles, and what we might be missing regarding support for the Common Good. He reminded me— it's my job, both as teacher and minister to emphasize what is best for all. I'll miss him. He kept me on my toes."

"All I hear about Phillip is complementary."

"Well, I've heard similar things about you. Apparently, you saved a young Security Officer's life and captured a brutal weapon."

"Yes, but another one lost his life. I thought the incident was not yet public. How did you learn about it?"

"It isn't public. I serve on a joint task force with the Security leaders, a coordination effort between Education and Security. The area Chief spoke highly of your actions in preventing collateral damage."

"Only trying to do my job."

Allison joins them. She had been in conversation with a couple of professors Vivi thought she might want to meet.

Marie introduces Allison to Dr. Samuel by saying, "This is A. Fulbright, my mother's best friend, visiting for a few days."

They shake hands. "Pleasure to meet you. Most people call me 'Pastor Sam,' we're a bit less formal."

"Well, in that case, it's Allison. A pleasure to be here."

"I see you are in science." nodding toward the dark red and two shades of gray on the front of Allison's Outer Garment

"Research."

"Anything interesting?"

"We are expecting some breakthroughs in the next few months."

Allison is giving more information than she realizes to this intelligent, connected man.

Marie says, "She's always expecting a breakthrough in the next few months—that keeps her plugging away."

Catching the hint Allison says, "Without a positive attitude we're stuck." The minister spots some other "new people" and excuses himself.

Allison and Marie exchange glances. The questioning expression drew a whispered comment from Marie. "He's more connected than one might guess."

The worship service is pleasant containing meditation and personal reflection. The music is mostly congregational singing plus a small band (drums, guitar, piano, and mandolin) and three singers provide two specials, heard regularly on the radio. The music is unknown to the visitors, but others resonate with the "sound." Liturgical prayers (from several traditions) are offered and "Thought Pieces" are designed to engage the mind.

The message comes from the Hebrew Scriptures: Micah 6:8 "… what does the Lord require of you but to do justice, and to love kindness, and to walk humbly with your God?" The Pastor points out "'Lord' can be translated whatever or whoever commands your ultimate loyalty and respect."

He suggests the three qualities are marks of a mature person showing commitments to the Common Good. Justice, love, and kindness produce positive benefits—including for the one who acts on behalf of others. Time is spent on "*walk humbly with your God.*" To be humble means not taking ourselves too seriously. "Also, remember, as you walk, take companions including whatever *calls* you to be a better person."

The discussion is opened for members to suggest ways to be more: just, loving, kind and humble. After several comments, one man sitting near the front added, "We must stop being complacent about our *benefits*. Our life is orderly and supports compassion for all. So we can mobilize our resources to address injustices largely because we are in a Structured State. But *a few* people in high places work every day to end this way of life. My relatives living in Unstructured States spend most of their time trying to make ends meet, or amassing wealth; leaving nothing for the weightier issues of life. It may sound selfish, but we must protect what we have. We need to watch for attempts to erode our orderly life—they are coming."

Another elderly woman asks, "Are you saying we should prevent other states from becoming structured, *so we can keep what is ours?*"

"No, I hope everyone joins The Plan—but powerful forces are trying to turn back history." Vivi, seated to Marie's right whispers, "That is Dr. Walter Derrick, he and his mate are professors in life sciences at the University. I introduced Allison to them while you were talking to the pastor."

At the end of the service, there are announcements including "Dr. Samuel will be away all September. The first half of the month he will be attending conferences for both his jobs; the remaining two weeks will be with the Arkansas work project. We are seeking volunteers to bring the message." Allison whispers to Marie, "You could do that." Marie responds, "Don't you *dare!*"

Reminders are given regarding study groups beginning in September or October. The final item concerns the meeting set for Monday evening with the Central Programmed States Updating Initiative. It's pointed out that Professor Derrick's earlier comment spoke to this situation. The group had been researched and found lacking any credibility either govern-mental or economic. Several university faculty members summarize the positions put forth by the "Updating Initiative." It's clear that most of those present plan to attend. Announcements conclude, and much informal discussion of the Monday Meeting ensues.

Catching the three women at the door, the minister attempts to persuade them to attend the presentation on Monday. All decline—for different reasons.

His buttonholing everyone causes me discomfort. A strong showing from the congregation will boost his status. He's ambitious—too ambitious. So do I return? Probably, he's an engaging speaker, shares his knowledge willingly, but harbors ambitions to be something else—maybe politics? Okay, I can be comfortable but cautious with him.

The women turn to the subject of a rental car. It's 10:33, and Marie is not due back at work until 4:00 PM. Vivi prompts, "So there is time for lunch? I know a quaint little restaurant about eight miles out of the shelter. They make excellent Gyros and salads."

"We had hoped to see the Flint Hills. Is the restaurant in that direction?"

"Yes, then it's settled."

They pick up a car on the east side of town at 10:50 and start driving northeast. While at the wheel, Marie reflects. *This is as "laid back" as I remember being. I'm with Mother and my new friend. What could be better?*

They reach the Gyro King Restaurant and find the food exquisite—especially the yogurt cucumber sauce. The scenery is beautiful. Many species of grass and wildflowers are still in bloom. Not a lot of green, because of the heat. The reduction of beef consumption means this reserve is seldom used for grazing.

The three women talk about flowers, politics, and Monday's meeting. They speak of travel, their favorite foods, and the calmness of the day. Shortly after 2:00 they turn back so that Marie will be home for her 4:00 PM shift.

The afternoon has been relaxing. A little work; time with Mother; another week starts. Next week is bound to be more normal—how can it not?

Fifty-Three
Phillip Tells More

After checking and correcting "Auto-Door" entries plus running a security sweep of the sector, Marie does a little reading. Allison is busy with calls regarding Dr. Robert Hildegard French, (Phillip's new identity). Dr. French, an astrophysicist who charts the movements of space objects, was in Wichita preparing for a year as a guest lecturer. He is being returned to Seattle because he lives near the city.

Dr. French's travels to other countries make fabricating his past simpler. Phillip's detailed work history allows Rudy and Allison to put together an electronic record for Dr. R. French. Bulla assists from the Seattle end by securing housing in his name. It's Bulla's "home" which she seldom uses, since she "lives" at Cyclops 95% of the time. Electronic documents create a paper trail indicating Dr. Robert French has been the mostly-absent owner for the last 12 years. The "paper trail," as it's still called, will hold up except under the closest scrutiny. Only someone looking for a renamed person would notice the inconsistencies. The people and computers "that count" believe Phillip died and was cremated.

Allison makes her calls; Marie works on some of the files Phillip created. After transferring the information to her laptop, Marie is ready to learn more of Phillip's secrets. The file labeled "Notes" is shortest, about 80 pages; the other named "Current Projects" contains more than 7300 pages according to the PA's estimates.

This file seems like gibberish. I'm beginning to understand how Phillip thought. Rather than adding layers of security at this point, Phillip wrote the file in a different computer language. No ... it's a trick Rudy taught me for sending messages before we had scramblers. Move each finger one key to the right and type as normal. I have a program to make this readable.

After a few keystrokes, the Notes file is intelligible. Two parts. The first is a journal about "packages."

Marie reads then notes the most important entries.

No contacts are named. Everyone is referenced by codes. The earliest entry is dated September 12, 2093.

"The network is making a final push, but interception attempts are constant. 11 packages remain. The western route is infiltrated. Only decoys are being sent through it.

"June 10: The East track is suspect, nothing going through.

"August 12: I may not live till morning. Four parcels arrived in the last 48 hours. I sent one through a friend to North 1, the other by an unorthodox method in luggage to a European contact. Both the remaining ones are in safe keeping until I survive or my replacement—probably M can make arrangements."

August 12 was his last entry. I'll copy all of those notes for Allison.

The second part of "Notes" is information about our nemesis. Berry said Bluefoot was not his real name. Perhaps Phillip unearthed the Senator's past. Marie reads silently.

James Jefferson Carver Bluefoot, his current name, did not exist before June 1, 2077. There is a paper trail leading to that date, but it is missing elements to create a stable history. I uncovered documents proving he was originally Carlos Veatos Rizzo, an Italian drug lord who attempted to enlarge his territory, becoming the target of assassination attempts. He faked his death in a June 10, 2073, explosion. His compound's 'safe house' was destroyed, and he was presumed to be in it. The bombing was, of course, blamed on a rival cartel. Rizzo was never heard from again. Four years later Bluefoot emerged from the shadows at age 49 complete with a history as an Import-Exporter residing in upper New York State. Those years were spent undergoing plastic surgery, and a complete identity makeover. Whoever pulled him out, set him up as a puppet so he could become the Senator most determined to undermine the 'Plan for the Future.' They are targeting the 2099 referendum in every state that will reaffirm, join, or remove each state from the "Structured Program Status."

Deciding to skim the remaining 50 pages of notes, Marie is brought up short by the phrase "genetic manipulation."

I obtained original documents from the 'Wallace/Ford/Remington Hearings' never released to the public or Congress. These documents prove beyond any doubt that the military used women without their consent or knowledge to produce a super race of soldiers.
Once the scandal broke, the organizers made plans to go deeper underground by using 'breeding sites' (their term for the women-mothers) in other countries. The children were taken to camps outside the countries of birth.

Phillip confirmed 200 babies had been born in 11 countries including Italy. "Women with specific genetic properties were identified, and the male counterpart was brought to them." Methods of impregnation included legal contracts, seduction, artificial insemination (with or without the woman's agreement) even rape.

I'll skip over the disgusting details. Apparently one male "engaged" nine women in Italy over a three-month period. It's possible that Carlos Rizzo is one of them.

A few pages later Phillip wrote:

Got it: the document connecting Rizzo with the military plan for super soldiers; that is the good news. The bad news: he is even more formidable than we thought. He possesses superior strength and is without emotion, compassion, or the *ability* to identify with anyone he hurts. He is also smart: he speaks five languages including English, Italian, and German like the natives. He needs less than four hours sleep per night and can survive in the desert heat in August without water or food except what he finds. He can live on roots, bugs, grass, getting moisture from leaves, dew, or even the animal dung. Apparently, his digestive track is more tolerant than 99% of the species.

In the end, Phillip indicated the person who had obtained these documents had been identified and was trying to escape with his life. Nothing from him since June 18, 2094.

At the end, a pop-up appears: "Daily Horoscope." It asks for name and birthdate.

Horoscope doesn't sound like an interest of Phillip's. I better check this out.

Typing Phillip's name and birthdate in a variety of formats produce only "ACCESS DENIED," messages.

Could it be set up for me? Marie Cranton Ward 08/06/2075. The page opens.

Please excuse the ruse. Horoscopes are not "my thing." All the documents I mentioned are safe. My attorney can access them. You will find my attorney—I left only one clue, but you will solve it. People died for these papers. Before you retrieve them, set up a place of safety. *Do not go alone.* You know a man who can help. Get his help and never be alone with the documents. People need these. You will determine who they are. The whole case against BF must be complete before any of this is exposed. He must be hit with a tsunami of facts, or he will beat the charges.

You cannot be too careful. If you have doubts about someone *don't* include them. Keep your circle small. Everyone in the circle is in danger, especially you. Be careful, be smart and stay alive. Sorry, I got you into this, but you are better equipped than anyone alive for this task. *You must succeed.* God be with you.

Feels like I've been hit in the gut with a brick. I can hardly breathe. It's overwhelming.

An avalanche. How do I stay ahead of it? Hold on! I've been here before; felt this way two days ago. I found a way to live with the expectations—take one issue, one problem, one step at a time. Maybe it works for this too.

I have a few more pieces of the puzzle; know a bit more about what must be done. I'm also reminded to seek help. I believe it'll be there—people, insight, energy reading, and talents I haven't discovered yet. What is happening to me? I'm usually calm. People expect that of me.

What just happened? An emotional meltdown started, but I stopped it. Mind and spirit are working together to keep me focused and reasonable.

Allison finishes her contacts, turns to find her daughter strangely introspective. Marie's vision appears unfocused, and she is still.

"Are you alright?"

"Yes. Some more unsettling responsibility has been laid on my shoulders and I started to 'fall apart;' as the other day. Somehow reason calmed me down. Perhaps I'm growing up."

Marie scrolls back to the top and passes Allison the computer. Allison reads and says, "Tomorrow evening Rudy will be here, will read this file, and help make plans. Abe will be here later. You and he will figure out the trip, and the protection you will need."

She takes an incoming call from Wessel.

"DK 86."

"Wessel here, announcing your chariot will pick you up from the theater at the west door number two at 7:30 PM. You should recognize your driver. You met last week."

"Thank you. I'll try to be on time."

"Anytime you want pizza, let me know."

"In fact, it's my regular Sunday evening meal. I'm about to order one. You're invited."

"May I bring a friend, and some drinks?"

"Of course. I prefer vegetarian with white sauce, do you insist on *pepperoni* on yours?"

"*No.* I saw a pepperoni growing in a field once. You don't want to eat that. I like ham or bacon, but I won't refuse anything you put in front of me."

"Ok, one with ham, pineapple, and black olives, and one regular."

They click off.

It's almost 6:00 PM. Pizzas are ordered. Allison puts salads together. Marie checks sector 86, using security cameras.

Guests start arriving about 6:20; pizzas a few minutes later. In addition to Marie and Allison at the table are Wessel and his mate, Dave, also known as Security 17, and Dr. Abraham Norris. Marie thinks about the "small circle" Phillip mentioned. *Any of these would fit into the circle. Dave and Wessel both have enough stresses and issues in their lives; I'll not add my secrets. Dr. Norris seems like a natural choice, as do Allison and Rudy. Abe Norris already knows about past packages, about some of the enhancements to friend, and new security Rudy put in place. He may suspect I'm HMP.*

Dave thanks Marie for her role in getting him aid when he was injured. Wessel adds, "And he wanted to get out of the house. He says I'm driving him crazy, but I'm always at work, so what's the problem?"

"You tend to *hover* anytime you're around."

Marie says, "Thanks for your comments. Trying to do my job. Returning the kindness shown me when I was running late."

The meal is relaxed and pleasant. Wessel brought drinks: Beer, Ginger Ale, and "… milk for the child among us."

Marie retorts, "It's legal to drink beer at 18, but I can't understand why anyone would want to—it's disgusting. The milk will be handy for my tapioca pudding if Central Services ever brings tapioca."

"I'm sorry, we're out. Few people *cook* tapioca—most like the instant. We will have some next week. I promise."

About 7:10 Wessel and Dave start to leave. Everyone says their farewells, and the two of them are away. By prior arrangement, Dr. Norris will monitor from Marie's console her comings and goings while leaving the rental car for Rudy's use tomorrow. Marie's Supervisor asks her for the out of shelter camera codes. He explains, "I assumed you'd be ready for tomorrow's task."

Marie provides the codes then changes into her least defining SOG, lots of yellow and minimal Keeper colors. She carries a travel bag lest she is spotted entering the airport without luggage. People in the workforce do not carry; the exception is when flying. Robots are available to carry checked luggage but most day travelers prefer a small carry-on with a few items.

This "carry-on" includes three small electronic items—from Rudy. Two are scanners: one to check for listening or tracking devices that might now be on the vehicle, the other checks for incendiary devices. *Can't be too careful. I may be the target of powerful and determined people with the ability to place such devices in the car. If I were gone, they might think they could find what Phillip left in the house.*

The car is parked less than a block away in a public parking area. There are spaces for five vehicles. Only one is occupied. Marie sets her PCD to transmit everything she says or hears to her console where Dr. Norris listens. Using both scanners as she approaches then walks around the car. Satisfied the vehicle is bug and bomb free she puts the scanners in her overnight bag, saying out loud, "Not a blip—clean except for standard tracker." Most vehicles are rental, so trackers are built in for the agents to track a car that goes missing or is involved in an accident.

The third item in her little bag is a small device to plug in under the dashboard. The purpose normally is to alter the tracking signal so only a particular service can locate the vehicle. For example, Central Services vehicles may not be tracked by anyone else. The one Rudy gave Marie however, has been modified to fool the tracking system in the car. Once plugged into the rental car, tracking will think the vehicle is still in the parking spot. When Rudy returns to this space tomorrow afternoon, he will remove the device, removing the record of the airport trip and return.

Marie's communicator indicates a text message.

Not-dozen is monitoring Security 1's communication. Jerkhead's Lieutenant told him 'watch the girl. We think Wessel is holding out.' Message back from S1 'my people are following her every move.' Be careful A

Marie sees a four-person pod from downtown headed west on 3rd Street. Marie erases the message and says, "Pod heading my direction. Would be good to know who's in it. I'm out of sight." Marie recited the codes to listen and follow a pod. It passes without slowing down.

Dr. Norris says, "The two occupants are mated and reside about two miles west. Here's their conversation as they reached and passed your location."

"A woman said, 'This is silly. The car hasn't moved. We could do this all night; then what?'

"The man replies, 'We must do this even if it *is* ridiculous.'

"'Yeah, but I need the toilet.'

"'So we'll go home, and then call another pod.'"

Supervisor says, "Both work for the census bureau. They have traveled up and down 3rd street since 1:30 PM."

Marie says, "I'll use a different route so that I won't pass them."

"Let's show them the sights of southern Wichita; I'll alter their pod's trip."

"Thanks."

Marie starts the car. *Don't mess with Doorkeepers. They know how to do stuff.*

Leaving the shelter requires driving into a "tube" capable of holding up to five vehicles. The tube is open on the shelter side, and there is a Central Services van waiting at the closed end. Marie says, "I think the van is the one I'll return in, but perhaps it should be checked?" The back end of the tube closes, and the front opens.

"Latisha is driving the van from Central Service." Marie slows a bit to give some space between them. On her way to the Airport, five vehicles going toward town pass. As she reaches each one, Dr. Norris indicates who is in the vehicle, and their destinations. None are suspicious. Unknown to Marie, he also checks the flight manifests to confirm their arrivals. Employees completing a shift are cross-checked against "routines" to assure Dr. Norris their trip is legitimate. Rudy tapping into the satellite system monitors a wider area for "anomalies."

Marie finds a parking space in the overnight parking. By using the sensor glasses, she finds a spot out of active camera view. With her bag in hand, Marie enters the airport terminal heading for the restroom. Emerges after an appropriate interval checking for active cameras while walking toward the exit. Her appearance is casual yet purposeful. While still a child, Rudy taught her how to disappear in plain sight. Well, anyone as attractive as Marie never becomes completely invisible. Casually meeting her in the airport, you would know *she* has an agenda, and *you* aren't on it.

At 7:31 Marie walks through the door. The van rounds the corner. Marie gets in the passenger side.

"Sorry I'm late, one of the robots had the wrong pallet. Not many people want to eat airplane repair parts."

"So robots make mistakes," Marie responds. The two women get reacquainted quickly. Latisha, filling in because of illnesses, is pleased to see Marie again. The trip back seems much faster. Marie is soon home.

Dr. Norris admits her. "When I sent the couple south they called using the phone in the pod. I intercepted and told them transportation had an automatic router fail, and we were correcting manually. They ended up at a Laundromat. They called again complaining about where they were, and I told them it was too congested around the theater where they wanted to go. So they said 'take us home.' I did, and they got out. They are now back in a different pod and heading toward your parking spot."

From the console speaker, they hear a male voice, "The car is gone. Now what?"

"I guess you better call him."

"What do we say? We lost her?"

"Maybe she just took it back to the rental place."

"It was signed out till Tuesday afternoon."

"So we call Security and let them find her."

"We can't involve the locals."

"Why not?"

"Because he *said* not… something about them all being under her spell."

"So what do you suggest 'Mr. brains of the operation?'"

"I say we tell him nothing. Pretend it didn't happen."

"What if he can access those cameras?"

"He wouldn't make us follow her if he had the cameras."

"Well, you have a point."

"If we call him and tell him we lost her, we'll end up owing him more. This was supposed to square us with him. We wait for the car to come back then follow her."

"What if it doesn't come back?"

"She is on duty tomorrow. She must come back."

"We are going to call in sick tomorrow aren't we?"

"We can't call in sick and be seen riding a pod up and down all day."

"What if we rent a car and park next to her, or where we can view those spots? At least one of us gets a little sleep while the other 'guards.'"

"That's a good idea. We can drive by her house every once in a while."

"We can't tell much from the outside, but it beats sitting and waiting. So when we reach downtown, we'll transfer to car rental." The pod became quiet now.

Allison says, "We gave their ID scans to Rudy. Their names are Barbie and Ken."

"You mean like the dolls?"

"Yes. Rudy found some info on them. It seems they were investing in some risky offshore companies. Some of their friends made a 'bundle.' It's illegal for government workers to make such investments. They lost their investment, and Security 1 heads a task force investigating such behavior. He caught them and some of their friends. Their friends all had made profits, so they paid a "fine." The 'dolls' could not pay, so Security 1 graciously lent them the money, on the condition they would perform some 'special work' and report only to him. They agreed, so here they are."

Dr. Norris says, "Another case of the corrupt corrupting others." The rest of the evening is much less stressful. They go over details for Monday and arrangements for a trip to Baltimore. At nine Marie is ready to turn in. Abe and Allison talk for a while. A little after midnight Allison comes to bed, and Marie takes the couch since she has "reactivation" the next morning at 4:00 AM.

Tomorrow starts a new week.

Fifty-Four
Nightmare

Marie begins sleep believing her life has become more orderly. The perception of "normality" evaporates during the night.

She wakes in a sweet and confused. *Wait ... where am I? Wichita on my couch ... Mother is here. It's only a frightening dream.*

In an instant, Allison is beside her. "You cried out, what happened?"

"A nightmare ... about tonight. The presentation was mostly lies; everything designed to sow doubt. In the comment time Mr. James Calhoun, Dr. Norris and Security 53 each tried countering their misinformation. But their answers were academic and factual. Suspicions of our leaders increased from the students and others. The organizers were dismissive and rude.

"Finally, they dropped the bombshell, 'Did you know a Wichita Security Officer died while following the orders of an inexperienced Doorkeeper? But of course, you didn't; you live in a *Controlled* State. Wake up before it's too late.'

"Everyone started shouting at once. It was chaos. Arrests were made for 'interfering with an investigation.' People, especially the students, were with the presenters.

"The dream feels like a warning."

After some discussion of options, it's decided that Marie will talk to Dr. Norris.

Using security cameras, she checks for unusual activity. Only the "doll family" parked near the space where Marie's rental had been.

A message to Rudy gives vehicle location in the airport parking lot and the suggestion that he park two blocks south.

He agrees.

Marie asks Allison, "Does that man ever sleep?"

"He varies his rest hours to be unpredictable. Another spy skill."

At 2:50 AM the Personal Assistant speaks. "Good Morning Marie, are you ready to begin the day? The Activation Specialist is due to arrive in 40 minutes."

"I slept on the couch so my guest could use the bed. How did you know I'm awake?"

"Your voice."

Of course, PA monitors the home and surrounding area while I sleep.

Marie says, "Yes, I'm up for the day. My houseguest will leave this morning, and another will arrive later."

"Noted. Would you like to receive your daily summary, information regarding the Central Program States Updating Initiative, or the unusual activity on your block during the night."

"Start with the 'unusual' occurrence."

"You instructed me to observe movements of individuals and vehicles on this and surrounding streets. The pole at the northeast corner had a repair robot climb leaving an object at the top. The cameras, lights, communication devices, and sensors on this poll were functioning appropriately before and after the climb. The permanent components were *not* examined."

"Do you have video?"

"Already sent to third screen."

"Thank you."

Marie and Allison view the arrival of a "Community Services" vehicle; a robot glides from the back and attaches itself to the pole. At the top in 10 seconds carrying a small box about one inch cubed and attaching it to the top with a metal band. Both objects are gunmetal gray: same as the pole. The climber remains while his handler on the ground tests something with a work-pad. Marie gets a good look at operator's face and prints his picture. After a slight adjustment to the angle of the box, the driver and machine are back in the vehicle. The whole process took less than two minutes. She takes another picture of the van's logo and identification number."

Allison says, "As a non-city dweller, I'm showing my ignorance but what is Community Services? Is this one of Wessel's vehicles?"

"Community Services are a counterpart to Central Service. Wessel's operation is sometimes called 'personal services.' They deal with anything people need to live, such as food, furniture, appliances, cleaning, and repairs. Community Services is responsible for everything outside the home: streets, sidewalks, the shelter and overall infrastructure. They are repairing the damage to the shelter from the explosion. We also have Regional Services: dealing with roads, railways, and air traffic between cities.

"Doorkeepers work very closely with Central Services. We also coordinate Transportation, which technically is under Community Services, but do little else with them."

"The cameras you access outside the homes are Security's?"

"Correct."

"Who else can access them?"

"I'm not sure. I need to find out."

While talking, Marie looks more closely at the box on the top of the pole. *It's a camera aimed at my front door.*

She says, "Someone wants to see who is coming and going here; likely somebody *without* security camera access. I can get details anytime someone uses a permanent camera."

Marie checks the other utility poles in Sector 86 and the adjacent sectors. None have additional cameras. She sends Rudy, and Security 23, a message containing the pictures. "PA recorded the encounter. A Fulbright will depart through a vacant house."

So I must get Allison across the courtyard without attracting attention. Problem: adults do not carry. Mother's luggage needs to be handled by a robot. I don't have one. One of the three construction robots are at 91 2nd Street will do. So ... I need an activation code from Wessel.

Marie contacts Central Services.

"Central Services, this is Gloria."

"Don't you ever sleep?"

"Hello Marie, I take the midnight shift twice a week, and you are the only one who calls at this hour."

"Sorry, I don't mean to be a pest, but I need to borrow a robot for a couple of hours."

"How soon do you need it?"

"Now. There is one at 91 2nd Street. The operation code is all I need. Will I need to talk to Wessel?"

"Wessel *does* sleep, and it's much better for everyone when he gets his 'beauty rest.' I'll find what you need."

She gives Marie the numbers for operation. Marie promises, "He will be back about 6:00 AM."

Gloria says, "Workmen are not due until 9:00 AM to finish up." Both say 'thanks' and click off.

In two minutes the machine is activated and out the door. In another four minutes, it's at the door of 37 Iris, and Marie brings it inside, out the back door, and across the courtyard to Marie's back door. Allison opens the sliding door in the bedroom. It is parked in a corner until needed.

A message from Rudy.

The 'workman' is a low-level thug Cotton uses for simple electronic tasks. Too bad there is no trans-sprectro-analizer 15.

The last is Rudy's way of suggesting using the spectro-analyzer he left with Marie. The longer name, misspelling, and number are to confuse whoever might be reading the message.

With 10 minutes before needing to prepare for 'reactivation,' Marie plugs the tool into the console camera function. In seconds she obtains the exact frequency of the transmission for the spy camera. Satellite scanning locates the receiver about four miles away. Marie relays this information to Rudy and Security 23.

Marie heads for her shower, instructing her PA to admit Rowena when she arrives.

Rowena enters just as Marie completes the chem-shower routine, dry and robed. *I plan to practice reading the emotional spikes of those I encounter at least twice daily. I'll set aside my dream and stick to my practice plan. Rowena's nearly a stranger: a fruitful practice subject.*

Following protocol, Marie removes her robe and stands facing the Activation Closet. *Rowena experiences an immediate spike in emotions. What is the emotion? Is it lust? That can't be right. I must be misreading something.... No, she is physically attracted to me.*

The scanner is being guided less than a half inch away from my skin. Across my shoulders, back, waist, hips, and legs.

Rowena asks, "Did you experienced any redness, itching or bleeding from any of the 'activation sites'?

"None."

"Did you wear the portable device a lot?"

"Most of the time. My console was not signaling properly."

"Must be the cause. So far you are 100% take. Extremely rare from a first Activation."

Rowena scans Marie's arms (held out to each side) and her sides from armpit to thigh. She hands Marie a filmy garment designed much like a gee-string. Marie steps into it.

Being naked is not a problem for me, but it is for her. She's uncomfortable, so I'm feeling embarrassed.

"Please turn around, Marie."

I'll not look in her face. Another huge spike in emotions. She is standing still, holding her breath.... She's breathing now ... probably 20-seconds.

Scanning from neckline through the topside of her breasts takes about 15 seconds. Rowena says, "I must lift each breast slightly to examine the underside without the probe touching you. I'll be gentle and quick, okay?"

"Of course."

Rowena is wearing soft cotton gloves to prevent skin-to-skin contact. She is working quickly, including the abdomen and front of my thighs. She checks data on a work pad and hands me my robe while looking away. Rowena checks supervisor's cameras, before speaking.

"Marie, you are 100% activated. Meaning I'll not return for 30-days. So I'll see you one month from today. Please keep the garment and put it on next time before I arrive."

Pausing for a moment, looking at the floor in front of Marie's feet she adds, "I could lose my career for saying this. You are beautiful, and I'm in a committed relationship, but I would start an affair with you in a heartbeat. If you are ever interested, tell me."

She glances up at me fearing she will find outrage on my face.

"I'm flattered, but to be honest, I'm so confused about *my* sexuality I dare not begin any relationship. I'm seeing a counselor. Once I understand some things about myself, I'll tell you. Please, don't expect quick results."

"Fair enough. We don't need to speak of this again. My offer is out of line. Thanks for understanding."

Marie smiles saying, "You picked up an extra 45 minutes, so maybe you can spend them with your mate?"

"I would love to, but unfortunately she has an early meeting, and left before I did."

It's 4:15 AM.

Friend gives the regular report of weather (hot) winds (moderate), and the possibility of a rainstorm Tuesday afternoon. Some vents will be opened to allow rain inside the shelter. This occurs when no severe weather or high winds are expected. Transportation and Doorkeepers have additional duties during an "Open Shelter Rain" including tracking flooding in low-lying areas and checking all exterior electrical circuits.

Friend made an appointment with Dr. Kildare for Marie's annual medical checkup: Friday at 10:00 AM.

Marie says, "I could get used to having an intelligent machine doing research and making appointments for me."

"Me too," says Allison. "Don't you think a Nobel Prize winner should receive a Personal Assistant?"

449

"I think one should come with the award. After only a week I can't imagine my life without her."

"As soon as you learn how to duplicate her capabilities tell me. She could save a lot of time, particularly if we must battle Jerkhead and his allies."

To both women's surprise, the Personal Assistant joined the conversation, "There are no Personal Assistants *like* me."

Marie says, "You are a prototype: one of a kind. But eventually, we'll produce something similar to you for Doorkeeper's so why not for medical researchers?"

"Of course, I wanted to save A Fulbright the disappointment of dealing with a lesser model."

"Understood."

Mother and daughter continue their conversation. "I've loved having you with me," says Marie.

"Glad to see your home and work. Our research data is safe, and we have a fighting chance of heading off the disaster. Thanks to you."

"And my predecessor."

"He played a hand, but the responsibility was yours, and you performed."

"Help our friend. He deserves better."

"Agreed. Michael is the best … my colleague who will care for him."

They chat about the people they met and the "new angel" they recruited. About Cranberry, her letter, energy trails and they speculate about Phillip's documents.

Marie says, "This morning it 'hit me,' *I may have a brother, sister and other siblings.* Wouldn't you like to know what happened to them?"

"If it's possible Rudy will find them. He has more pressing issues at the moment."

"Oh, I'm in no rush. I'm still getting used to the idea there may be 'another' related to me."

At 5:30 Allison announces, "Time to go." The out of service pod is due at 5:35 at the vacant house across the courtyard. The robot carries her luggage. They hug. Allison promises to text when back at Cyclops. Both say, "See you soon." *Something tells me we will be together much earlier than either of us can predict. No idea why.*

The plan is Allison's *only contacted* if a problem appears. There are none. The trip to the University hospital proceeds without a hitch. From the Medical Center to the Airport, also without issue.

Rudy had "vetted" the pilots and the aircraft to make certain neither is a "ringer." Using infrared and magnetic resolve, Marie scans the plane for hidden devices or increased density of the shell. Tires, fuel tanks, the gurney containing the patient, the two nurses accompanying them, all equipment, even Allison are scanned. There is nothing out of place for this flight.

The Medical Air Jet takes off on time. Marie uses the satellite imagery and technology to follow the flight all the way to Seattle. She will do the same for Rudy's plane when he leaves for Wichita in less than an hour. Rudy will change planes in Denver arriving in Wichita about 3:00 PM.

Marie returns the robot to its proper location, and sends a private message to Dr. Norris "Please call at your convenience." Vivi is at the door, and her communicator sounds. She answers the call and admits Vivi.

"This is Marie."

"You rang?"

"Wanted to share our friends are airborne."

"Any trouble?" Vivi is leaning in close to hear.

451

"No trouble. I'm reaffirming my decision not to attend tonight."

"Why?"

"I had a nightmare about tonight. One of the three makes accusations about an officer being killed while following the orders of 'an inexperienced Doorkeeper.' It became chaos. We were losing the students. *Their* goal is sowing doubt among the students. I think I should stay away."

"Don't let your anxiety which manifest itself as a dream keep you away."

"You don't understand. *I never dream.* Of course, I dream, but I don't remember them when I awake. The exception is when bad things are happening. I've remembered three dreams in my life. One, the night my father died. Another, the day a fellow student was killed in a skiing accident and this one.

"I don't want to mess everything up. My absence should preclude bringing up the death of a Security Officer."

"Well, the incident is not public. How would they know?"

"In my dream, Security 53 arrests the one who breaks the news. Everyone was shouting. It was horrible."

"Trust your instincts." After more conversation, Dr. Norris arranges for Marie to text him anything that might be helpful for the defenders in the room.

Marie and Vivi talk as Marie watches over the plane. Vivi is unaware Allison is on a medical plane with Phillip. Marie tells Vivi about the unauthorized camera pointed at her front door. Vivi and several other joggers enter and leave by the front door. The watching camera observes the activity.

Security 23 calls Marie. "The camera signal ends in a van with recording equipment. Everything is being recorded but is unattended. I'm setting up an 'arresting robot."

"A what?"

"An arresting robot monitors the van and signals me when someone enters. If they try to leave before I arrive, the robot detains them. Coiling wire around them and attaching to a magnetized robot arm does the trick. It can hold someone for 20 minutes. Anyway, we will discover who is behind this."

"We can guess."

"Yes, but we need proof."

"Thanks for the info. Anything else?"

"Not at the moment." They disconnect.

Marie monitors Allison's plane until it lands. Rudy is on the way to Denver. Both are without incident. From Denver Rudy messages "All is well."

Marie eliminates A Fulbright's reservation on the afternoon flight by moving it to a flight completed earlier the same day.

The flight from Denver lands ahead of schedule. With only carry-on luggage, Rudy gets to the rental car and texts Marie, "found the 'roller-skate.'" Marie sends the key from her PCD. *I'll hear from him when he is ready to enter the vacant house. Need to update Dr. Norris again. I can return to regular duty.*

Dr. Norris replies, "Auto-Door is handling, for now, pick up at five."

At 3:10 PM. Marie receives a message from Allison, "The book is in the library." *Dr. Robert Hildegard French is now under medical care in Seattle.*

Marie asks Friend for a report on Ken and Barbie. Because they are in a rented car, the PA has been tracking their movements all day. *They've gone up and down 3rd Street rarely venturing to their home for food or rest stops, and only once passed 36 Jasmine. I feel a bit sorry for them expending all this futile effort. Their body language says they are not "happy campers."*

Rudy arrives, using the vacant house.

The console signals an outside call from Security 23, Fenton J.

Dr. Norris steps up to her front door. Marie admits Dr. Norris and answers the call.

"We know who's watching your front door."

"There are two others here who would be interested in what you have learned."

"I'll come over so we can talk in person."

"Want to use the vacant home at 37 Iris?"

"Not necessary. Rudy taught me how to do a 'cover shot' so we can come and go without being detected. I'll give you the set-up."

This home will soon be the scene of another planning summit. Need to "rustle up" some food. High-level decisions always make us hungry. I may be short on food since my regular supply is not due until tomorrow. We can always do pizza or oriental. Let's see what I can find.

Fifty-Five
Showdown

Marie assembles the makings of a self-service snack supper on the kitchen counter. Guests will be invited to help themselves.

Fenton J, Security 23, arrives and is formally greeted. Similar greetings are extended her other two guests. Fenton says, "I've been here so often it feels like I'm no longer a 'guest.'"

Rudy responds, "Well, I like it. Until greeted I'm never sure whether she wants me around or I'm merely tolerated." Everyone laughs, Marie the longest. "Thanks, Rudy, I needed to laugh. Things were getting too serious."

What a change of intensity of emotion that comment made. This is one of my practice times for energy reading. But only an hour, I want to be able to turn it off.

Fenton J starts, "We know who set up the camera to spy on this address. C Crystal arrived today with the other two leading tonight's session. After leaving their *private jet,* he went directly to the van attempting to retrieve the recording. We had a chat.

"He admitted he came to retrieve the chip. He's to check again before leaving tomorrow giving them to a courier bound for Cotton, Bluefoot's right-hand man.

"I created a visual loop, to prevent identification of anyone we don't want them to know about." Fenton gives each of them the activation sequence. So far the camera recorded the arrival and departure of Rowena here for sixteen minutes and eleven joggers each staying six to ten minutes.

"Speaking of spies ..." Marie reports on the activities of Barbie and Ken. The Automated Personal Assistant provided a chart of all their movements from the times since they picked up the rental car. Friend is also monitoring their conversations and changes made in their daily routine to cover their illicit activities.

Rudy reports, "The three people who will 'lead the session' tonight are Charles Crystal, Doug Burner, and Franklin Favor; employees of Grog Foundation. I have dossiers on each of them. None of their histories go back more than a dozen years when their 'current identities' were created. None are wearing SOGS."

Dr. Norris adds, "They will say wearing Smart Garments makes us easier to track. Dr. Throne provided transcripts of two similar presentations from other locations. They claim to be part of a task force reviewing the conditions in the "Programmed States," the pejorative term they use to describe "Full-Plan-States." Then they will make recommendations for the 'new law' after the referendum. Then they say 'let's tell you what we've learned from other places.' This allows them to present their agenda making it sound like *others* raised these points.

"We found only students and faculty attended those presentations. In the 'forum' part no one questioned the credibility or authority of the presenters. Few of their inaccurate facts were challenged. So they may be surprised tonight; I count, about 200 community folk attending."

They talk about Marie's concerns. Laying out her dream in some detail, they come to agree that Marie's absence seems wise.

Marie addresses her supervisor, "If I were to go, I would address the university population. I think I can pull them back to reality. I'm willing to come if we start losing them."

He responds, "Your earlier decision not to attend seems prudent. How can they accuse you if you are absent?"

"Perhaps a broad generalization like, 'If doorkeepers are so great why was a Security Officer killed here last week following a DKs instructions?'"

Fenton J says, "Anyone saying that *will* be arrested."

"The youth will buy into their cover-up theory even more. I don't want the accusation to happen, but if it does, I can't leave it to others to respond."

After more pondering, Norris says, "Suppose we leave it like this—if they accuse, *then* you speak. I think you're right about your reaching the younger listeners. Be careful not to reveal anything contained in the reports."

Rudy asks, "How long before the reports will be out?"

"We are working on the addendums and recommendations. All such reports are due on the last day of the month of the event. One week from tomorrow. We'll be done before then."

Rudy says, "Suppose I stay with her. If it goes badly, I'll get her there in 11 minutes, and provide protection."

All agree. It's a plan.

They are agreeing, thinking it won't be necessary. But it will.

A message comes from Allison that Marie puts through the scrambler and reads aloud. "I'm back at C. headquarters. My friend indicates new research in this type of injury. We may see significant results in about a month. Keep you posted."

Marie responds, "Message received. Sharing with R, A, and 23."

Ready for the evening their attention turns to Marie's need to go to Baltimore for Phillip's documents. They listen to Phillip's audio message on the computer.

"How soon do we need to do this?" Rudy asks.

Norris responds, "The sooner, the better. The trip will be a 'special assignment.'"

"What's on for this week Marie?" asks Rudy.

She pulls up her routine. "Lunch tomorrow, with the Records Assistant who accessed Phillip's Records. Might learn something."

"You should keep the lunch date," says Dr. Norris.

"Annual check-up on Friday and therapy on Saturday."

"So we have about two and one-half days. Rudy, can you be back Tuesday at noon?"

"Yes. Barely."

"Should we use public air, or let Rudy arrange something?"

Security 23 says, "Baltimore is at a high check level. Marie might be scanned while in the city. If there's no record of her arrival, a red flag goes up. Public flight seems best."

After weighing the options, it's decided that Marie will travel as C. F. Fields." Rudy has researched and found a significant history for Dr. Fields. Nothing in the record raises questions.

Flight is arranged for her leaving Tuesday afternoon, arriving in Baltimore about Midnight. Fenton will join them Wednesday morning, bringing a makeup artist for Marie.

When checking about funds to pay for the trip, without raising a red flag—someone else paying for CF Field's expenses the PA is asked, "Does CF Fields have money?"

Friend responds, "Yes, CF is one of the owners of the three manufacturing facilities he started."

"What?" Everyone asks in unison.

"The liquid lava counters, electronic storage and delivery, and the laser imaging system. Manufactured separately but sold as 'compact kitchens.' Dr. Fields maintains a controlling percent. His return on investment is slightly more than a level 7 income. Dr. Fields is an "Option 2" participant in the economy."

Now Marie is confused. "What' does that mean?"

Rudy says, "Finally a question I can answer. We are all Option 1 people. Ninety-eight percent are Option 1: seven levels of income moving up the scale for merit and longevity, down for incompetence, retraining or retirement. Some people, however, invent something and take the risk of developing it to a marketable product. They usually need financial backers. Many of those investors come from outside our economy even other countries. They receive a percentage of profit based on the size of their contribution to the start-up costs.

"I thought no company made a profit from their production."

"If the economy accepts the project, it absorbs the cost of building the plants and developing the manufacturing process. No profit is realized, only a return of original costs. But when the economy makes no direct contribution to development and production the company can make a profit for ten years. During that time they must repay the investors including some interest. A reduced profit is allowed for another five years.

"If you believe the product is going to take off, you have a choice. Stay within the economy, or option two—perhaps making more. When President Earldrige financed the Smart Outer Garments, he chose to stay with option 1—so the cost of SOGS came down quickly. Our friend CF took her chances. So there will be money for her only if the products sell. Franklin A does the same thing."

"So someone *can* become wealthy in a structured state?"

"Not likely. CF can only use up to level 7—the rest must be reinvested, given to a recognized non-profit or accumulated."

"Seems like a lot of risks. What's the advantage of the second option?"

"Speed. There is a three-or-more-year backlog of requests for new products/projects under option 1. In option 2 the product is out faster, and you maintain creative control. It also encourages investments from outside—leaving economy funds for other projects."

"Thanks."

Seems I'll be going to Baltimore tomorrow. I should pack, but I own no luggage. All my things arrived in "transport cartons."

Marie says, "I'll need some luggage. Should I use my ID, or C.F. Field's?"

Fenton says, "Luggage is one of the few things where ID can be changed. People pass luggage down to children or give it to strangers when they obtain different, so the ID strip is relatively easy to change."

After checking the in-stock listing, Marie finds a medium and small case: dark red and black. She calls explaining to Wessel what she needs.

Wessel says, "Dr. Field's ID is on file. I'll deliver the items personally on the way to the 'ambush.'"

"Thanks."

Everyone snacks. Preparing for her shift Marie checks Auto-Door and is "studying up" on the Grog Foundation.

All her company except Rudy depart. Wessel stops by with her luggage. Marie says, "I'll be taking a trip tomorrow. So what about food for the next week, since I expect to be gone most of the week?"

"We'll send the standard allotment, and adjust the following week."

"There is much I took for granted while in school. Now I must think about food, packing, luggage and whatever."

"Welcome to adulthood."

"I'm not complaining. Things keep surprising me."

At 8:50 Dr. Norris contacts Marie, "The hall is filling up rapidly. It holds about 500 people. I expect it to be full by the time the session starts at 9:00."

At one minute after nine, three men take their places seated at a table on the stage.

The leader, Crystal, introduces himself as Harry James, and his two colleagues as Virgil Wise, and Sidney Cast, all false names. They're not wearing SOGS; less obvious with them seated at a table.

"James" welcomes everyone saying how "pleased" he is with the turnout. Dr. Wise is requested to outline the "methodology" being employed to gather data from a "vast cross-section of America."

"Dr. Wise" basically says we are holding meetings to listen to your concerns and take notes on everything said. We plan to return in a few months to outline the "new plan."

Next Sidney Cast, who is now "Professor Cast," is called on to explain the "philosophical issues" which the Update Initiative addresses. Cast "explains" while The Plan proposes many good intentions, and has "… in fact alleviated numerous *marginal* societal problems… unfortunately, it produced some *unintended* consequences, which must be rectified."

He identified the consequences as including but not limited to: stifling of creativity; removing the incentive to challenge the status quo; increasing dependence on government; diminishing perception of personal accomplishment and satisfaction; removing the sense of responsibility; and turning the *economy* into an all-powerful force ultimately controlling our lives.

He adds, "Communism made similar mistakes. This is our opportunity to make necessary changes lest we go the way of communism."

Marie thinks *this is all beginning to sound familiar.* "Rudy this is where my dream started—with the comments about feeling a lack of 'satisfaction.'"

Next, the one calling himself Harry James takes charge to begin sharing "...what we learned so far. In other words, the issues others are raising." Marie is saying the words in unison with him.

Rudy silently ponders, "Where is this coming from? This child I've known from birth now dreams the future? Last week I was unsettled by her ability to tell me things I thought and said, miles away. What surprise will she reveal next? I *will not fail her* like I did her parents."

James talks about "... lack of privacy—cameras everywhere—even in your homes—even as you sleep." Next, the "nutritional mandates" are attacked. You are told what to eat; food comes from only one source ... and who assures that food is safe and free of unwanted drugs?"

Marie texts Dr. Norris:

This is almost word for word my dream. Next, he will talk about the 'Joy of home ownership.' How are the students responding?

He texts back:

The lips I read say, 'Never thought of that,' and 'Why hasn't anyone told us?'

Rudy asks, "What about your reading the emotions of that group through Norris' PCD?"

"Worth a try." Marie texts back asking him to angle his camera toward some students.'

Marie receives a live view of about 20 undergraduates.

These emotions are easy to read: mostly "confusion" followed by a feeling of being "violated," "lied to" or "mislead" by the established leaders.

Marie texts: *"On my way."*

To Rudy, "We better go. We're losing them." Rudy heads toward the front door.

"If we go out the way you came in, technically I'm still here."

Rudy spins around heading for the courtyard door, "Glad one of us is thinking."

Friend locks the courtyard door instructed to admit no one, but them. Rudy drives.

As they drive, Marie hears the presenter wrap up his argument with another reference to "lost freedoms" and the proposal that compensation should match responsibility. Question and Comment time is next.

Mr. James Calhoun starts by pointing out the presenters "Total misinterpretation the Financial Sector's functional role." He speaks about home ownership: nearly everyone owns or is purchasing their home. Explaining the principle of "stable home values," based on "construction costs." The concept of "Equity Transfer" is defined, "as everything paid on one residence will be transferred to a different home in the future." In short, his response is too academic for this time of night and does little to dislodge the presenter's position that everyone rents "all your lives."

Next Security 53 points out the high degree of safety and the virtual non-existence of crime under The Plan.

From the stage comes the question, "So why do we need so many officers?"

Unprepared for the question—the Chief stammers—then responds, "Our job is to protect and serve. There are many tasks other than crime prevention."

"Yeah, they always say 'protect and serve' when there is no real justification."

Wessel takes the floor to counter the insinuation that Central Services people "rifle through your things while you are out." Wessel also defends the single source for food as saving "time, money, energy and ensuring high nutritional value." No verbal challenges come from the table, but shoulder shrugs do more to undermine than words.

Dr. Norris takes the floor to speak about the broad range of value added by the presence of Door Services. He points out a Doorkeeper interfaces with Transportation, Location Services, Medical, Central Services, Disaster Preparedness, and Security. He is about to speak about the strict use of cameras when the comment comes from the platform. "If Doorkeepers are so good for safety then why was an officer killed here last week while following the instructions of an *inexperienced* Doorkeeper?"

Gasps of surprise are everywhere. Then pandemonium breaks out. Security 53 is yelling at the presenters, "You're interfering with an ongoing investigation. How did you find out?" Without a microphone the Chief's words are lost on all but a hand-full of people; most people only see the Chief shaking his fists, yelling and red-faced.

"Henry James," with a microphone, feigned an apology, "Oh, I'm sorry—I forgot people aren't supposed to *know* what their public servants are doing."

Rudy finds a parking space across from the entrance. Glancing at Marie, he sees a look of determination rarely seen before. Facial appearance combined with her most austere SOG gives her the appearance of being five years older.

They are heading for the entrance as Dr. Norris begins speaking. Marie knows when the interruption will come as she focuses on what's happening in the room 20 feet away. The lobby is filled with people listening and commenting. She approaches with an air of power and resolve, producing a parting like the Red Sea for Moses. Rudy behind and to her left says, "Got your back—whatever you need." No response is necessary. The challenge comes from the speaker's table. Marie is standing at the double door with only a campus-security-trainee blocking her way.

The officer says, "No seats available. I can't let you in."

Marie responds, "I'll not be sitting."

Rudy says, "She's the next speaker."

"Well OK!" The officer steps aside.

The insincere "apology" is ringing out over the speakers as Marie and Rudy step through the double doors. A dozen people are waiting for an opportunity to leave. Rudy says, "You'll want to hear what she says."

Rudy's voice offers no threat, but he impresses people as the kind of person you *want* to agree with. They return to their seats as Marie starts forward. A wave of silence sweeps in with her as many turn to see the stranger marching to the front. Where did she come from? What will she do? Fenton J calmed his Chief enough to whisper, "Marie is coming."

"We can't subject her to this."

Fenton nods toward the door saying, "She's here." Security 53 turns, glances, and sits down saying, "Well I'll be damned."

Dr. Abraham Norris holds the microphone and moves toward Marie a few rows up the aisle. He asks, "Are you sure about this?"

"I can do no other."

"Alright." He hands her the mike. Unknown to either of them their exchange is overheard by everyone—because of the quiet and the amplification.

Marie takes an instant to measure Dr. Norris' emotions. *Concern for me, but mostly relief. I know the first thing to say and have a checklist of other points. Here goes.*

Moving to the front and her left, she turns to face a section containing primarily undergraduates. "I want to talk to the students. The rest of you (gesturing to her left) can listen in—but *no interruptions ...*" 180 degree turn to face the platform she adds *"especially from you three."* The two closest to her with their elbows on the table involuntarily retreat in their seats from her intensity. A few smiles and a little laughter followed Marie's first comment, but more laughter and light applause accompany her message to the stage.

Turning she says, "I want to talk to the students, because this whole event is about *you*."

From the stage comes, "State your name and position!"

Marie moves to the center aisle again and turns facing the elevated structure, "What part of NO INTERRUPTIONS do you not understand? Is it the NO part? Does no one ever say 'NO' to your half-truths and baseless suspicions? Or perhaps it's *interruptions* you don't understand. It *is* a big word. It means when someone else has the floor you shut ... your ... mouth." Marie finishes, and the room erupts with laughter and applause, this time, some coming from the younger attenders. Three Security Officers 23, the Chief, and 93 get up moving to the dais. Fenton leans over to the one in the center saying, "interrupt her again and you'll be getting up from the floor." The three officers take 'parade rest' stances behind those at the table.

Marie says, "This is an open forum. The Open Meetings Act of 2063, Article 3 Paragraph 4 provides that no person may be compelled to give their identity *as a condition* for participation in an open forum. Therefore, I'm *not* required to give my name, position, gender, age, nationality, degrees or favorite sports team." This produces a rousing laugh from the whole group.

I gained some respect from those over 30. No one will call me on my ad-lib chapter and verse till later.

Back to the section primarily filled with university personnel. "As I was saying before we were so rudely interrupted, I'm here to talk to the students because this whole session is designed around you. These guys and others like them are traveling from campus to campus, trying to sow seeds of doubt and suspicion in our minds. They want us to vote *no* when the referendum comes in 2099. Somehow they think those who never lived *one day* in the 'Time of Confusion' can be persuaded to try it. How bad could it be?

"But I'm getting ahead of myself. You see—six and one-half weeks ago, I was one of you. Completing my training to become a Doorkeeper at the end of June, I began my time as a Teaching Assistant July first. I was helped greatly by TAs when I started my education and wanted to return the favor to the next class.

"That all changed a week ago last night. While sitting in the commons room enjoying my weekly personal pizza and root beer, waiting for my card-playing friends to arrive an announcement called me to a temporary office."

The students are listening. I know their lives. Their trust is growing.

"Arriving at the office, I was asked if I would be willing to take an assignment. From the first days of school, we are taught to say and believe, 'It's my pleasure to serve.' Be careful what you say when you get called away from your pizza." This brought laughter and smiles, especially from the younger listeners.

"I said what I'd been taught. So here I am. The need occurred at this unusual start time because one of our Doorkeepers occupies a 'hole of completion.' Well, that's sad. People do die, sometimes unexpectedly.

"After arriving, I learned my predecessor had been *kidnapped and murdered.*" The phrase hangs for a few seconds as the room fills with gasps and expression of astonishment, many are asking their neighbor, "Did you know?"

Marie continues, "Now, these guys didn't mention *his death*, because … well … they're responsible. Not *these* specific guys but others who think *like* them hired three goons to do the deed. They are part of the movement to destroy the Structured States. The ones behind me are in the 'Lie to the Students' branch, which *is so much* more respectable than the 'Kill off the Smart Ones' branch. But be sure … they are part of the same movement; taking instruction from the same people.

"I raise this to help give a little perspective to how the death of a Security Officer acting under the direction of a Doorkeeper might occur. The Chief told you, though most of you couldn't hear due to the disrespect, the Officer's death is still under investigation. I can say nothing more. But the death of my predecessor *is not* under investigation, so I'm able to speak about it.

"But before I do, I must go back to something I said earlier: you are the reason for this whole event. *These forums are held on College and University campuses.* Why? Obviously, they want students and few others. Another reason occurs to me. The rule on a campus of learning is 'Truthfulness at all times.' Anyone heard that?" Laughter everywhere.

"So when you come to class your ultimate goal is to arrive at a better understanding of *truth*... and get a good grade. When your instructors tell you something, it's supposed to be to the best of their ability ..." Marie opens her hands to the group in an inviting gesture and many of group answers "*true.*"

"You check sources for information in your field they are supposed to be ... " (same gesture).

The group responds more loudly "*true.*"

"And when you come to a Forum in a University Hall with three outside experts they are supposed to tell you the ..." (same gesture).

Some say, "*true*" others "*truth.*" They laugh a bit over the confusion.

Ok, I got everyone's attention: time for some truth.

"But the guys at the table haven't spoken one ... word ... of truth since they arrived." There were sharp intakes of breath.

I don't need to be reading energy trails to feel the rising distrust toward the presenters, particularly from this side of the room.

"Let me correct myself. They are right about one thing: this is Wichita." Laughter.

"How many of you were under the impression these men represent a Governmental Agency?" Every student's hand goes up and two-thirds of the others. "They were extremely careful *not* to *say* they are government connected, but they intended to leave that impression. *Truth: they are not.*"

"They are not wearing Smart Outer Garments like the rest of us? Partly because if they wore SOGS when they deplaned the *private jet* their actual identities would be revealed. The names they gave are false. The one in the center is named something Crystal, I don't remember the other two, but not what they told you."

"So you may wonder how I know so much about them? You see they could not hide the identity of the jet—owned by Grog. So a simple Internet search. Anyone know the Grog Foundation?"

A "graduate fellow" in the 3rd row says, "Yes. I'm doing my dissertation on Grog and three other right-wing groups exercising undue influence on the political activity of 3rd world nations."

"We probably can't hear your whole dissertation, but would you answer one question? Is Grog's agenda friendly toward The Plan's Structure?"

"Absolutely NOT. They have sworn to bring down the Program States, as they call them, by any means possible."

"Does anything our panel presented sound like Grog's platform?"

"Yes, since you mention it—*everything*: they want to return to the way things were before The Plan."

"Do you think we should try their way for a while?"

"Hell no! This country tried that way from 1492 until 2050. It did not work for most people then, and it certainly won't work now." Marie has been holding the microphone so he could be heard throughout the hall. She steps back saying, "Thank you."

"Well, it's getting late. Only a few more things I want to say. First, if you think Doorkeepers are spying on you, sit with me for a 10 and half hour shift. I don't get time to eat or go to the bathroom, much less spy on you. Second, anytime I turn on a camera I *must* document *the reason*. Plus my Supervisors can watch my work anytime, and they can copy what is happening at my workstation without my even knowing it.

"Third, Wessel's people work hard. They clean our homes, bring our food, make repairs and do our laundry. When they deliver they are not messing with your stuff—they're as busy as I am. Random checks are made on their work, just like mine.

"Lastly, our Security people are outstanding. Mr. Crystal had a question about 'so many officers.' Well, per capita, there are three times as many police in non-structured states, yet they still have violent crime."

"Now, I need to go back to work, because some of you are going to need admission to your houses, and that takes a Doorkeeper. My final word: *stop the lies.*"

Marie was hoping to leave without saying more about either death.

A young woman in the fourth row stood before Marie could reach the aisle. Her colors indicate a graduate student in social work. "Wait, don't leave us hanging, how did your predecessor get kidnapped?"

Marie sighs and takes a deep breath, "When the Central Services people come to a home while the residents are out they use a 'keycard' for entry. The card works only once; it must be recharged before it functions again.

"Back when physical keys were no longer opening doors, someone had the idea of making some 'master keycards' to open *any* door, *anytime.* Security, FBI, TAS, groups like that would have them for emergency use. Well, some cards were made, and when President Earldrige found out about it, he scuttled the idea. All cards were collected and destroyed; *except one.* It was used to open the door of my predecessor's home after he had gone to bed, and was *not* wearing a SOG. So he was kidnapped."

"Is that card still out there."

"Yes, it is." Gasps of fear come from all quarters. "But let me tell you how smart my predecessor was. Knowing people

471

might try to invade his home, he programmed his Automated Personal Assistant to capture the codes from the keycard that opened his door. They were stored where they could not be erased. The invaders tried, but were unable to delete the card details."

"When Security and their electronics experts got the details, they created a fix. All homes in Wichita, and by now most places in North America have received the repairs sent out by satellite. So the card cannot open *your* door or any door. Wherever it is—it's useless."

There is resounding applause. Marie says, "Don't applaud me! Applaud Security; applaud Central Services; the anonymous electronics people, some of whom are here, and my predecessor. I'm the fortunate one who stumbled on all this good work."

Marie departs or tries to. People want to stop her along the way to ask something or say thanks. Rudy is at her side in an instant acting as a combination bodyguard/battering ram. Marie responds to questioners in a weak voice, "I'm sorry, I'm exhausted." Her exaggeration is minimal. In the lobby, some people seem ready to follow them. Rudy says, "I think the President is about to speak." They fall for the ruse and head back toward the hall. Rudy and Marie run to the car and are out of sight before anyone realizes they have been misdirected. The vehicle's lights are left off until they are beyond the hall. Taking a different route, avoiding the Dolls and parking in a different location come automatically after years of practice.

"My long day is almost over. I can relax for a while." *Why do I feel relaxing will not last long?*

Fifty-Six
After Session

Marie and Rudy sit down: Marie at her console to check Auto-Door and Rudy with his communicator, at the table.

"Friend, anything noteworthy since we left?"

"Barbie and Ken went to their home. They drove by this address and received a voice message from the person called 'one.' He instructed them to view an Internet site for University events and asked, 'Is that Marie?' They admitted losing the car but 'She must be home, or the camera would show her leaving.' Obscenities were uttered. One told them to check out other parking areas."

"Thank you. Continue surveillance." Marie does a security sweep of the area. Pic lines are busy bringing people back from their various activities. Marie listens in to a couple of transports. "Oh, crap ... everyone is talking about a 'speech' at the University Center."

A call comes from Ann.

"You were wonderful, no one but me recognized you. I'll keep your secret. Our instructors encouraged us to attend expecting information about real changes for the future."

"I don't know what you're saying, I've been here all evening."

"Sure."

Ann will not blow my cover. She enjoys being a co-conspirator.

Wessel, Dr. Norris, and Fenton J. are coming up the walk. Marie admits them.

"We have company." Marie nods toward the front door as the three men enter.

"Welcome again, gentlemen, but of course, you're not here are you?"

Fenton J responds, "Not according to the hidden camera, but your PA may think otherwise."

"She's so nosey."

Marie asks her supervisor, "How much trouble am I in?"

"None from me. Fenton, is she in trouble with you?"

"No. Three things you should be aware of: 53 arrested Crystal. He will spend the night in a cell. Security 93 and 23 plan to accompany you. We located the student with the Grog information. I need to confirm his safety." Fenton leaves promising to return.

Rudy turns to Marie asking, "How did you remember the exact reference to the open meetings law?"

"I knew what I said, but I made up section numbers."

"Well, Article 3 Paragraph 4 says: 'Insuring open dialogue without threat of repercussion to any individual speaking at a public forum is essential to the free exchange of ideas. No person, resident, alien, visitor, or foreign citizen, will be required to identify themselves by name, position, education, place of residence, or work status. All speakers will be granted up to 15 minutes during which time they will be accorded respect and attention without interruption.'"

"How did those numbers come to me?"

I may know, but I'm afraid to say it. Did I somehow tap into my energy trail when reading the act? Can I tap into all my trails? That would be my whole life!

Friend announces, "Barbie and Ken have located Marie's rental car."

"Thank you." Marie turns on the surveillance cameras confirming the Personal Assistant's assessment and says, "This could be a problem."

Wessel says, "We thought something similar might happen. I'll let Fenton J explain when he gets back. Oh, heck why should he get all the fun? I can activate a code making their PA 'think' there is a fire in their house activating the sprinklers. Of course, nothing is on fire. So they will be called home, to find the mess, and pack for temporary relocation, while the electronic people 'sort out the snafu' and clean up. Security will conveniently locate them just before Rudy needs to leave."

Dr. Norris adds, "So when Marie leaves as Fields through the vacant address the computers will place her here all week."

"What about the 'service days?' I can't be here when they come."

Wessel says, "No service this week—damn computers."

"That's most of it ... who's covering my shifts?"

"Dr. Kim Sam Rea and Jeffery will split your duties.

"Okay—thanks."

Wessel chimes in, "What is your feeling about being famous?"

"What are you talking about?" *Please be joking.*

"The video of your speech is all over the Internet."

"Just local, right? It'll go away with the next good cat video."

"Not likely—100,000 downloads so far."

Dr. Norris is also on his communicator looking at something. "The New York Times publishes at midnight. Here is what it says: 'Publication delayed until 3:00 AM due to late breaking news.' Want to bet what the story is?"

Marie is feeling overwhelmed. She distorts her face trying not to let fear show, but to no avail, the tears flow, and she hears herself say, "Oh God help me, what've I done?" Her prayer's answer is immediate.

Abraham Norris, Dean of Door Service Supervisors, comes to her side placing a hand on her shoulder. "You did what *had* to be done. You did what we all *tried* to do but *couldn't*. Every word, every action, every facial expression—all were perfect."

"All I ever wanted to do was open doors and help people with their problems. Look at all the trouble I'm causing."

"You opened a door tonight the whole nation will walk through. We're with you. But you are key, and we'll protect you."

Marie relaxes—the voice in her head repeats: *Remember your plan. One issue, one problem, one step at a time.*"

Marie says, "I'm sorry. I never wanted to be one of those people who cries all the time."

"I'm glad to see the tears. I was worried your focus on the task had caused you to push away your emotions."

"You wouldn't if you'd been here for my meltdowns—after reading stuff from Phillip. If I can remember my plan—one problem at a time—I'll be ok. So what's next?"

Wessel says, "We all need to see this." Wessel's communicator has a Broadcast News Report, all-hours information service.

The news anchor sits at a desk, with the word "Editorial" diagonally repeated across a board behind him. He begins, "This is an editorial, *only* because we are still *confirming* some of the *related* facts. In the years to come, tonight's happening will be remembered as 'ground zero' of a process changing our world for good or ill.

"One thing about working the overnight shift at Broadcast News is always looking for the next big story. This time it comes from the relatively quiet city of Wichita, Kansas." He goes on to explain the late night forums; providing extra credit for students who attend.

He describes the Central Program States Updating Initiative, pointing out there are also "Eastern" and "Western" branches. These groups account for 30 sessions held on University Campuses this year. He reads the stated purpose as gathering data from the attendees and sharing the emerging vision for the future structure.

He then says, "In reality, it's a transparent attempt to indoctrinate the students and anyone else who will listen." The main points of their vision are listed using clips from the presenter's words.

He then shows a clip of Wessel explaining why a single food source is good with the background of the disrespect. Followed by a clip of the presenter saying, "If Doorkeepers increase safety why was a Security Officer killed...." Next, is the scene of confusion and Security 53's angry retort.

The anchor says, "Then this happened."

The clip shows Marie entering the room with the noise and shouting ending as she walked straight toward Dr. Norris. It cuts to the confrontation with the panel including her refusal to give her name and her reason.

The anchor says, "She is correct. In further reading of the Open Meetings Act, it should be noted the *only* people required to identify themselves are the up-front leaders. The act also says organizations must, and I quote, "reveal all its sponsors, financial supporters, and any organization providing data, or research." They must also declare "any contractual agreement with any organization maintaining an interest in the outcome of the group's findings."

The video cuts to Marie asking the audience how many thought the presenters were part of an official government agency. Most hands are up. She identifies the group as connected to the Grog Foundation. Next, the graduate student saying Grog is "sworn to bring down the Program States, as they call them, by any means possible."

The commentator concludes. "What you just saw has been verified. Some, I dare say, most have viewed the video of the whole meeting, at least from the arrival of the young Doorkeeper. We excluded much of the video because factual verification is incomplete. We do know this much: Grog Foundation finances all the operations of the Program States Update Initiative forums. If you attended one of these forums earlier and thought you heard facts about an anticipated future for Structured States; I suggest you reconsider any conclusions you may have reached. Our speaker points out that holding the sessions on a university campus *implies* those on a stage speak truth—but not in this case. They presented a plan for the future formulated by Grog Foundation. Their vision is not based on research; no opinions are being solicited.

"So who is Grog Foundation? They took down their website so you can't see. However, Broadcast News captured the content of their site before they closed it. You can view it at BroadcastNews.org/Grog. You may not want to read it—it's pretty grim stuff.

"This Doorkeeper opened a door. We cannot close it again. Some people for personal gain would send us back to the time when banks, insurance, advertising and political half-truths dominated our society. The truth is they would like to make us economic slaves.

"We must not let hers be the only voice of sanity. Now it's time for the rest of us to take up the cause—creating a movement. It starts tonight. Message your Representatives, Senators, Governors, President and Vice President. Tell them to root out the attempts to undo The Plan. I'm Rich Goodman—no I'm not. Goodman has been my broadcast name for years. My real name is Sylvester Cleats; Rich Goodman does sound better."

Half way through the broadcast Fenton J returned. "The student is being relocated to a home with a Doorkeeper for his safety."

Rudy suggests Marie get some sleep.

"Sounds good to me."

Rudy will tell me what I need. Tomorrow will be another "abnormal day." Feels like I may never have another "typical day."

As Marie's head hits the pillow she reflects, *I'm grateful for my friends. I can rest because they will keep me safe.*

Fifty-Seven
Imminent Danger

"Bleep, Bleep, Bleep, Marie wake up *Imminent Danger, Imminent Danger.*"

Rudy is at her side. "Change of plans we are leaving *now.* You're with me. Friend, how long?"

"One to two hours."

Marie had packed for three days away, including one SOG. Rudy empties her dresser into her bag.

Everyone talks at once. Through the jumble of words she understands:

"New York Times named you as the only Doorkeeper fitting the details.

"Security 1 ordered 53 to arrest you, for interference in an investigation. He flatly refused. So 'One' is sending Officers from outside our area. The Chief deployed forces to block their entrance into the district—buying us some time."

"Wessel and Security 17 will live here while you're away. They will have the stunning cannon."

"The makeup artist will meet us in Baltimore, probably Wednesday."

Marie asks, "What about Barbie and Ken?"

"Stalking is still a crime; they're being arrested. A deal will likely be cut for testimony against Security One. Our chief filed a petition with the Security Oversight Board for the Grand Chief's removal."

Marie, wearing C.F. Fields' SOG, hands the two packages to Rudy, who places them in his computer case. Friend says, "With the 'travel memory chip' in place on your laptop, we will be able to communicate without detection." Marie runs to the kitchen and removes the strange spherical object. Everyone gawks at the orb.

"Oh, none of you have seen this." Pausing a few seconds. "This is what it takes to access the PA space unless you are me." It's placed it in the floor opening then closed. Time is taken for embraces. The tears come as Marie says, "I owe you guys my life."

They are out the door heading for the car. *The carry robot is superfast; we are trotting to keep up.* In the car, Rudy says, "We're about 40 minutes ahead of them."

Marie says, "Fingerprints. If they enter the apartment, they'll find my fingerprints and DNA."

"Wessel has a crew there cleaning up. By the time they finish no one can prove you ever walked in."

"My Portalock where's my Portalock?"

"In the drawer *where it belongs*. You are not going to be opening any doors for a while."

Marie laughs, "Of course, I'm obsessing, as usual. My sensor glasses, we'll need them."

Rudy opens the top of his SOG and hands her the glasses. "Dr. Norris thought of everything. Now I need your help watching for anyone following us."

He mostly wants to distract me, so I'll stop obsessing. They reach the airport, and Rudy drives up to a side entrance with a guard. Rudy hands him an ID The guard says, "Good Morning Col. Masters, I was unaware you had a passenger."

481

"There is no passenger, only 'my package.' I'm assisting emergency relocation services."

"Very good sir."

"I may be followed by some people *claiming* to be Security."

"You were never here sir."

"Very good." They salute. Rudy drives through the gate. Shortly they reach the plane. Three guards flank the aircraft: two of them step forward to carry luggage. "In the cabin," Rudy instructs.

In the cockpit, Rudy takes the pilot's seat and Marie the co-pilot's. "You can fly a plane?" Rudy asks.

"You know I can't."

"I thought perhaps they taught something useful in Keeper School." Marie laughs.

"I'll teach you."

They started through the pre-flight checklist. Two-thirds of the way through a message came from Marie's PA. "Security One diverted four cars to the airport. ETA fifteen minutes."

Rudy clicked the mike to the tower, "Bravo, Tango, Delta 8686 requesting clearance for takeoff."

"You are cleared. Nearest traffic is 50 miles."

"Understood."

They continue the checklist as they taxi. At the end of the runway, Rudy does a 95-degree turn and hits the throttle. They are airborne in seconds, climbing at a nearly 50-degree angle. Rudy says, "We are military; we must fly that way."

Marie holds the incline while Rudy removes three electronic components from his briefcase. He pulls out connecting wires from behind the instrument panel and plugs in the components. They reach 29,000 feet and level off. After 5 seconds Rudy flips a switch on one of the "add-ons." Dropping to 24,000 feet, Rudy hands Marie a work-pad displaying a map with a line from Wichita to Seattle with two minor course changes.

"We are going to Seattle?" Marie asks.

"No, but the plane is." After an instant of confusion, she understands. "Watch the line. Tell me of any blips outside the line." Rudy engages a second switch beginning a gradual turn to the right, heading north then northeast. After three minutes Rudy asks, "Any blips?"

"None."

"OK, now let's climb a little." They climb and hear a "pinging" sound followed immediately by a "swoosh." Rudy explains, "The ping is radar hitting us, the swooshing sound indicates signal is matched and counteracted. In other words, we are invisible to radar."

Flight Operation calls on a secure frequency, "People arrived at the tower claiming to be Security Officers, searching for convicted felons. Your enemies are powerful. Suggest radio silence." Rudy soundlessly pushes and releases his mike button to acknowledge.

Marie says, "Well the 'Select Tribunal' believes in swift injustice. I wonder what I'm guilty of now?"

"I think your crime is speaking the truth."

"Your electronics adaptations are impressive. How long did those take?"

"Wish I could claim credit, but they're standard issue. This is how we get diplomats out of 'harms way.'"

They fly in silence for a half-hour.

For the first time since I was tapped for this job, I know what's going to happen next. What a comfort. There are obstacles ahead, but now I can name them. I'm supported and protected, and for the moment no one is threatening me.

During the flight, they receive several secure messages. From Friend, "Security One has been relieved of all duties, pending further investigation. Dispatched Security personnel are recalled. Barbie and Ken are testifying about the Grand

Chief's efforts to track Marie. Sector 86 Keeper's home was not entered."

Allison is called to bring her up to date. She had seen the video of Marie "telling some truth." They talk about Marie's dream, her compulsion to speak, and the unintended consequences. Rudy adds, "Our timeline is shorter. We'll be lucky to have two weeks to fortify our case."

Marie mentions how she used the energy trails to guide what she did and said next. Allison, the scientist, still wants to find a way to measure them but is grateful they are working.

The news about Phillip is more encouraging than anticipated—he asked for "water"—the first word he's uttered. A long way from the genius developing liquid lava countertops and the most sophisticated Automated Personal Assistant ever.

Marie asks her PA to contact the Department of Records and Inquiries with a message for Records Assistant 186. "Tell her I need to reschedule our lunch."

Ten minutes later Friend texts:

RA 186 understands. She added the following: "I obtained the *sealed court document* for our friend's trial. It is blank. Hidden ink maybe microchip? I used to be a document authenticator for museums, so I took it to the museum and borrowed their equipment. Nothing. I checked the case number: not registered anywhere. Also the court: bogus. I suspect you knew. Stay safe." Message ends. Shall I respond?

"Tell her thanks, stay safe."

To Rudy, she says, "I understand about the false radar images going toward Seattle, but what happens when no plane lands in Seattle. Will someone be looking for a downed aircraft?"

"No, when it's time to enter the Seattle airspace the signal disappears. So Seattle Air Traffic Control never gets a plane, so nothing is missing."

"Since we are invisible how do we land?"

"That is what the third switch does. Once we're close, the third device creates a flight path, not the real one of course, and radar again sees us."

"Fascinating."

"Thought you'd like it. Are you ready to fly this thing?"

"We're on autopilot, right?"

"Yes."

"Well, I can do that."

Rudy shows Marie how to practice maneuvering the aircraft. She finds it relatively easy. "Of course," Rudy says, "you will 'perceive' a bank to the right, or other change."

"I already do. Remember when I was five or six you and Dad took me to an amusement park. We'd been on several rides and were waiting in a long line for the rollercoaster. I watched one group do the full ride. So I said, 'I don't need to go. I rode with the last group.' I wondered why you all seemed confused.

"I thought everyone had the same experiences when mindfully observing. So as we practiced, I felt the turns, dives, and everything."

Rudy muses, "Wasn't that the same time you cleaned out the sharpshooter's booth of stuffed animals? Then gave them all away to a group of scruffy kids outside the gate?"

"Yes."

"I never understood what happened."

"Didn't I tell you guys? Perhaps not, well the operator was cheating; he had set the barrel of the gun off at an angle, so if you aimed dead center—your shot misses. After the first shot, I corrected for his deception and hit all the rest. You and Dad were funny trying to carry all those prizes."

"Yeah, we couldn't see where we stepped. We kept dropping them. Then we got to the exit, and you gave them away."

"The only one I wanted was the big polar bear. All the bigger kids pushed up. When toys were gone, one little girl remained. She was about three, barefoot, dirty dress, smudged face, hair in tangles—blond like me. She started crying. The bear was bigger than her. It was bigger than me."

"You told her 'don't let anyone take this away from you. It's yours forever.' Our backup was Harris. He carried her bear home. The three older brothers were scheming how to sell their animals. Harris said he was from the 'stuffed animals protection league' or something similar. 'This bear is endangered; if you touch it, an alarm will go off, and I'll come and hang you by their feet and put red ants down your pant legs."

"I never thought of Harris as funny."

"Oh, he wasn't joking. He even put a sensor in the bear's neck and told the girl she had to hug it every day, around the neck. If she missed a day, an alarm would go off, and he would return for the bear.

"Your Dad thought the Roller Coaster frightened you. That was the confusion."

"I thought everyone was like me. Recently I got the idea—maybe I'm different. I've taken so much for granted. I *am* sorry."

"Don't apologize. We knew you were HMP. The experts said you would not experience any of your specialness before puberty—well not you because they didn't know about you."

"I wanted that bear."

"I'll buy you one."

"Where would I put it? I'm a homeless fugitive."

After a moment of quiet Marie asks, "No one knows I'm HMP? People were aware of Berry's pregnancy. Even when she did not come back, surely some suspected there was a child."

"Berry's post mortem. Allison told you?"

"About the poison and how she kept it out of her breast milk, yes."

"Allison erased evidence of the pregnancy."

"But she had two other children."

"No records, but the ones she gave you. No paper trail: nothing happened."

"Wow, I am alone. Oh, I don't mean from you guys…"

"I understand. We'll find your brother and sister if they are still alive, but not this week."

"I'm feeling odd, and I just figured out why. This is the first time since I entered Primary 1 that I can choose what I do for the next few moments."

"There are always choices."

"Not so! After I decide what to study all my 'free time' priorities are made. I might read one article before another, but I *will* read them both."

"You *could* simply *not* read and digest everything on the syllabus."

"*You do* remember me, don't you? If it can be learned, I want to learn it. Isn't this true for everyone?"

"You can't be *serious*?"

"Yes, I am. Why would anyone pass up the chance to learn to fly a plane, build a circuit board, understand an artist's motivation, or talk to the divine, or…. '

"You are the *ideal* of 'The Plan,' but that is far from reality for many people."

"Ask me not to learn; you might as well ask me not to breathe."

"Marie, I love you for it. But you are different. I must admit sometimes I'm intimidated being around you. I don't measure up to your level of intensity."

"What? You're the most intensely *loyal* person I know; to me, Allison, and 'Not-a-Dozen.' You will learn everything needed to protect those you care for. Not intense? Come on. Anyway, you changed my diapers—I can't intimidate you."

"I *tried* to change your diapers a few times, but someone always had to be rescued. *That task* is intimidating."

They both laugh and Marie decides to work on her journal, with some of her "free time."

An hour later—journal work is completed. Marie asks, "How much longer?"

"We'll be there around noon your time."

"How were you going to meet me in Wichita at 4:00 PM?"

"My original plan was to leave the packages with an intermediary, who would take the last leg. Since you're with me, might as well go the distance. We'll spend the night at the center and go to Baltimore tomorrow getting there in the evening. Twenty-three and crew will meet us at our hotel in Baltimore. It'll be Thursday before you see the Attorney."

"I assumed our destination to be Newfoundland, Labrador or maybe Nova Scotia, but we're over water. Where are we going?"

"Iceland."

"Alright, a new place to visit."

Marie goes to the restroom. On the way back finds a cooler of sandwiches and juices: vegetarian for Marie and turkey for Rudy.

"Who made these?"

"Wessel's crew."

"You guys thought of everything."

"I told you we are g-o-o-o-d."

Sometime later Rudy shows Marie how they become "visible" again.

"Bring us down to 34,000 feet; slow and gradual, we want to appear like an airliner now." At 38,000 feet, Rudy toggles the third switch. "We are a passenger aircraft. Our trajectory shows us coming from New York. Rudy instructs Marie how to adjust the course in a gradual descent: over a glacier and a level plain finally around a mountain flying into a gap between two peaks. A lighted landing strip carved out of the side of the mountain appears. Marie lands like she has done it for years—reversing engines and braking.

We need a longer runway. I better be ready to power up. There was a snap, and the plane abruptly stops.

Rudy says, "I forgot to tell you about the hook. Nobody lands here without a tail-hook." The parking area is large enough for two planes. Marie parks in the first space.

After the shutdown procedures, as they gather their belongings, Rudy asks, "Are you ready for this adventure?"

"What does it involve?"

"Nothing you can't handle."

Fifty-Eight
Data Assimilation Site

Looking out the cabin windows confirms my impression: we are in the middle of nowhere. No people, planes or hangers. Nothing makes this a place to keep an aircraft. "I could swear the runway had lights when we landed."

"It did. Activated by a sensor when we turned the mountain; going off two minutes after the cable is snagged. Our first destination is the shed. Be prepared—it can be windy."

Lowering the plane's stairs, a blast of cold greets them. Wind-chill is 10 degrees though the thermometer reads 34 Fahrenheit. Face-shields snap up for wind protection, and the SOGs begin heating. Marie reaches the shed with her cases, slides the door open, and steps into warmth.

Rudy closes and locks the aircraft. A gust of wind strikes him as he turns. He pauses for a moment—back to the wind. Rudy shuffles two cases in tow. Marie meets him half way taking a bag. Once inside the shelter, the door is closed.

There is an oxygen tank with hoses and four masks. Each takes a few drags to assist adjusting to the thin air.

Rudy opens the oversized clothing locker containing thermal garments. In five minutes both are dressed for the cold with no exposed skin. They wrap the computer cases in heat generating packages. Everything is loaded into what appears to be a golf cart, merged with a snowmobile. Rudy opens a door on the "mountain side" of the shed. Marie drives through it, and Rudy closes the door behind them.

The "cart" maneuvers through the snow filled crevice between two sections of the mountain. From this cavern, they pass through a barn-like door, to a roadway leading toward a village looking like a New England Christmas card picture.

Six buildings are arranged around a central circle featuring an obelisk surrounded by a retaining wall. Rudy pulls up to the second building, on the left side. The sign reads "Bed and Breakfast" in three languages. The entry area is like a living room with a staircase on each side leading upstairs. There is a small table to the right of the entrance door with a bell and a hand printed sign, "Ring for Service" also in three tongues.

Rudy taps the bell. After the ringing stops, a matronly woman comes out of a side room. "May I help you?"

Rudy hands her a "business card" saying, "We would like the Three-Day-Special." She glances at his card and removes a stack of similarly sized cards from a drawer in the little table. The hostess shuffles through the well-worn cards until she finds a match.

"Ah, Yes, Mr. Carlton. Pleased to have you back. Young lady, you are also welcome."

"Thank you."

They walk up the right stairs, carrying their luggage to the third door on the right. The room is small. Containing a double bed, a dressing table with mirror and bench at one end where luggage is placed, a small closet, and a door promising to be a bathroom.

After each has a turn using the facilities, Rudy says, "The thin air combined with our arriving as the landing strip moves into shadow created a problem. The winds rise to hurricane force through the passage almost every day for a few minutes. I realize my nearly perfect plan for this trip has one flaw."

"What's that?"

"I must be alive for it to work. We weren't in danger, but the gust knocked me off balance. I realized, 'if I die here, so will you.' No one would miss us until Allison called the center. They would not find us in time. I intended to save you some stress by telling only what you 'needed to know;' but I was wrong. You *need it all.*"

For the next 40 minutes, Rudy lays out every aspect of his plan: every step, protocol, code, and escape route. Also, she learns how to access the plane, avoid congested radar areas, obtain fuel, and what to do if intercepted by while in invisible mode. In short, every contingency plan, and how they work.

No notes are taken. Occasionally Rudy checks critical points with a question. Marie gives necessary details plus interpretation. When finished Rudy adds, "I don't know about you, but I'm more comfortable."

"Again I'm in awe of your thoughtful and complete care for me. *I'm sorry* I said mean things to you about your safeguards while I was in school. You are the best at what you do. I'm grateful. There are no words."

Rudy's eyes have tears. *My thoughtlessness could have killed her, but* she *thanks* me. "You help me believe my life is more than one long run from disaster."

They embrace—holding each other, experiencing joy in the other's presence. Both are thinking what might happen next if the age gap between them was 20 years smaller. Rudy realizes "Marie could be 'reading' my emotions. I don't want her to know my lustful feelings toward her." Rudy tries ending the embrace, but Marie hangs on. With her ear on his chest, she says, "It's not impossible … but not now. I need to understand myself before I can be intimate with anyone. It would

492

be unfair to you." Marie breaks the hug holding Rudy at arms distance looking into his face. "I didn't mean to pry into your private feelings, but I had the same ones."

"You *did?*"

"Yes."

"Something to *live* for."

"Me too."

Two deep sighs, smiles, and back to work.

The next step is to make dinner reservations. A secret compartment in the wall contains an old style telephone. The reservation is made and confirmed for 7:30 PM. They have traveled six time zones to the east. When leaving the room, they take their luggage. Whether they return tonight will depend on what they learn at dinner.

A tunnel leads from the back of the B & B to the restaurant. The dining area is small. Two other couples are dining when they arrive. Menus are offered. Rudy says, "We'll take the daily special."

"Excellent choice," responds the waiter. This and several more events are part of the protocol. Marie has no idea what they ordered. What arrives is a shepherd's pie. One of the other couples introduces themselves welcoming the newcomers.

After they leave, Rudy says, "He is the Head of Security. The conversation indicates we are cleared for the center tonight."

The "check" arrives with two visitor's badges and a key. The latter operates a vehicle parked in a heated garage connected by another tunnel. They leave with their luggage heading to the garage. There are two vehicles. Theirs is the newer, meaning made this century. Rudy checks the gas, the warmth and puts their bags in the front seat between them. They don insulated clothing including facemasks and start off. It's only four miles but takes 20-minutes to make the trip. They pull up to a card reader station about 8:20 PM local time. Their visitor cards are scanned, and the gate rises. Rudy heads directly toward a wing of a farmhouse. A tree blocks their way, but Rudy drives "over" the tree as it flattens into the snow. A section of the wall opens providing a place for their vehicle. Eight feet inside they stop, and the wall closes behind them. They are in a garage. They get out and walk to what appears as a wild-west style jail cell complete with bars.

Baggage is placed in a drawer and pulled through. The attendant scanning their bags appears similar to the one at the B & B. The visitors are ushered into the cell. The door is locked behind them. Another door begins to form out of the "solid" stone wall; opening with all the gravity worthy of an "Indiana Jones" style lost tomb. First through the door is a carry-robot "… to take your luggage." The visitors want their computer cases with them. The robot insists, "I will deliver luggage to your rooms and return the smaller cases and follow you as long as necessary."

Behind the robot is a woman Marie thinks she knows. The newcomer says, "Hi 'Rude Man,' glad you're here."

"Hi, 'Sandpaper.' Still trying to rub me the wrong way with that nickname." They hug. She turns to Marie. "And this is Marie, all grown up. Must be nine or ten years. Are you finished with school yet?"

Rudy says, "Are you the only one on the planet who doesn't know this woman?"

Marie perceives embarrassment coming. "Can't we leave it like that for now? I would like an hour of anonymity."

"Of course, it's your story to tell, I apologize." Now, the two older women are curious.

Marie says, "Tell me about your work. Allison is excited about what you are doing here."

"Let's go inside," Sandy suggests. All four step through the opening that closes up again.

Seeing the robot return with their computer bags, Rudy says, "But first..." He opens his bag, removing two 14x12 envelops—handing them to Marie.

Caught off guard by this gesture, Marie says, "On behalf of a grateful nation, and some who are ungrateful, I present the final packages of data." Sandy reaches for them, but Marie continues, "As you take these remember there is blood on them. Four people died, and others were willing to die to ensure their safe arrival. I give these into your care so your work can continue with a prayer that the bloodletting is ended."

Sandy is stunned. She thinks, "This is not the carefree child I remember; smart and serious, but always joyous and optimistic."

She says, "What happened to you?"

"My TA role ended abruptly a week ago Sunday. I'm still trying to adjust to the changes."

That is not exactly right, but close enough for Sandy to accept.

Sandy gives Marie a guided tour of the process that takes the raw data and inputs it into several models. "Each model builds on one approach to cure or eradicate the viruses. The computer runs each against the seven viruses. We send the results from each model to the super computer.

They go to the "Scaling Room" where the super computer compares every entry with every other entry. There are three walls lined with panels filled with small colored lights appearing as dots: 300 in each column, thousands of columns—many still blank.

"The computer searches for things the resistant plants and animals have in common. All the darker colors are common characteristics for those succumbing to the disease. As you can see many negative finds." One whole left wall plus half of the end wall are filled with dark colors.

"The lighter colors are the hits for positive characteristics. Common factors identified in the resistant organisms. You see far fewer results." The right wall reserved for those lights is almost blank. "The best we have is 10 to 20 hits."

"What about these?" Marie asks looking at half of the end section with thousands of lights.

"Oh." says Sandy, "Those are the frustrating ones. A single hit, all the yellow-green is one single positive feature—not duplicated anywhere else. We hope with new data more duplicates will be found."

Marie is puzzled, so Sandy starts to explain why the computer would note all those individual occasions of something positive. Marie says, "I understand, but which one is the single anomalies?"

"The yellow-green."

"But *which* yellow-green." Suddenly Marie understands. "Don't tell me I'm the only person in this room who sees four distinct shades of yellow-green on this board?"

Everyone seems dumbfounded, so Marie points out the four different colors and which one is darker or lighter than the other. Sandy says, "We need to read the colors by pixel counts." A few keystrokes and they find the exact arrangement Marie had noted. More importantly, almost 90,000 hits for one common factor in plants resistant to at least four of the viruses.

Everyone celebrates the find. Marie says, "I don't want to be rude, but I need some sleep?" It's 9:45 PM at DAS center but only 3:45 PM Wichita. Marie has slept only four hours in the last forty-one. She and Rudy are guided to their rooms by the robot. Marie asks, "When must we leave in the morning?"

"We are not traveling tomorrow. A weather system is moving in; I checked while you were getting the first part of the tour. The best we can hope is to be out of here on Thursday."

"Oh, thank God, I need to let my spirit catch up with me." *I'm unsure what that means, but it feels right.*

Rudy asks, "Do you sense anyone here is not what they claim? Anyone, we should be suspicious of?"

"You mean a spy? No. I find no one with a hidden agenda. Of course, I've not met everyone, but the energy trails I crossed are clean and healthy."

"Sandy runs the data program of the Center. Virginia runs everything else and when Sandy is absent data as well. She says the packages we brought contain useful data. All data is clean. It'll take a month to input it from the paper copies." They reach their rooms after walking in silence. Rudy says, "Lock the hall door but leave the adjoining door unlocked. Perhaps ajar would be even better. I think you're safe, but that is when we get lax."

I learned more things about myself today. Flying, even landing came easily. I'd like to be a pilot. I'm amazed that others do not see the colors I do. Energy trails are becoming easier. I wonder what I'll learn tomorrow? Marie drifts off to sleep.

Fifty-Nine
The Movement

Marie sleeps over nine hours. No PA to wake and give her daily news summary.

Where am I? Oh yes, a sleeping room at DAS. Physically: more rested, warm, and hungry. Goals for the day: this is an extra day due to weather—nothing on the agenda. How long since I had an entire day free? Did I ever?

Hearing her stirring Rudy taps on the connecting door. "Morning Marie. Sleep well?"

"Yes, but now I'm hungry."

"Get dressed. I'll let them know we're ready for breakfast."

Two minutes later she steps out of her room and is greeted with applause. *They are making fun of me for oversleeping. No everyone has seen "the video."*

Words cannot express their appreciation for Marie's insight and courage—so they clap their hands. They smile, hug, high-five, and say thanks. The last is Sandy who takes both her hands, gazes into her eyes saying, "I'm so glad I know you."

At breakfast, Marie giggles.

Rudy asks, "What's that about."

"I had this silly thought. Before getting back to Wichita, I'll be interviewed on Public Radio by Teresa Graves, on 'New Air.'"

"Still waiting for *the silly* part." Musing for a moment, he says, "You're inspired. *Eventually*, you must tell the story your way. Why not pick your venue. Would you do her show?"

"Of course, she's been an inspiration since I was a kid. I shouldn't mention that should I? I even listen to the earlier versions with Terry Gross during the times of confusion."

"I'll see what I can arrange."

So begins the first day of the rest of Marie's life. The world now knows her as the Doorkeeper who speaks truth to power, credited with founding the "Stop the Lies" movement.

Her words are all verified. Commentators are comparing her to a modern day M.L. King, Gandhi or Earldrige. She accepts none of the comparisons but understands that others do. *People need a hero. I can fill the slot if needed. We need our fantasies; as long as I don't start believing them.*

Today she will experience the joy of helping pinpoint a discovery in the fight against the clambering viruses—minor breakthrough, but real progress nonetheless. *Now I understand why Allison loves her life of research.*

Tomorrow, Thursday, August 26th she will pilot a 100 million dollar aircraft to Baltimore, and meet Phillip's attorney. In silence, the attorney, Miranda Crayborne, will read the pages from Phillip. Following his instructions, they will communicate back and forth using work pads to make plans and decisions.

On Friday, August 27th they will meet at 9:30 AM at an "empty" apartment. Rudy and Miranda's security agencies will scan the building block, and roadways near the housing complex in Cockeysville, Maryland. Once they followed all of

Phillip's safety precautions, the custody of the documents will exchange to Marie.

On that morning the two women will talk about Phillip. Miranda will confess she wanted to marry Phillip back in graduate school, but he found another, and she found no other. Marie will share Phillip's genius and the legacy he left.

On that day Marie will receive the keys to eight four drawer file cabinets bolted to the floor, wall, and ceiling, in a secret basement. It will take hours to relocate the documents to a secure storage unit under Marie's control.

Marie, Rudy and later a legal assistant (arranged by Security 53) will clock about a hundred hours each reading and sorting documents before September 2nd.

Some papers added to what Rudy, Allison, and Not-A-Dozen had already collected resulting in a Special Federal Grand Jury. Marie, Dr. Norris, Security 23, Rudy, Mr. James Calhoun, and Dr. Allison Ward among others will testify between August 30 and September 6th.

Ultimately Marie will play a primary role in seeing that Phillip's wishes are honored and that his work is used to benefit the Common Good. By accepting the responsibility, she unwittingly becomes a significant force in assuring the well being of the economy and supporting The Plan.

Sixty
Now—The Future

On Tuesday, September 6, 2094, Marie meets Teresa Graves at a Public Radio Studio near Harrisburg, Pennsylvania to record an interview.

"Today on New Air our guest is the young woman everyone is talking about. Monday, August 22nd she walked into a heated debate, called the presenters liars, and proceeded to expose a concerted conspiracy to undo 'The Plan for the Future.'

"She is sitting across the table from me. I must say you appear even younger in person than in the video."

"I'm nineteen."

"There's been much speculation about your identity. Will you tell us your name?"

"My name is Marie. I'm the Doorkeeper and Security Coordinator for Residential Sector 86 in Wichita, Kansas."

"The room was filled with authority figures trying to dispel the let's say 'differences of opinion.' They seem unsuccessful, what made *you* think people would listen to you."

"Our sector leaders deserve *respect*. Their answers *satisfied* seasoned citizens. But I had been in school recently enough to understand—they weren't reaching the students. For 45 minutes the presenters told the students 'you're being lied to and taken advantage of.' So when the sector heads attempted to address the presentation's errors, the youth thought, 'those guys say different. They must be right because they are on stage and you're not.' It all comes back to Universities being *places for truth telling*."

"What America seems most curious about is *how* did you come by all the information you shared?"

"Happened to be in the *right* place doing my job. I wrote reports on each situation, listened to and read other's evaluations of the situation. In the process, I made connections others had not yet noticed.

"Part of my work is to ensure the safety of the whole sector. If I see something threatening the peace, I must act. I explored my predecessor's background, and what he was working on at the time of his disappearance. I learned all I shared by paying attention."

"Let's change the subject a bit. Reporters have been trying to find out things about you. Some talked to your fellow students. Many are extremely complimentary, but some of your classmates say you enjoyed being the center of attention. How do you respond?"

"If learning the answers to questions you are sure will come up in class is attention seeking. Well, guilty as charged. Several of my instructors said I never volunteered an answer unless an important point was being overlooked."

"So you are saying you tried to be a model student."

"I'm a *conscientious* student. Doorkeepers' never stop learning. No one else should either."

"One person claimed 'you cheated' and so they 'got rid of you' because the faculty was embarrassed."

Marie glances at a timepiece. "I can answer his charges in about half an hour."

"Something is happening in the next half hour, determining whether you cheated in school?"

"Oh, sorry. It does sound like I'm evading. For now, I'll say — I don't cheat. Why would I when learning is so much fun. Shortly I *may* be able to tell you some things about the man who charges me with cheating. So can we return to the subject after a break?"

The interview proceeds for another hour. Questions include the threats to Marie, and the safety measures being taken, Phillip's demise, the Security Officer's death, and what it feels like to be the founder of a movement.

Asked what political figure she admires she answers James Earldrige because of The Plan and his generosity.

They take a break, during which Marie checks on the indictments, and suggests her host do the same to share with her listeners.

"We took a brief break and are back now. While we've talked, major news has happened. Marie, you knew about this?"

"I did. The Grand Jury's full report is being released as we speak. Your listeners should be told, I testified on some of the points we've discussed earlier."

"Well here is the news: A Special Federal Grand Jury indicted Senator Bluefoot and 16 of his staff plus 21 others. Charges include murder, kidnapping, torture, treason, election tampering, diverting public funds to illegal weapon programs, falsifying expenses, manipulating economic protocols, money laundering, and attempted intimidation of members of Congress. Other charges as well. Marie anything to add?"

"One of those named is a Mr. Thornton on the payroll of one of the Senator's staff. He had applied for the position of Keeper at sector 86 in Wichita. His credentials were falsified indicating experience and degrees he does not possess.

"He actually 'washed out' of Door Facilitation Training in one year.

"Some Sector 86's residents have high-level sensitive responsibilities. As a Doorkeeper, Mr. Thornton could have opened doors for his fellow conspirators for any reason.

"This is the same person claiming he knew me as a child, and that I cheated my way through School. I'll let your listeners decide which of us to believe."

"Marie, after the indictments and our interview airs, you are going to be even more on everyone minds. How are you coping with your sudden fame?"

"Fame is fleeting. I have to face myself in the mirror each day. I need to be able to say, 'I did the best I knew how.'"

"Thank you, Marie. I'm Teresa Graves; this is 'New Air.'"

The interview finishes about 4:00 PM. Marie is looking forward to a secluded evening with Allison, Rudy, Wessel, and Dr. Norris. Today's hotel is near Frederick, Maryland.

The Grand Jury report and all the arrests are on every channel. Marie's interview is to air at 9:00 PM. Broadcast News announces: "We will carry it in its entirety."

Marie thinks, *surely the other outlets will stick with the indictments.* Not so: the Doorkeeper from Wichita *is* the big story.

Rudy takes a call from one of the operatives working with the Federal Prosecutor's office. Rudy reports, "Some bad news: Bluefoot was not at his office, home, or his vacation house on the Cape. Interpol is checking his homes in France and Switzerland. We also lost Cotton and 'Chuck-ee.' Of course, we still don't know enough about the shadowy figure called 'the General,' the real power."

Wessel asks, "So the only ones of Phillip's kidnappers available for trial are the electronics guy and Cotton's twin brother?"

"I'm afraid so."

Dr. Norris says, "Perhaps Bluefoot's disappearance is not all bad. *If he* were on trial, his counsel would use diversions and delay tactics. The other trials will be less media grabbing. So we can keep the focus on the Reaffirmation of Structured States vote."

Wessel asks, "You think there will still be attacks on the Structured State provisions?" All say, "Yes."

Dr. Norris responds, "They will regroup. With the General's money and influence, they won't stop now. These are not the kind of people to cut their losses and go live in luxury."

They "see" the New Air interview. Broadcast News carries it with the view of whoever is speaking on screen. Marie speaks candidly with clarity and reveals herself to be dedicated, intelligent, resourceful, compassionate and respectful.

The broadcast ends leaving everyone speechless, except Marie. She turns off the "viewing device" and says, "I want to thank each of you for your love and support. Without it, I couldn't have survived these last 23 days." Looking at Allison and Rudy she adds, "... or 19 years without you two."

Rudy says, "Marie, I forgot to tell you. There may be a call on your communicator. I gave your contact information to someone who might call with a message of appreciation."

"Who?"

"You'll recognize the voice if the call comes."

"Okay."

Rudy would never endanger me. So I'll forget it. Then her communicator sounds.

Marie answers, "How may I help you?"

From the PCD comes a familiar voice.

"You already have."

"Mr. President?"

"They used to call me that."

"Mr. President … My name is Marie."

"My name is Jim. How may *I* help *you*?"

THE END

MORE SECRETS WILL BE REVEALED
IN *THE DOORKEEPER'S MIND*